THE SMURFS

Peyo

VENGEANCE!
WHAP
RUN FOR YOUR SMURFS!
CRAAAC

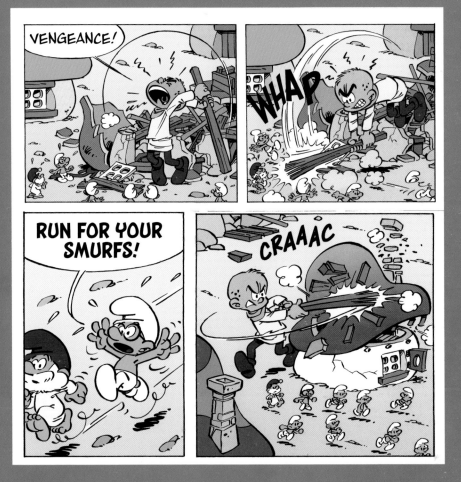

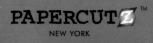

PAPERCUTZ™
NEW YORK

THE SMURFS TALES #1

SMURF™

"The Smurfs and the Bratty Kid"
BY PEYO
WITH THE COLLABORATION OF MIGUEL DÍAZ VIZOSO AND
THIERRY CULLIFORD FOR THE SCRIPT,
JEROEN DE CONINCK FOR THE ART,
AND NINE CULLIFORD FOR THE COLORS

"The Horde of the Crow"
BY PEYO
WITH THE COLLABORATION OF YVAN DELPORTE AND
THIERRY CULLIFORD FOR THE SCRIPT,
ALAIN MAURY FOR THE ART,
AND NINE CULLIFORD AND STUDIO LEONARDO FOR THE COLORS

"The Smurf Gags"
BY PEYO

"The Hanged Man's Inn"
BY PEYO

Joe Johnson, SMURFLATIONS
Bryan Senka and Wilson Ramos Jr., LETTERING SMURFS
Léa Zimmerman, SMURFIC PRODUCTION
Matt. Murray, SMURF CONSULTANT
Ingrid Rios, SMURF INTERN
Jeff Whitman, MANAGING SMURF
JayJay Jackson, SMURFTASTIC THANKS
Jim Salicrup, SMURF-IN-CHIEF

HC ISBN: 978-1-5458-0618-0
PB ISBN: 978-1-5458-0619-7

PRINTED IN MALAYSIA
JULY 2021

Papercutz books may be purchased for business or
promotional use. For information on bulk purchases
please contact Macmillan Corporate and Premium
Sales Department at (800) 221-7945 x5442.

DISTRIBUTED BY MACMILLAN
FIRST PAPERCUTZ PRINTING

THE SMURFS AND THE BRATTY KID

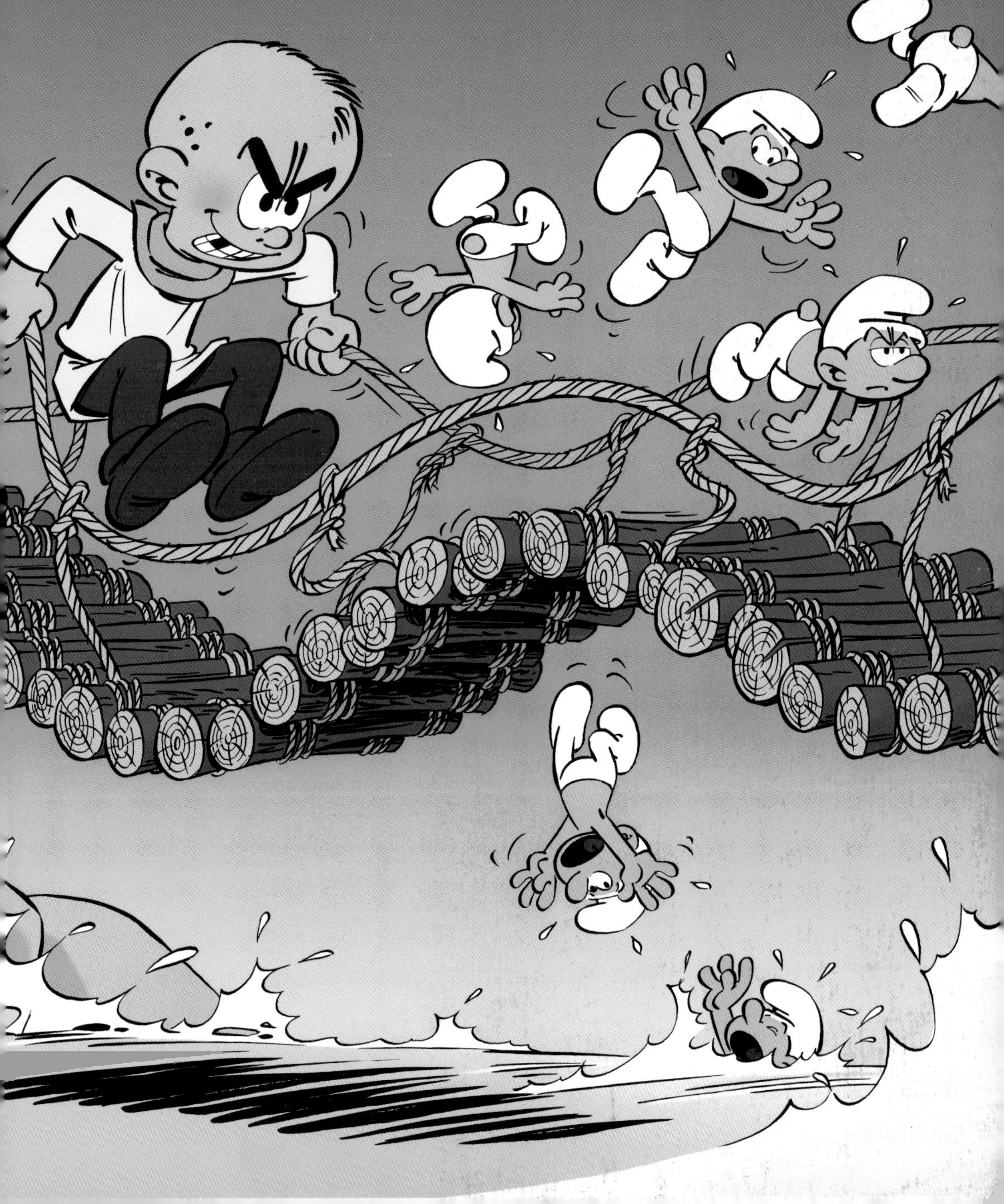

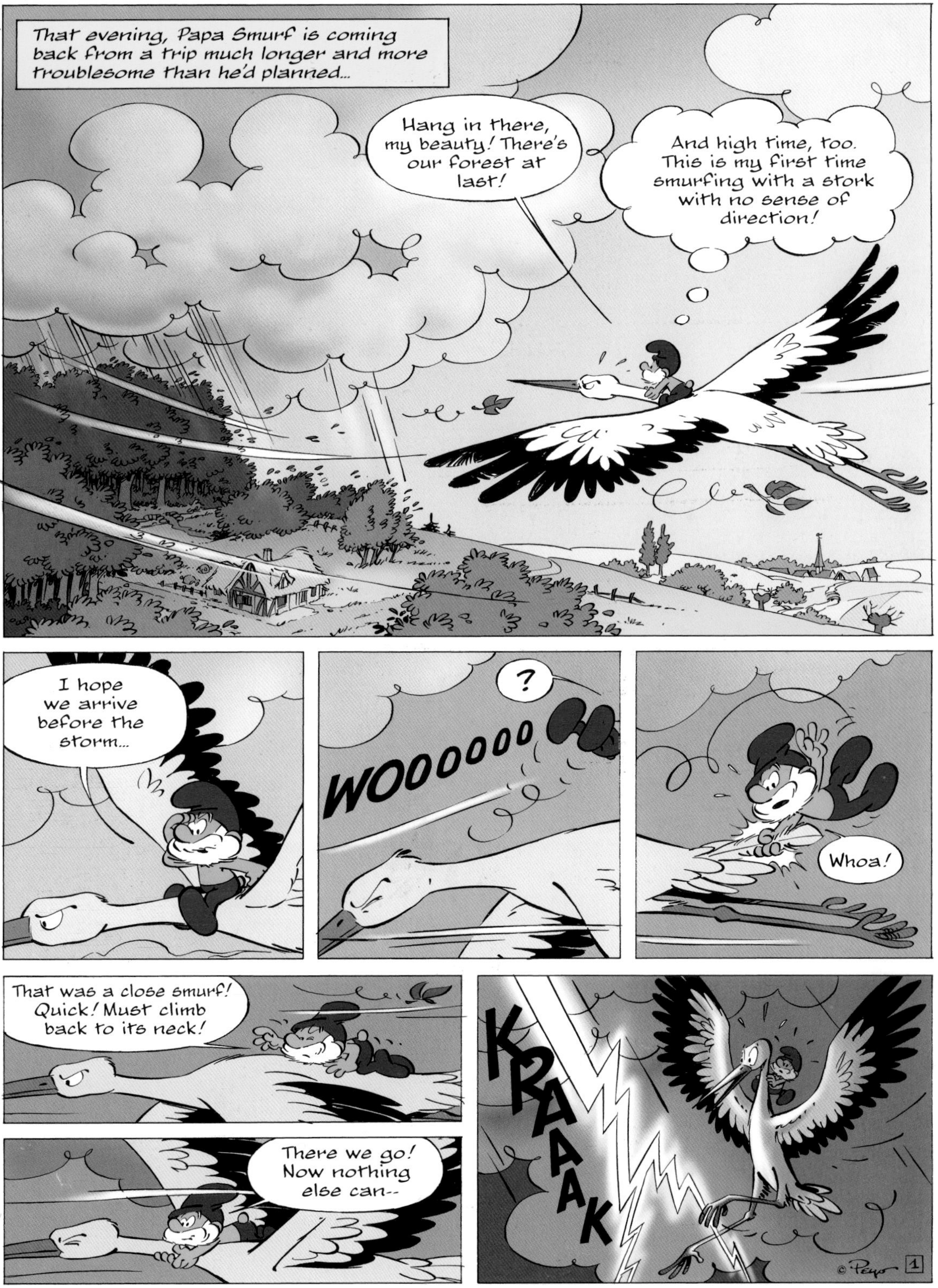
That evening, Papa Smurf is coming back from a trip much longer and more troublesome than he'd planned...
Hang in there, my beauty! There's our forest at last!
And high time, too. This is my first time smurfing with a stork with no sense of direction!
I hope we arrive before the storm...
?
WOOOOOO
Whoa!
That was a close smurf! Quick! Must climb back to its neck!
There we go! Now nothing else can--
KRAAAK
© Peyo
1

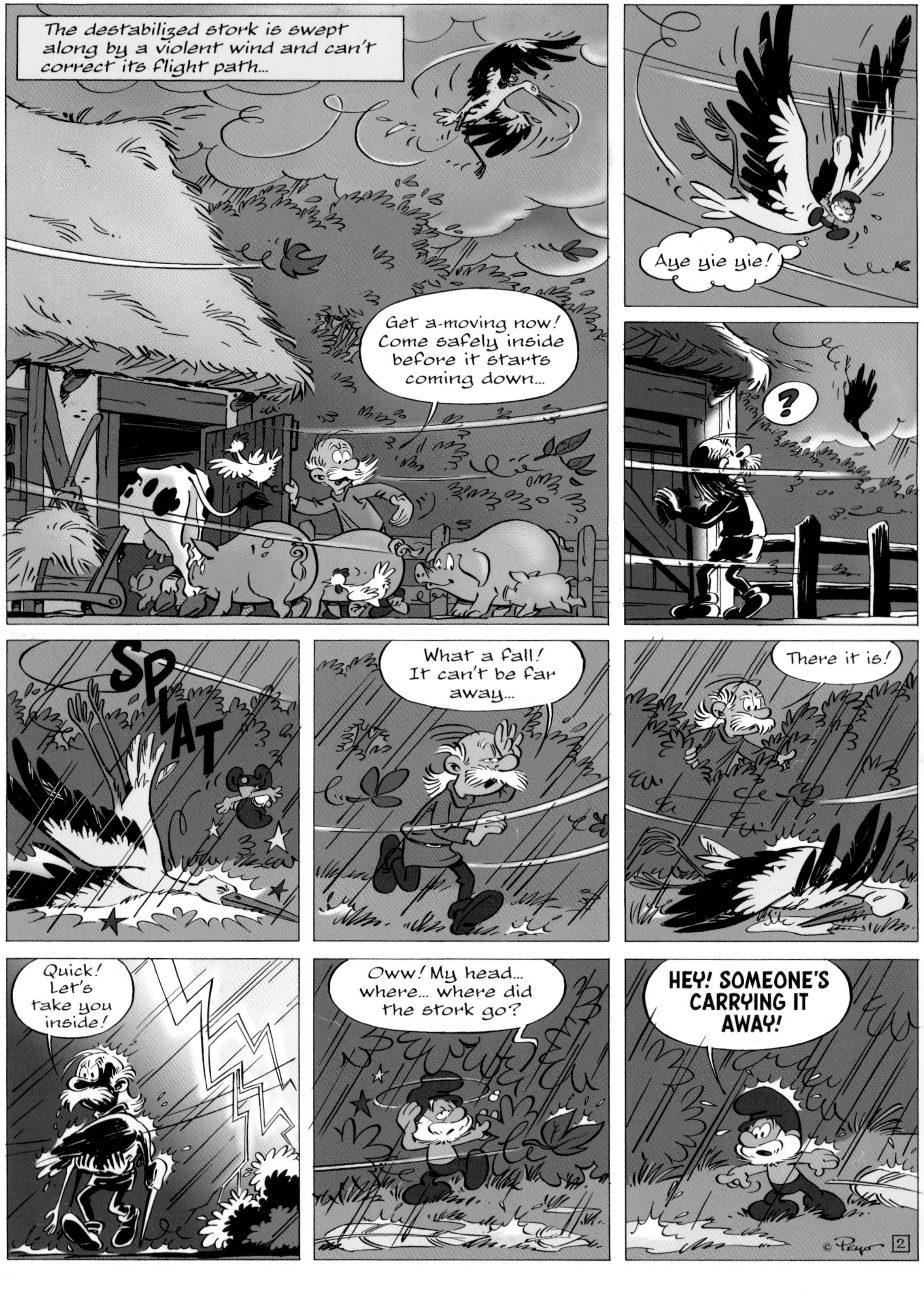
The destabilized stork is swept along by a violent wind and can't correct its flight path...
Get a-moving now! Come safely inside before it starts coming down...
Aye yie yie!
?
SPLAT
What a fall! It can't be far away...
There it is!
Quick! Let's take you inside!
Oww! My head... where... where did the stork go?
HEY! SOMEONE'S CARRYING IT AWAY!
© Peyo
2

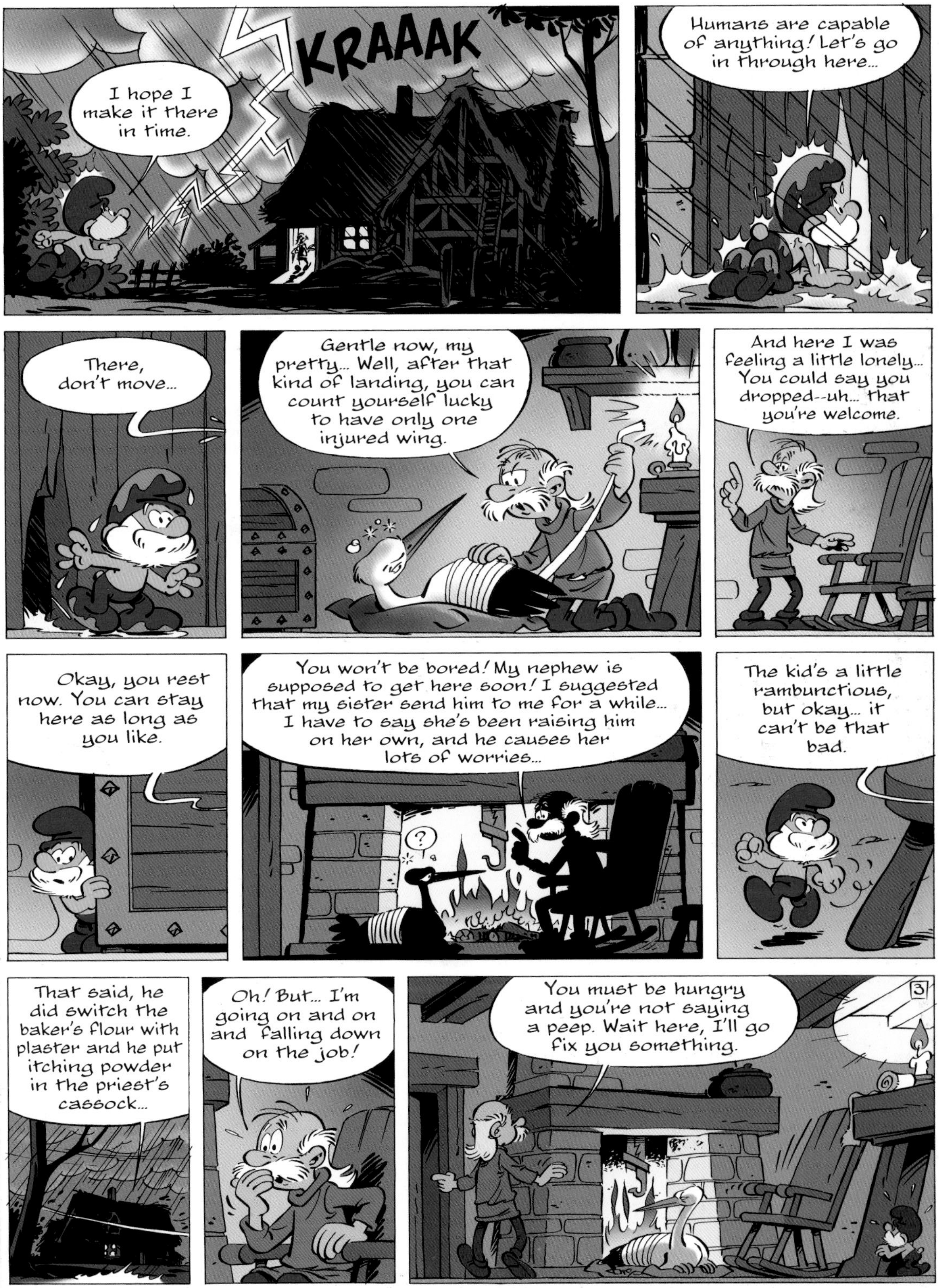
KRAAAK
I hope I make it there in time.
Humans are capable of anything! Let's go in through here...
There, don't move...
Gentle now, my pretty... Well, after that kind of landing, you can count yourself lucky to have only one injured wing.
And here I was feeling a little lonely... You could say you dropped--uh... that you're welcome.
Okay, you rest now. You can stay here as long as you like.
You won't be bored! My nephew is supposed to get here soon! I suggested that my sister send him to me for a while... I have to say she's been raising him on her own, and he causes her lots of worries...
?
The kid's a little rambunctious, but okay... it can't be that bad.
That said, he did switch the baker's flour with plaster and he put itching powder in the priest's cassock...
Oh! But... I'm going on and on and falling down on the job!
You must be hungry and you're not saying a peep. Wait here, I'll go fix you something.
3

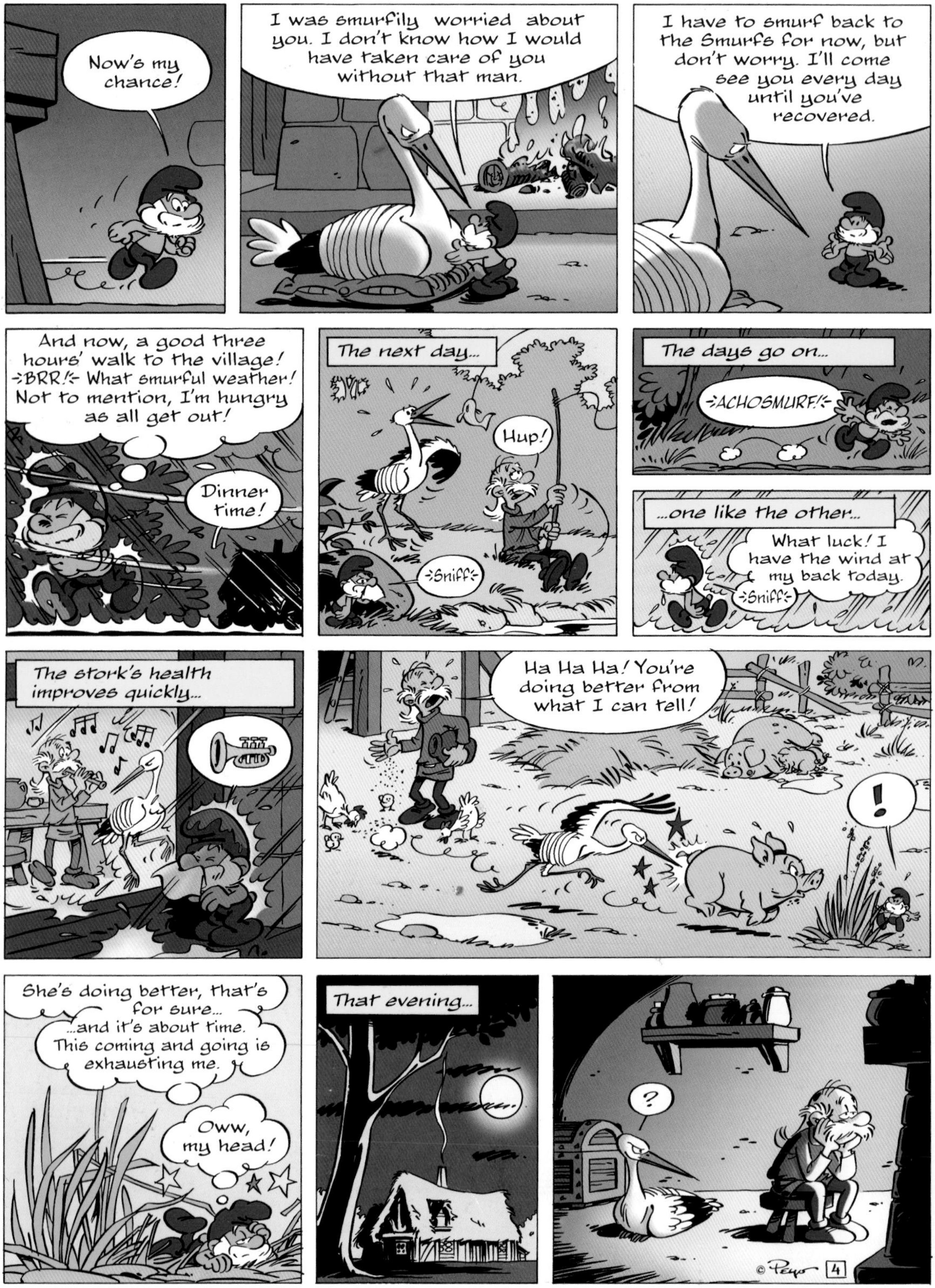

Now's my chance!
I was smurfily worried about you. I don't know how I would have taken care of you without that man.
I have to smurf back to the Smurfs for now, but don't worry. I'll come see you every day until you've recovered.
And now, a good three hours' walk to the village! -BRR!- What smurful weather! Not to mention, I'm hungry as all get out!
Dinner time!
The next day...
Hup!
-Sniff-
The days go on...
-ACHOSMURF!-
...one like the other...
What luck! I have the wind at my back today.
-Sniff-
The stork's health improves quickly...
Ha Ha Ha! You're doing better from what I can tell!
!
She's doing better, that's for sure...
...and it's about time. This coming and going is exhausting me.
Oww, my head!
That evening...
?
© Peyo 4

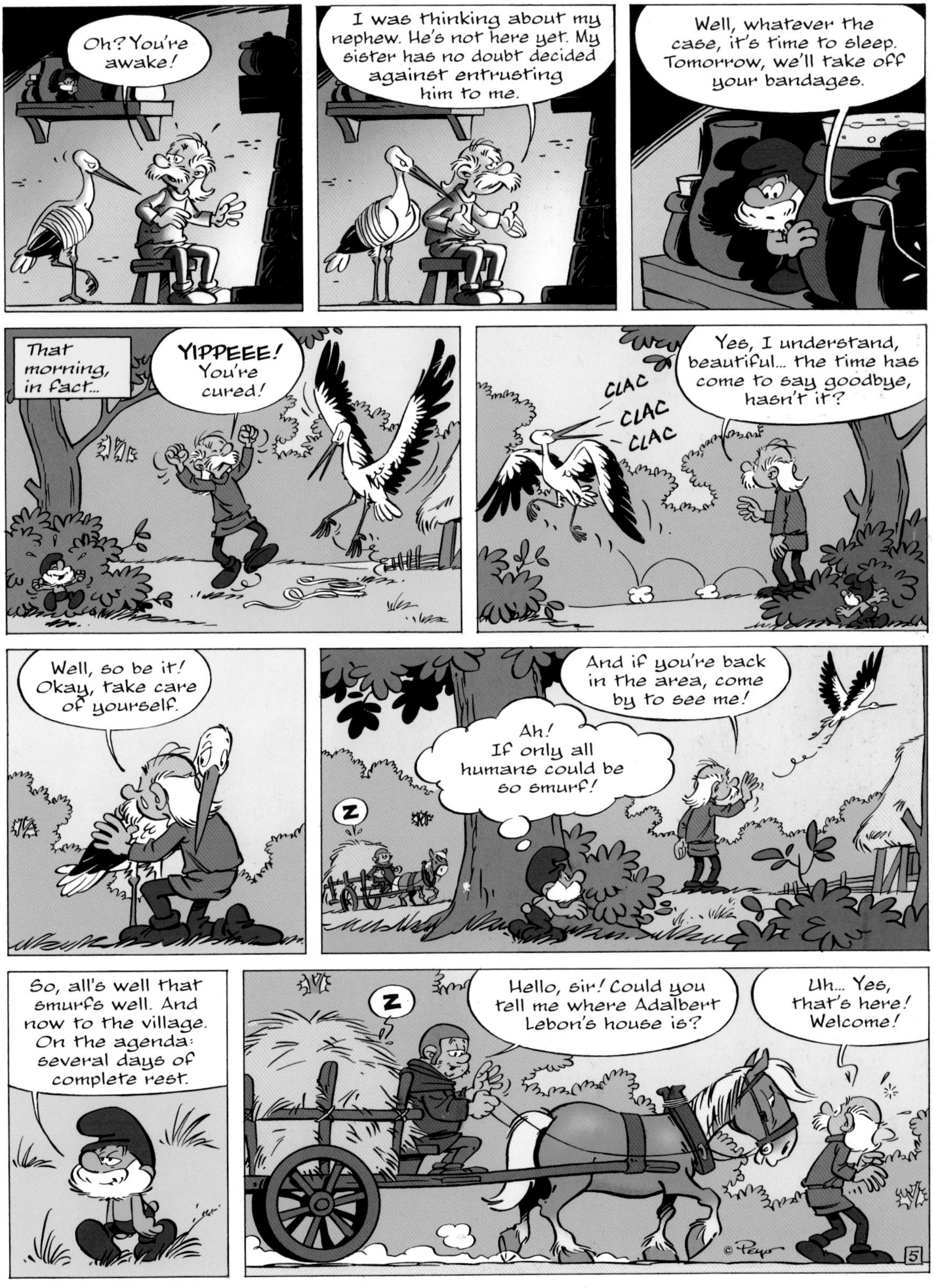
Oh? You're awake!
I was thinking about my nephew. He's not here yet. My sister has no doubt decided against entrusting him to me.
Well, whatever the case, it's time to sleep. Tomorrow, we'll take off your bandages.
That morning, in fact...
YIPPEEE! You're cured!
CLAC
CLAC
CLAC
Yes, I understand, beautiful... the time has come to say goodbye, hasn't it?
Well, so be it! Okay, take care of yourself.
And if you're back in the area, come by to see me!
Ah! If only all humans could be so smurf!
Z
So, all's well that smurfs well. And now to the village. On the agenda: several days of complete rest.
Z
Hello, sir! Could you tell me where Adalbert Lebon's house is?
Uh... Yes, that's here! Welcome!
© Peyo
5

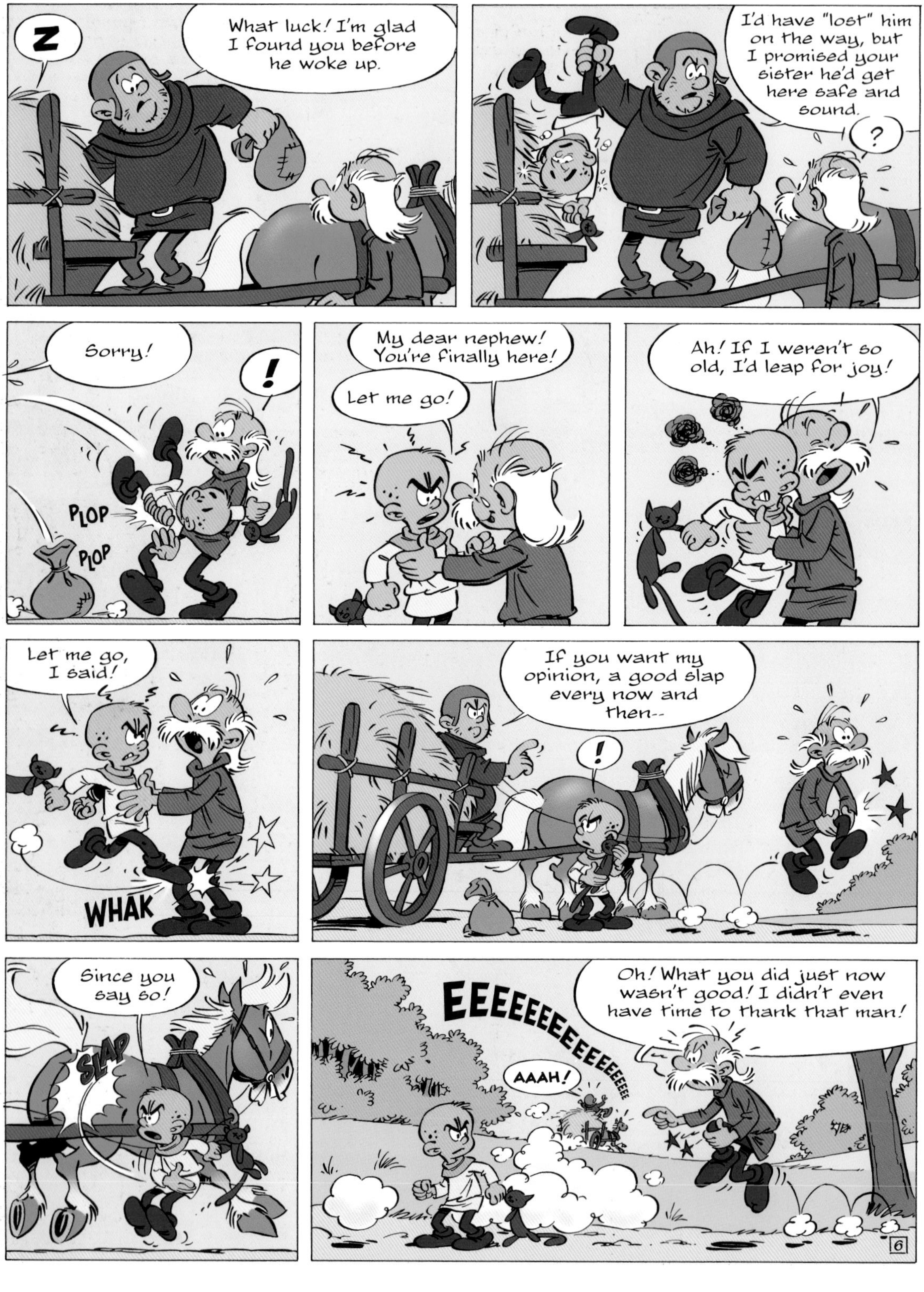
Z
What luck! I'm glad I found you before he woke up.
I'd have "lost" him on the way, but I promised your sister he'd get here safe and sound.
?
Sorry!
!
PLOP
PLOP
My dear nephew! You're finally here!
Let me go!
Ah! If I weren't so old, I'd leap for joy!
Let me go, I said!
WHAK
If you want my opinion, a good slap every now and then--
!
Since you say so!
SLAP
EEEEEEEEEEEEEEEEEE
AAAH!
Oh! What you did just now wasn't good! I didn't even have time to thank that man!
6

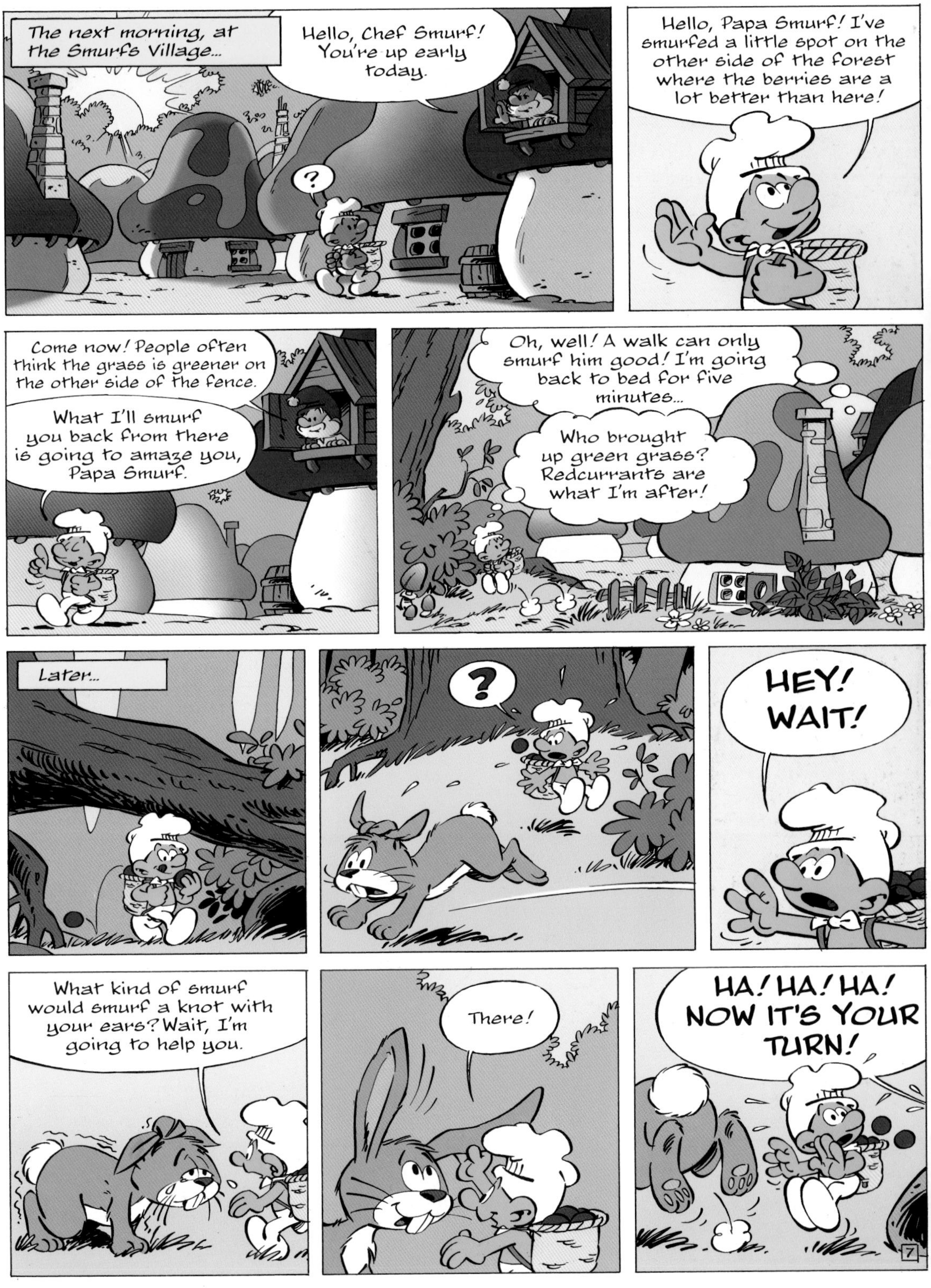
The next morning, at the Smurfs Village...
Hello, Chef Smurf! You're up early today.
?
Hello, Papa Smurf! I've smurfed a little spot on the other side of the forest where the berries are a lot better than here!
Come now! People often think the grass is greener on the other side of the fence.
What I'll smurf you back from there is going to amaze you, Papa Smurf.
Oh, well! A walk can only smurf him good! I'm going back to bed for five minutes...
Who brought up green grass? Redcurrants are what I'm after!
Later...
?
HEY! WAIT!
What kind of smurf would smurf a knot with your ears? Wait, I'm going to help you.
There!
HA! HA! HA! NOW IT'S YOUR TURN!
7

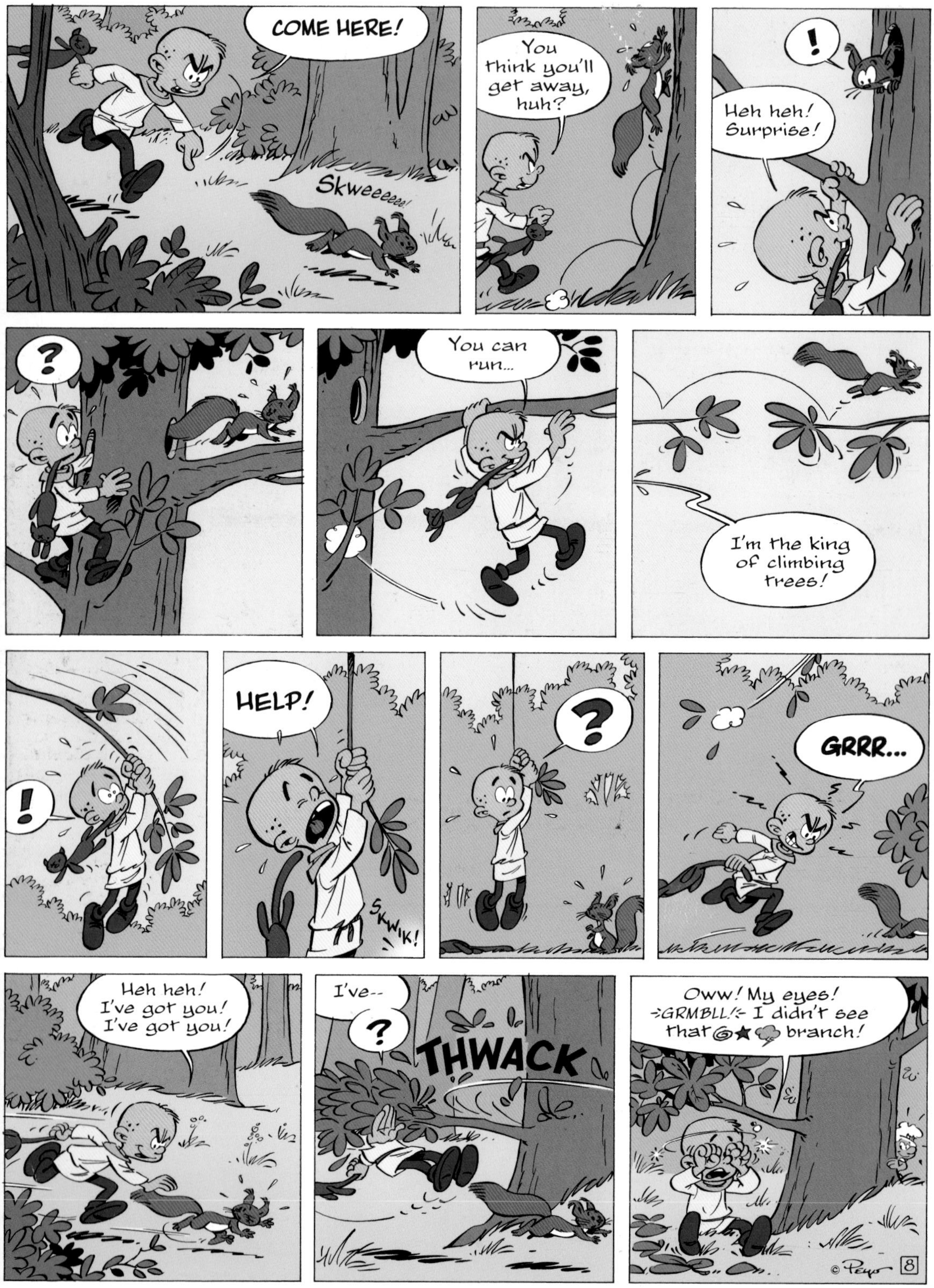
COME HERE!
Skweeeeee!
You think you'll get away, huh?
!
Heh heh! Surprise!
?
You can run...
I'm the king of climbing trees!
!
HELP!
SKWIK!
?
GRRR...
Heh heh! I've got you! I've got you!
I've--
?
THWACK
Oww! My eyes! -GRMBLL!- I didn't see that branch!
© Peyo
8

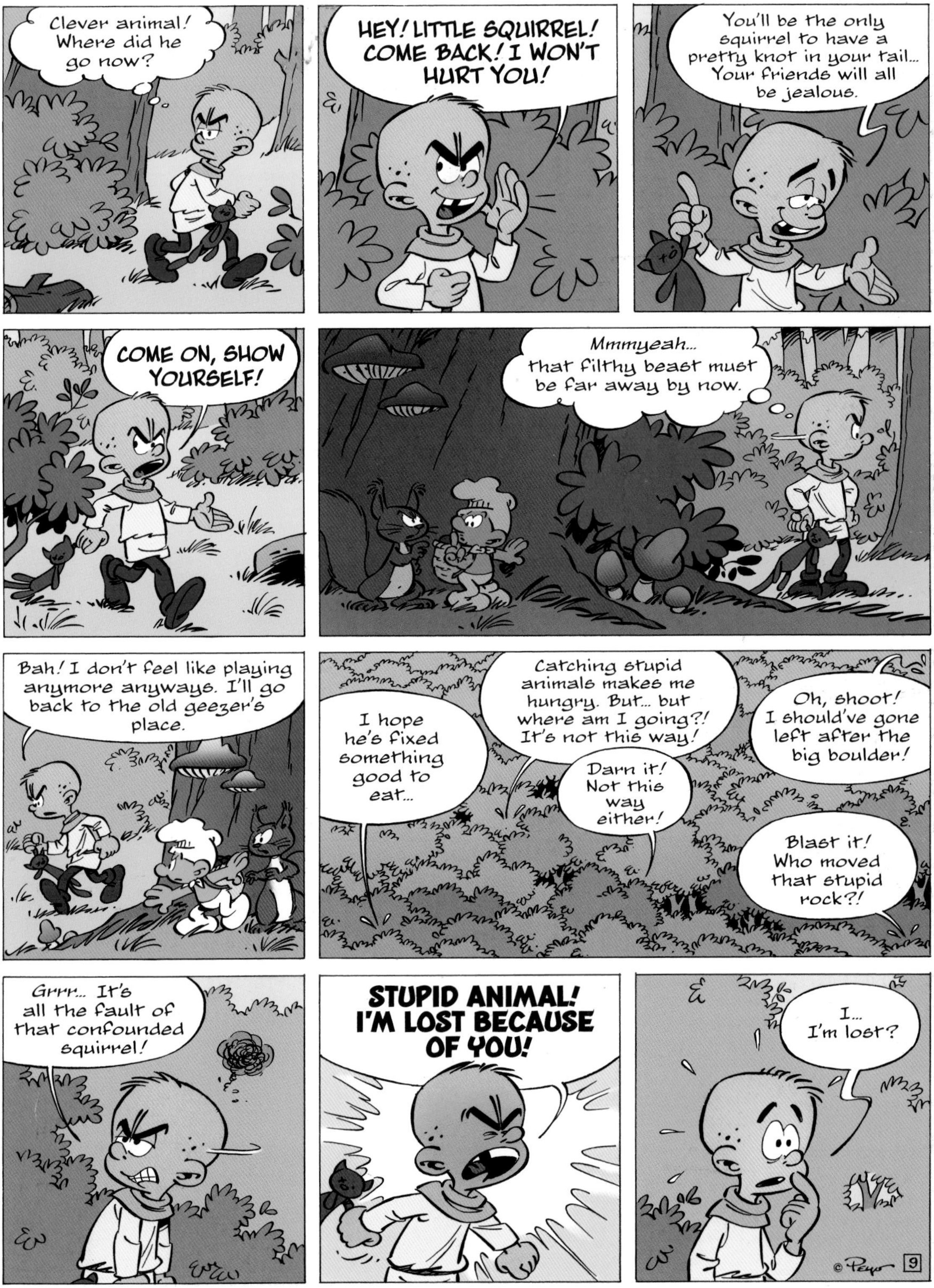

Clever animal! Where did he go now?
HEY! LITTLE SQUIRREL! COME BACK! I WON'T HURT YOU!
You'll be the only squirrel to have a pretty knot in your tail... Your friends will all be jealous.
COME ON, SHOW YOURSELF!
Mmmyeah... that filthy beast must be far away by now.
Bah! I don't feel like playing anymore anyways. I'll go back to the old geezer's place.
I hope he's fixed something good to eat...
Catching stupid animals makes me hungry. But... but where am I going?! It's not this way!
Darn it! Not this way either!
Oh, shoot! I should've gone left after the big boulder!
Blast it! Who moved that stupid rock?!
Grrr... It's all the fault of that confounded squirrel!
STUPID ANIMAL! I'M LOST BECAUSE OF YOU!
I... I'm lost?
© Peyo
9

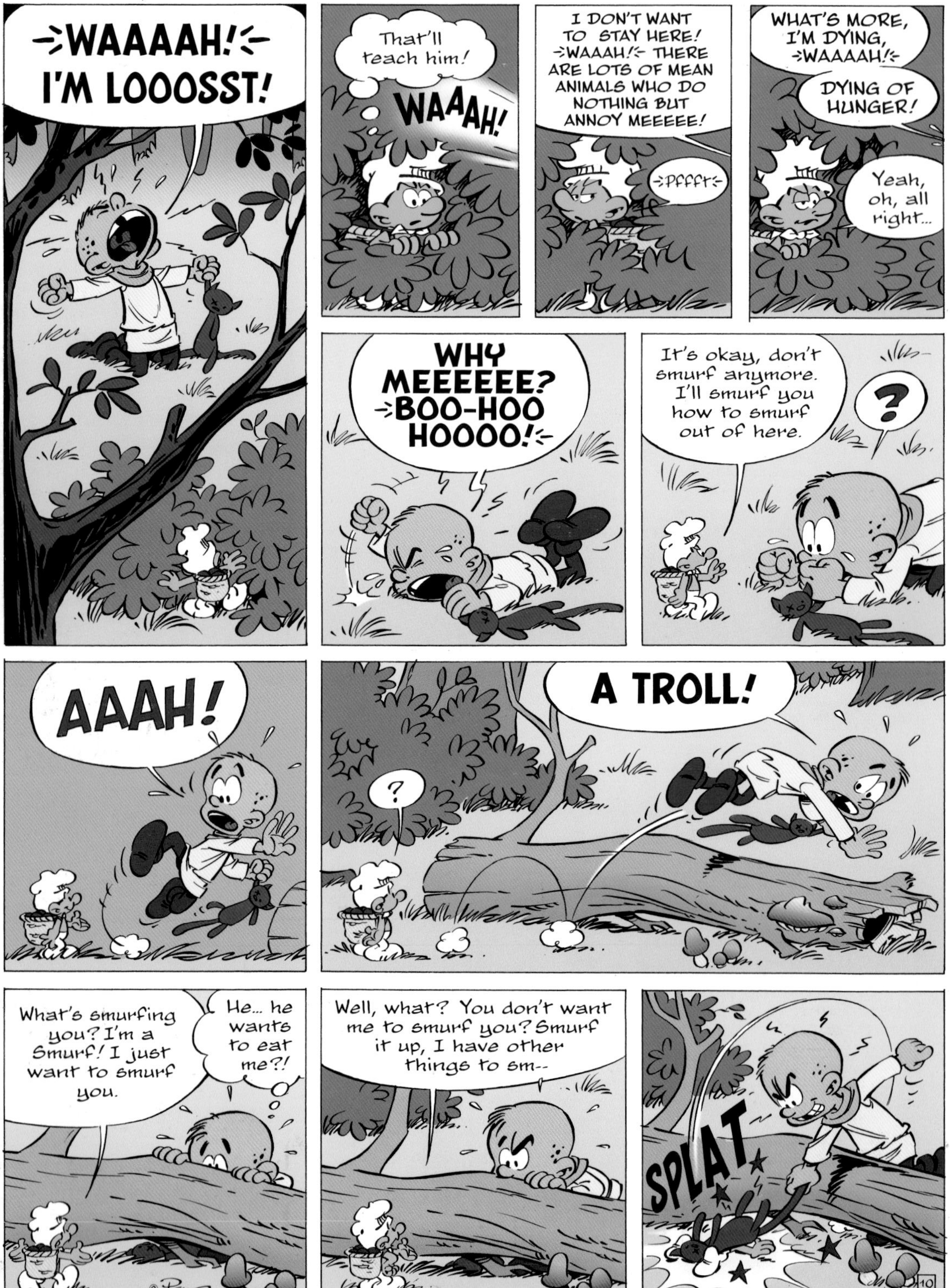
WAAAAH! I'M LOOOSST!
That'll teach him!
WAAAH!
I DON'T WANT TO STAY HERE! WAAAH! THERE ARE LOTS OF MEAN ANIMALS WHO DO NOTHING BUT ANNOY MEEEEE!
Pffft
WHAT'S MORE, I'M DYING, WAAAAH!
DYING OF HUNGER!
Yeah, oh, all right...
WHY MEEEEEE? BOO-HOO HOOOO!
It's okay, don't smurf anymore. I'll smurf you how to smurf out of here.
?
AAAH!
A TROLL!
?
What's smurfing you? I'm a Smurf! I just want to smurf you.
He... he wants to eat me?!
© Peyo
Well, what? You don't want me to smurf you? Smurf it up, I have other things to sm--
SPLAT
10

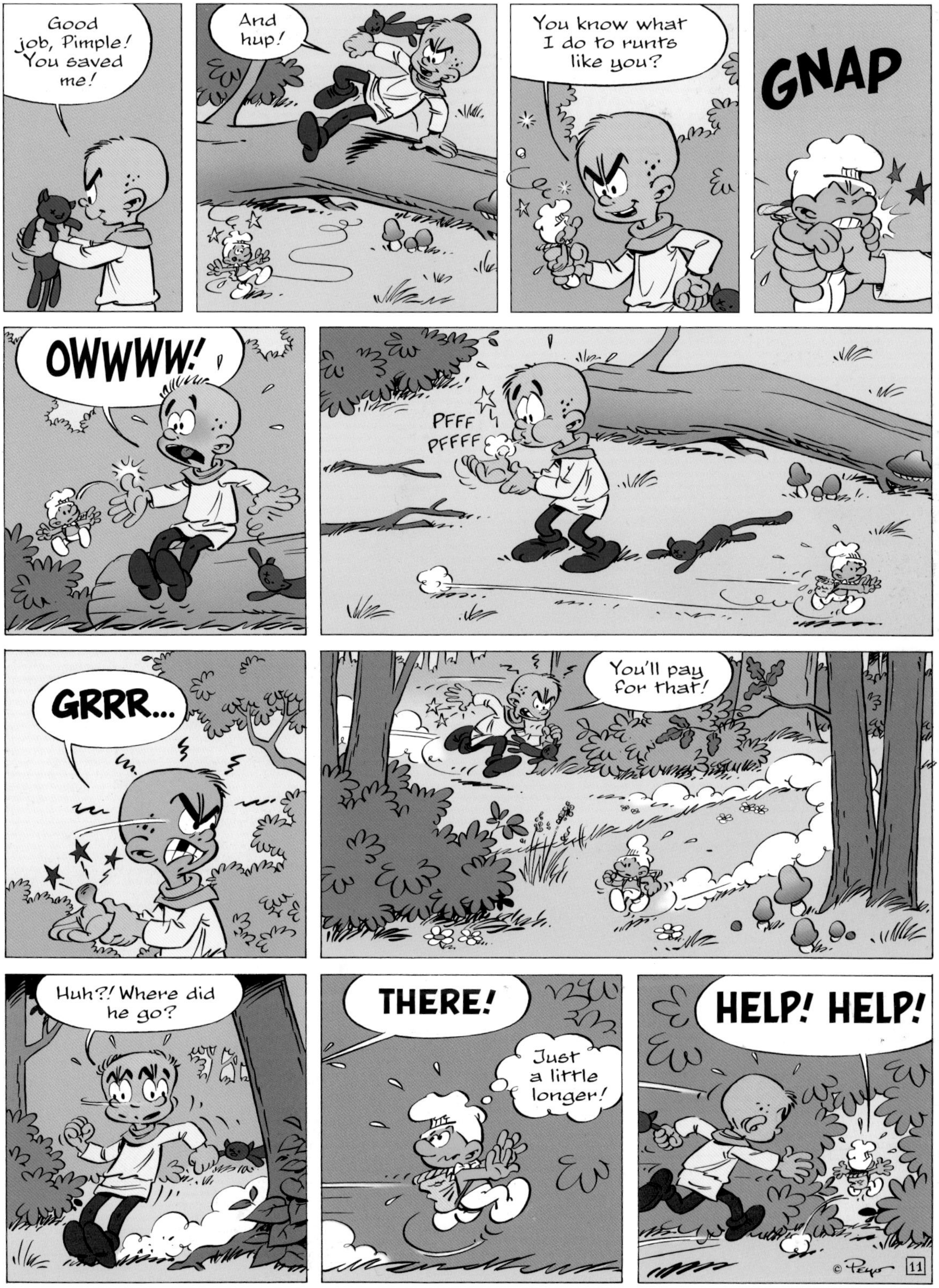
Good job, Pimple! You saved me!
And hup!
You know what I do to runts like you?
GNAP
OWWWW!
PFFF PFFFF
GRRR...
You'll pay for that!
Huh?! Where did he go?
THERE!
Just a little longer!
HELP! HELP!
© Peyo
11

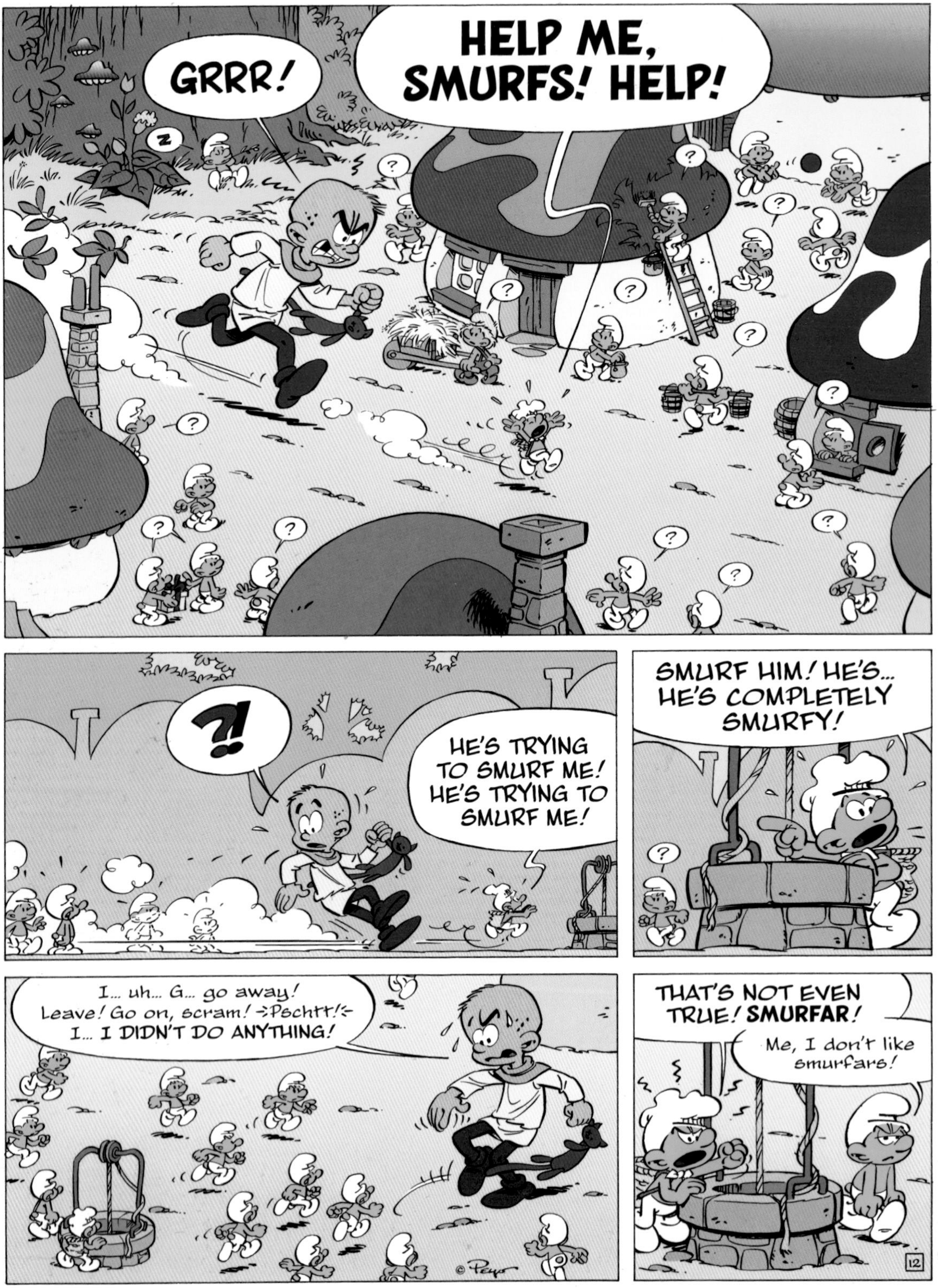
GRRR!
HELP ME, SMURFS! HELP!
?!
HE'S TRYING TO SMURF ME! HE'S TRYING TO SMURF ME!
SMURF HIM! HE'S... HE'S COMPLETELY SMURFY!
I... uh... G... go away! Leave! Go on, scram! -Pschtt!- I... I DIDN'T DO ANYTHING!
© Peyo
THAT'S NOT EVEN TRUE! SMURFAR!
Me, I don't like smurfars!
12

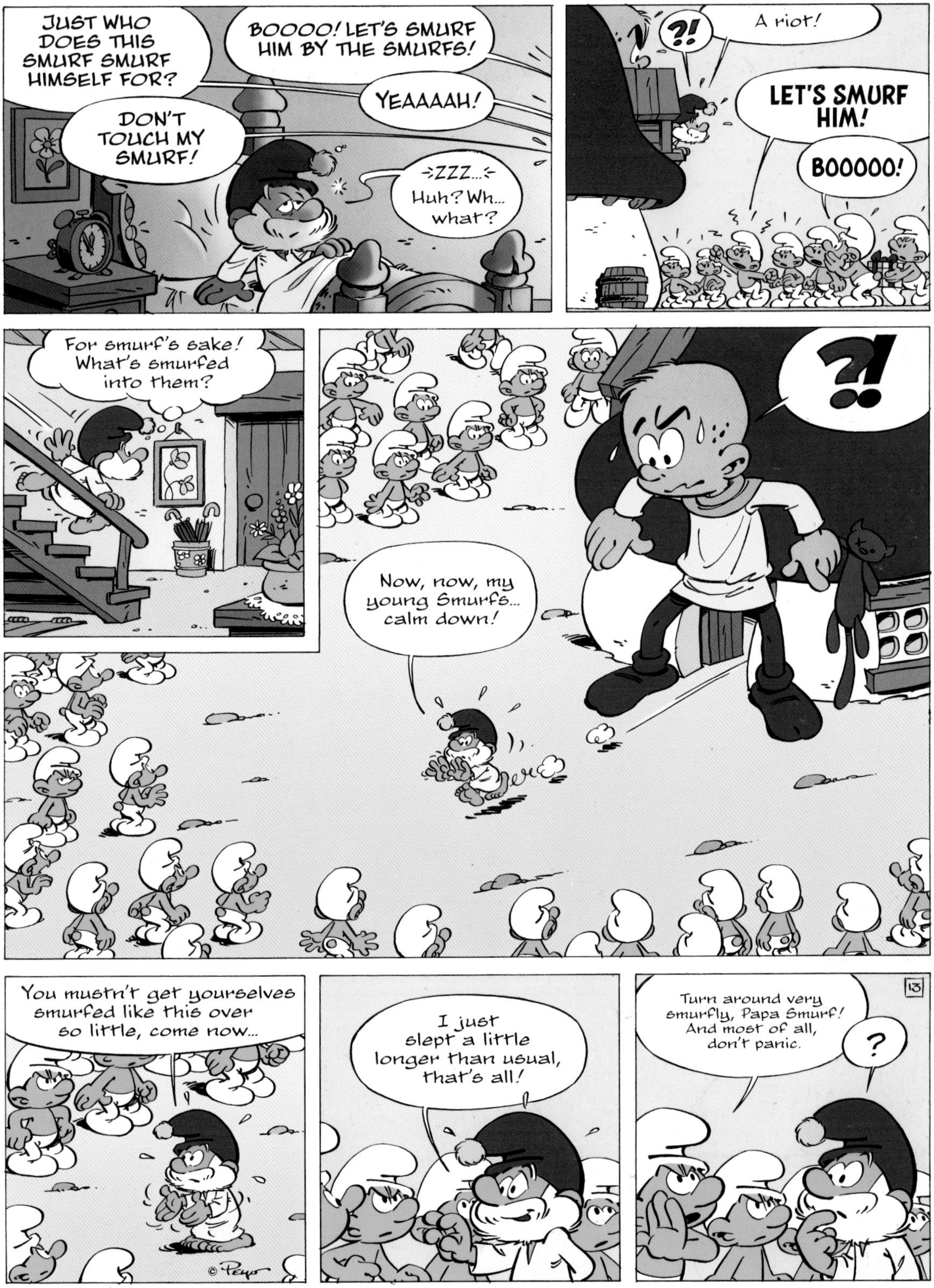
JUST WHO DOES THIS SMURF SMURF HIMSELF FOR?
BOOOO! LET'S SMURF HIM BY THE SMURFS!
YEAAAAH!
DON'T TOUCH MY SMURF!
ZZZ... Huh? Wh... what?
?!
A riot!
LET'S SMURF HIM!
BOOOOO!
For smurf's sake! What's smurfed into them?
?!
Now, now, my young Smurfs... calm down!
You mustn't get yourselves smurfed like this over so little, come now...
© Peyo
I just slept a little longer than usual, that's all!
Turn around very smurfly, Papa Smurf! And most of all, don't panic.
?
13

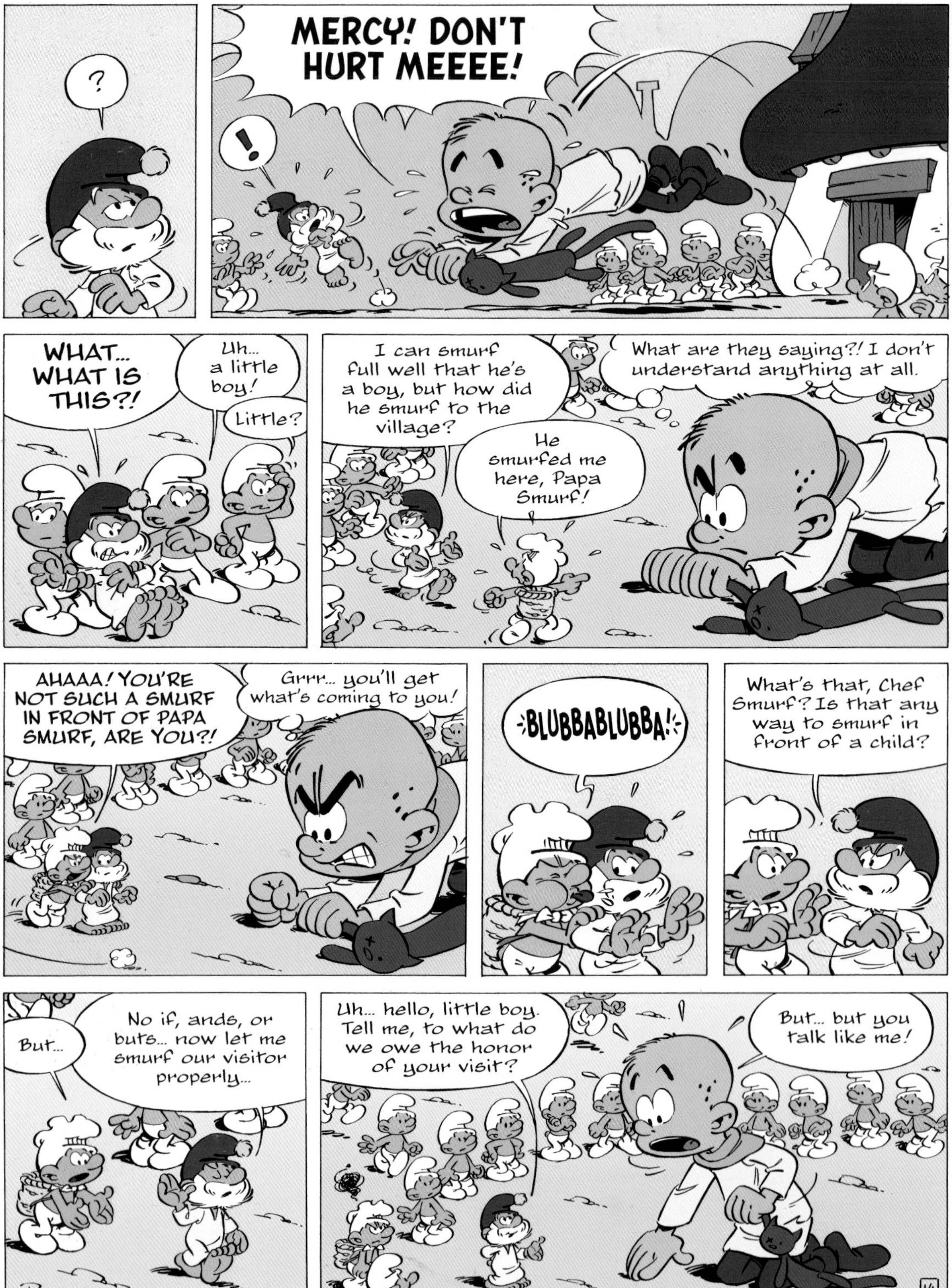
?
MERCY! DON'T HURT MEEEE!
!
WHAT... WHAT IS THIS?!
Uh... a little boy!
Little?
I can smurf full well that he's a boy, but how did he smurf to the village?
What are they saying?! I don't understand anything at all.
He smurfed me here, Papa Smurf!
AHAAA! YOU'RE NOT SUCH A SMURF IN FRONT OF PAPA SMURF, ARE YOU?!
Grrr... you'll get what's coming to you!
BLUBBABLUBBA!
What's that, Chef Smurf? Is that any way to smurf in front of a child?
But...
No if, ands, or buts... now let me smurf our visitor properly...
Uh... hello, little boy. Tell me, to what do we owe the honor of your visit?
But... but you talk like me!
© Peyo
14

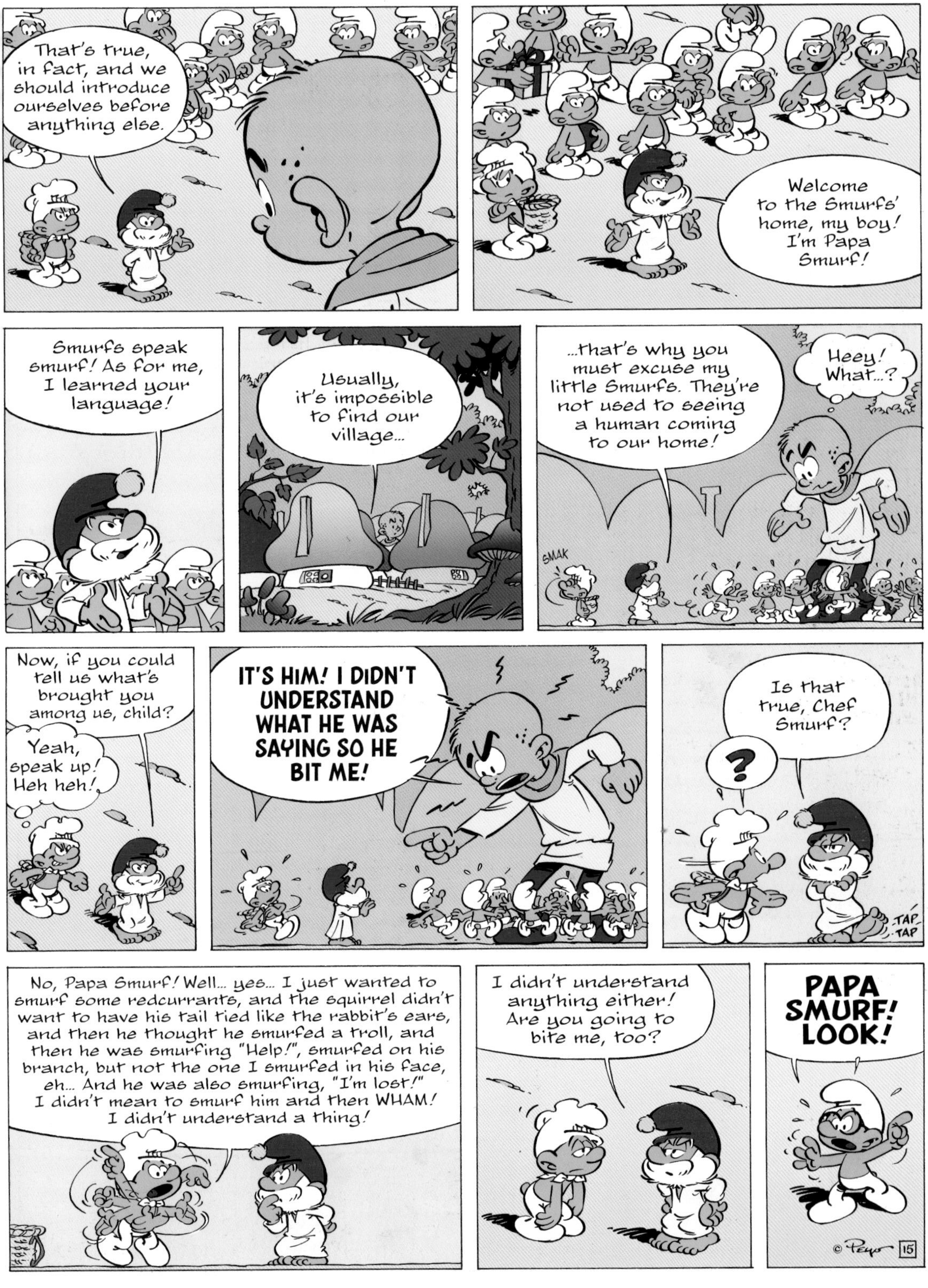

That's true, in fact, and we should introduce ourselves before anything else.
Welcome to the Smurfs' home, my boy! I'm Papa Smurf!
Smurfs speak smurf! As for me, I learned your language!
Usually, it's impossible to find our village...
...that's why you must excuse my little Smurfs. They're not used to seeing a human coming to our home!
Heey! What...?
SMAK
Now, if you could tell us what's brought you among us, child?
Yeah, speak up! Heh heh!
IT'S HIM! I DIDN'T UNDERSTAND WHAT HE WAS SAYING SO HE BIT ME!
Is that true, Chef Smurf?
?
TAP TAP
No, Papa Smurf! Well... yes... I just wanted to smurf some redcurrants, and the squirrel didn't want to have his tail tied like the rabbit's ears, and then he thought he smurfed a troll, and then he was smurfing "Help!", smurfed on his branch, but not the one I smurfed in his face, eh... And he was also smurfing, "I'm lost!" I didn't mean to smurf him and then WHAM! I didn't understand a thing!
I didn't understand anything either! Are you going to bite me, too?
PAPA SMURF! LOOK!
© Peyo 15

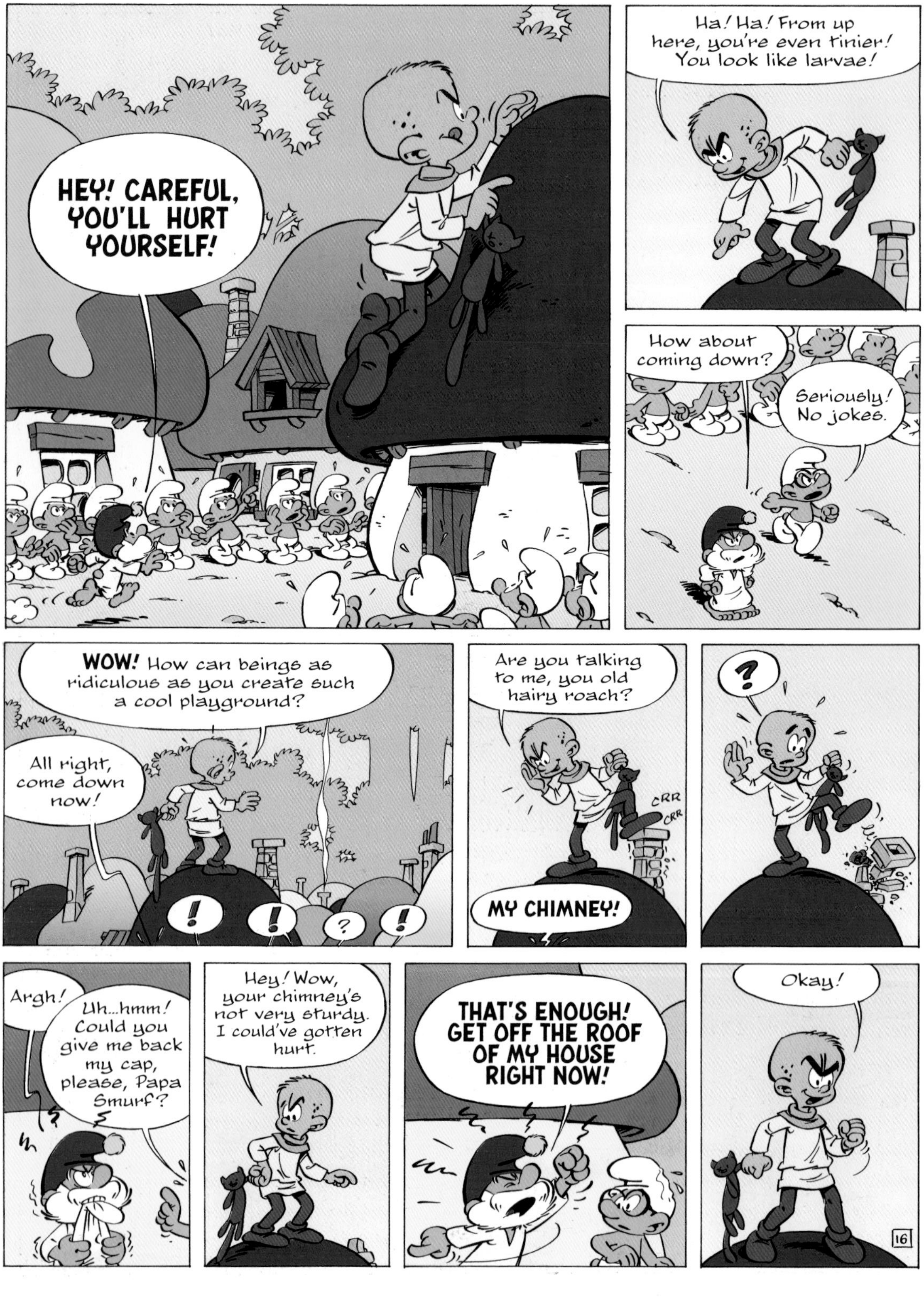
HEY! CAREFUL, YOU'LL HURT YOURSELF!
Ha! Ha! From up here, you're even tinier! You look like larvae!
How about coming down?
Seriously! No jokes.
WOW! How can beings as ridiculous as you create such a cool playground?
All right, come down now!
!
!
?
!
Are you talking to me, you old hairy roach?
CRR
CRR
MY CHIMNEY!
?
Argh!
Uh...hmm! Could you give me back my cap, please, Papa Smurf?
Hey! Wow, your chimney's not very sturdy. I could've gotten hurt.
THAT'S ENOUGH! GET OFF THE ROOF OF MY HOUSE RIGHT NOW!
Okay!
16

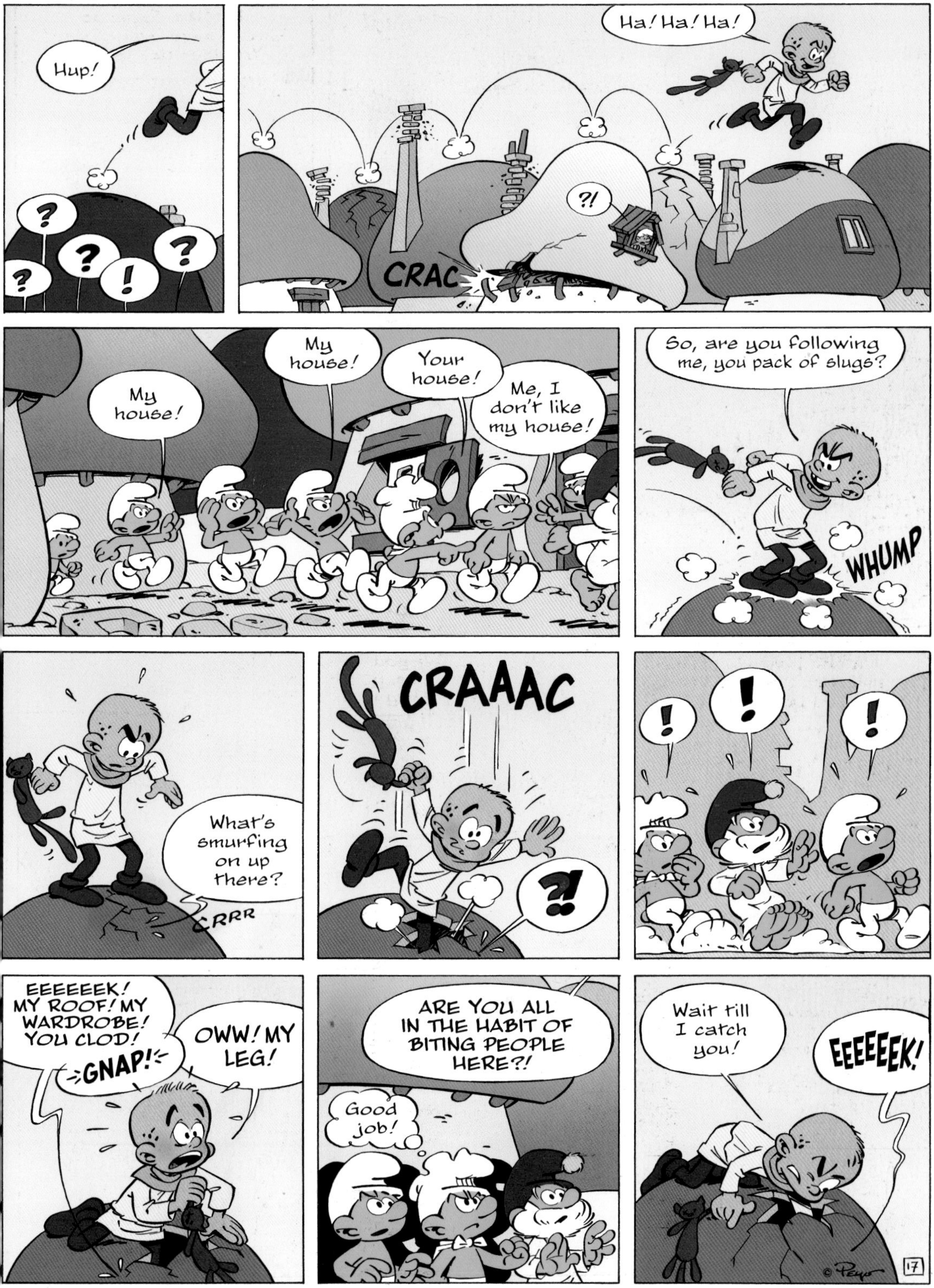

Hup!
?
?
?
!
?
Ha! Ha! Ha!
?!
CRAC
My house!
My house!
Your house!
Me, I don't like my house!
So, are you following me, you pack of slugs?
WHUMP
What's smurfing on up there?
CRRR
CRAAAC
?!
!
!
!
EEEEEEK! MY ROOF! MY WARDROBE! YOU CLOD!
GNAP!
OWW! MY LEG!
ARE YOU ALL IN THE HABIT OF BITING PEOPLE HERE?!
Good job!
Wait till I catch you!
EEEEEEK!
© Peyo
17

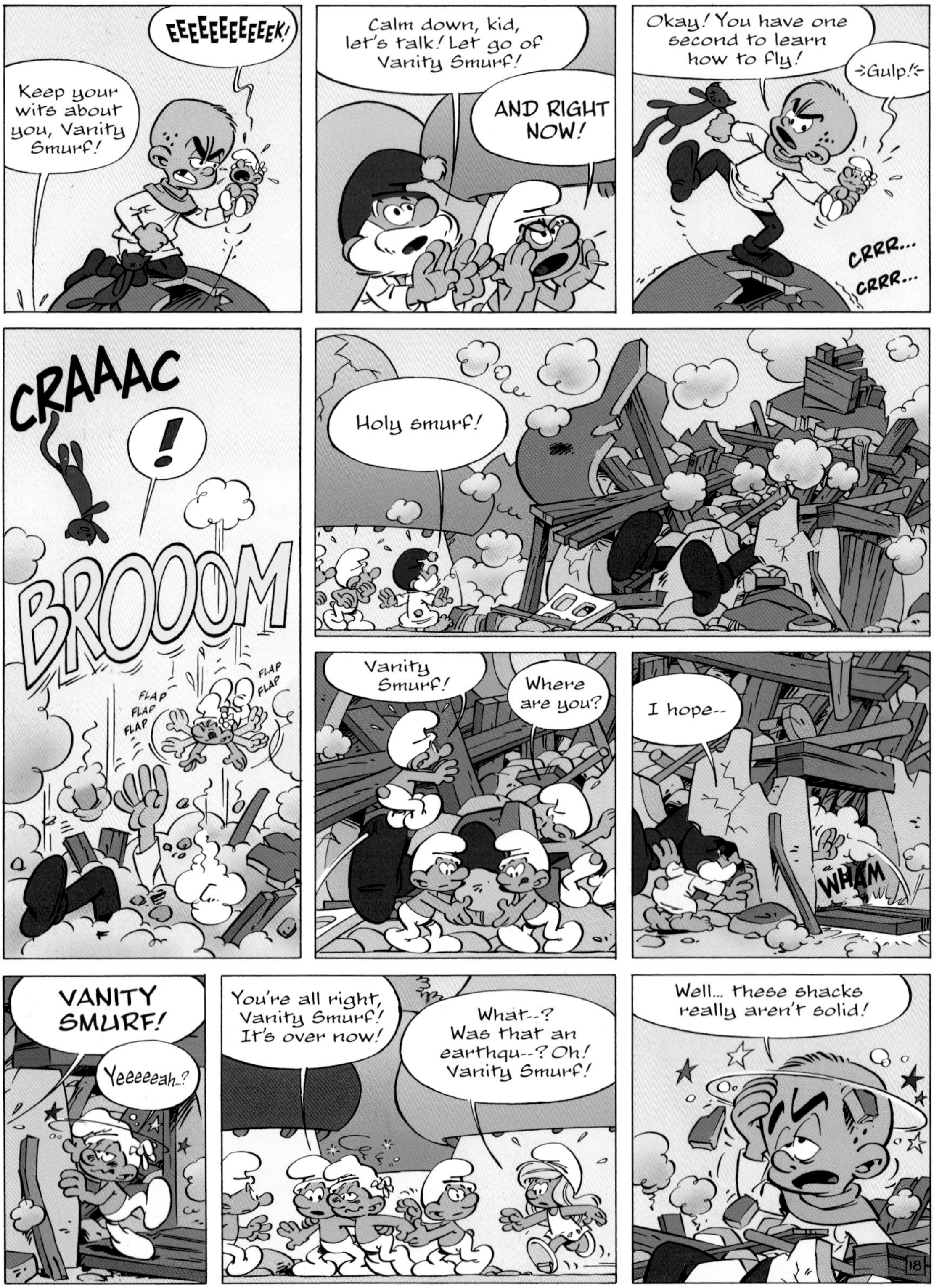
EEEEEEEEEEEK!
Keep your wits about you, Vanity Smurf!
Calm down, kid, let's talk! Let go of Vanity Smurf!
AND RIGHT NOW!
Okay! You have one second to learn how to fly!
Gulp!
CRRR... CRRR...
CRAAAC
!
BROOOM
FLAP FLAP FLAP
FLAP FLAP
Holy smurf!
Vanity Smurf!
Where are you?
I hope--
WHAM
VANITY SMURF!
Yeeeeeah...?
You're all right, Vanity Smurf! It's over now!
What--? Was that an earthqu--? Oh! Vanity Smurf!
Well... these shacks really aren't solid!
18

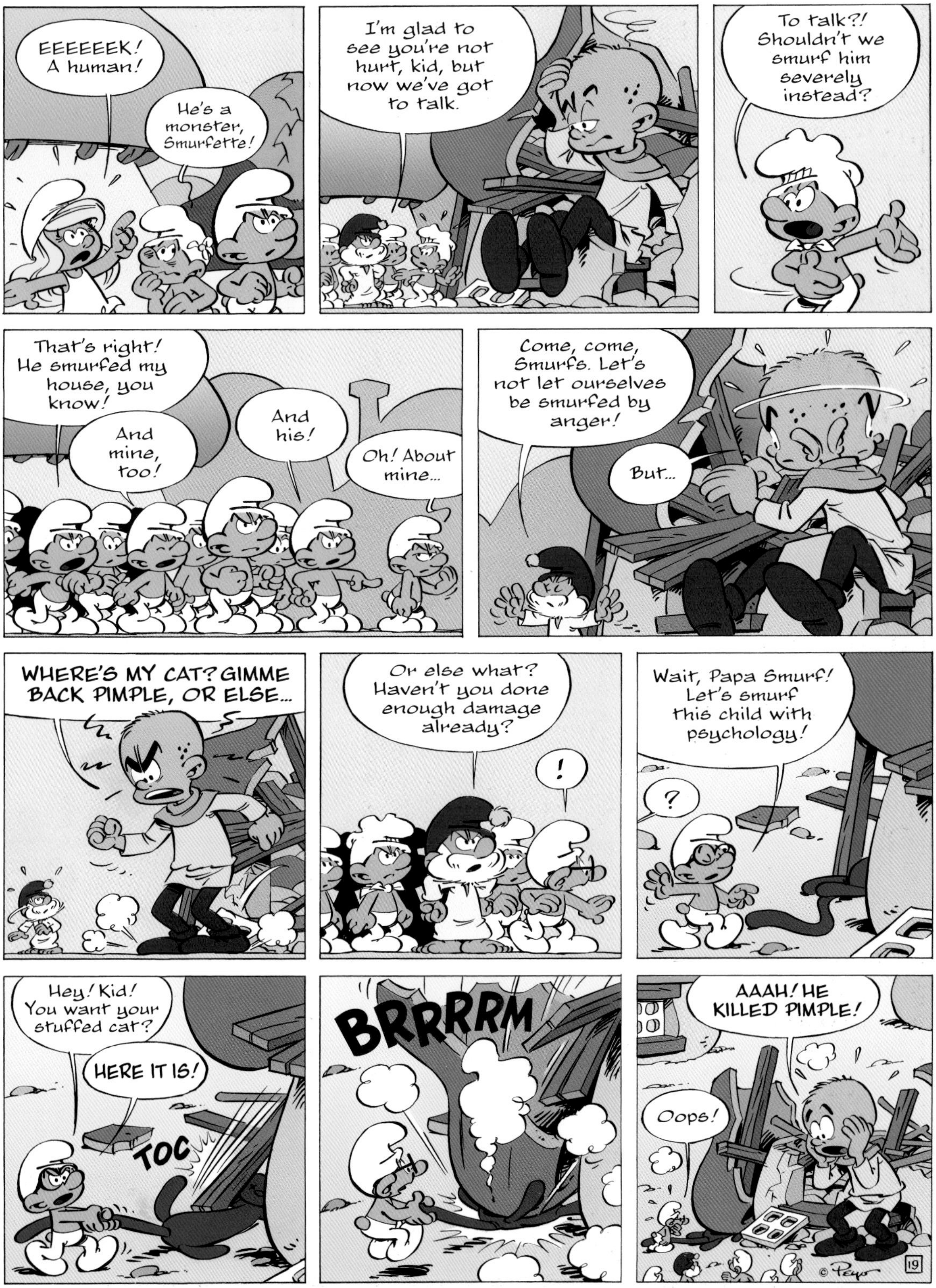
EEEEEEK! A human!
He's a monster, Smurfette!
I'm glad to see you're not hurt, kid, but now we've got to talk.
To talk?! Shouldn't we smurf him severely instead?
That's right! He smurfed my house, you know!
And mine, too!
And his!
Oh! About mine...
Come, come, Smurfs. Let's not let ourselves be smurfed by anger!
But...
WHERE'S MY CAT? GIMME BACK PIMPLE, OR ELSE...
Or else what? Haven't you done enough damage already?
!
Wait, Papa Smurf! Let's smurf this child with psychology!
?
Hey! Kid! You want your stuffed cat?
HERE IT IS!
TOC
BRRRRM
AAAH! HE KILLED PIMPLE!
Oops!
© Peyo
19

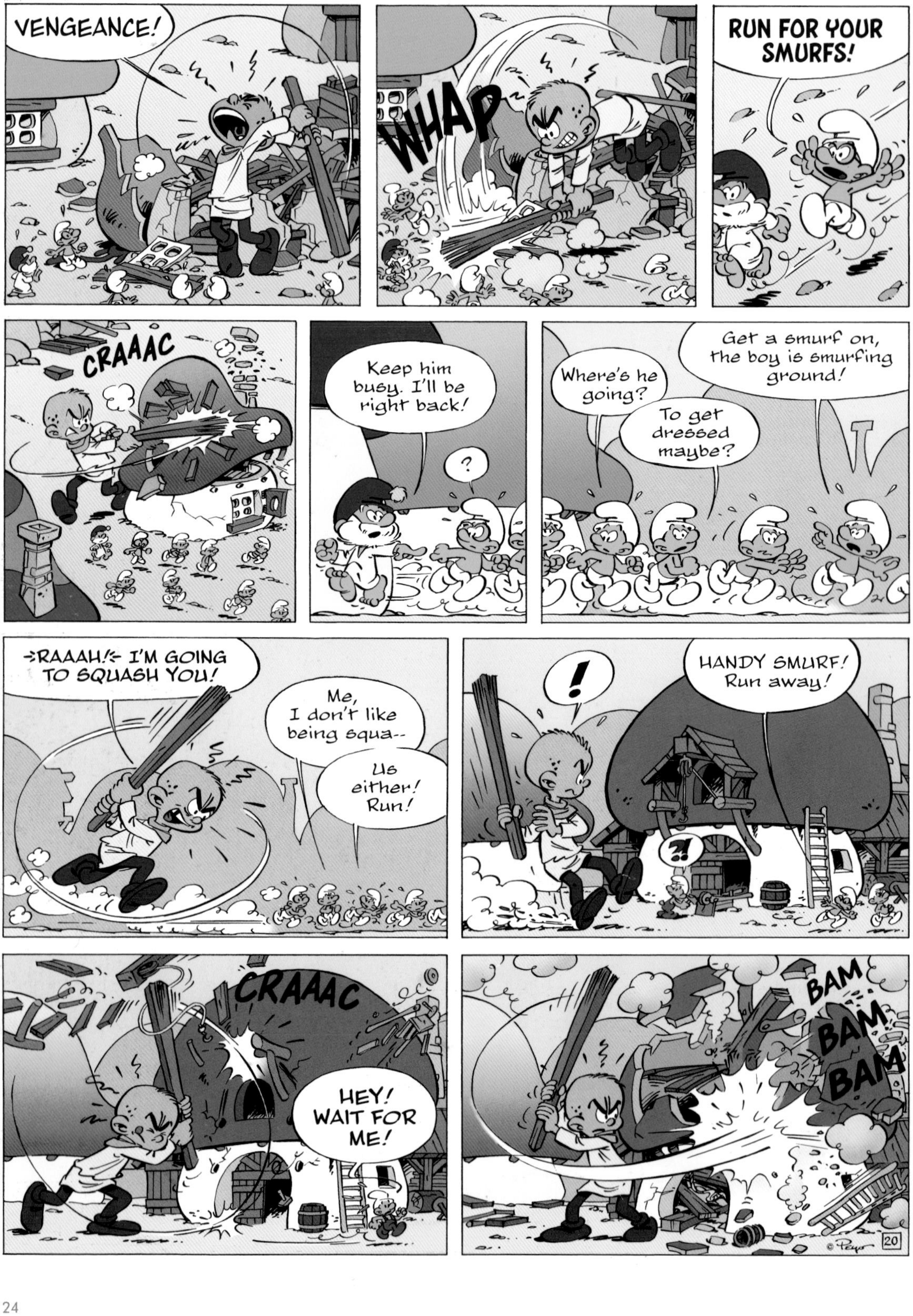
VENGEANCE!
WHAP
RUN FOR YOUR SMURFS!
CRAAAC
Keep him busy. I'll be right back!
?
Where's he going?
To get dressed maybe?
Get a smurf on, the boy is smurfing ground!
-RAAAH!- I'M GOING TO SQUASH YOU!
Me, I don't like being squa--
Us either! Run!
!
HANDY SMURF! Run away!
?!
CRAAAC
HEY! WAIT FOR ME!
BAM
BAM
BAM
© Peyo
20

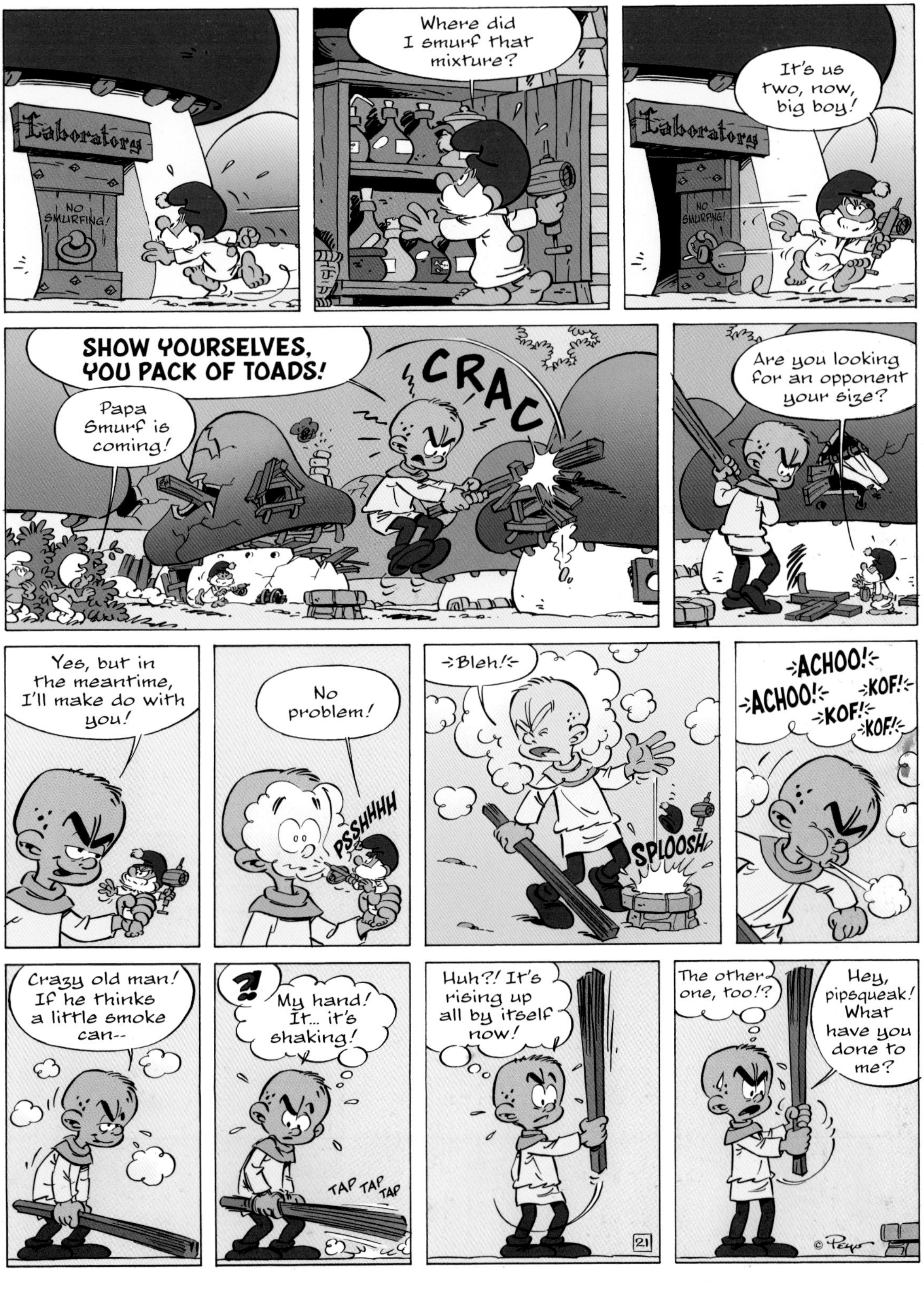
Laboratory
NO SMURFING!
Where did I smurf that mixture?
Laboratory
NO SMURFING!
It's us two, now, big boy!
SHOW YOURSELVES, YOU PACK OF TOADS!
Papa Smurf is coming!
CRAC
Are you looking for an opponent your size?
Yes, but in the meantime, I'll make do with you!
No problem!
PSSHHHH
Bleh!
SPLOOSH
ACHOO!
ACHOO!
KOF!
KOF!
KOF!
Crazy old man! If he thinks a little smoke can--
?!
My hand! It... it's shaking!
TAP TAP TAP
Huh?! It's rising up all by itself now!
21
The other one, too!?
Hey, pipsqueak! What have you done to me?
© Peyo

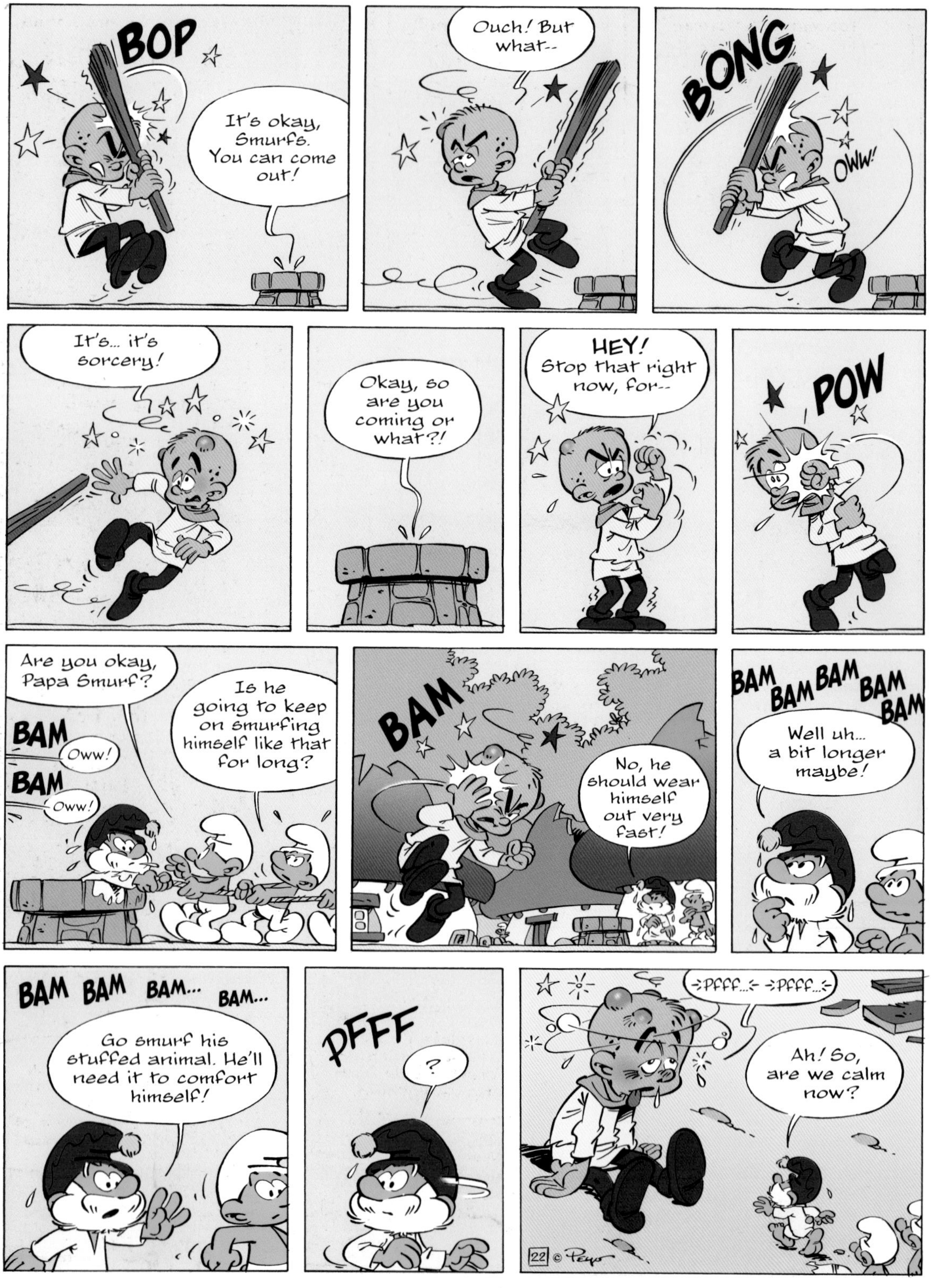
BOP
It's okay, Smurfs. You can come out!
Ouch! But what--
BONG
OWW!
It's... it's sorcery!
Okay, so are you coming or what?!
HEY! Stop that right now, for--
POW
Are you okay, Papa Smurf?
BAM
Oww!
BAM
Oww!
Is he going to keep on smurfing himself like that for long?
BAM
No, he should wear himself out very fast!
BAM BAM BAM BAM BAM
Well uh... a bit longer maybe!
BAM BAM BAM... BAM...
Go smurf his stuffed animal. He'll need it to comfort himself!
PFFF
?
PFFF... PFFF...
Ah! So, are we calm now?
22 © Peyo

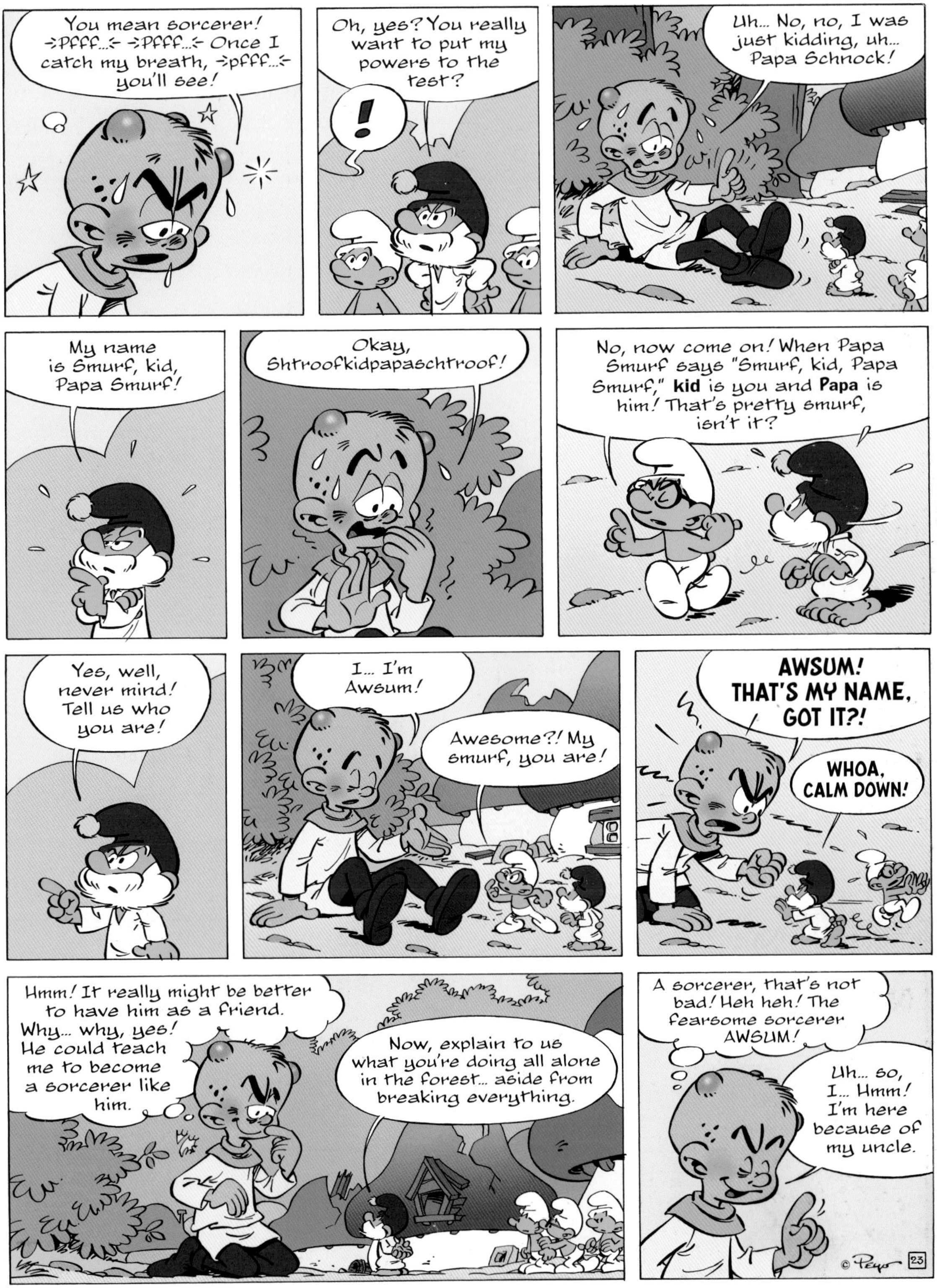
You mean sorcerer! ->Pfff...<- ->Pfff...<- Once I catch my breath, ->pfff...<- you'll see!
Oh, yes? You really want to put my powers to the test?
!
Uh... No, no, I was just kidding, uh... Papa Schnock!
My name is Smurf, kid, Papa Smurf!
Okay, Shtroofkidpapaschtroof!
No, now come on! When Papa Smurf says "Smurf, kid, Papa Smurf," **kid** is you and **Papa** is him! That's pretty smurf, isn't it?
Yes, well, never mind! Tell us who you are!
I... I'm Awsum!
Awesome?! My smurf, you are!
AWSUM! THAT'S MY NAME, GOT IT?!
WHOA, CALM DOWN!
Hmm! It really might be better to have him as a friend. Why... why, yes! He could teach me to become a sorcerer like him.
Now, explain to us what you're doing all alone in the forest... aside from breaking everything.
A sorcerer, that's not bad! Heh heh! The fearsome sorcerer AWSUM!
Uh... so, I... Hmm! I'm here because of my uncle.
© Peyo
23

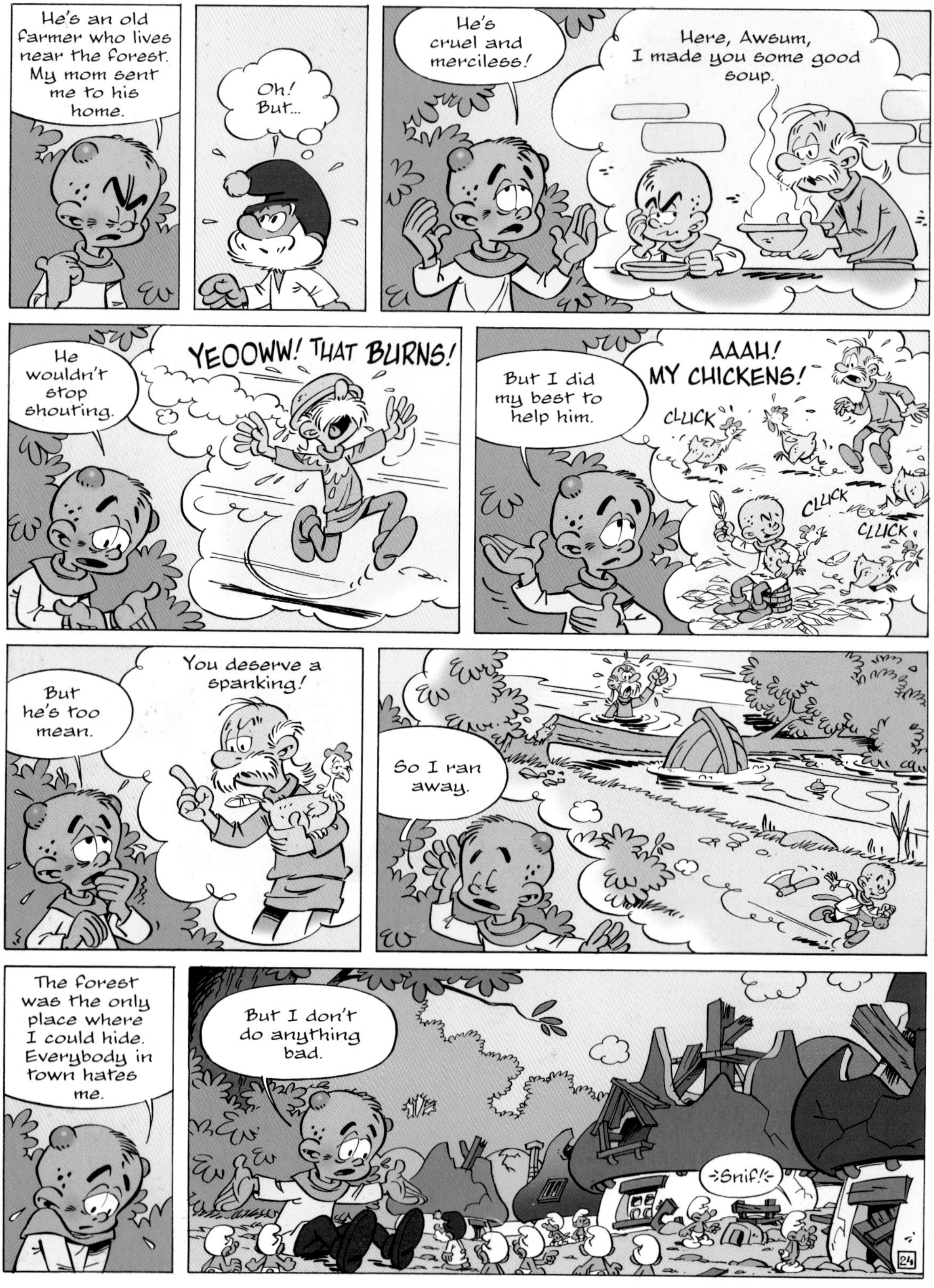
He's an old farmer who lives near the forest. My mom sent me to his home.
Oh! But...
He's cruel and merciless!
Here, Awsum, I made you some good soup.
He wouldn't stop shouting.
YEOOWW! THAT BURNS!
But I did my best to help him.
AAAH! MY CHICKENS!
CLUCK
CLUCK
CLUCK
But he's too mean.
You deserve a spanking!
So I ran away.
The forest was the only place where I could hide. Everybody in town hates me.
But I don't do anything bad.
Snif!
24

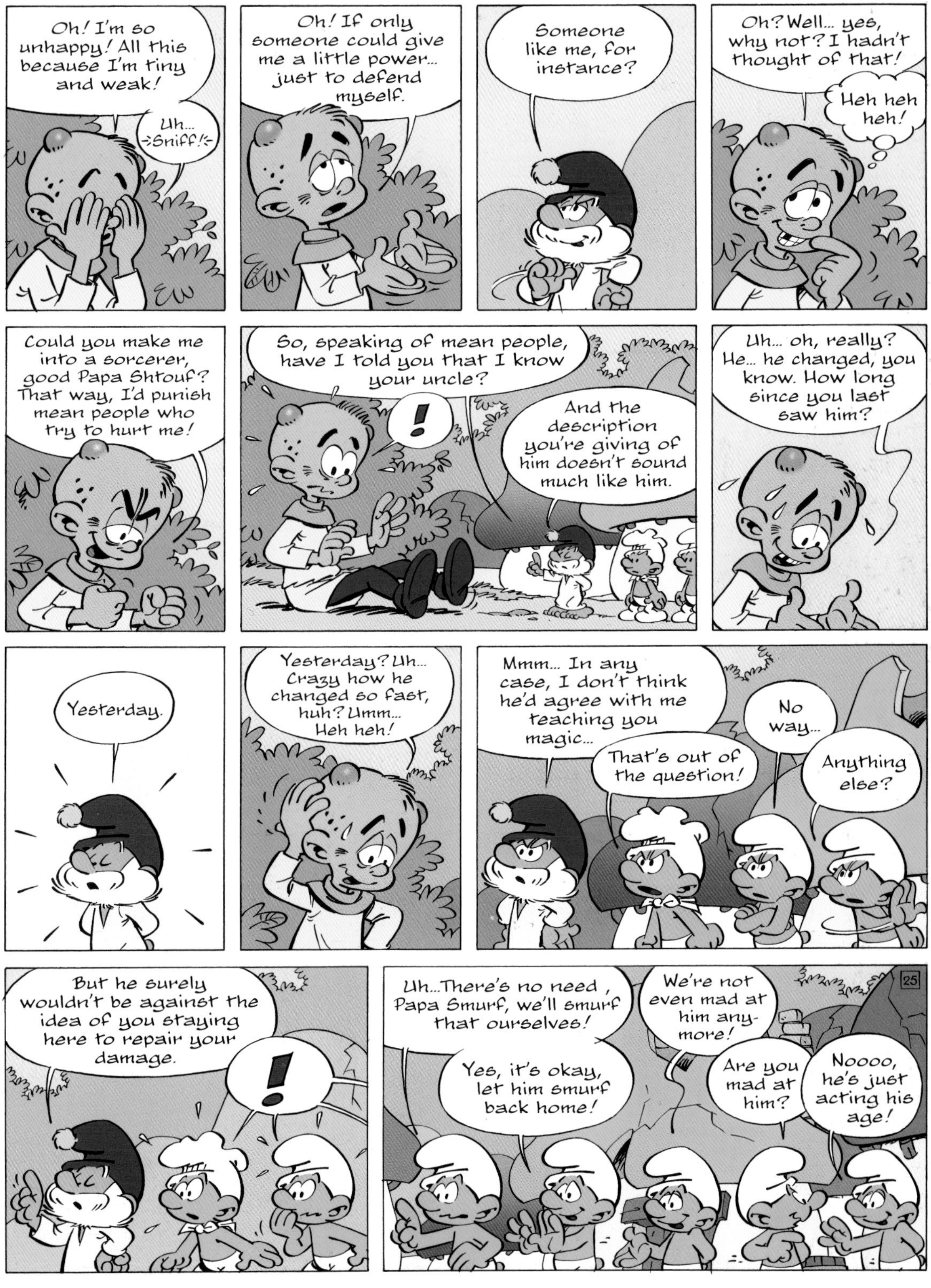
Oh! I'm so unhappy! All this because I'm tiny and weak!
Uh... -Sniff!-
Oh! If only someone could give me a little power... just to defend myself.
Someone like me, for instance?
Oh? Well... yes, why not? I hadn't thought of that!
Heh heh heh!
Could you make me into a sorcerer, good Papa Shtouf? That way, I'd punish mean people who try to hurt me!
So, speaking of mean people, have I told you that I know your uncle?
!
And the description you're giving of him doesn't sound much like him.
Uh... oh, really? He... he changed, you know. How long since you last saw him?
Yesterday.
Yesterday? Uh... Crazy how he changed so fast, huh? Umm... Heh heh!
Mmm... In any case, I don't think he'd agree with me teaching you magic...
That's out of the question!
No way...
Anything else?
But he surely wouldn't be against the idea of you staying here to repair your damage.
!
Uh... There's no need , Papa Smurf, we'll smurf that ourselves!
Yes, it's okay, let him smurf back home!
We're not even mad at him any-more!
Are you mad at him?
Noooo, he's just acting his age!
25

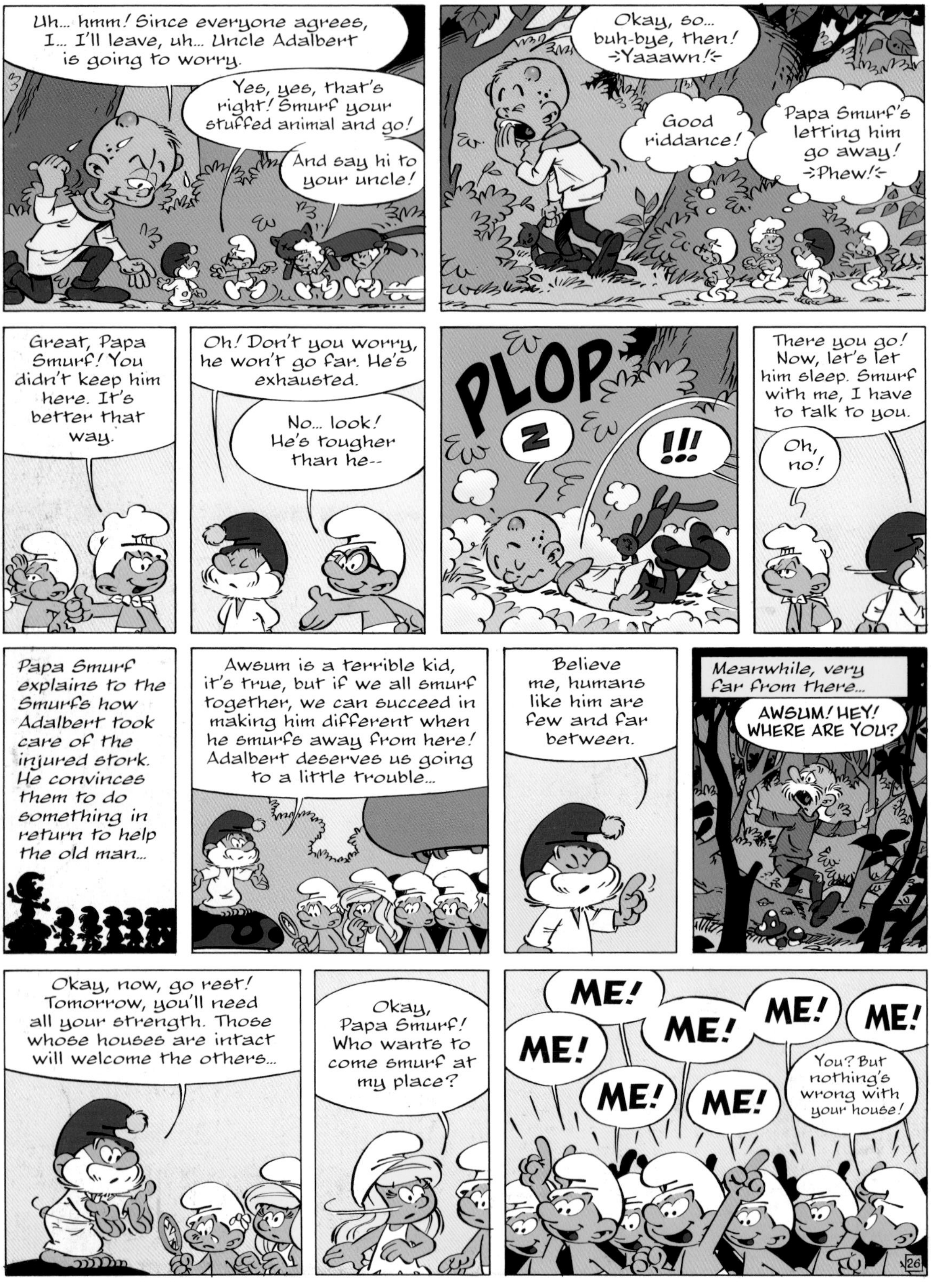
Uh... hmm! Since everyone agrees, I... I'll leave, uh... Uncle Adalbert is going to worry.
Yes, yes, that's right! Smurf your stuffed animal and go!
And say hi to your uncle!
Okay, so... buh-bye, then! ~Yaaawn!~
Good riddance!
Papa Smurf's letting him go away! ~Phew!~
Great, Papa Smurf! You didn't keep him here. It's better that way.
Oh! Don't you worry, he won't go far. He's exhausted.
No... look! He's tougher than he--
PLOP
Z
!!!
There you go! Now, let's let him sleep. Smurf with me, I have to talk to you.
Oh, no!
Papa Smurf explains to the Smurfs how Adalbert took care of the injured stork. He convinces them to do something in return to help the old man...
Awsum is a terrible kid, it's true, but if we all smurf together, we can succeed in making him different when he smurfs away from here! Adalbert deserves us going to a little trouble...
Believe me, humans like him are few and far between.
Meanwhile, very far from there...
AWSUM! HEY! WHERE ARE YOU?
Okay, now, go rest! Tomorrow, you'll need all your strength. Those whose houses are intact will welcome the others...
Okay, Papa Smurf! Who wants to come smurf at my place?
ME!
ME!
ME!
ME!
ME!
ME!
ME!
You? But nothing's wrong with your house!
26

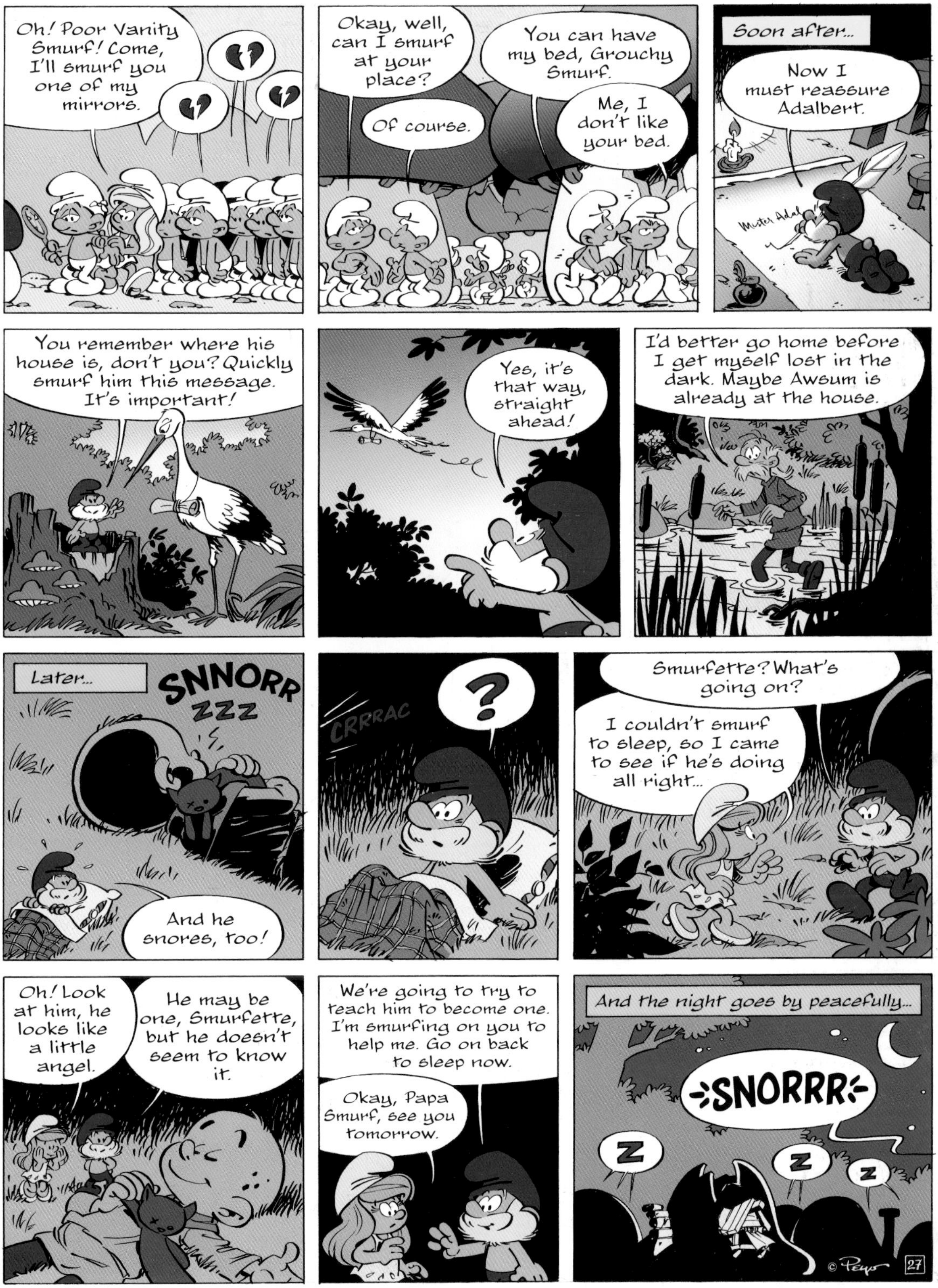
Oh! Poor Vanity Smurf! Come, I'll smurf you one of my mirrors.
Okay, well, can I smurf at your place?
Of course.
You can have my bed, Grouchy Smurf.
Me, I don't like your bed.
Soon after...
Now I must reassure Adalbert.
Mister Adal
You remember where his house is, don't you? Quickly smurf him this message. It's important!
Yes, it's that way, straight ahead!
I'd better go home before I get myself lost in the dark. Maybe Awsum is already at the house.
Later...
SNNORR
ZZZ
And he snores, too!
CRRRAC
?
Smurfette? What's going on?
I couldn't smurf to sleep, so I came to see if he's doing all right...
Oh! Look at him, he looks like a little angel.
He may be one, Smurfette, but he doesn't seem to know it.
We're going to try to teach him to become one. I'm smurfing on you to help me. Go on back to sleep now.
Okay, Papa Smurf, see you tomorrow.
And the night goes by peacefully...
SNORRR
Z
Z
Z
© Peyo
27

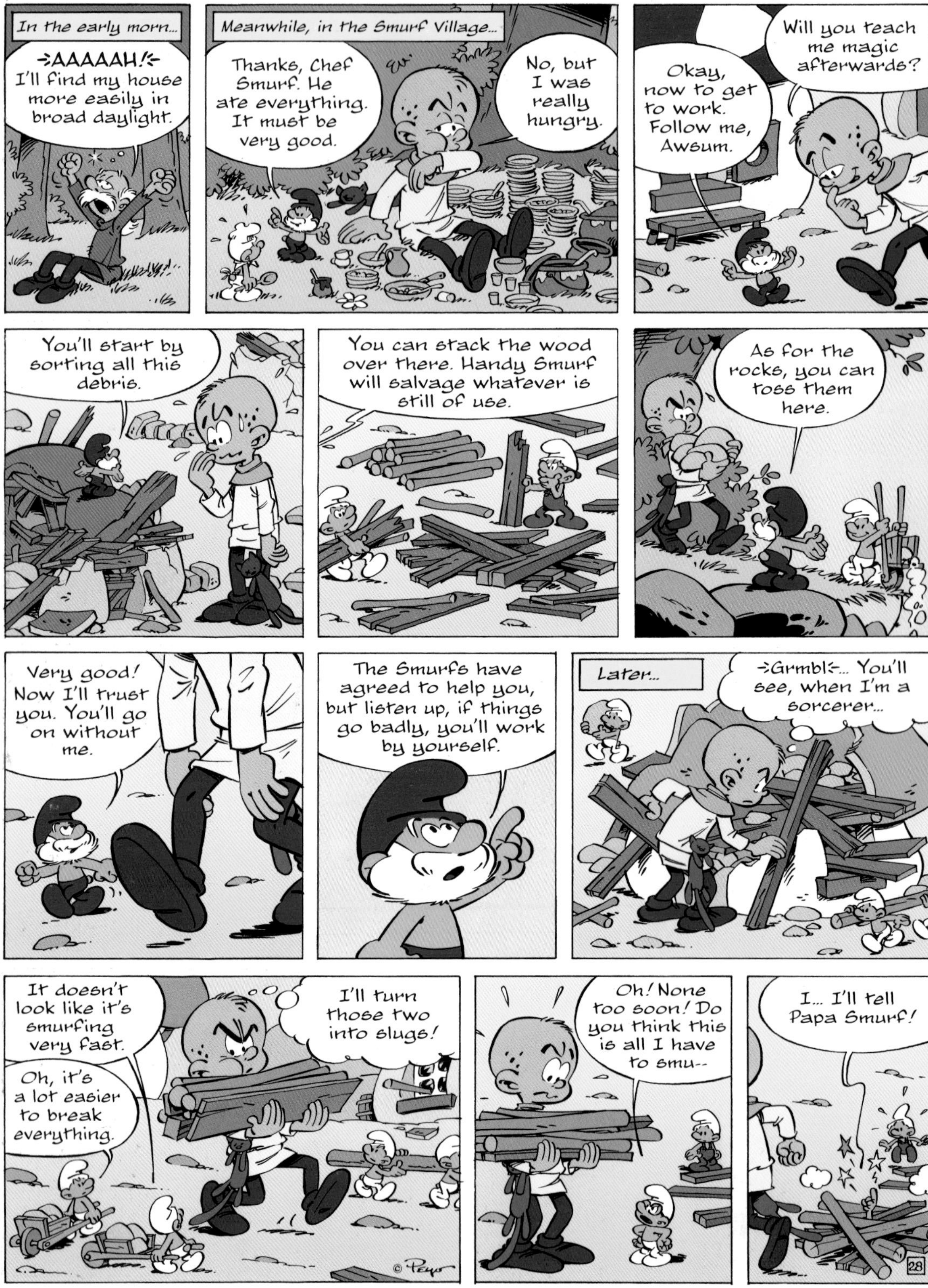

In the early morn...
-AAAAAH!- I'll find my house more easily in broad daylight.
Meanwhile, in the Smurf Village...
Thanks, Chef Smurf. He ate everything. It must be very good.
No, but I was really hungry.
Okay, now to get to work. Follow me, Awsum.
Will you teach me magic afterwards?
You'll start by sorting all this debris.
You can stack the wood over there. Handy Smurf will salvage whatever is still of use.
As for the rocks, you can toss them here.
Very good! Now I'll trust you. You'll go on without me.
The Smurfs have agreed to help you, but listen up, if things go badly, you'll work by yourself.
Later...
-Grmbl-... You'll see, when I'm a sorcerer...
It doesn't look like it's smurfing very fast.
Oh, it's a lot easier to break everything.
I'll turn those two into slugs!
Oh! None too soon! Do you think this is all I have to smu--
I... I'll tell Papa Smurf!
© Peyo
28

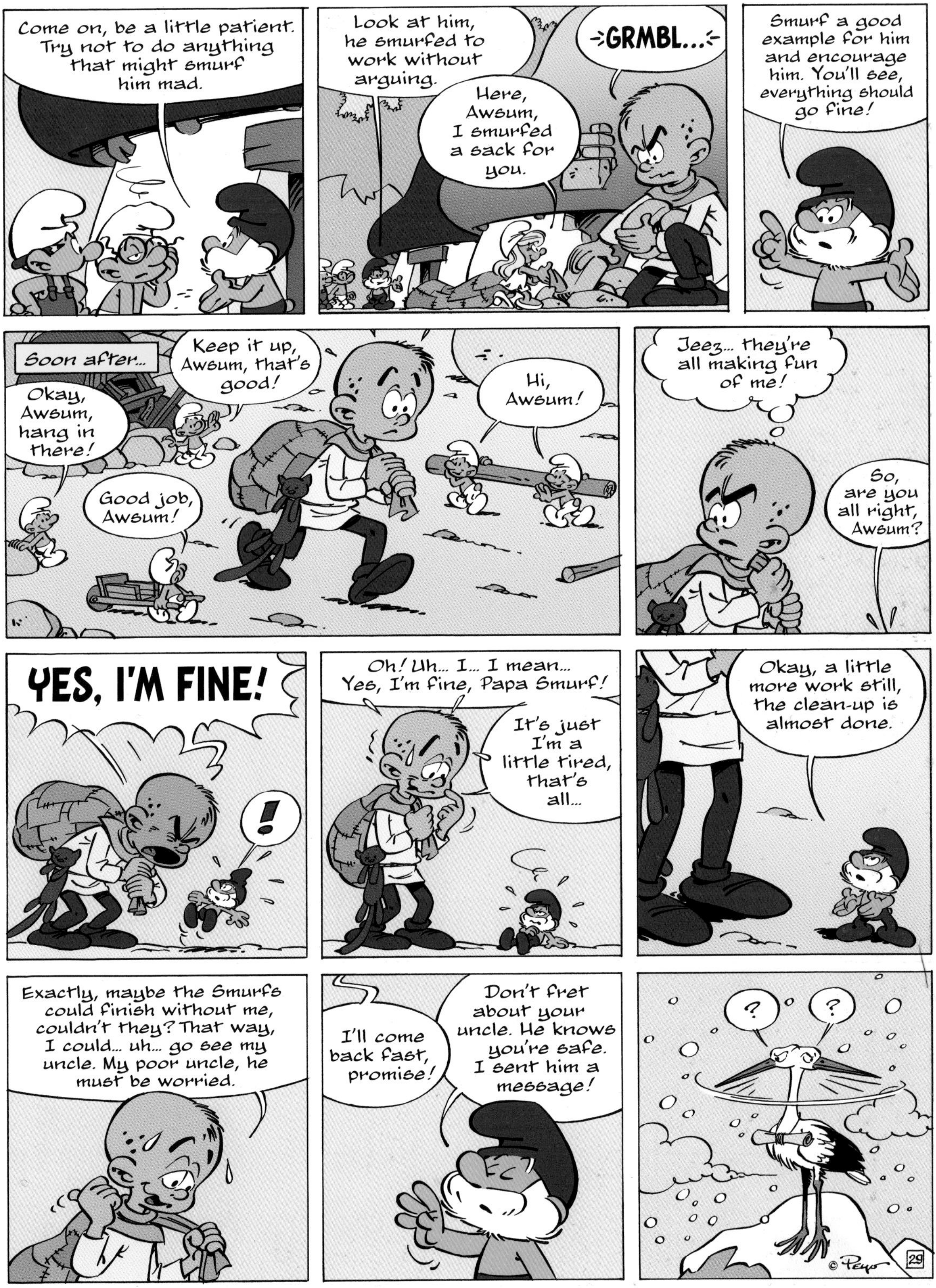
Come on, be a little patient. Try not to do anything that might smurf him mad.
Look at him, he smurfed to work without arguing.
Here, Awsum, I smurfed a sack for you.
GRMBL...
Smurf a good example for him and encourage him. You'll see, everything should go fine!
Soon after...
Okay, Awsum, hang in there!
Keep it up, Awsum, that's good!
Good job, Awsum!
Hi, Awsum!
Jeez... they're all making fun of me!
So, are you all right, Awsum?
YES, I'M FINE!
!
Oh! Uh... I... I mean... Yes, I'm fine, Papa Smurf!
It's just I'm a little tired, that's all...
Okay, a little more work still, the clean-up is almost done.
Exactly, maybe the Smurfs could finish without me, couldn't they? That way, I could... uh... go see my uncle. My poor uncle, he must be worried.
I'll come back fast, promise!
Don't fret about your uncle. He knows you're safe. I sent him a message!
?
?
© Peyo
29

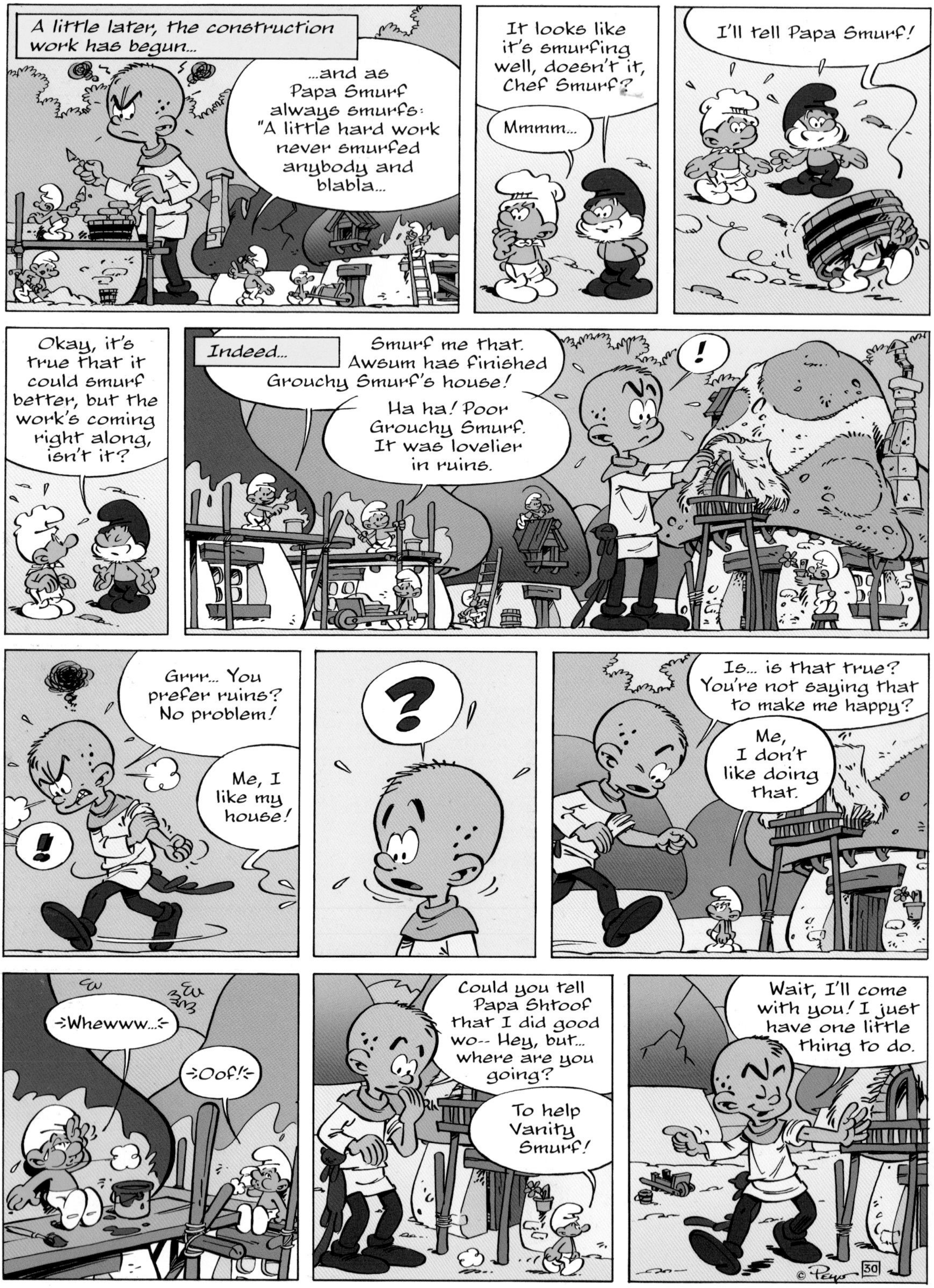
A little later, the construction work has begun...
...and as Papa Smurf always smurfs: "A little hard work never smurfed anybody and blabla...
It looks like it's smurfing well, doesn't it, Chef Smurf?
Mmmm...
I'll tell Papa Smurf!
Okay, it's true that it could smurf better, but the work's coming right along, isn't it?
Indeed...
Smurf me that. Awsum has finished Grouchy Smurf's house!
Ha ha! Poor Grouchy Smurf. It was lovelier in ruins.
!
Grrr... You prefer ruins? No problem!
!
Me, I like my house!
?
Is... is that true? You're not saying that to make me happy?
Me, I don't like doing that.
Whewww...
Oof!
Could you tell Papa Shtoof that I did good wo-- Hey, but... where are you going?
To help Vanity Smurf!
Wait, I'll come with you! I just have one little thing to do.
© Peyo 30

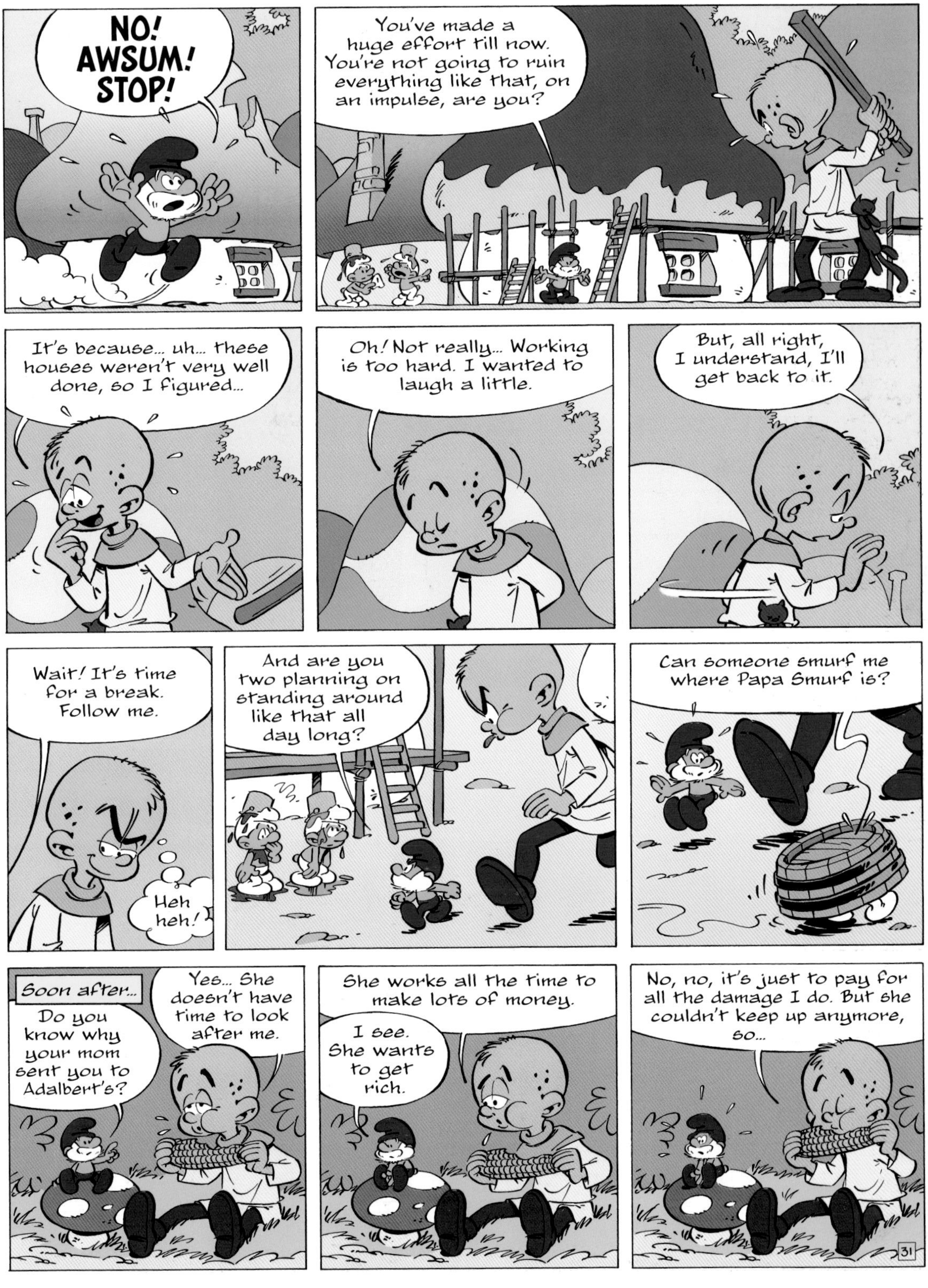
NO! AWSUM! STOP!
You've made a huge effort till now. You're not going to ruin everything like that, on an impulse, are you?
It's because... uh... these houses weren't very well done, so I figured...
Oh! Not really... Working is too hard. I wanted to laugh a little.
But, all right, I understand, I'll get back to it.
Wait! It's time for a break. Follow me.
Heh heh!
And are you two planning on standing around like that all day long?
Can someone smurf me where Papa Smurf is?
Soon after...
Do you know why your mom sent you to Adalbert's?
Yes... She doesn't have time to look after me.
She works all the time to make lots of money.
I see. She wants to get rich.
No, no, it's just to pay for all the damage I do. But she couldn't keep up anymore, so...
31

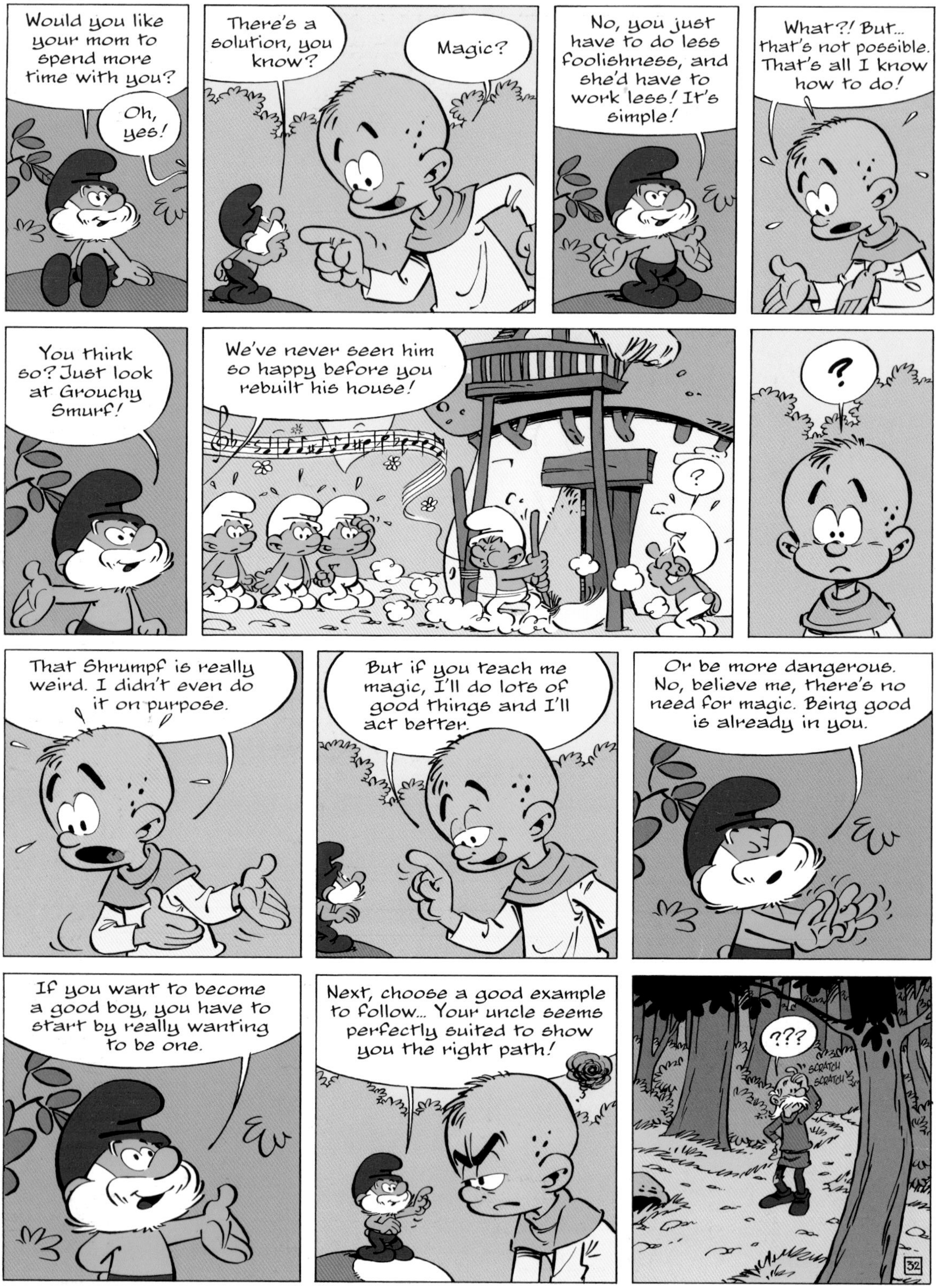
Would you like your mom to spend more time with you?
Oh, yes!
There's a solution, you know?
Magic?
No, you just have to do less foolishness, and she'd have to work less! It's simple!
What?! But... that's not possible. That's all I know how to do!
You think so? Just look at Grouchy Smurf!
We've never seen him so happy before you rebuilt his house!
?
?
That Shrumpf is really weird. I didn't even do it on purpose.
But if you teach me magic, I'll do lots of good things and I'll act better.
Or be more dangerous. No, believe me, there's no need for magic. Being good is already in you.
If you want to become a good boy, you have to start by really wanting to be one.
Next, choose a good example to follow... Your uncle seems perfectly suited to show you the right path!
???
SCRATCH
SCRATCH
32

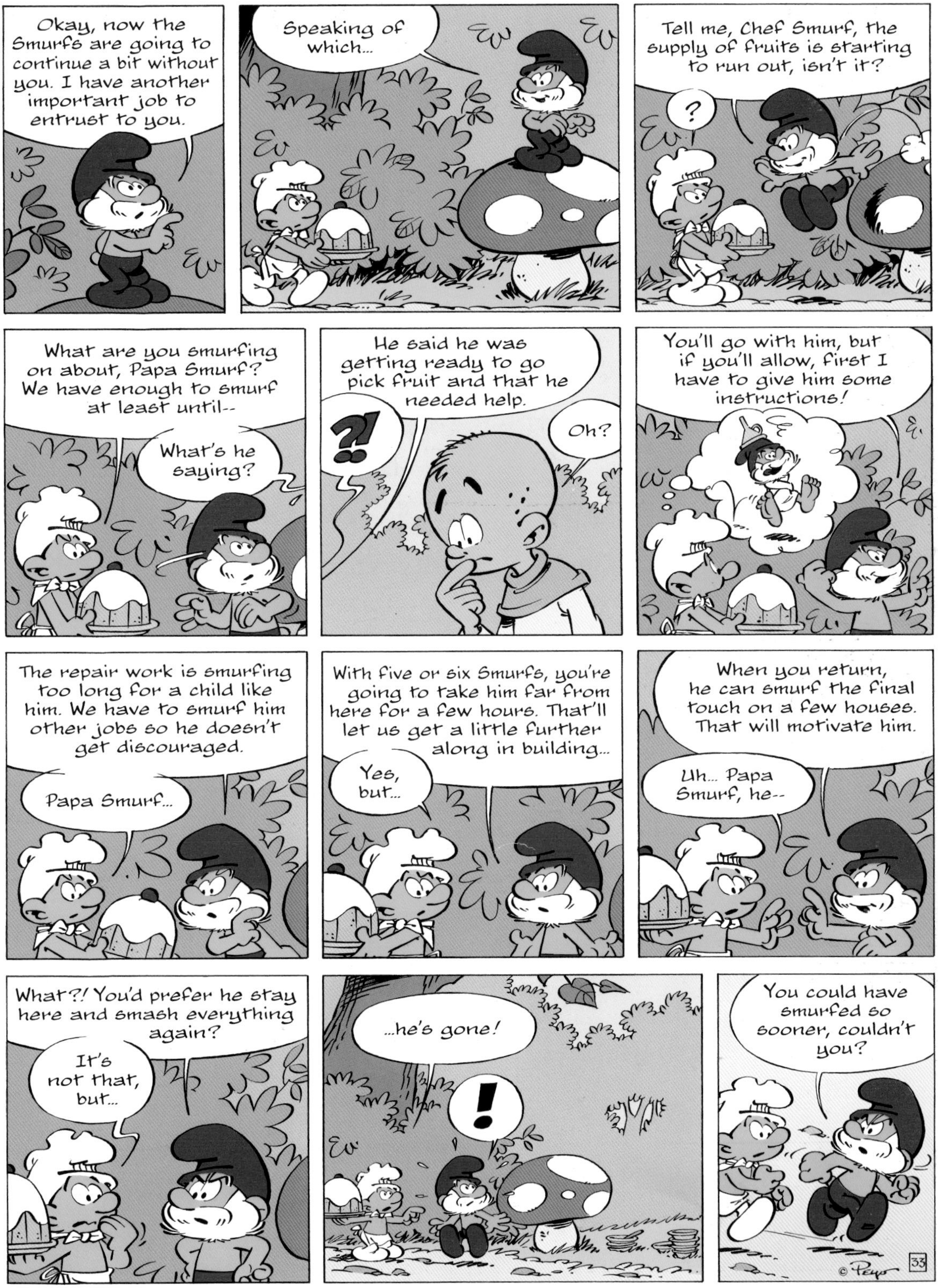
Okay, now the Smurfs are going to continue a bit without you. I have another important job to entrust to you.
Speaking of which...
Tell me, Chef Smurf, the supply of fruits is starting to run out, isn't it?
?
What are you smurfing on about, Papa Smurf? We have enough to smurf at least until--
What's he saying?
He said he was getting ready to go pick fruit and that he needed help.
?!
Oh?
You'll go with him, but if you'll allow, first I have to give him some instructions!
The repair work is smurfing too long for a child like him. We have to smurf him other jobs so he doesn't get discouraged.
Papa Smurf...
With five or six Smurfs, you're going to take him far from here for a few hours. That'll let us get a little further along in building...
Yes, but...
When you return, he can smurf the final touch on a few houses. That will motivate him.
Uh... Papa Smurf, he--
What?! You'd prefer he stay here and smash everything again?
It's not that, but...
...he's gone!
!
You could have smurfed so sooner, couldn't you?
33
© Peyo

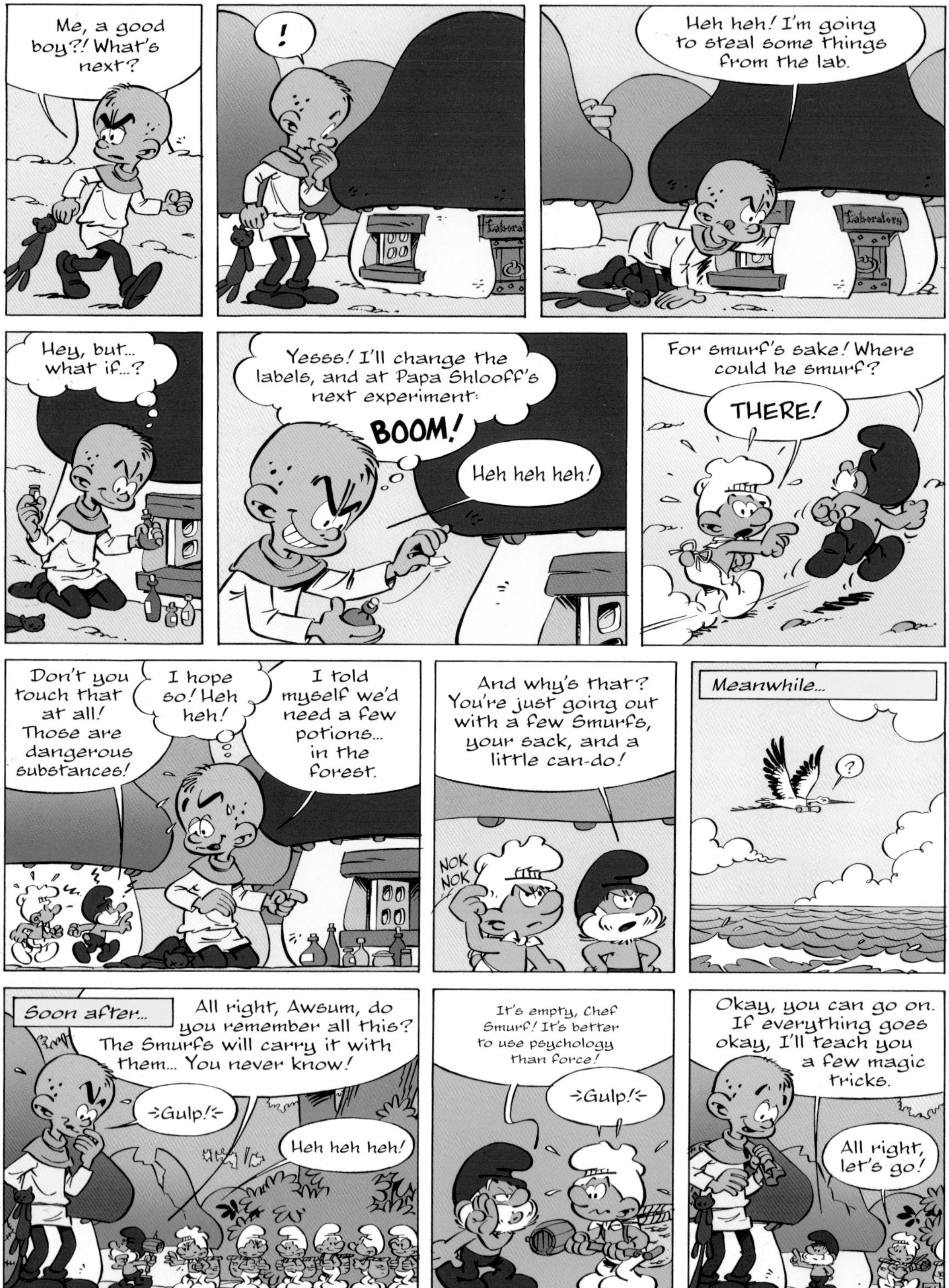

Me, a good boy?! What's next?
!
Heh heh! I'm going to steal some things from the lab.
Laboratory
Hey, but... what if...?
Yesss! I'll change the labels, and at Papa Shlooff's next experiment:
BOOM!
Heh heh heh!
For smurf's sake! Where could he smurf?
THERE!
Don't you touch that at all! Those are dangerous substances!
I hope so! Heh heh!
I told myself we'd need a few potions... in the forest.
And why's that? You're just going out with a few Smurfs, your sack, and a little can-do!
NOK NOK
Meanwhile...
?
Soon after...
All right, Awsum, do you remember all this? The Smurfs will carry it with them... You never know!
Gulp!
Heh heh heh!
It's empty, Chef Smurf! It's better to use psychology than force!
Gulp!
Okay, you can go on. If everything goes okay, I'll teach you a few magic tricks.
All right, let's go!
34

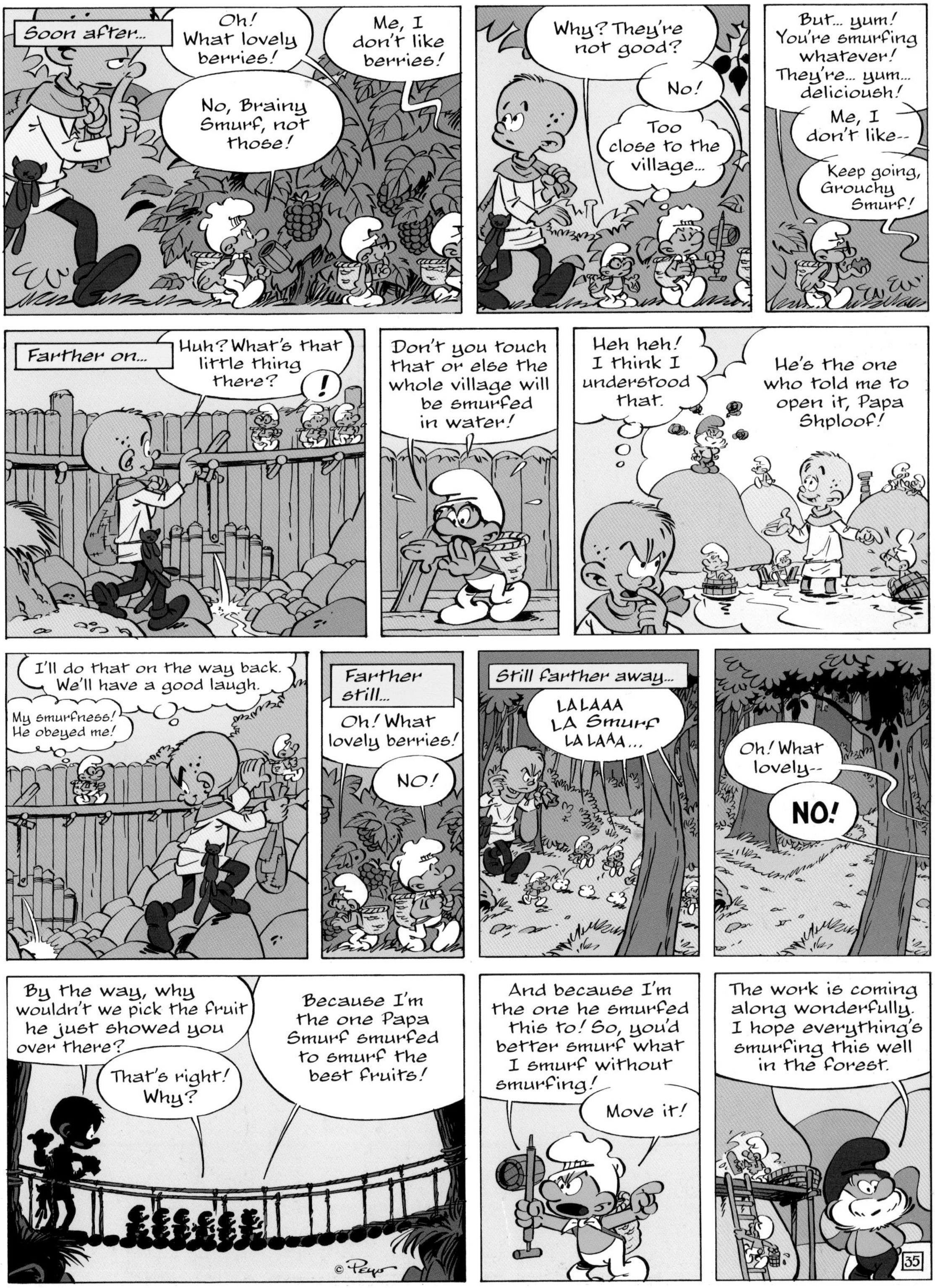

Soon after...
Oh! What lovely berries!
Me, I don't like berries!
No, Brainy Smurf, not those!
Why? They're not good?
No!
Too close to the village...
But... yum! You're smurfing whatever! They're... yum... delicioush!
Me, I don't like--
Keep going, Grouchy Smurf!
Farther on...
Huh? What's that little thing there?
!
Don't you touch that or else the whole village will be smurfed in water!
Heh heh! I think I understood that.
He's the one who told me to open it, Papa Shploof!
I'll do that on the way back. We'll have a good laugh.
My smurfness! He obeyed me!
Farther still...
Oh! What lovely berries!
NO!
Still farther away...
LA LAAA LA Smurf LA LAAA...
Oh! What lovely--
NO!
By the way, why wouldn't we pick the fruit he just showed you over there?
That's right! Why?
Because I'm the one Papa Smurf smurfed to smurf the best fruits!
© Peyo
And because I'm the one he smurfed this to! So, you'd better smurf what I smurf without smurfing!
Move it!
The work is coming along wonderfully. I hope everything's smurfing this well in the forest.
35

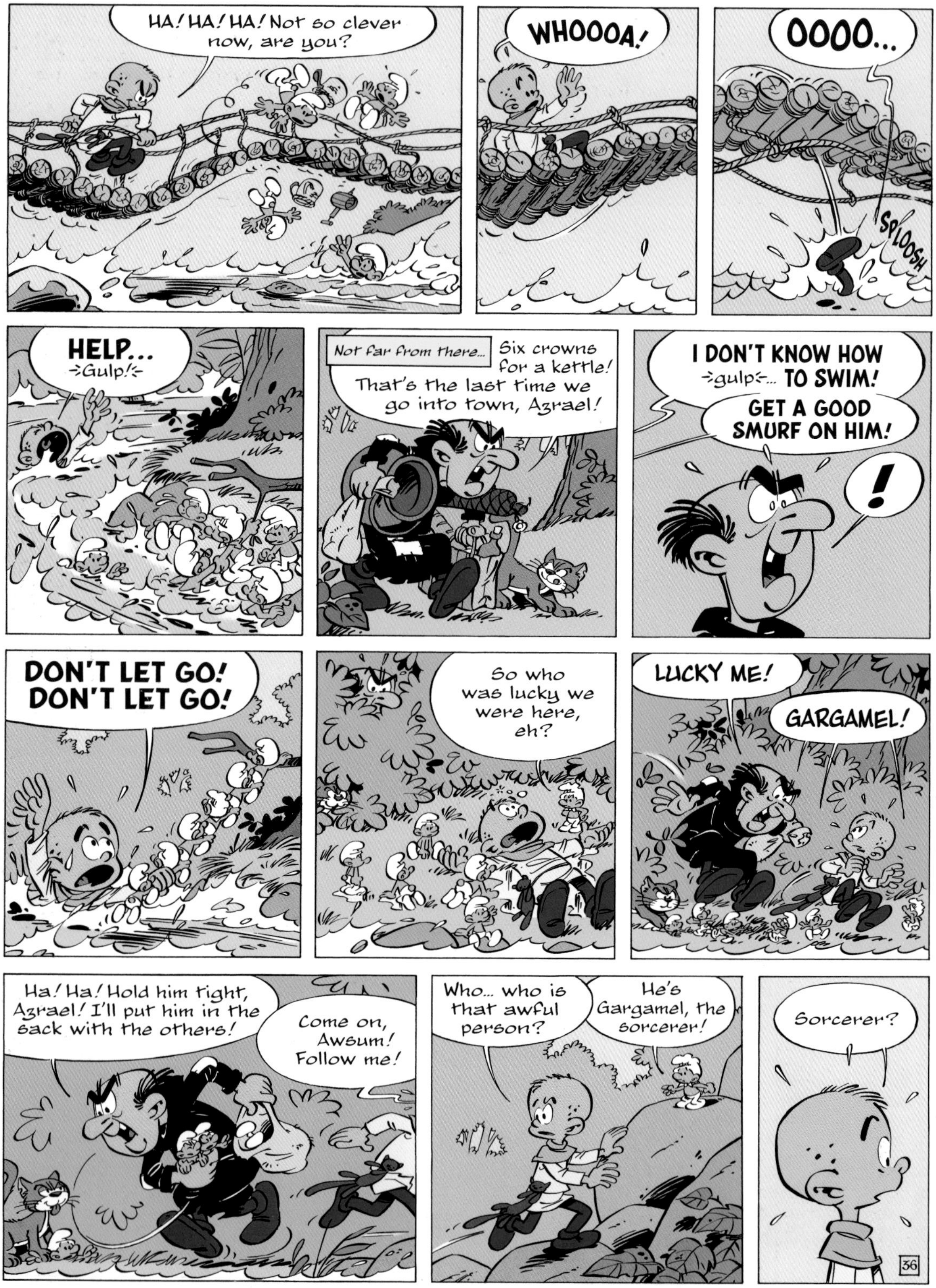
HA! HA! HA! Not so clever now, are you?
WHOOOA!
OOOO...
SPLOOSH
HELP... ›Gulp!‹
Not far from there...
Six crowns for a kettle! That's the last time we go into town, Azrael!
I DON'T KNOW HOW ›gulp‹... TO SWIM!
GET A GOOD SMURF ON HIM!
!
DON'T LET GO! DON'T LET GO!
So who was lucky we were here, eh?
LUCKY ME!
GARGAMEL!
Ha! Ha! Hold him tight, Azrael! I'll put him in the sack with the others!
Come on, Awsum! Follow me!
Who... who is that awful person?
He's Gargamel, the sorcerer!
Sorcerer?
36

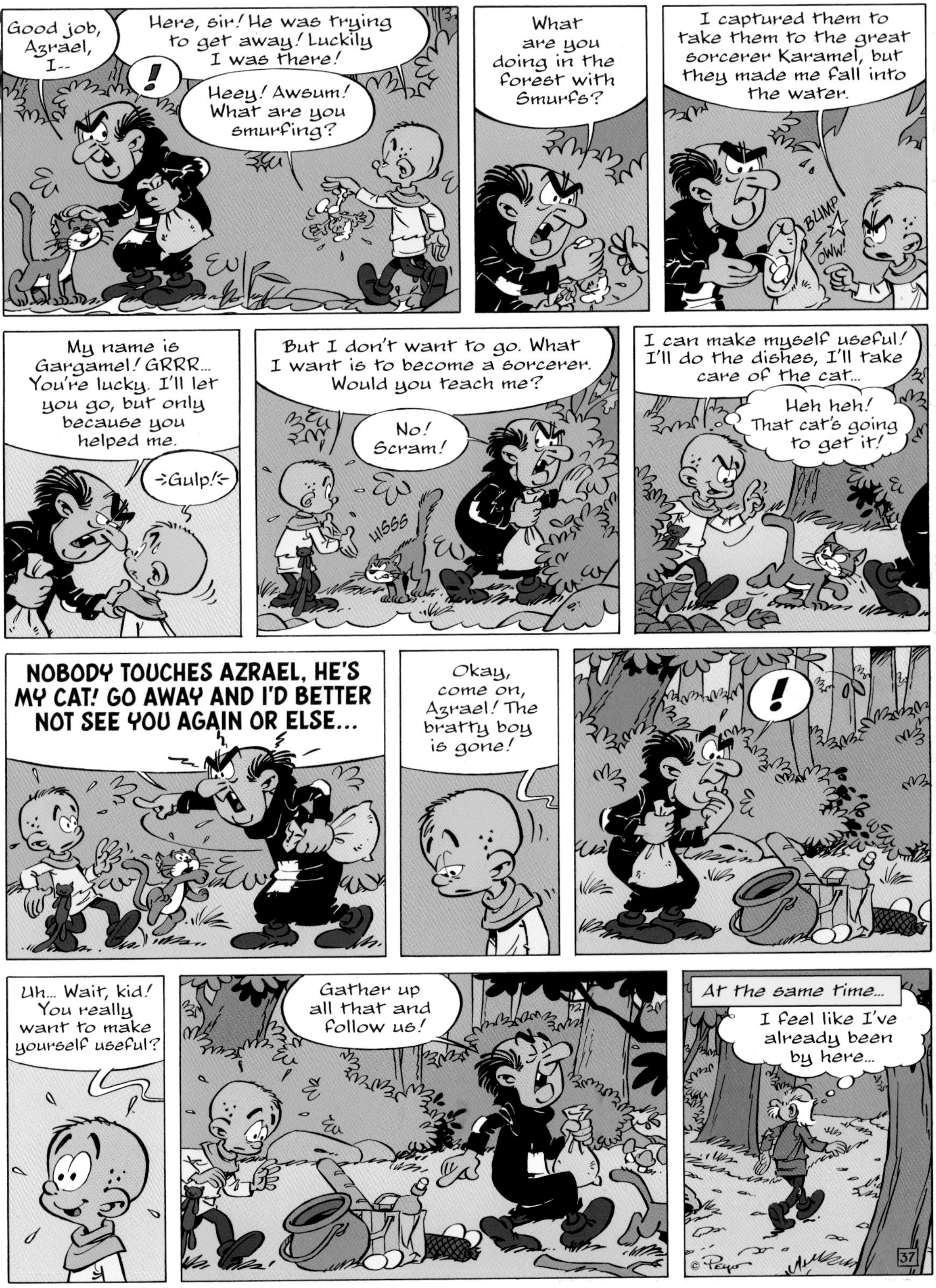

Good job, Azrael, I--
Here, sir! He was trying to get away! Luckily I was there!
!
Heey! Awsum! What are you smurfing?
What are you doing in the forest with Smurfs?
I captured them to take them to the great sorcerer Karamel, but they made me fall into the water.
BLUMP
OWW!
My name is Gargamel! GRRR... You're lucky. I'll let you go, but only because you helped me.
Gulp!
But I don't want to go. What I want is to become a sorcerer. Would you teach me?
No! Scram!
HISSS
I can make myself useful! I'll do the dishes, I'll take care of the cat...
Heh heh! That cat's going to get it!
NOBODY TOUCHES AZRAEL, HE'S MY CAT! GO AWAY AND I'D BETTER NOT SEE YOU AGAIN OR ELSE...
Okay, come on, Azrael! The bratty boy is gone!
!
Uh... Wait, kid! You really want to make yourself useful?
Gather up all that and follow us!
At the same time...
I feel like I've already been by here...
© Peyo
37

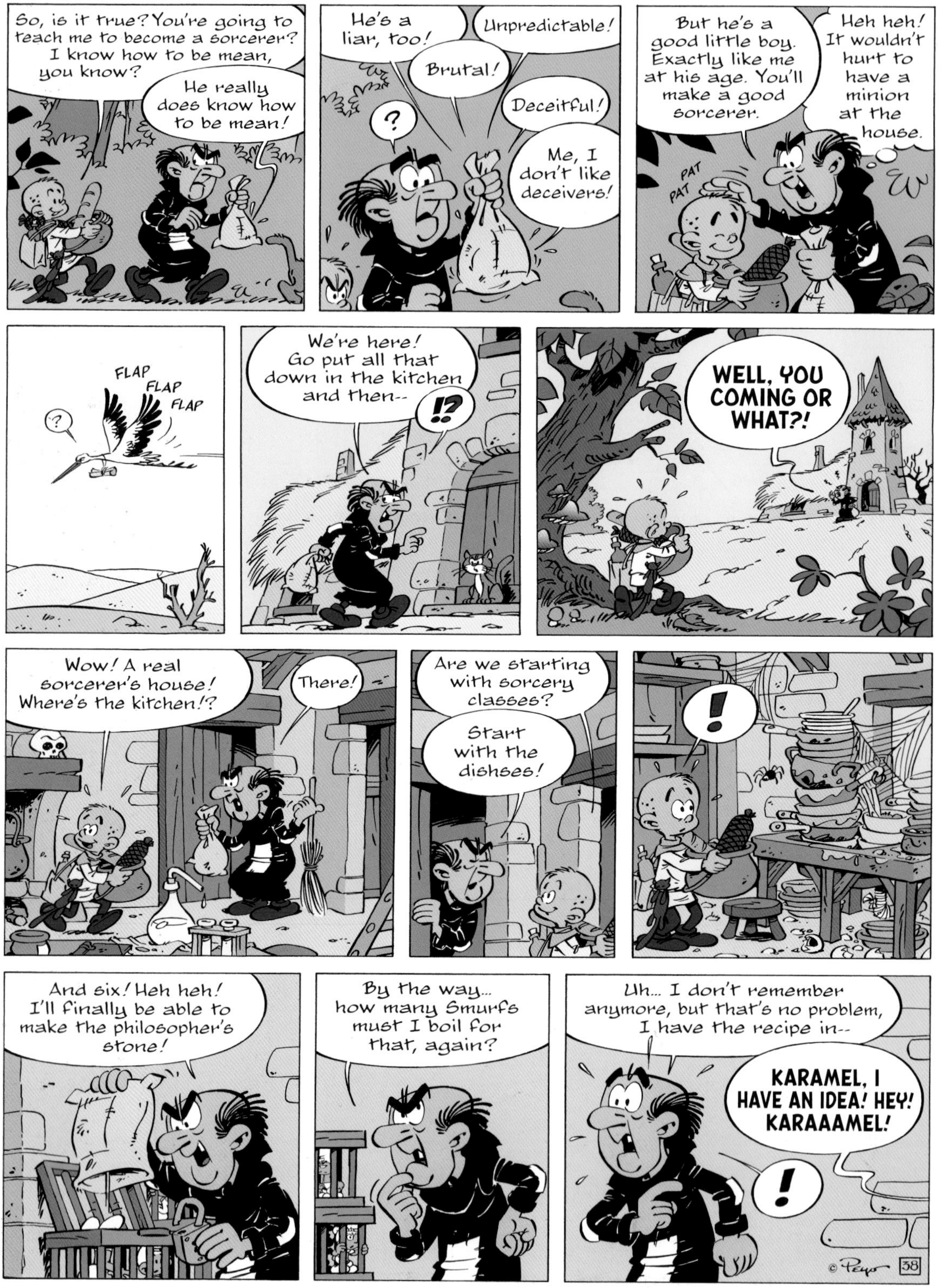
So, is it true? You're going to teach me to become a sorcerer? I know how to be mean, you know?
He really does know how to be mean!
He's a liar, too!
Unpredictable!
Brutal!
?
Deceitful!
Me, I don't like deceivers!
But he's a good little boy. Exactly like me at his age. You'll make a good sorcerer.
Heh heh! It wouldn't hurt to have a minion at the house.
PAT
PAT
FLAP
FLAP
FLAP
?
We're here! Go put all that down in the kitchen and then--
!?
WELL, YOU COMING OR WHAT?!
Wow! A real sorcerer's house! Where's the kitchen!?
There!
Are we starting with sorcery classes?
Start with the dishses!
!
And six! Heh heh! I'll finally be able to make the philosopher's stone!
By the way... how many Smurfs must I boil for that, again?
Uh... I don't remember anymore, but that's no problem, I have the recipe in--
KARAMEL, I HAVE AN IDEA! HEY! KARAAAMEL!
!
© Peyo
38

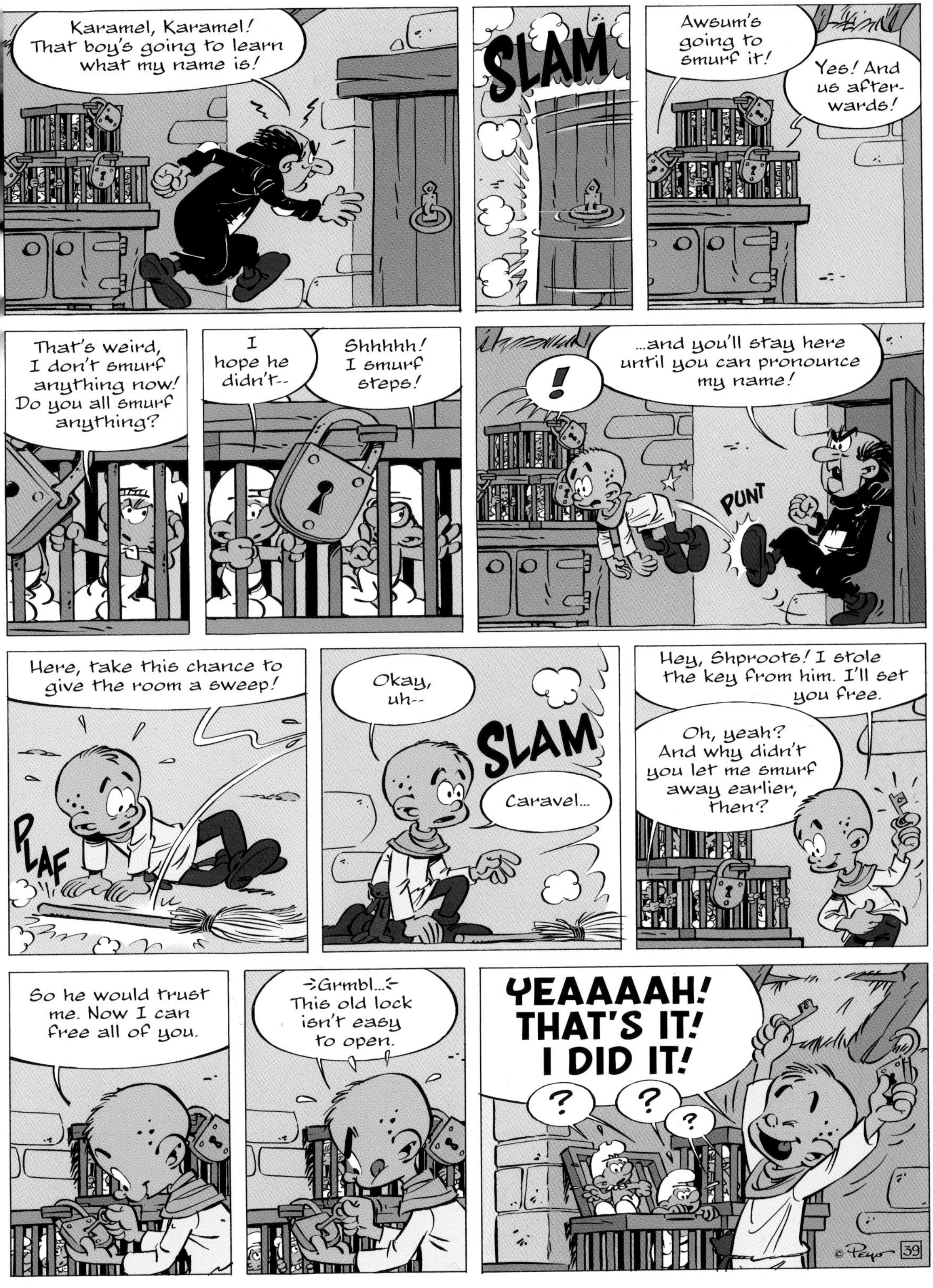
Karamel, Karamel! That boy's going to learn what my name is!
SLAM
Awsum's going to smurf it!
Yes! And us afterwards!
That's weird, I don't smurf anything now! Do you all smurf anything?
I hope he didn't--
Shhhhh! I smurf steps!
...and you'll stay here until you can pronounce my name!
!
PUNT
Here, take this chance to give the room a sweep!
PLAF
Okay, uh--
SLAM
Caravel...
Hey, Shproots! I stole the key from him. I'll set you free.
Oh, yeah? And why didn't you let me smurf away earlier, then?
So he would trust me. Now I can free all of you.
Grmbl... This old lock isn't easy to open.
YEAAAAH! THAT'S IT! I DID IT!
?
?
?
© Peyo
39

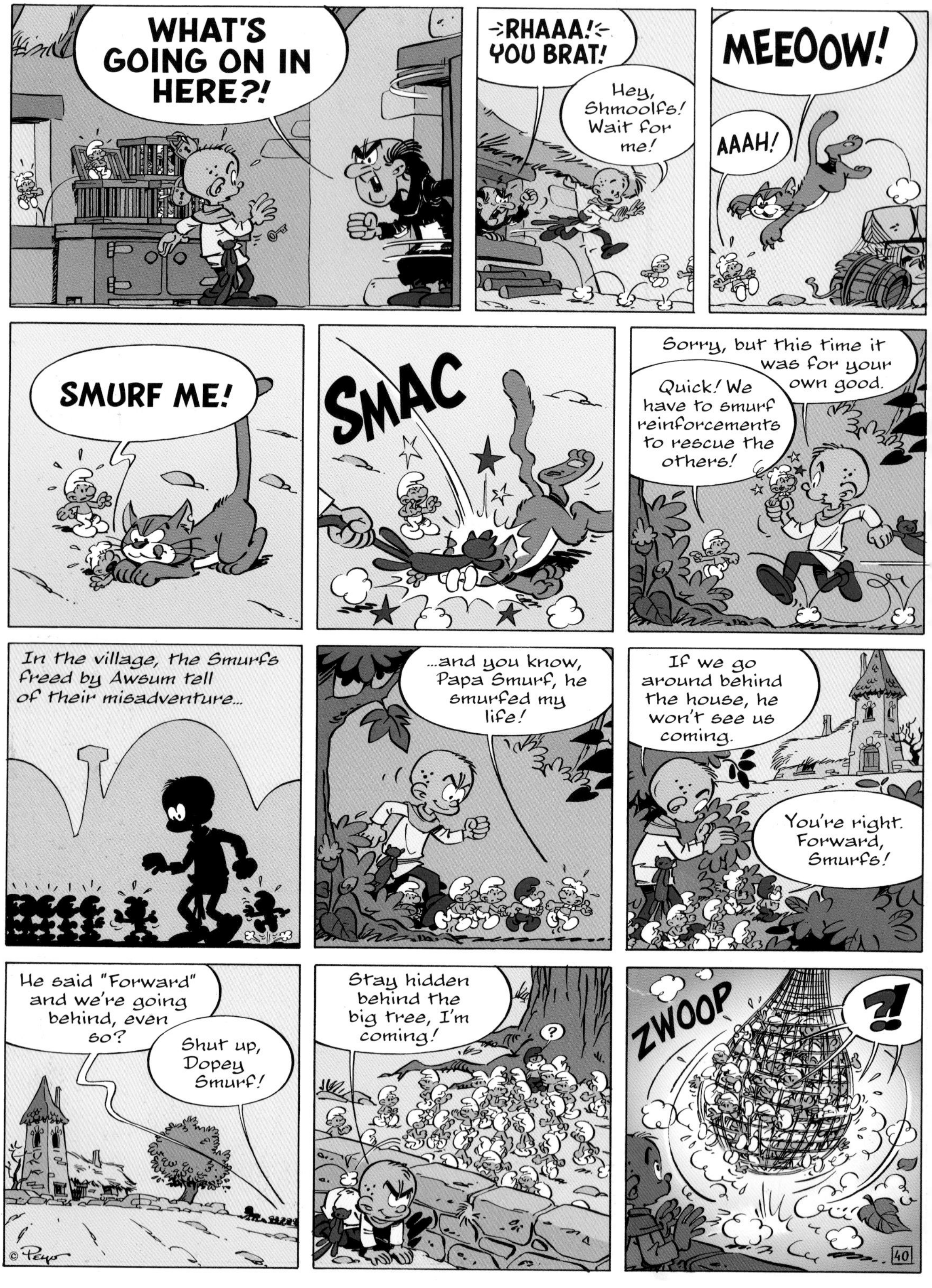

WHAT'S GOING ON IN HERE?!
RHAAA! YOU BRAT!
Hey, Shmoolfs! Wait for me!
MEEOOW!
AAAH!
SMURF ME!
SMAC
Sorry, but this time it was for your own good.
Quick! We have to smurf reinforcements to rescue the others!
In the village, the Smurfs freed by Awsum tell of their misadventure...
...and you know, Papa Smurf, he smurfed my life!
If we go around behind the house, he won't see us coming.
You're right. Forward, Smurfs!
He said "Forward" and we're going behind, even so?
Shut up, Dopey Smurf!
© Peyo
Stay hidden behind the big tree, I'm coming!
?
ZWOOP
?!
40

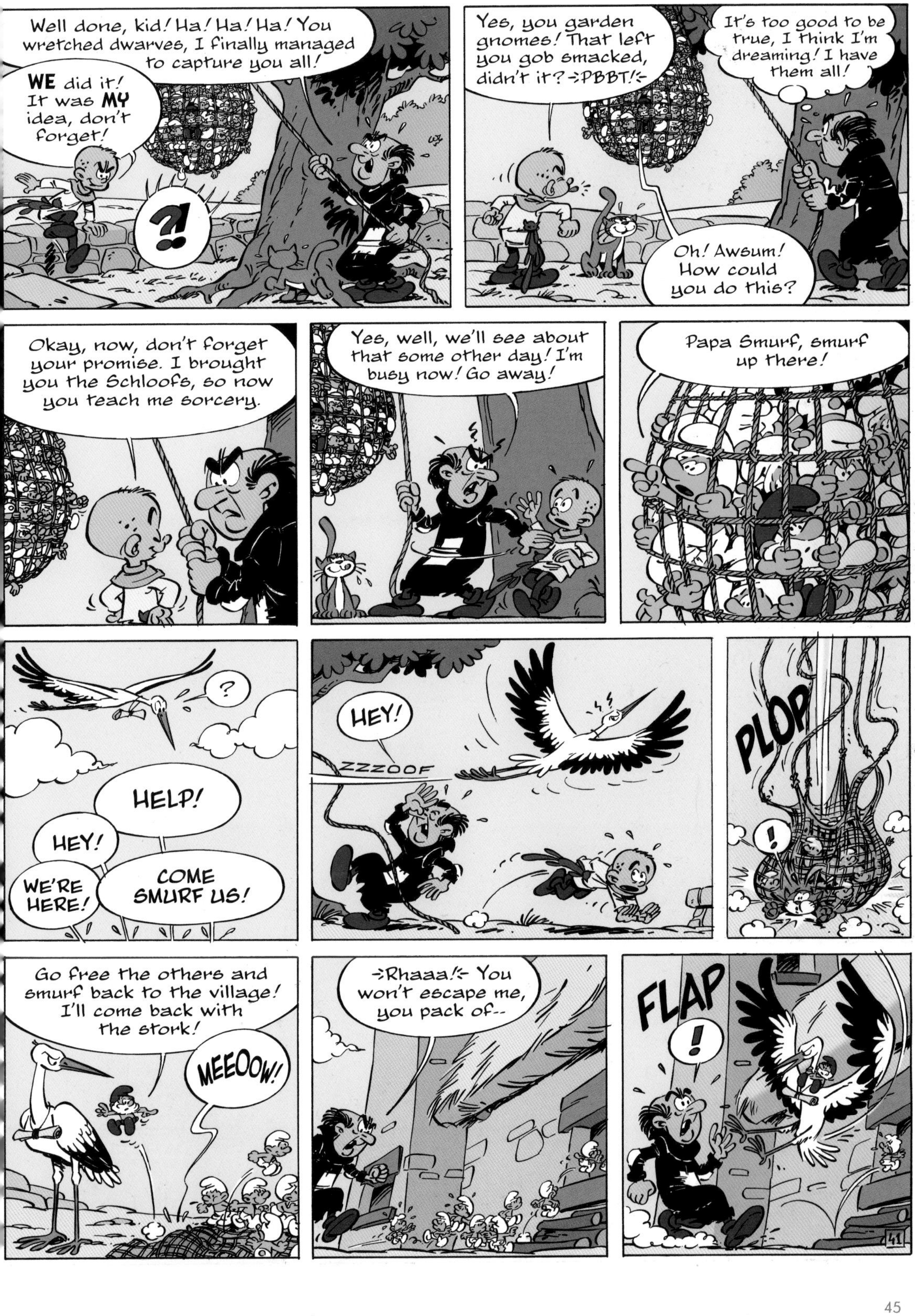
Well done, kid! Ha! Ha! Ha! You wretched dwarves, I finally managed to capture you all!
WE did it! It was MY idea, don't forget!
?!
Yes, you garden gnomes! That left you gob smacked, didn't it? -PBBT!-
It's too good to be true, I think I'm dreaming! I have them all!
Oh! Awsum! How could you do this?
Okay, now, don't forget your promise. I brought you the Schloofs, so now you teach me sorcery.
Yes, well, we'll see about that some other day! I'm busy now! Go away!
Papa Smurf, smurf up there!
?
HELP!
HEY!
WE'RE HERE!
COME SMURF US!
HEY!
ZZZOOF
PLOP
!
Go free the others and smurf back to the village! I'll come back with the stork!
MEEOOW!
-Rhaaa!- You won't escape me, you pack of--
FLAP
!
41

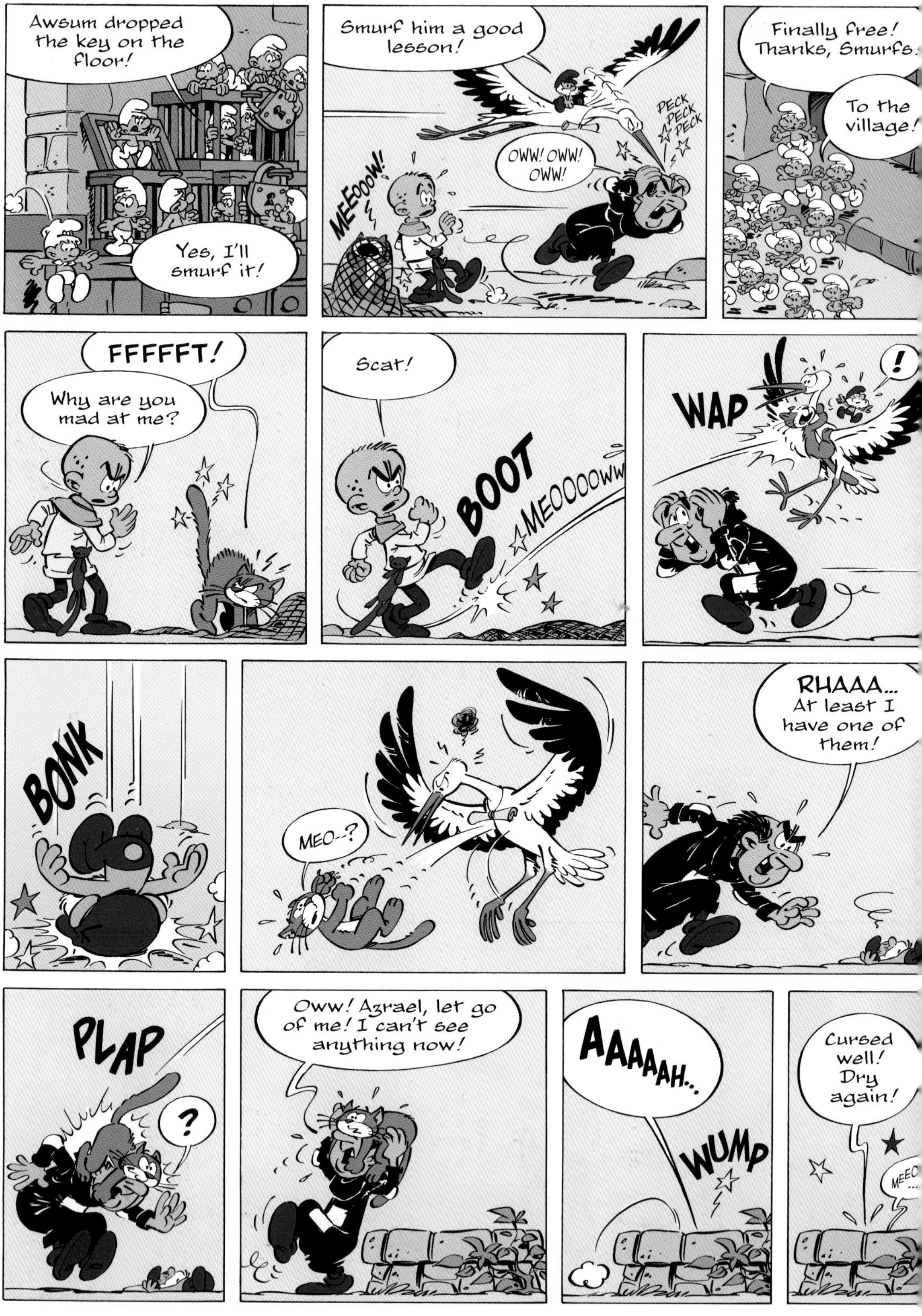
Awsum dropped the key on the floor!
Yes, I'll smurf it!
Smurf him a good lesson!
PECK PECK PECK
OWW! OWW! OWW!
MEEOOOW!
Finally free! Thanks, Smurfs!
To the village!
FFFFFT!
Why are you mad at me?
Scat!
BOOT
MEOOOOWW
WAP
!
BONK
MEO--?
RHAAA... At least I have one of them!
PLAP
?
Oww! Azrael, let go of me! I can't see anything now!
AAAAAH...
WUMP
Cursed well! Dry again!

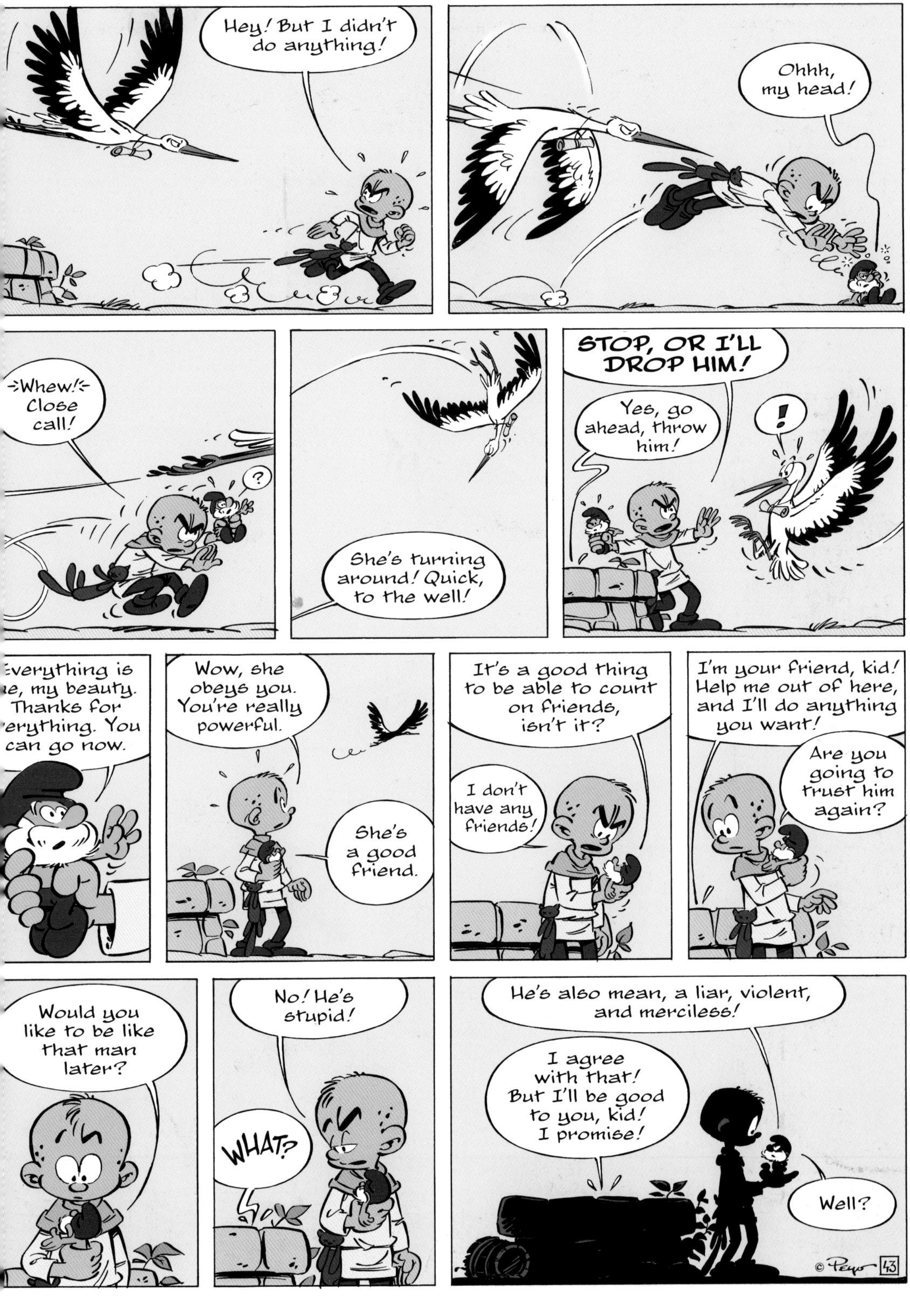
Hey! But I didn't do anything!
Ohhh, my head!
Whew! Close call!
She's turning around! Quick, to the well!
STOP, OR I'LL DROP HIM!
Yes, go ahead, throw him!
!
Everything is e, my beauty. Thanks for erything. You can go now.
Wow, she obeys you. You're really powerful.
She's a good friend.
It's a good thing to be able to count on friends, isn't it?
I don't have any friends!
I'm your friend, kid! Help me out of here, and I'll do anything you want!
Are you going to trust him again?
Would you like to be like that man later?
No! He's stupid!
WHAT?
He's also mean, a liar, violent, and merciless!
I agree with that! But I'll be good to you, kid! I promise!
Well?
© Peyo 43

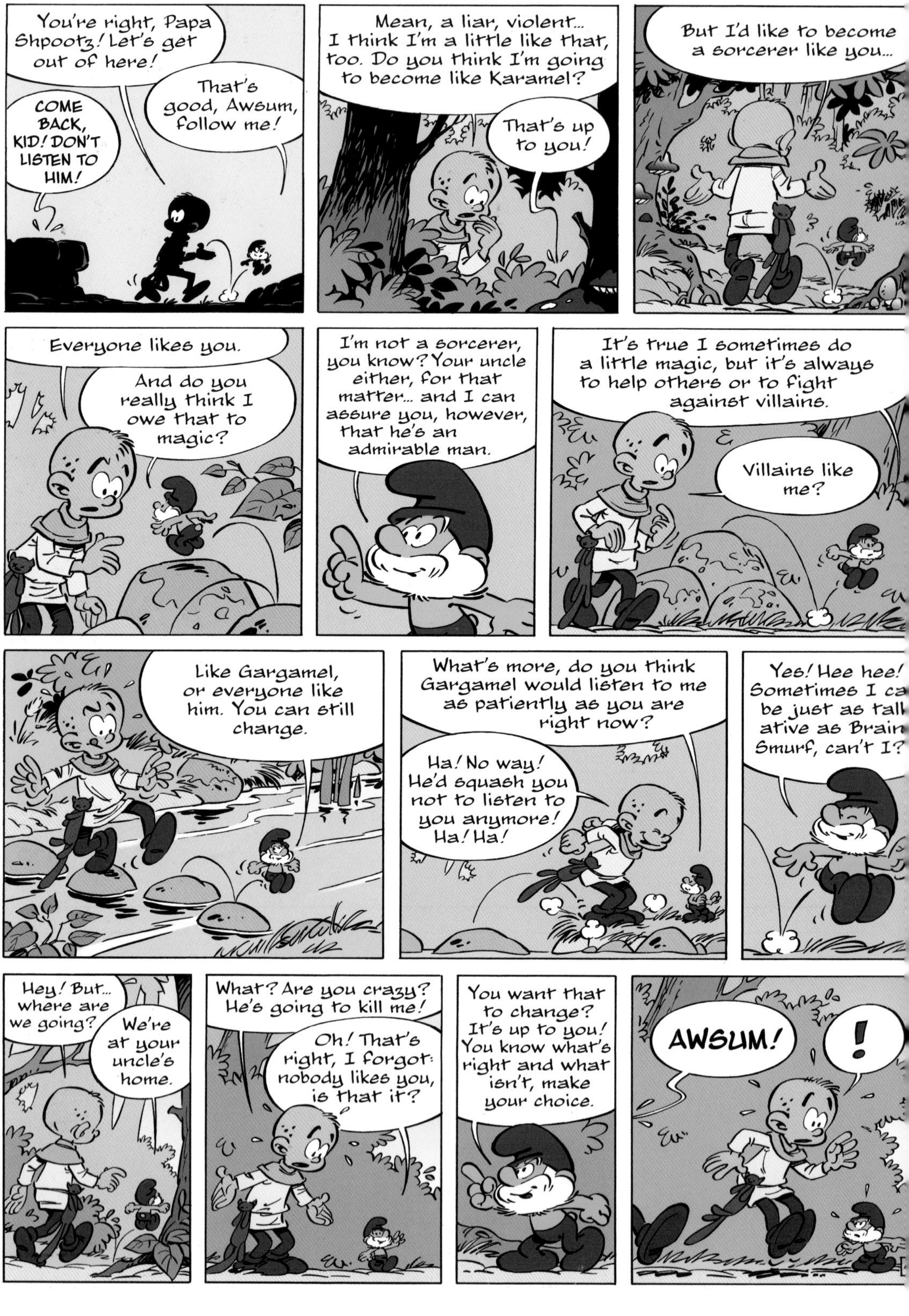
You're right, Papa Shpootz! Let's get out of here!
That's good, Awsum, follow me!
COME BACK, KID! DON'T LISTEN TO HIM!
Mean, a liar, violent... I think I'm a little like that, too. Do you think I'm going to become like Karamel?
That's up to you!
But I'd like to become a sorcerer like you...
Everyone likes you.
And do you really think I owe that to magic?
I'm not a sorcerer, you know? Your uncle either, for that matter... and I can assure you, however, that he's an admirable man.
It's true I sometimes do a little magic, but it's always to help others or to fight against villains.
Villains like me?
Like Gargamel, or everyone like him. You can still change.
What's more, do you think Gargamel would listen to me as patiently as you are right now?
Ha! No way! He'd squash you not to listen to you anymore! Ha! Ha!
Yes! Hee hee! Sometimes I ca be just as tall ative as Brain Smurf, can't I?
Hey! But... where are we going?
We're at your uncle's home.
What? Are you crazy? He's going to kill me!
Oh! That's right, I forgot: nobody likes you, is that it?
You want that to change? It's up to you! You know what's right and what isn't, make your choice.
AWSUM!
!

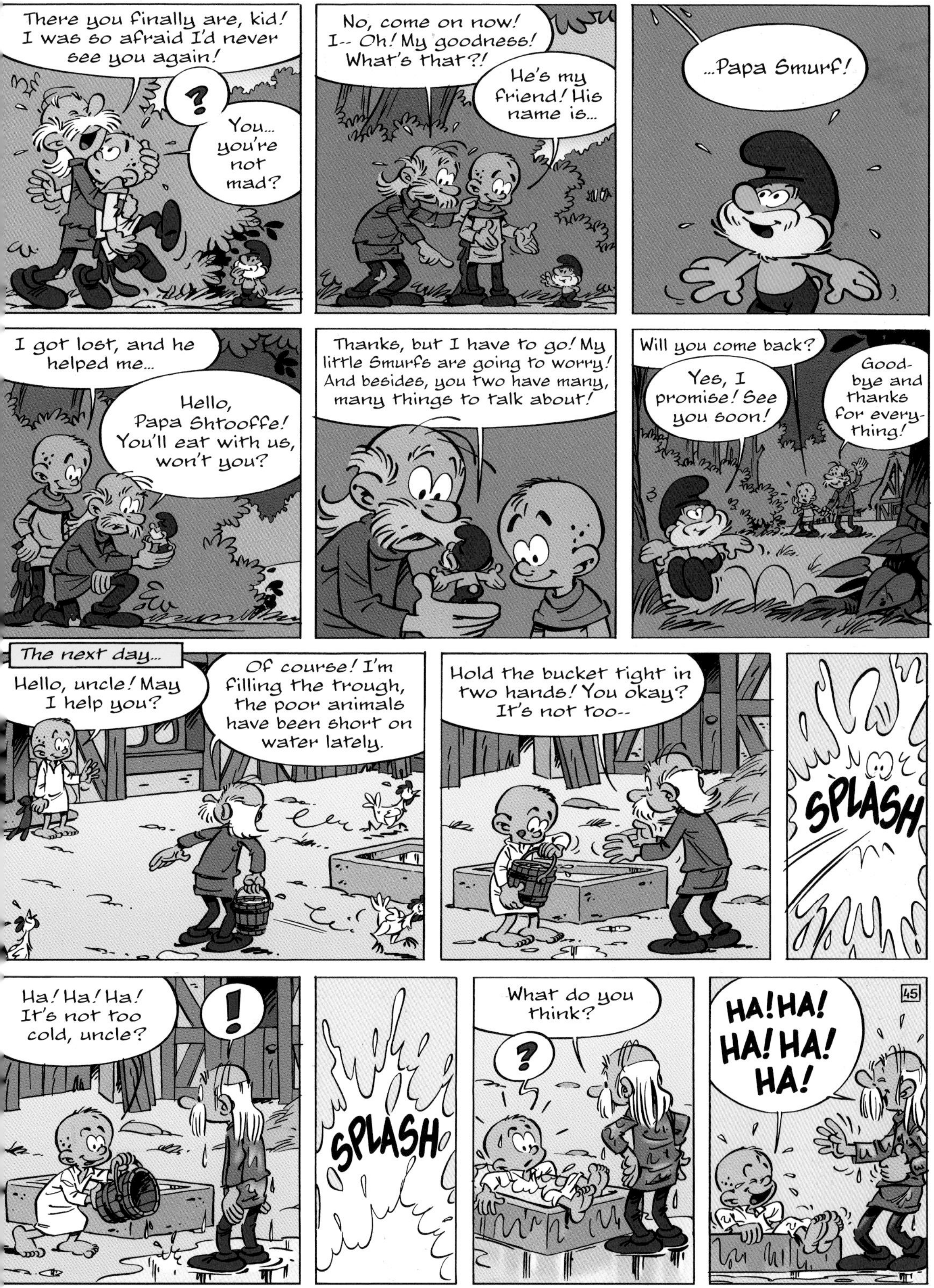
There you finally are, kid! I was so afraid I'd never see you again!
?
You... you're not mad?
No, come on now! I-- Oh! My goodness! What's that?!
He's my friend! His name is...
...Papa Smurf!
I got lost, and he helped me...
Hello, Papa Shtooffe! You'll eat with us, won't you?
Thanks, but I have to go! My little Smurfs are going to worry! And besides, you two have many, many things to talk about!
Will you come back?
Yes, I promise! See you soon!
Good-bye and thanks for every-thing!
The next day...
Hello, uncle! May I help you?
Of course! I'm filling the trough, the poor animals have been short on water lately.
Hold the bucket tight in two hands! You okay? It's not too--
SPLASH
Ha! Ha! Ha! It's not too cold, uncle?
!
SPLASH
What do you think?
?
45
HA! HA! HA! HA! HA!

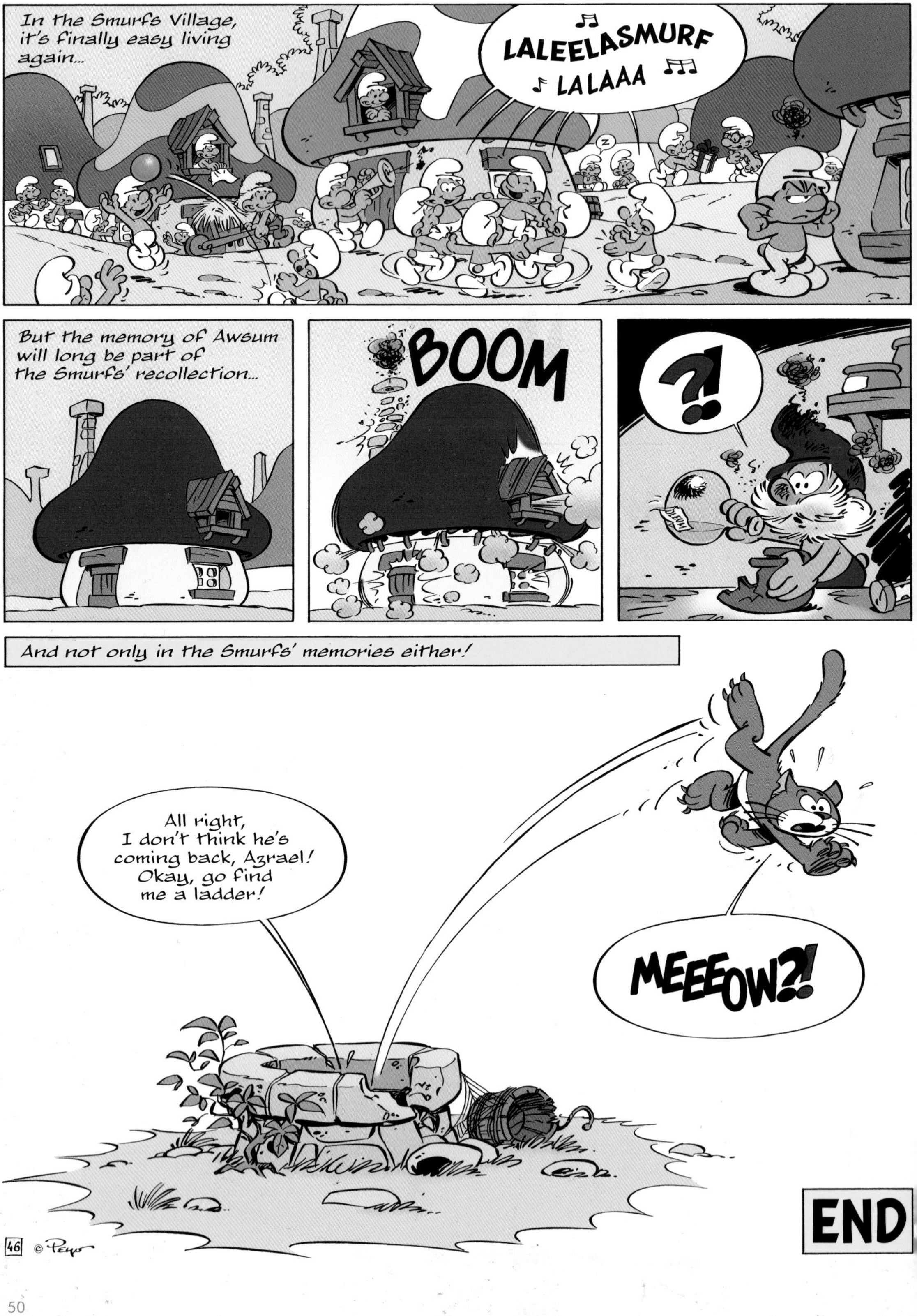
In the Smurfs Village, it's finally easy living again...
LALEELASMURF LALAAA
But the memory of Awsum will long be part of the Smurfs' recollection...
BOOM
?!
And not only in the Smurfs' memories either!
All right, I don't think he's coming back, Azrael! Okay, go find me a ladder!
MEEEOW?!
END
46 © Peyo

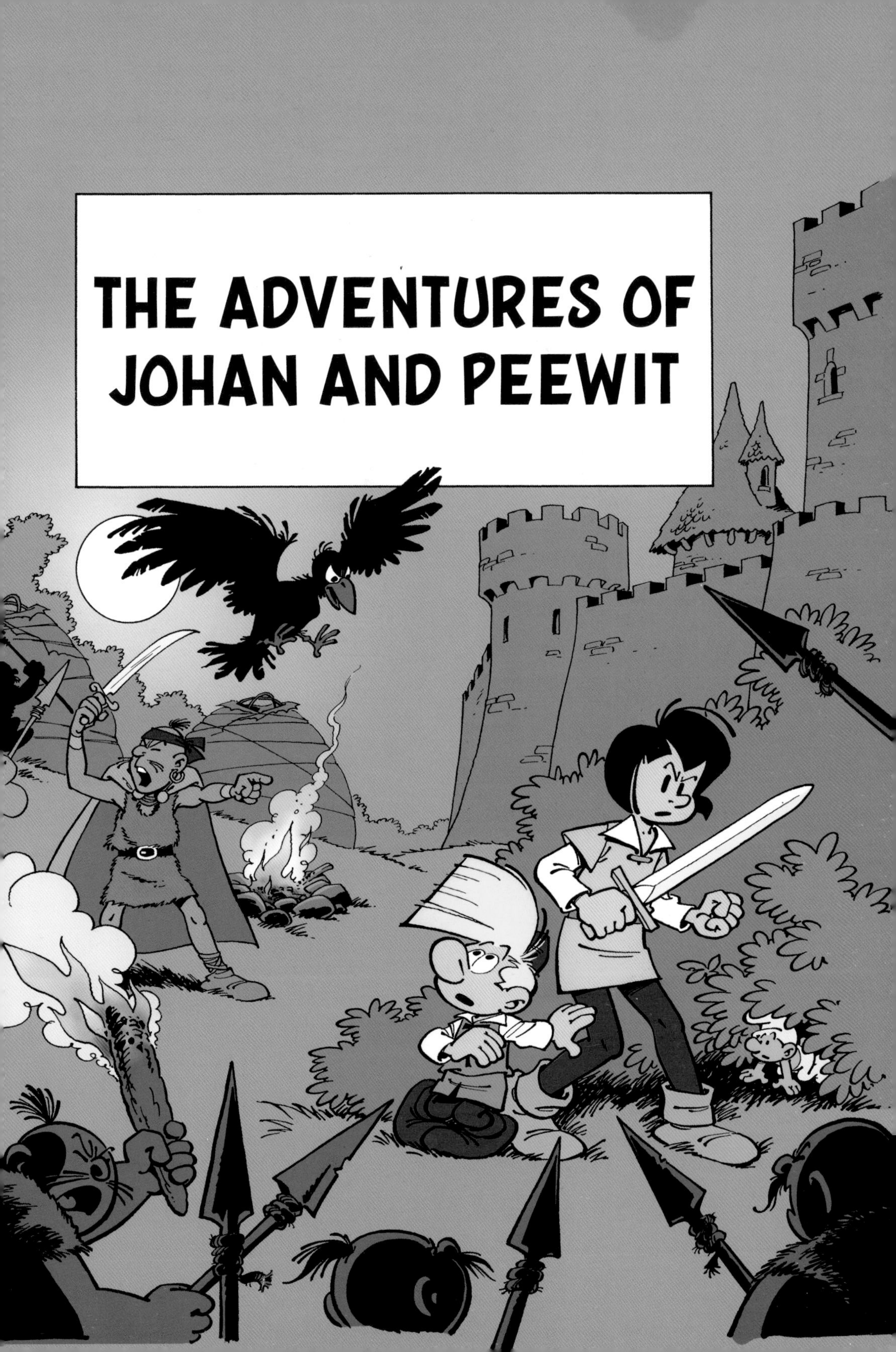
THE ADVENTURES OF
JOHAN AND PEEWIT

Peyo

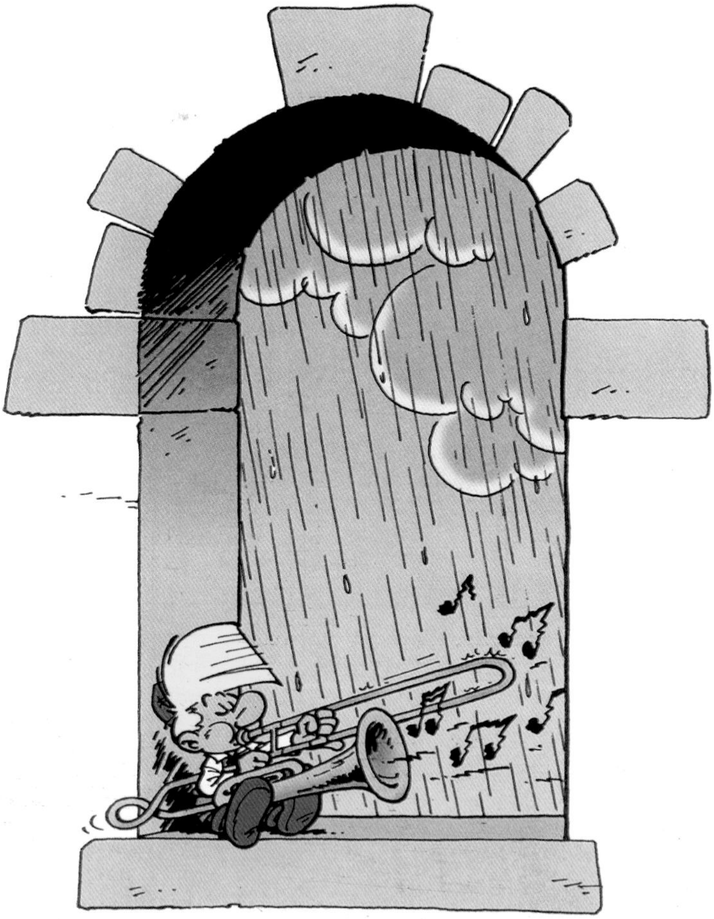

THE HORDE OF THE CROW

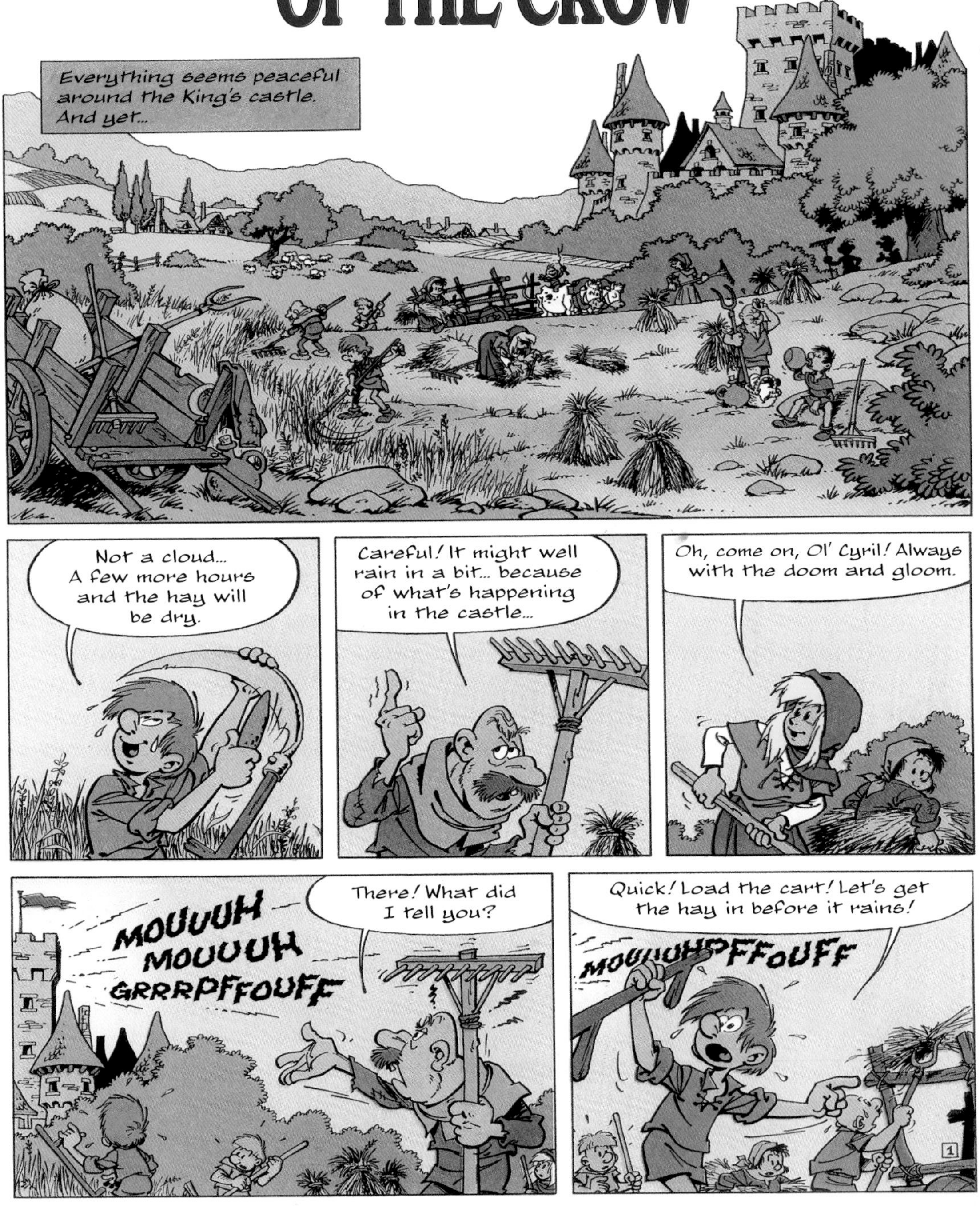

Everything seems peaceful around the King's castle. And yet...
Not a cloud... A few more hours and the hay will be dry.
Careful! It might well rain in a bit... because of what's happening in the castle...
Oh, come on, Ol' Cyril! Always with the doom and gloom.
MOUUUH
MOUUUH
GRRRPFFOUFF
There! What did I tell you?
MOUUUHPFFOUFF
Quick! Load the cart! Let's get the hay in before it rains!
1

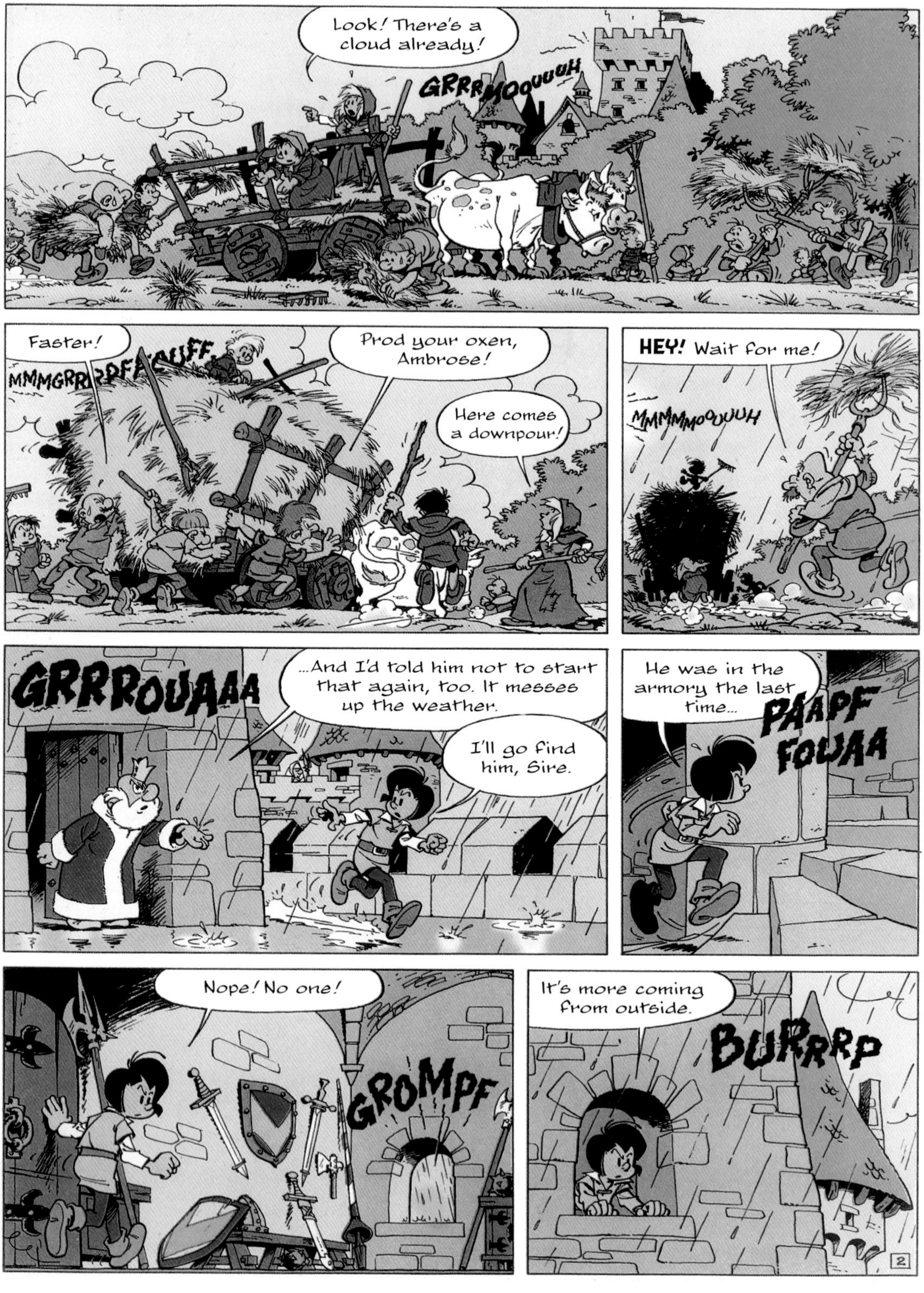
Look! There's a cloud already!
GRRRMOOUUUH
Faster!
MMMGRRRPFFOUFF
Prod your oxen, Ambrose!
Here comes a downpour!
HEY! Wait for me!
MMMMMOOUUUH
GRRROUAAA
...And I'd told him not to start that again, too. It messes up the weather.
I'll go find him, Sire.
He was in the armory the last time...
PAAPF FOUAA
Nope! No one!
GROMPF
It's more coming from outside.
BURRRP
2

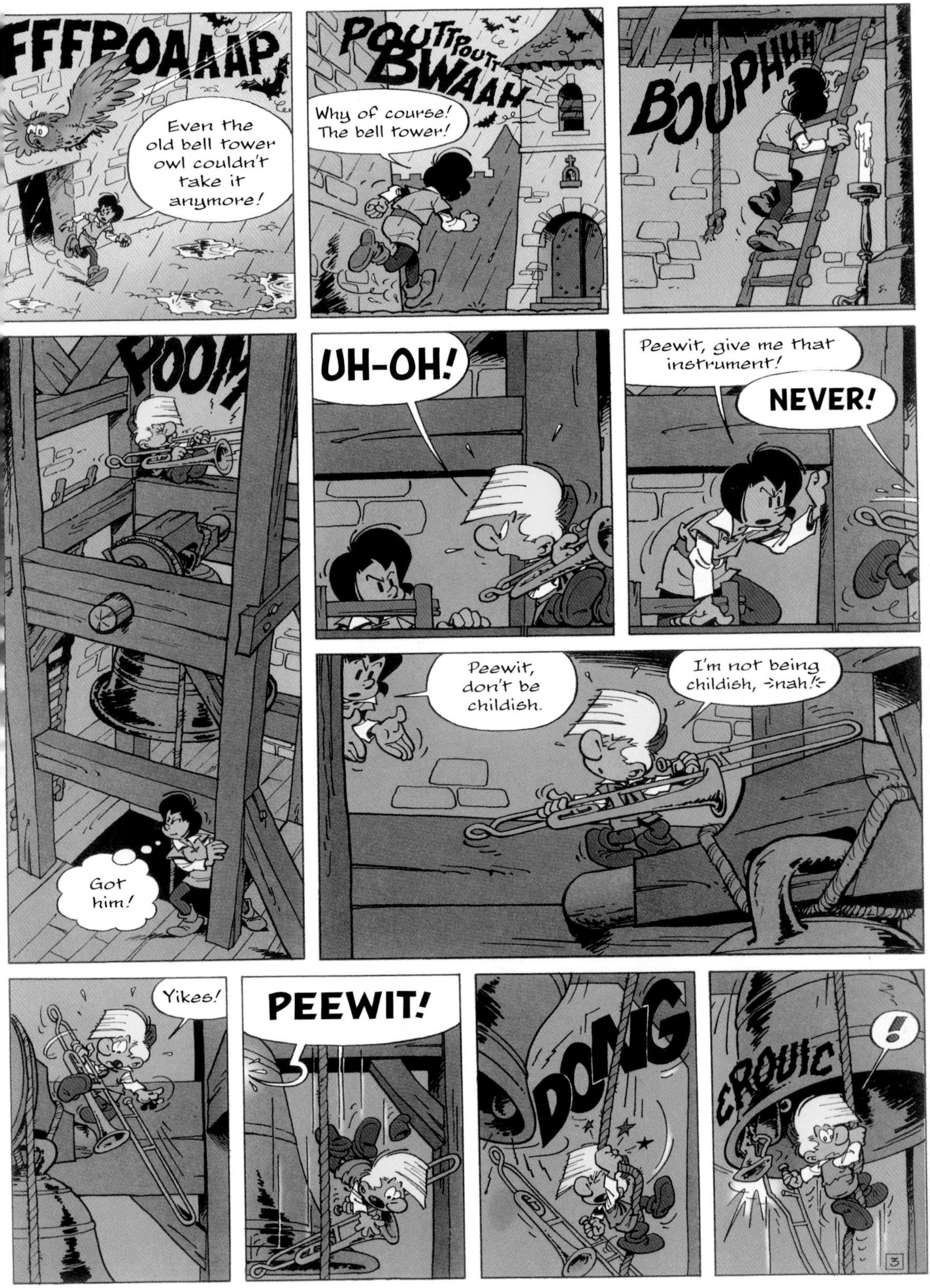
FFFPOAAAP
Even the old bell tower owl couldn't take it anymore!
POUTTPOUTT BWAAH
Why of course! The bell tower!
BOUPHHH
POOM
Got him!
UH-OH!
Peewit, give me that instrument!
NEVER!
Peewit, don't be childish.
I'm not being childish, nah!
Yikes!
PEEWIT!
DONG
CROUIC
!
3

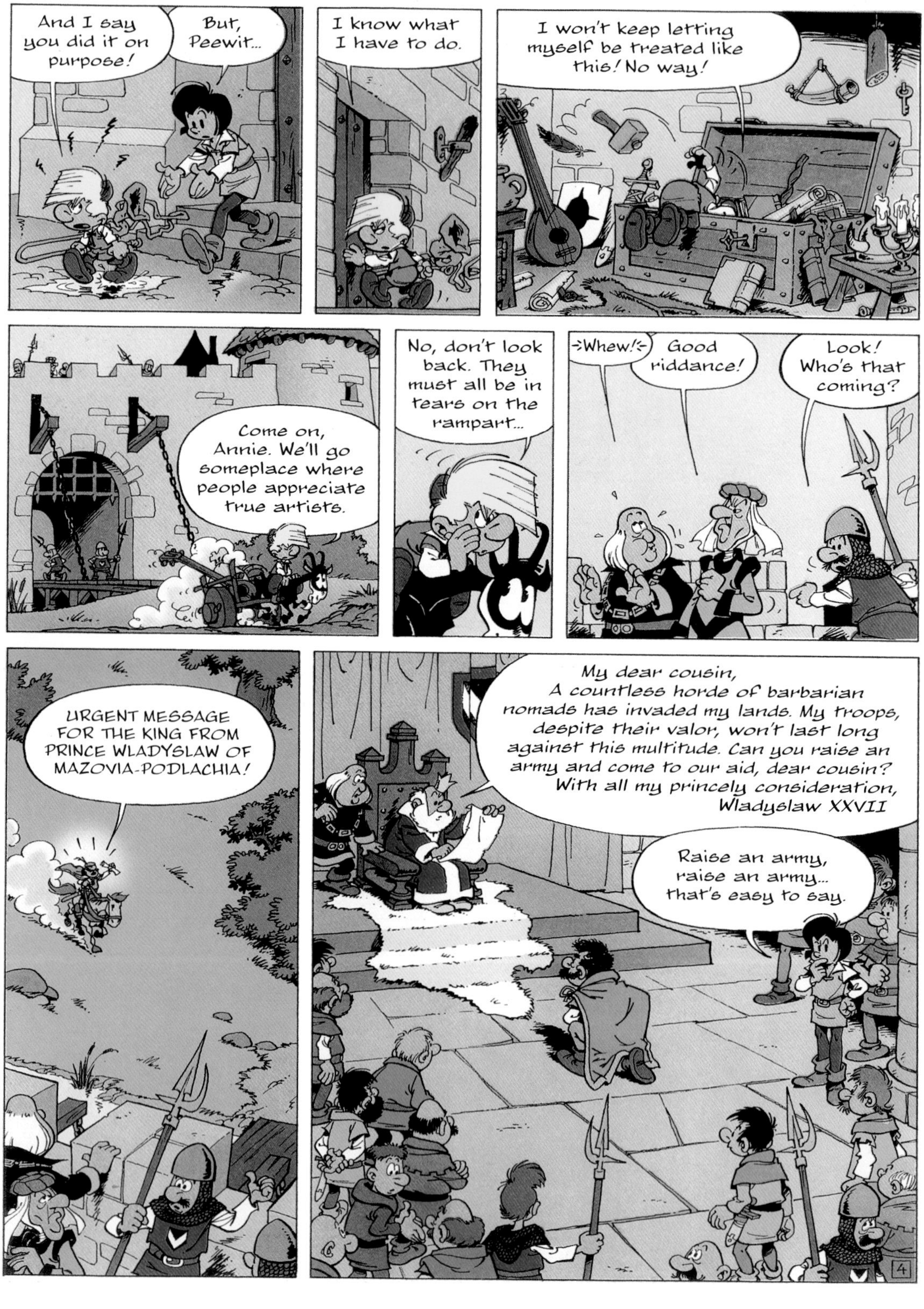
And I say you did it on purpose!
But, Peewit...
I know what I have to do.
I won't keep letting myself be treated like this! No way!
Come on, Annie. We'll go someplace where people appreciate true artists.
No, don't look back. They must all be in tears on the rampart...
Whew!
Good riddance!
Look! Who's that coming?
URGENT MESSAGE FOR THE KING FROM PRINCE WLADYSLAW OF MAZOVIA-PODLACHIA!
My dear cousin,
A countless horde of barbarian nomads has invaded my lands. My troops, despite their valor, won't last long against this multitude. Can you raise an army and come to our aid, dear cousin?
With all my princely consideration,
Wladyslaw XXVII
Raise an army, raise an army... that's easy to say.
4

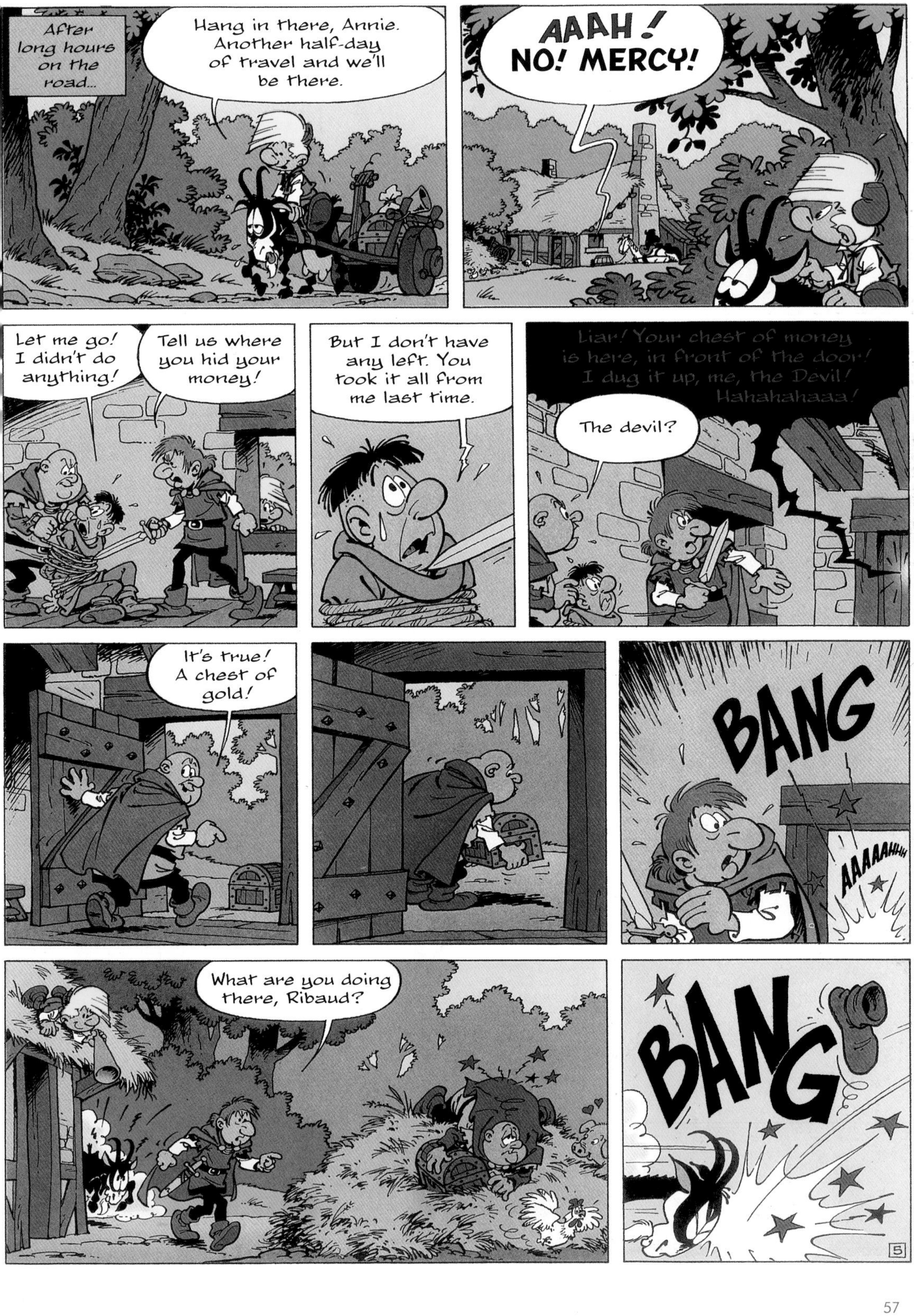
After long hours on the road...
Hang in there, Annie. Another half-day of travel and we'll be there.
AAAH! NO! MERCY!
Let me go! I didn't do anything!
Tell us where you hid your money!
But I don't have any left. You took it all from me last time.
Liar! Your chest of money is here, in front of the door! I dug it up, me, the Devil! Hahahahaaa!
The devil?
It's true! A chest of gold!
BANG
AAAAAHHH
What are you doing there, Ribaud?
BANG

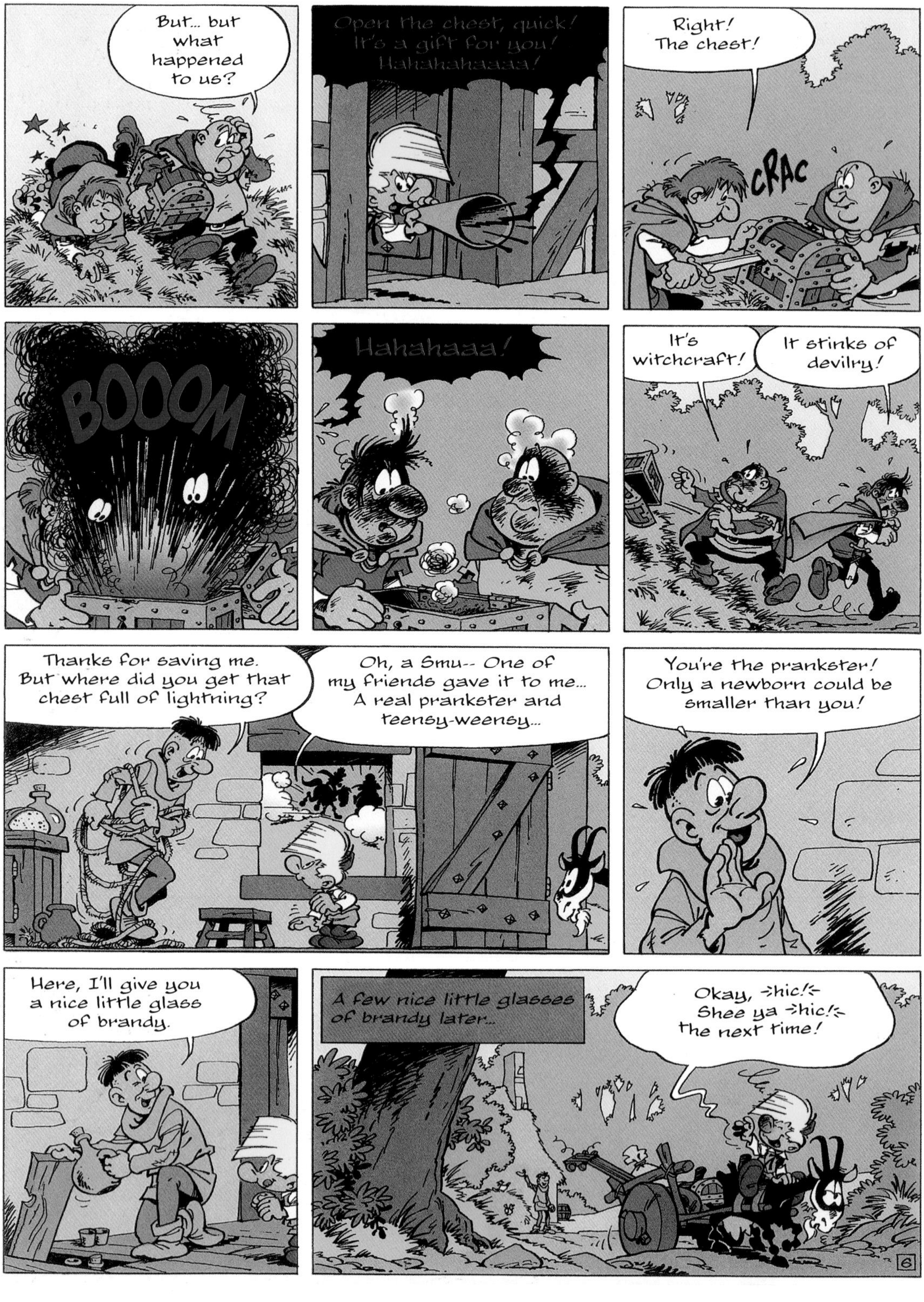
But... but what happened to us?
Open the chest, quick! It's a gift for you! Hahahahaaaa!
Right! The chest!
CRAC
BOOOM
Hahahaaa!
It's witchcraft!
It stinks of devilry!
Thanks for saving me. But where did you get that chest full of lightning?
Oh, a Smu-- One of my friends gave it to me... A real prankster and teensy-weensy...
You're the prankster! Only a newborn could be smaller than you!
Here, I'll give you a nice little glass of brandy.
A few nice little glasses of brandy later...
Okay, -hic!- Shee ya -hic!- the next time!
6

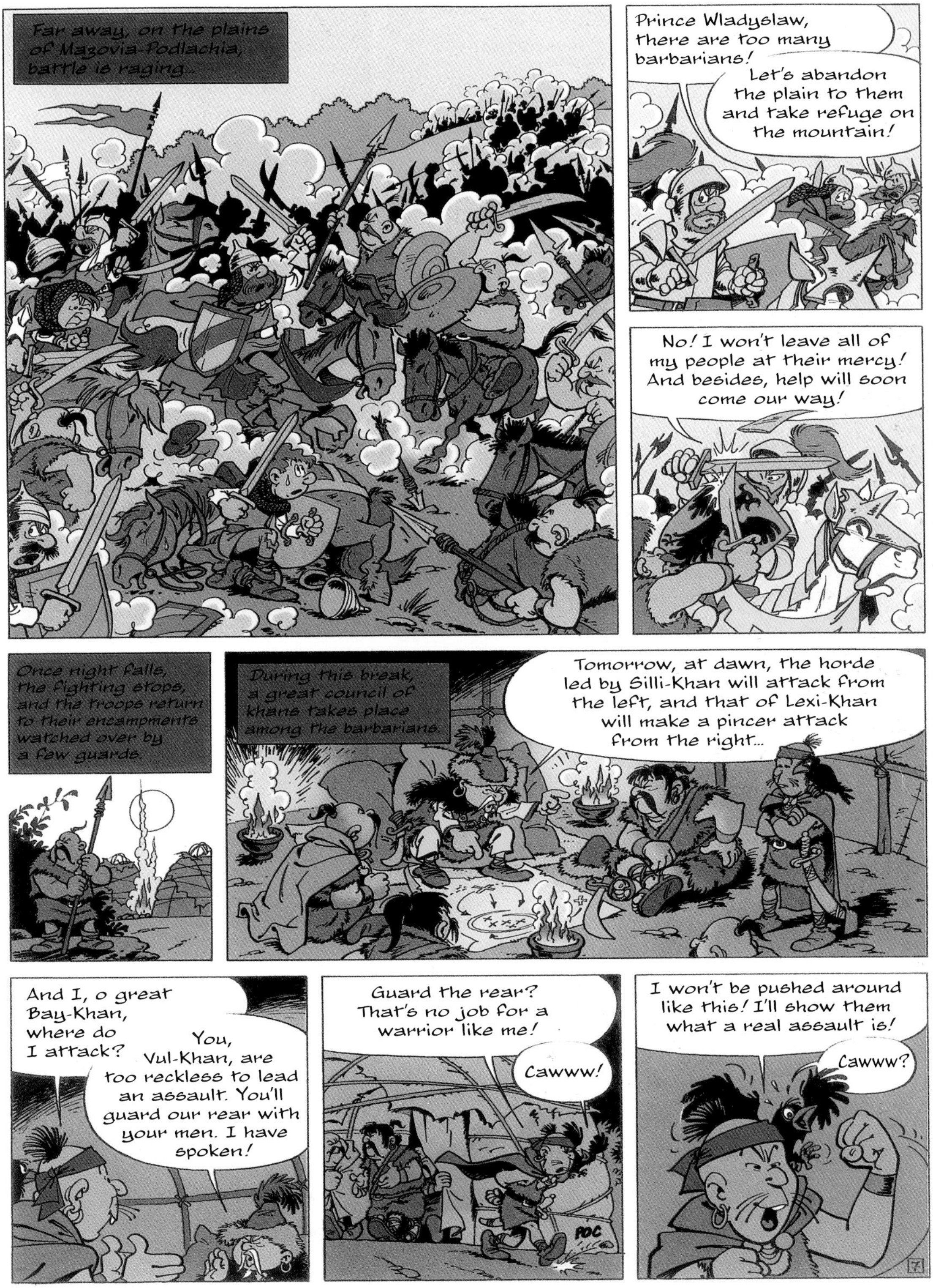

Far away, on the plains of Mazovia-Podlachia, battle is raging...
Prince Wladyslaw, there are too many barbarians!
Let's abandon the plain to them and take refuge on the mountain!
No! I won't leave all of my people at their mercy! And besides, help will soon come our way!
Once night falls, the fighting stops, and the troops return to their encampments watched over by a few guards.
During this break, a great council of khans takes place among the barbarians.
Tomorrow, at dawn, the horde led by Silli-Khan will attack from the left, and that of Lexi-Khan will make a pincer attack from the right...
And I, o great Bay-Khan, where do I attack?
You, Vul-Khan, are too reckless to lead an assault. You'll guard our rear with your men. I have spoken!
Guard the rear? That's no job for a warrior like me!
Cawww!
POC
I won't be pushed around like this! I'll show them what a real assault is!
Cawww?
7

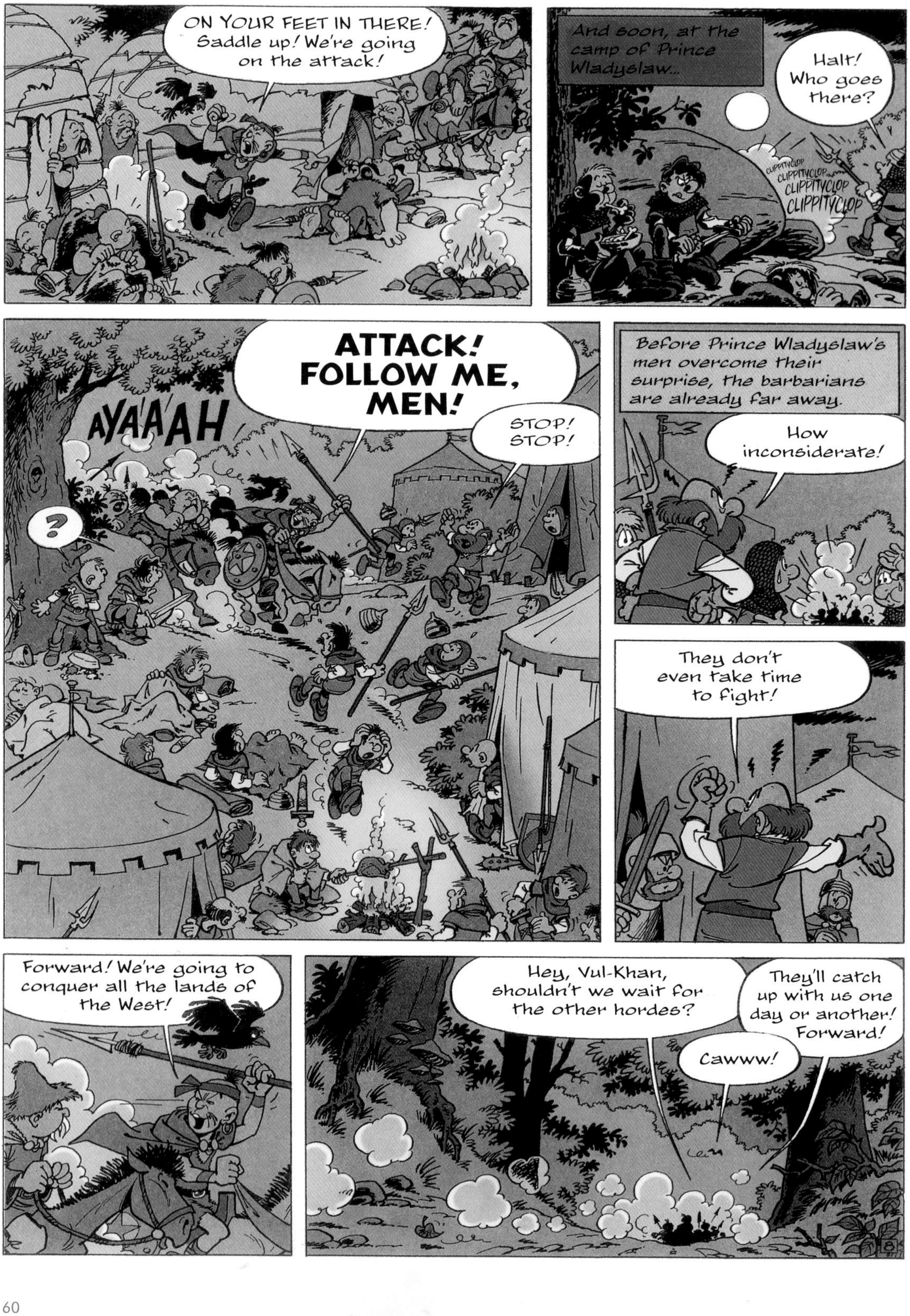
ON YOUR FEET IN THERE! Saddle up! We're going on the attack!
And soon, at the camp of Prince Wladyslaw...
Halt! Who goes there?
CLIPPITYCLOP CLIPPITYCLOP CLIPPITYCLOP CLIPPITYCLOP
AYAAAH
ATTACK! FOLLOW ME, MEN!
STOP! STOP!
?
Before Prince Wladyslaw's men overcome their surprise, the barbarians are already far away.
How inconsiderate!
They don't even take time to fight!
Forward! We're going to conquer all the lands of the West!
Hey, Vul-Khan, shouldn't we wait for the other hordes?
They'll catch up with us one day or another! Forward!
Cawww!

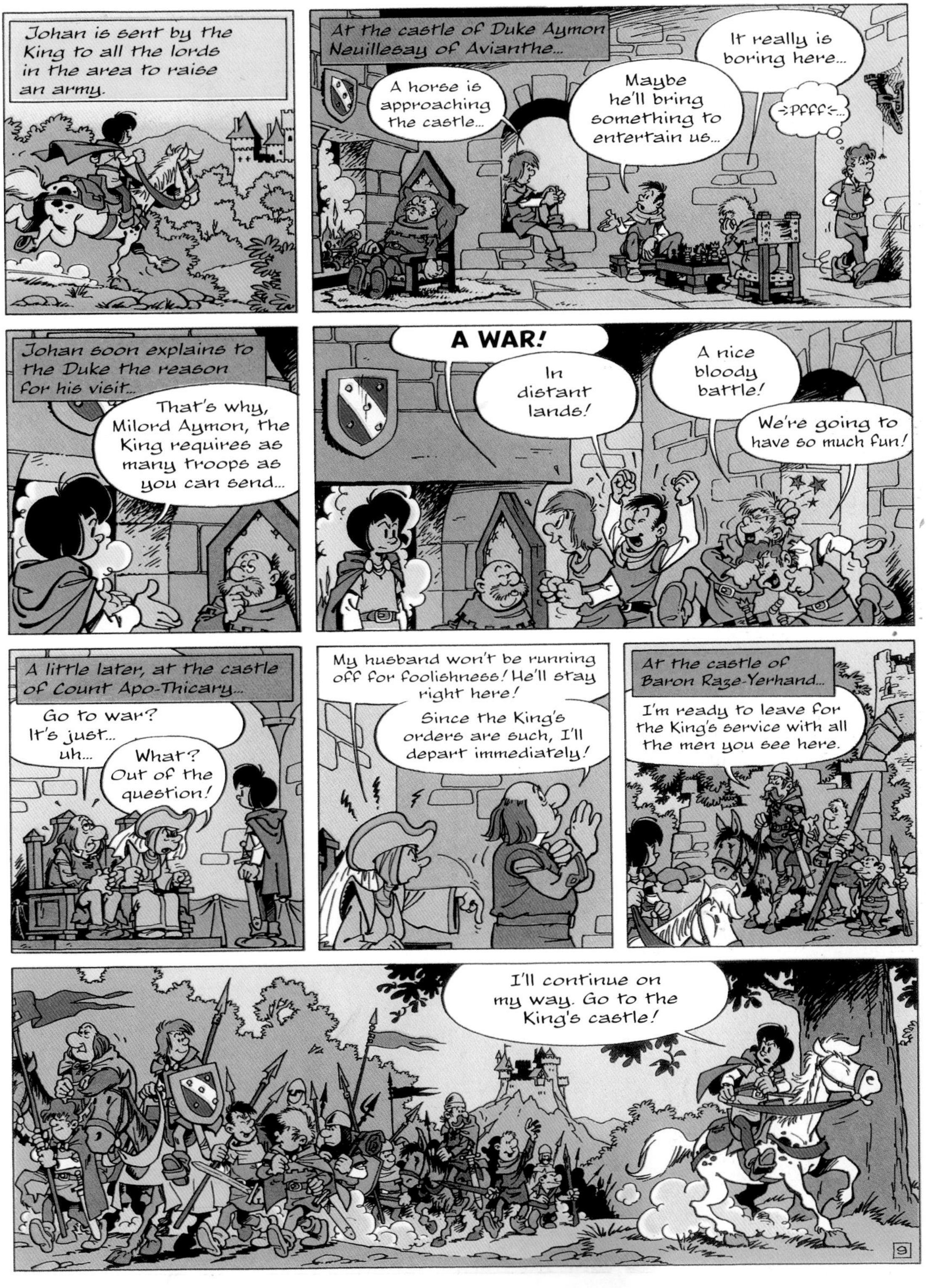

Johan is sent by the King to all the lords in the area to raise an army.
At the castle of Duke Aymon Neuillesay of Avianthe...
A horse is approaching the castle...
Maybe he'll bring something to entertain us...
It really is boring here...
PFFF
Johan soon explains to the Duke the reason for his visit...
That's why, Milord Aymon, the King requires as many troops as you can send...
A WAR!
In distant lands!
A nice bloody battle!
We're going to have so much fun!
A little later, at the castle of Count Apo-Thicary...
Go to war? It's just... uh...
What? Out of the question!
My husband won't be running off for foolishness! He'll stay right here!
Since the King's orders are such, I'll depart immediately!
At the castle of Baron Raze-Yerhand...
I'm ready to leave for the King's service with all the men you see here.
I'll continue on my way. Go to the King's castle!
9

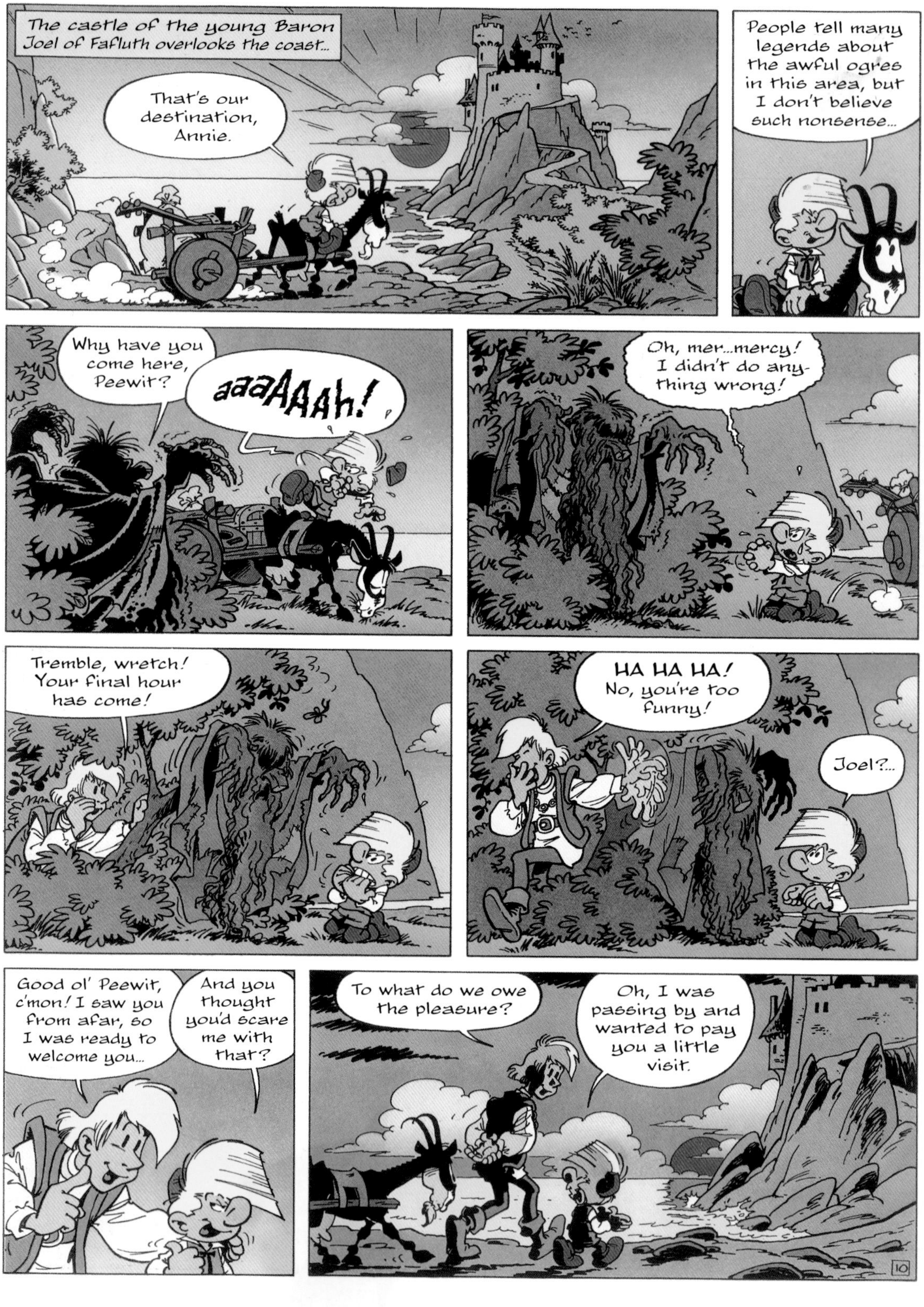
The castle of the young Baron Joel of Fafluth overlooks the coast...
That's our destination, Annie.
People tell many legends about the awful ogres in this area, but I don't believe such nonsense...
Why have you come here, Peewit?
aaaAAAh!
Oh, mer...mercy! I didn't do anything wrong!
Tremble, wretch! Your final hour has come!
HA HA HA! No, you're too funny!
Joel?...
Good ol' Peewit, c'mon! I saw you from afar, so I was ready to welcome you...
And you thought you'd scare me with that?
To what do we owe the pleasure?
Oh, I was passing by and wanted to pay you a little visit.
10

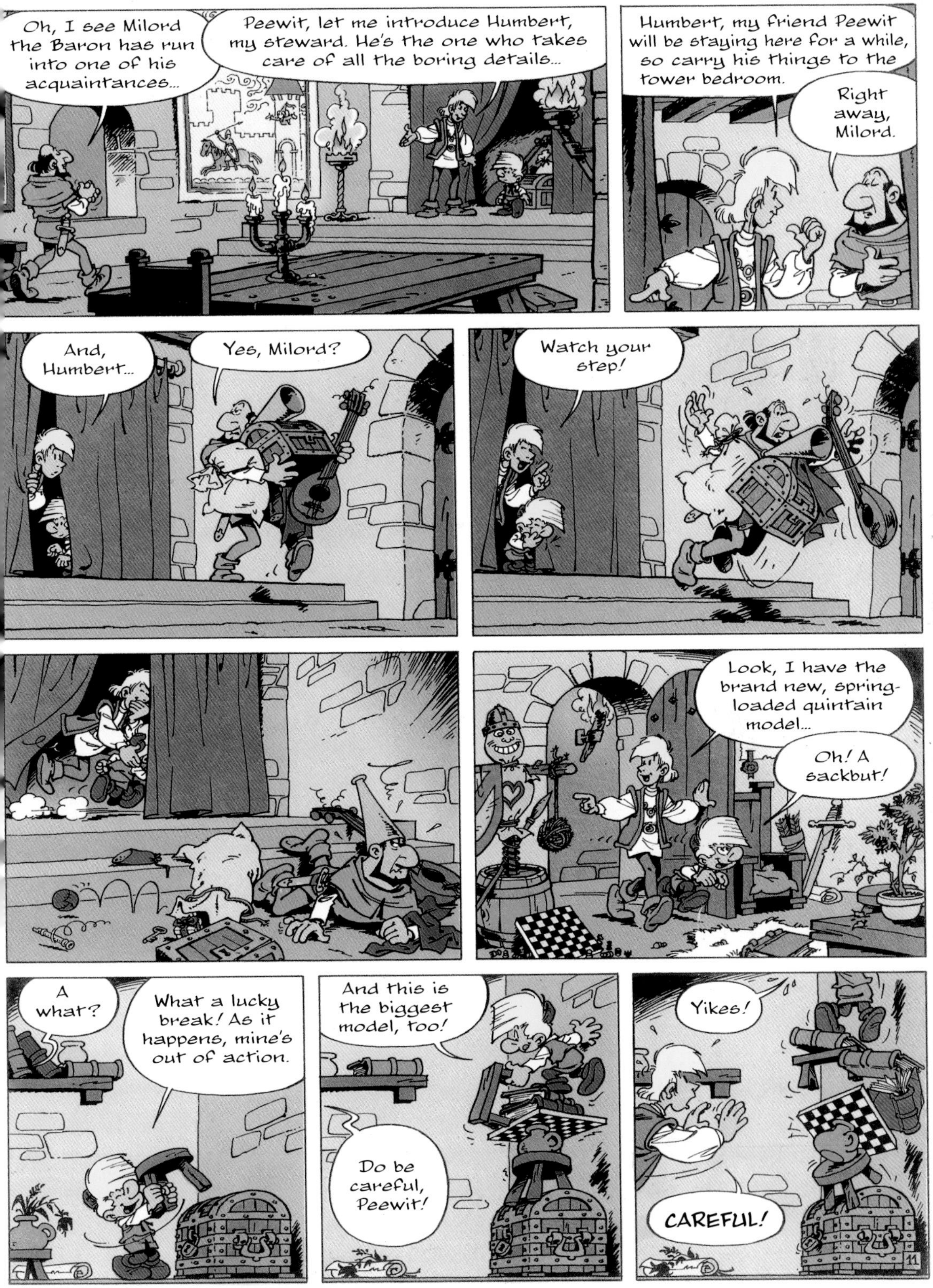
Oh, I see Milord the Baron has run into one of his acquaintances...
Peewit, let me introduce Humbert, my steward. He's the one who takes care of all the boring details...
Humbert, my friend Peewit will be staying here for a while, so carry his things to the tower bedroom.
Right away, Milord.
And, Humbert...
Yes, Milord?
Watch your step!
Look, I have the brand new, spring-loaded quintain model...
Oh! A sackbut!
A what?
What a lucky break! As it happens, mine's out of action.
And this is the biggest model, too!
Do be careful, Peewit!
Yikes!
CAREFUL!
11

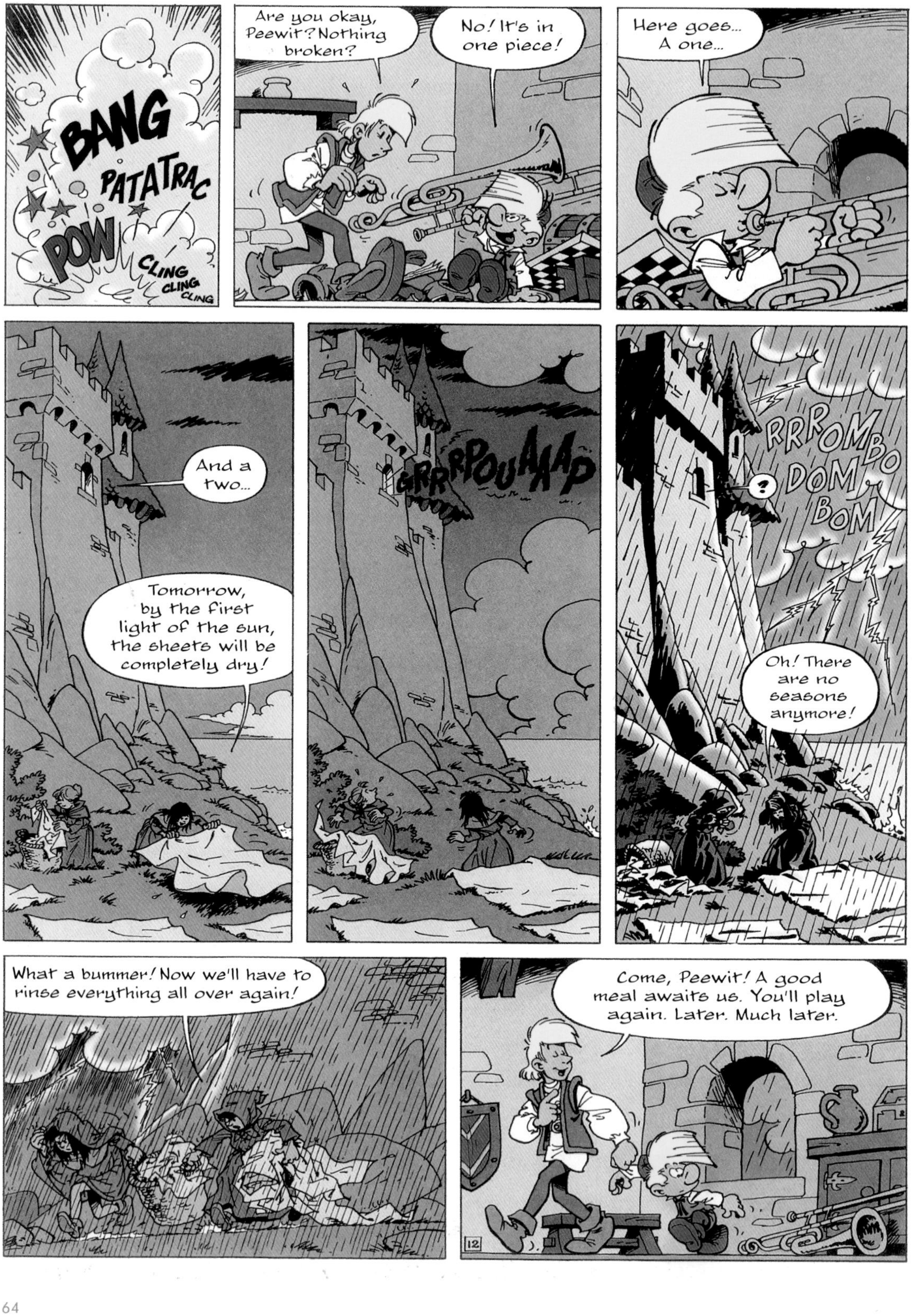
BANG
PATATRAC
POW
CLING
CLING
CLING
Are you okay, Peewit? Nothing broken?
No! It's in one piece!
Here goes... A one...
And a two...
Tomorrow, by the first light of the sun, the sheets will be completely dry!
GRRRRPOUAAAAP
RRROMBO DOM BOM
?
Oh! There are no seasons anymore!
What a bummer! Now we'll have to rinse everything all over again!
Come, Peewit! A good meal awaits us. You'll play again. Later. Much later.
12

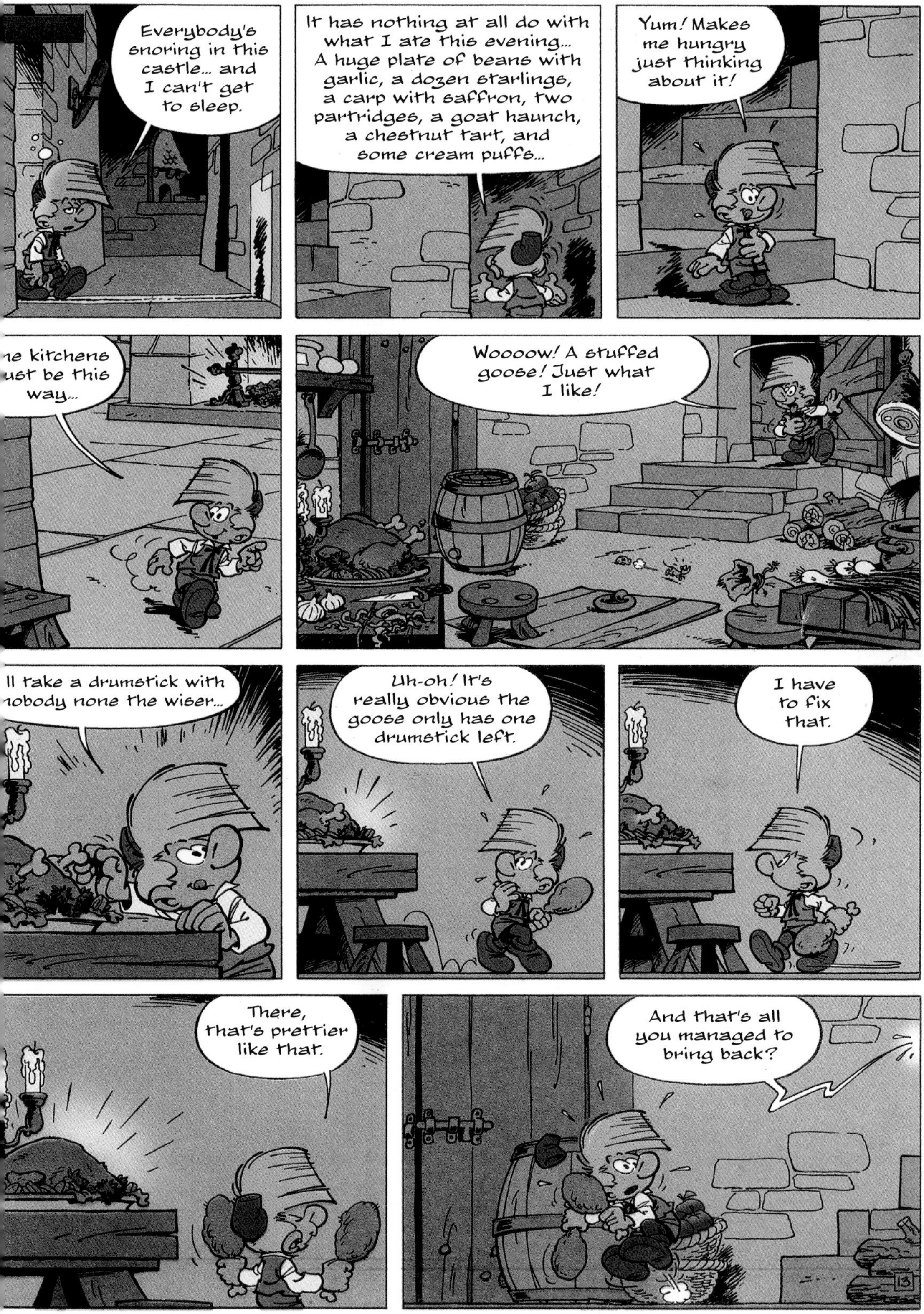
Everybody's snoring in this castle... and I can't get to sleep.
It has nothing at all do with what I ate this evening... A huge plate of beans with garlic, a dozen starlings, a carp with saffron, two partridges, a goat haunch, a chestnut tart, and some cream puffs...
Yum! Makes me hungry just thinking about it!
ne kitchens ust be this way...
Woooow! A stuffed goose! Just what I like!
ll take a drumstick with obody none the wiser...
Uh-oh! It's really obvious the goose only has one drumstick left.
I have to fix that.
There, that's prettier like that.
And that's all you managed to bring back?
13

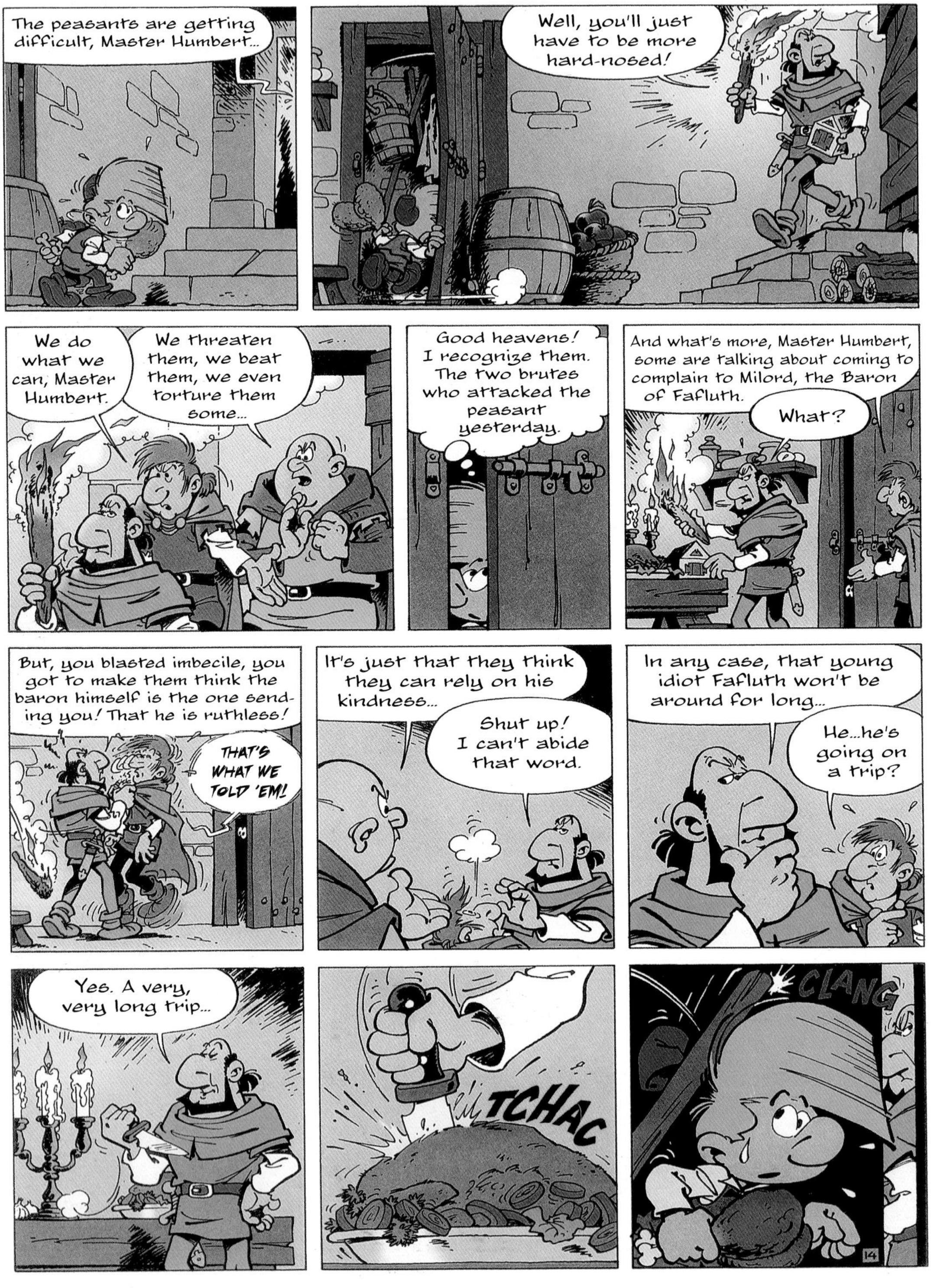

The peasants are getting difficult, Master Humbert...
Well, you'll just have to be more hard-nosed!
We do what we can, Master Humbert.
We threaten them, we beat them, we even torture them some...
Good heavens! I recognize them. The two brutes who attacked the peasant yesterday.
And what's more, Master Humbert, some are talking about coming to complain to Milord, the Baron of Fafluth.
What?
But, you blasted imbecile, you got to make them think the baron himself is the one sending you! That he is ruthless!
THAT'S WHAT WE TOLD 'EM!
It's just that they think they can rely on his kindness...
Shut up! I can't abide that word.
In any case, that young idiot Fafluth won't be around for long...
He...he's going on a trip?
Yes. A very, very long trip...
TCHAC
CLANG
14

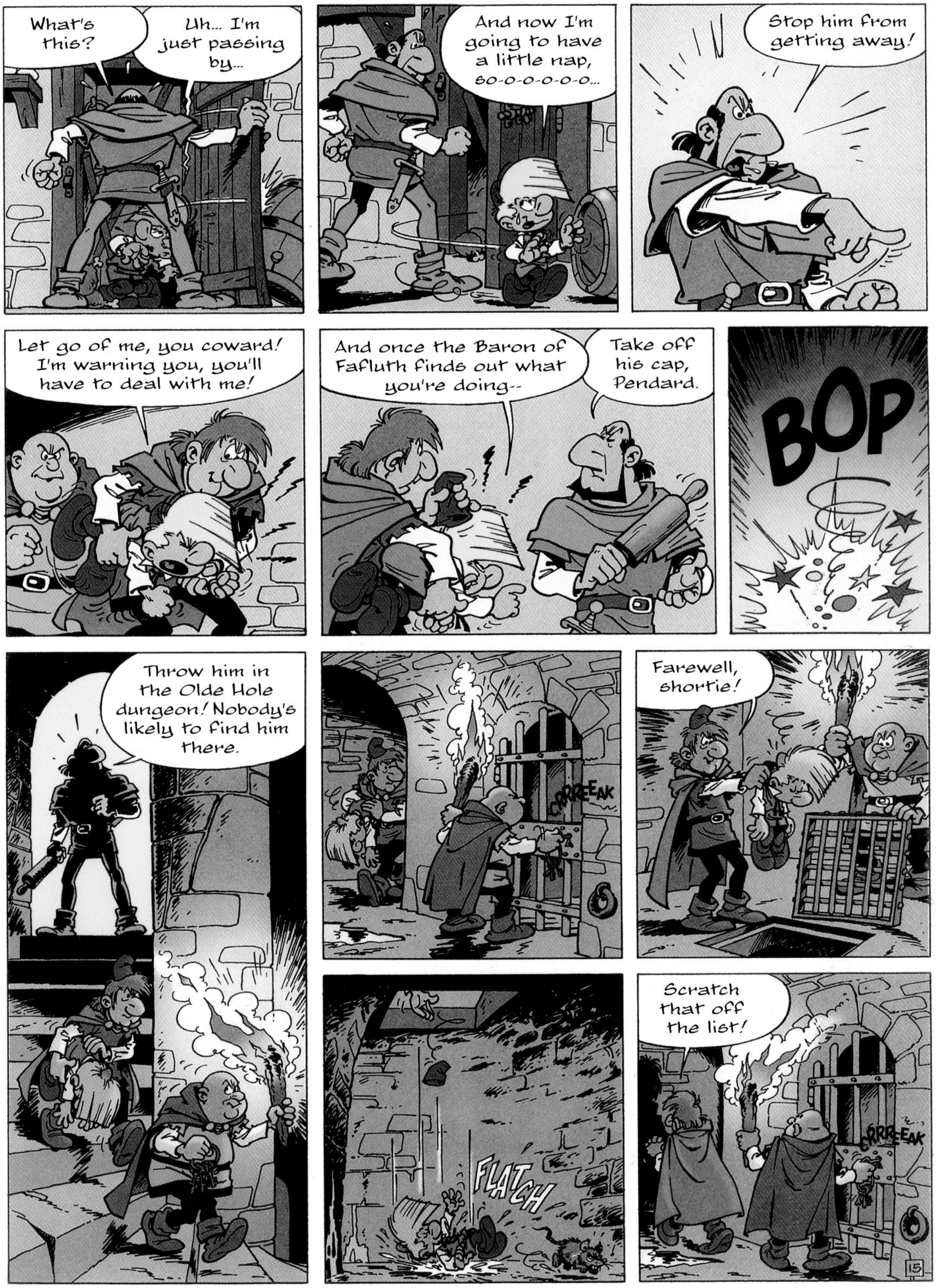

What's this?
Uh... I'm just passing by...
And now I'm going to have a little nap, so-o-o-o-o-o-o...
Stop him from getting away!
Let go of me, you coward! I'm warning you, you'll have to deal with me!
And once the Baron of Fafluth finds out what you're doing--
Take off his cap, Pendard.
BOP
Throw him in the Olde Hole dungeon! Nobody's likely to find him there.
CRRREEAK
Farewell, shortie!
FLATCH
Scratch that off the list!
CRRREEAK
15

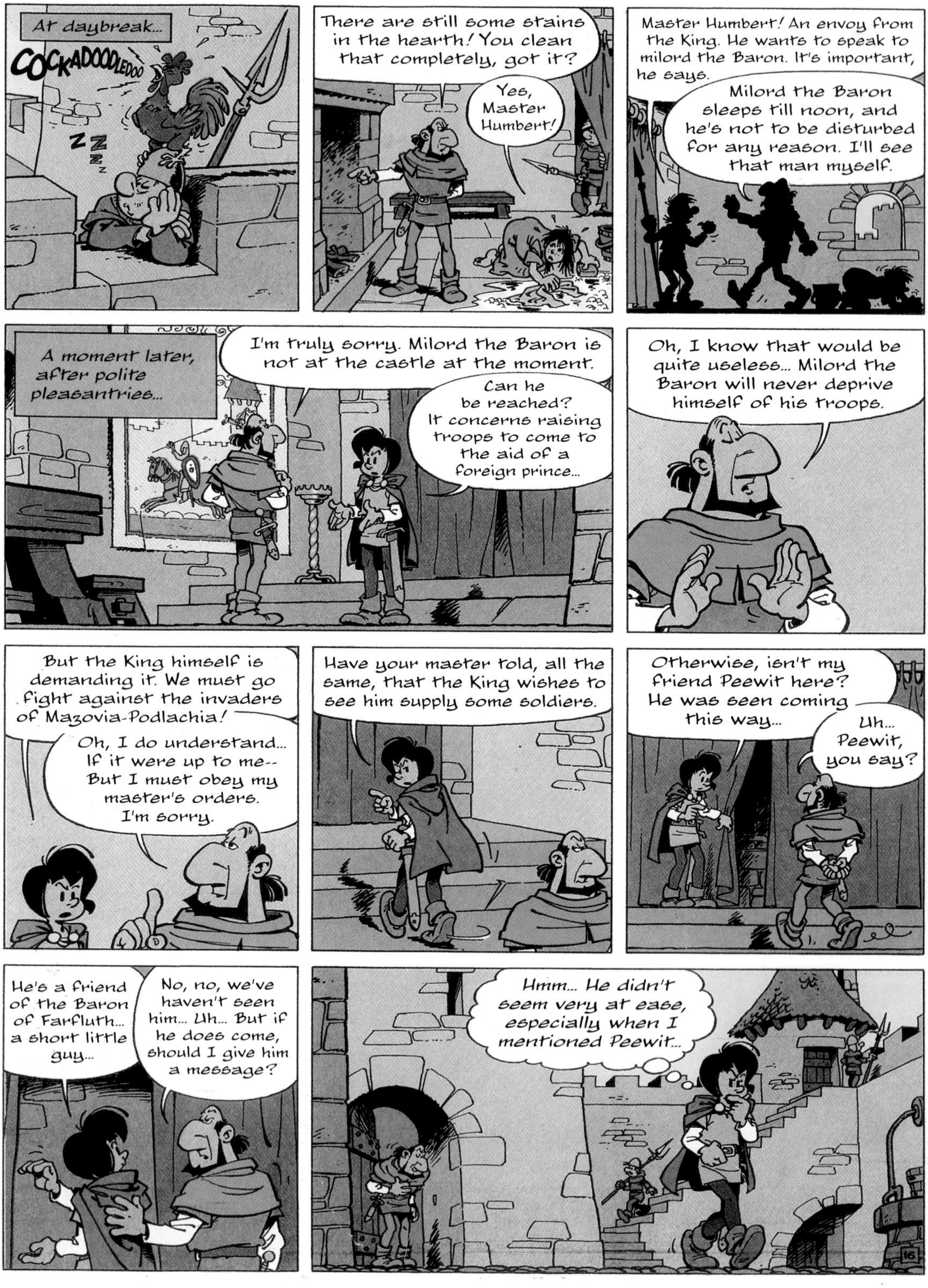
At daybreak...
COCKADOODLEDOO
ZZZ
There are still some stains in the hearth! You clean that completely, got it?
Yes, Master Humbert!
Master Humbert! An envoy from the King. He wants to speak to milord the Baron. It's important, he says.
Milord the Baron sleeps till noon, and he's not to be disturbed for any reason. I'll see that man myself.
A moment later, after polite pleasantries...
I'm truly sorry. Milord the Baron is not at the castle at the moment.
Can he be reached? It concerns raising troops to come to the aid of a foreign prince...
Oh, I know that would be quite useless... Milord the Baron will never deprive himself of his troops.
But the King himself is demanding it. We must go fight against the invaders of Mazovia-Podlachia!
Oh, I do understand... If it were up to me-- But I must obey my master's orders. I'm sorry.
Have your master told, all the same, that the King wishes to see him supply some soldiers.
Otherwise, isn't my friend Peewit here? He was seen coming this way...
Uh... Peewit, you say?
He's a friend of the Baron of Farfluth... a short little guy...
No, no, we've haven't seen him... Uh... But if he does come, should I give him a message?
Hmm... He didn't seem very at ease, especially when I mentioned Peewit...

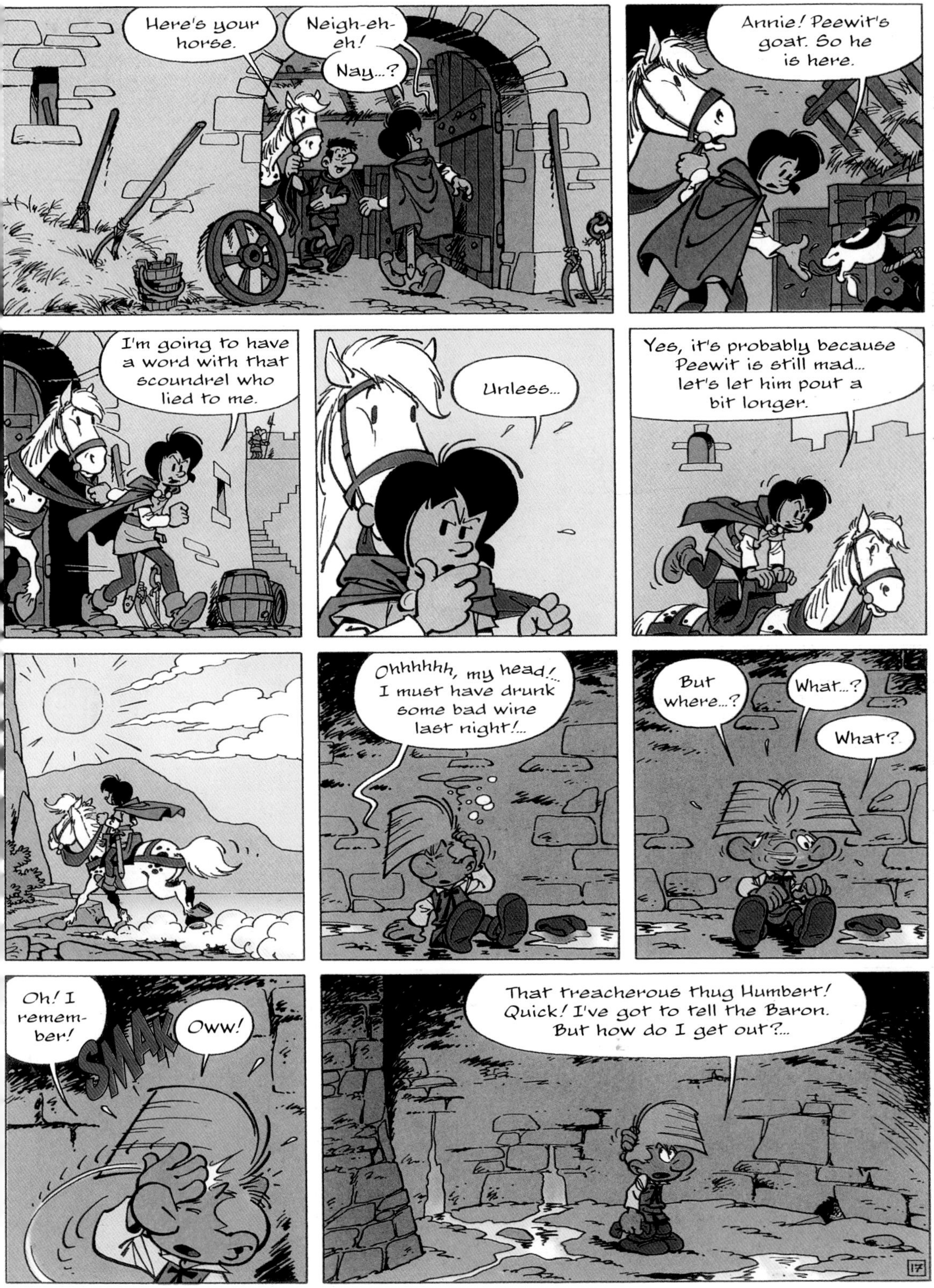

Here's your horse.
Neigh-eh-eh!
Nay...?
Annie! Peewit's goat. So he is here.
I'm going to have a word with that scoundrel who lied to me.
Unless...
Yes, it's probably because Peewit is still mad... let's let him pout a bit longer.
Ohhhhhh, my head!... I must have drunk some bad wine last night!...
But where...?
What...?
What?
Oh! I remem-ber!
SMAK
Oww!
That treacherous thug Humbert! Quick! I've got to tell the Baron. But how do I get out?...
17

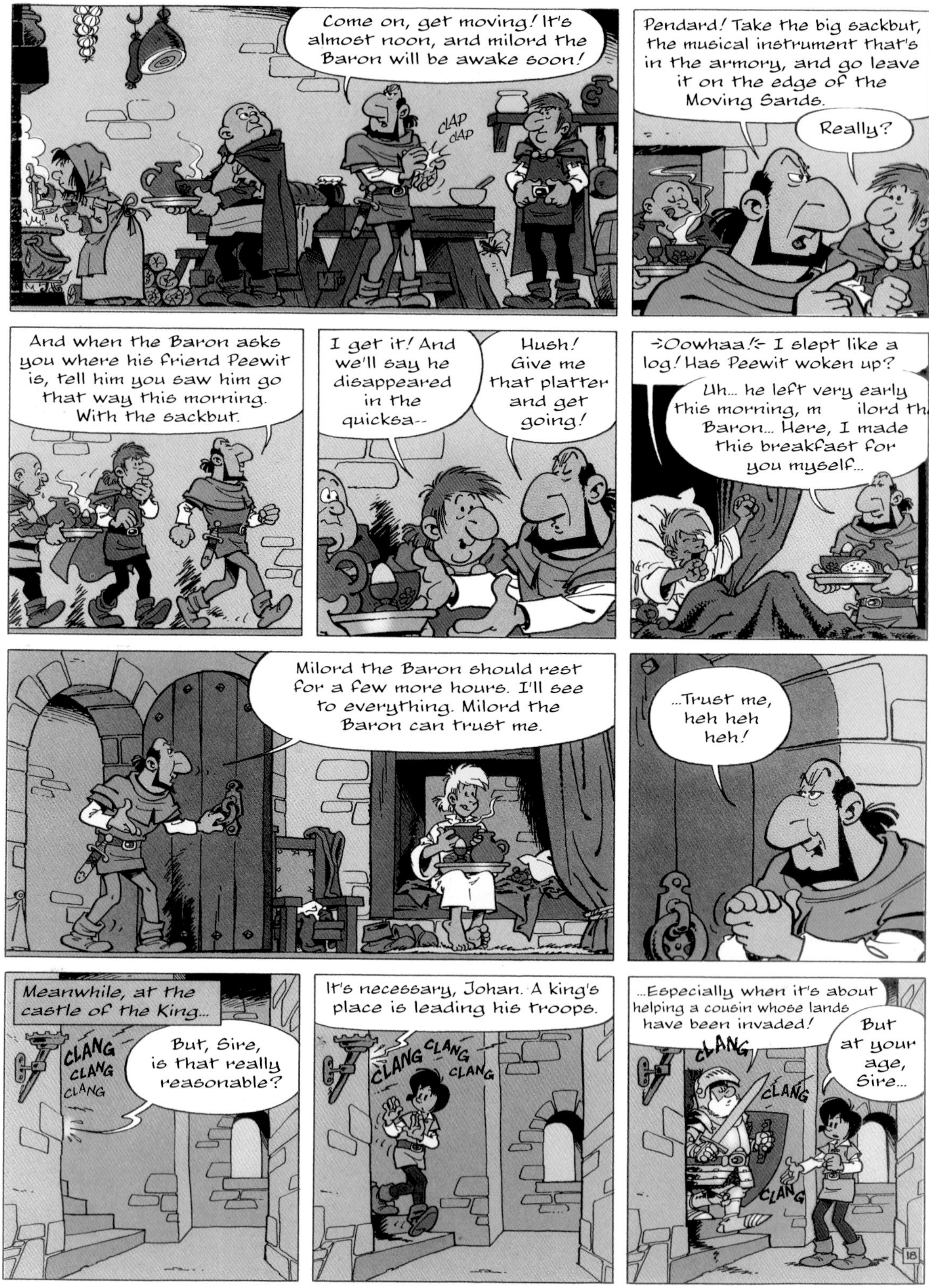
Come on, get moving! It's almost noon, and milord the Baron will be awake soon!
CLAP CLAP
Pendard! Take the big sackbut, the musical instrument that's in the armory, and go leave it on the edge of the Moving Sands.
Really?
And when the Baron asks you where his friend Peewit is, tell him you saw him go that way this morning. With the sackbut.
I get it! And we'll say he disappeared in the quicksa--
Hush! Give me that platter and get going!
-Oowhaa!- I slept like a log! Has Peewit woken up?
Uh... he left very early this morning, milord the Baron... Here, I made this breakfast for you myself...
Milord the Baron should rest for a few more hours. I'll see to everything. Milord the Baron can trust me.
...Trust me, heh heh heh!
Meanwhile, at the castle of the King...
CLANG CLANG CLANG
But, Sire, is that really reasonable?
It's necessary, Johan. A king's place is leading his troops.
CLANG CLANG CLANG CLANG
...Especially when it's about helping a cousin whose lands have been invaded!
CLANG
But at your age, Sire...
CLANG
CLANG
18

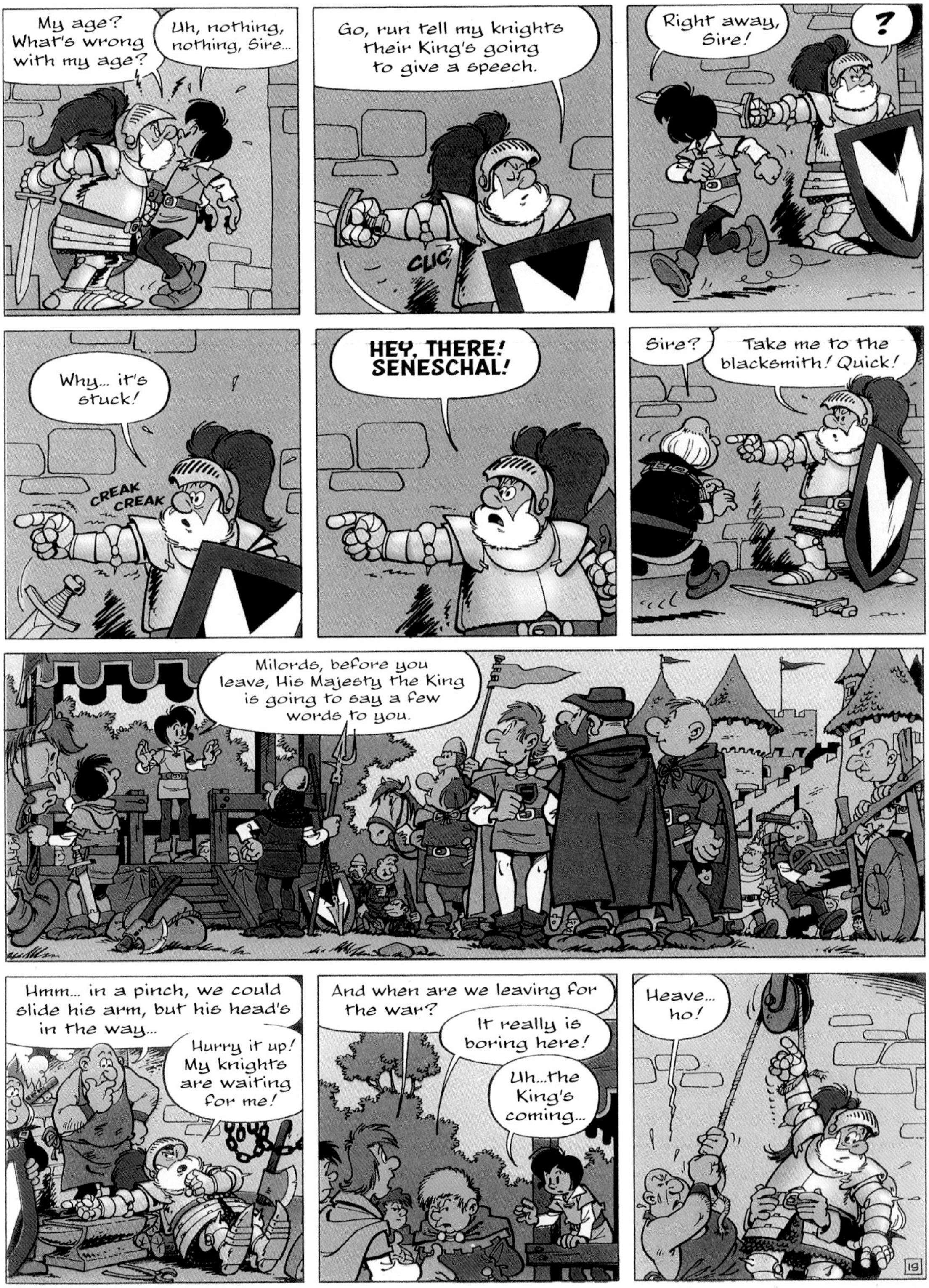

My age? What's wrong with my age?
Uh, nothing, nothing, Sire...
Go, run tell my knights their King's going to give a speech.
CLIC
Right away, Sire!
?
Why... it's stuck!
CREAK CREAK
HEY, THERE! SENESCHAL!
Sire?
Take me to the blacksmith! Quick!
Milords, before you leave, His Majesty the King is going to say a few words to you.
Hmm... in a pinch, we could slide his arm, but his head's in the way...
Hurry it up! My knights are waiting for me!
And when are we leaving for the war?
It really is boring here!
Uh...the King's coming...
Heave... ho!
19

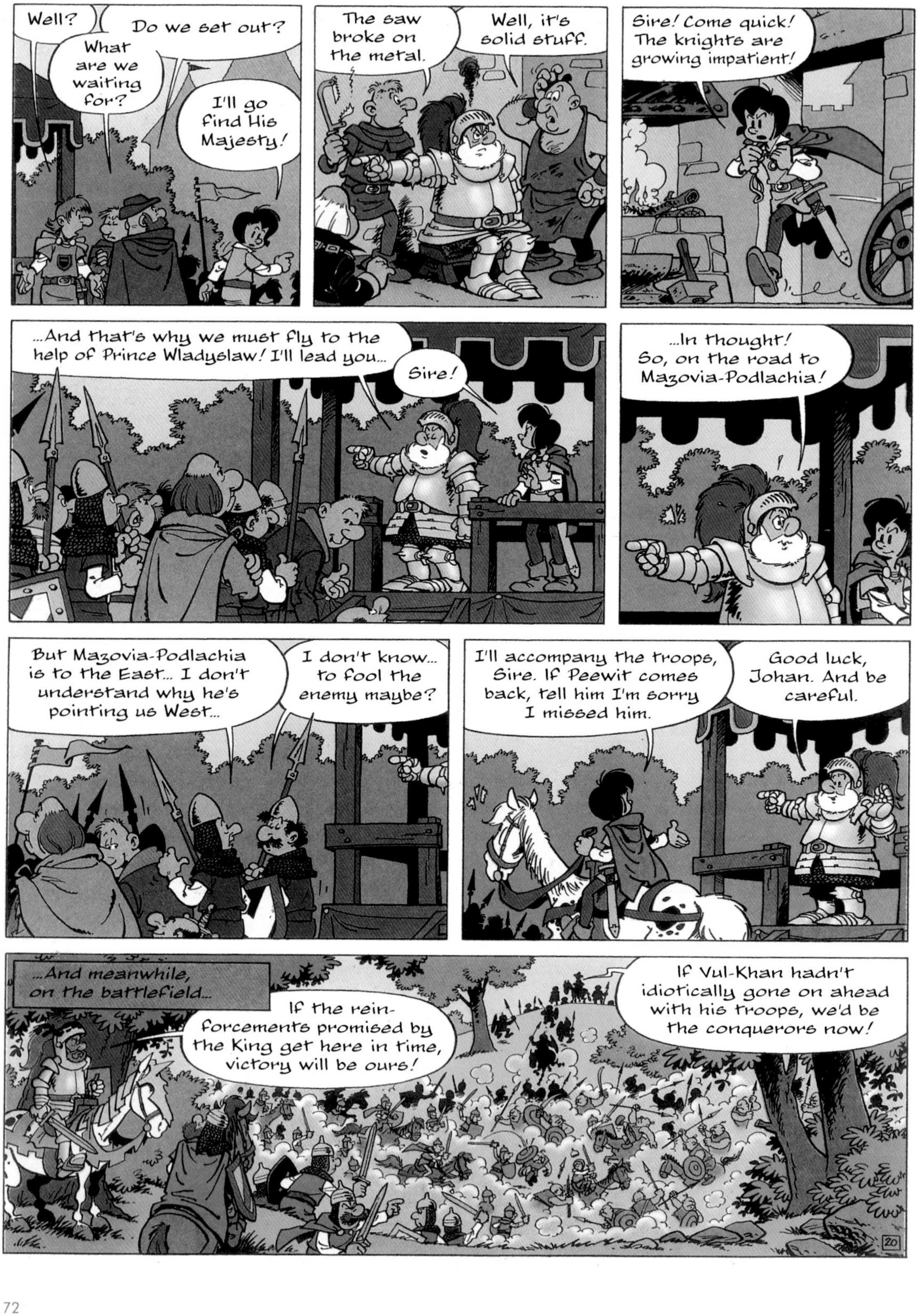

Well?
What are we waiting for?
Do we set out?
I'll go find His Majesty!
The saw broke on the metal.
Well, it's solid stuff.
Sire! Come quick! The knights are growing impatient!
...And that's why we must fly to the help of Prince Wladyslaw! I'll lead you...
Sire!
...In thought! So, on the road to Mazovia-Podlachia!
But Mazovia-Podlachia is to the East... I don't understand why he's pointing us West...
I don't know... to fool the enemy maybe?
I'll accompany the troops, Sire. If Peewit comes back, tell him I'm sorry I missed him.
Good luck, Johan. And be careful.
...And meanwhile, on the battlefield...
If the reinforcements promised by the King get here in time, victory will be ours!
If Vul-Khan hadn't idiotically gone on ahead with his troops, we'd be the conquerors now!
20

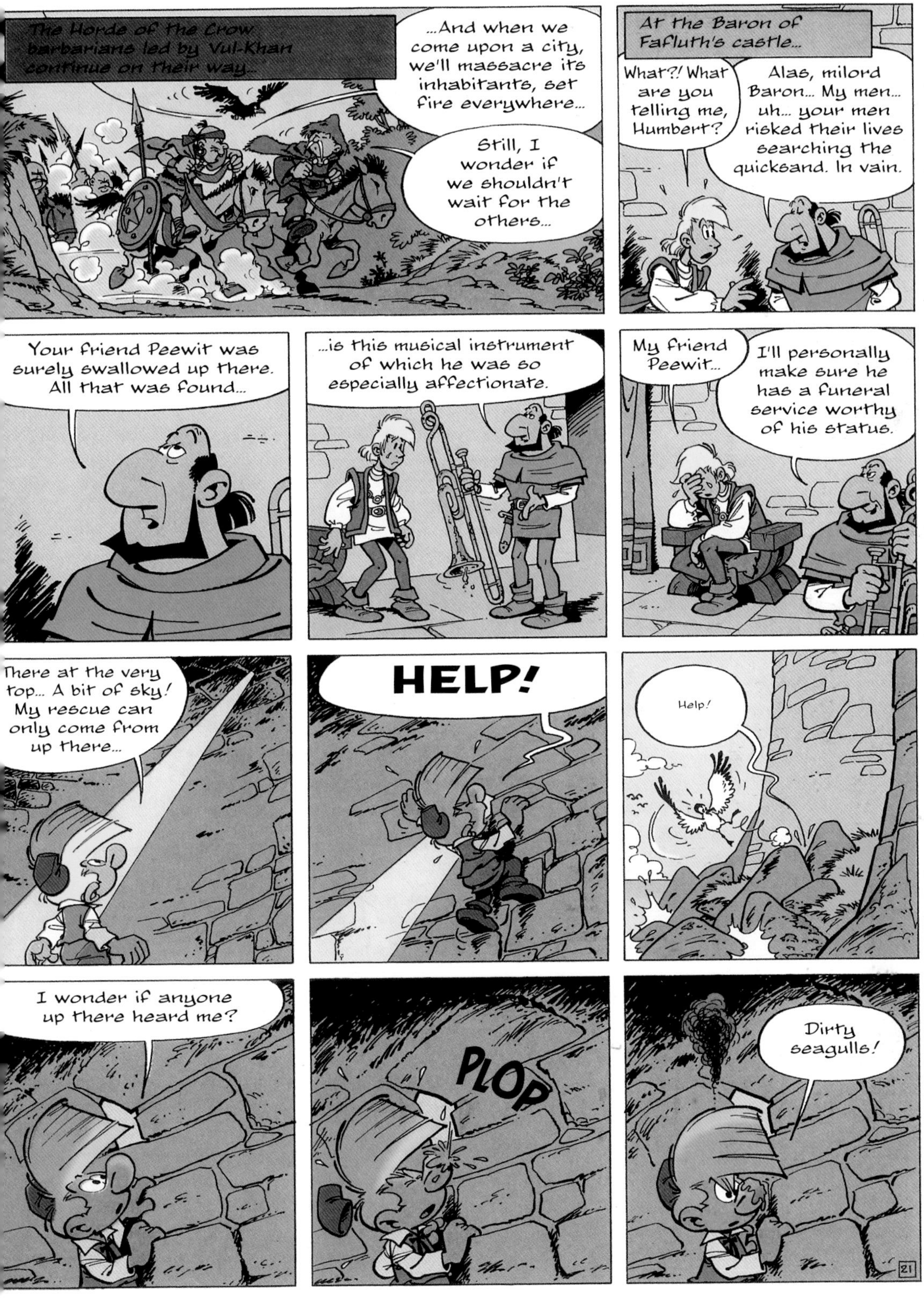
The Horde of the Crow barbarians led by Vul-Khan continue on their way...
...And when we come upon a city, we'll massacre its inhabitants, set fire everywhere...
Still, I wonder if we shouldn't wait for the others...
At the Baron of Fafluth's castle...
What?! What are you telling me, Humbert?
Alas, milord Baron... My men... uh... your men risked their lives searching the quicksand. In vain.
Your friend Peewit was surely swallowed up there. All that was found...
...is this musical instrument of which he was so especially affectionate.
My friend Peewit...
I'll personally make sure he has a funeral service worthy of his status.
There at the very top... A bit of sky! My rescue can only come from up there...
HELP!
Help!
I wonder if anyone up there heard me?
PLOP
Dirty seagulls!
21

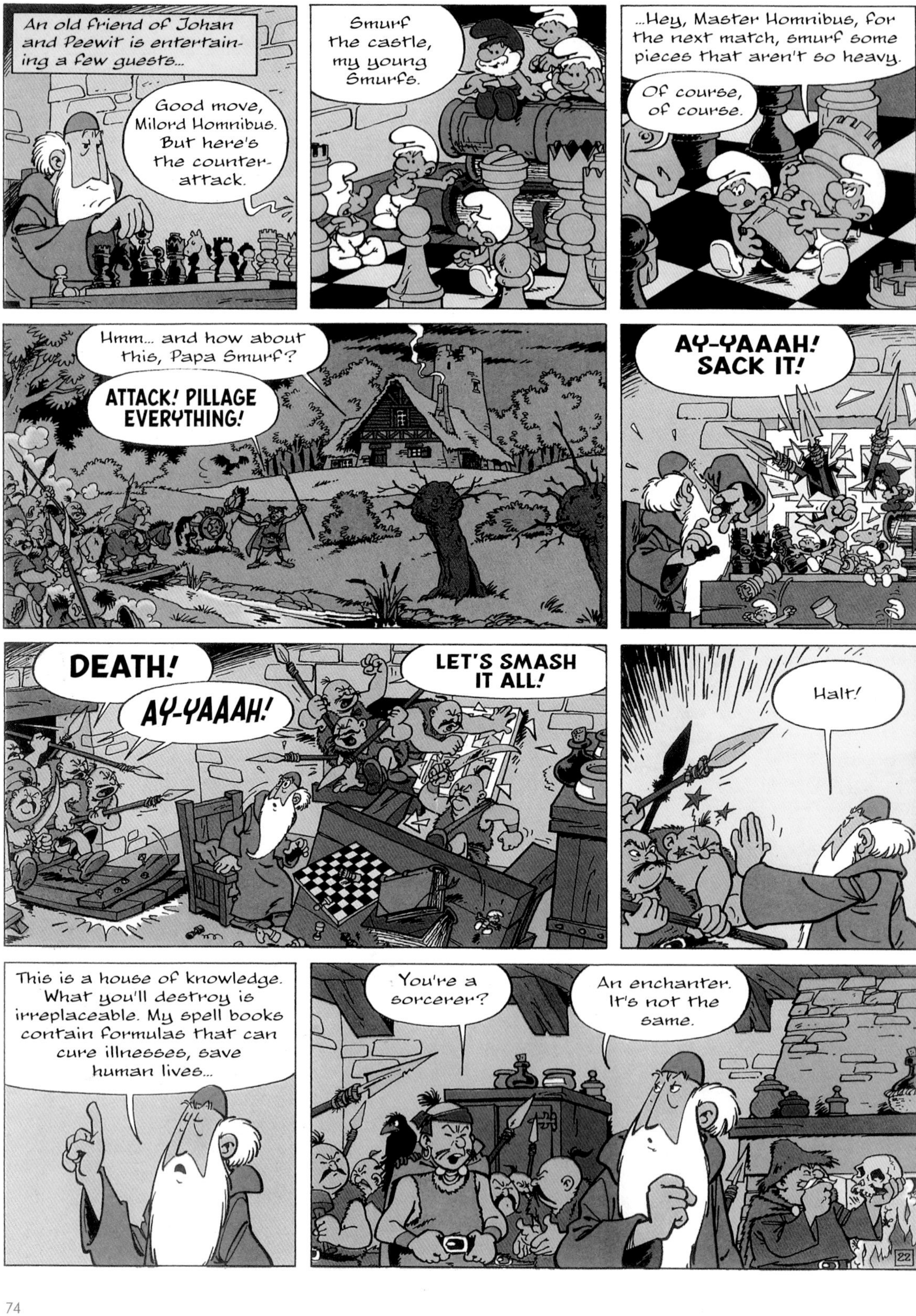
An old friend of Johan and Peewit is entertaining a few guests...
Good move, Milord Homnibus. But here's the counter-attack.
Smurf the castle, my young Smurfs.
...Hey, Master Homnibus, for the next match, smurf some pieces that aren't so heavy.
Of course, of course.
Hmm... and how about this, Papa Smurf?
ATTACK! PILLAGE EVERYTHING!
AY-YAAAH! SACK IT!
DEATH!
AY-YAAAH!
LET'S SMASH IT ALL!
Halt!
This is a house of knowledge. What you'll destroy is irreplaceable. My spell books contain formulas that can cure illnesses, save human lives...
You're a sorcerer?
An enchanter. It's not the same.
22

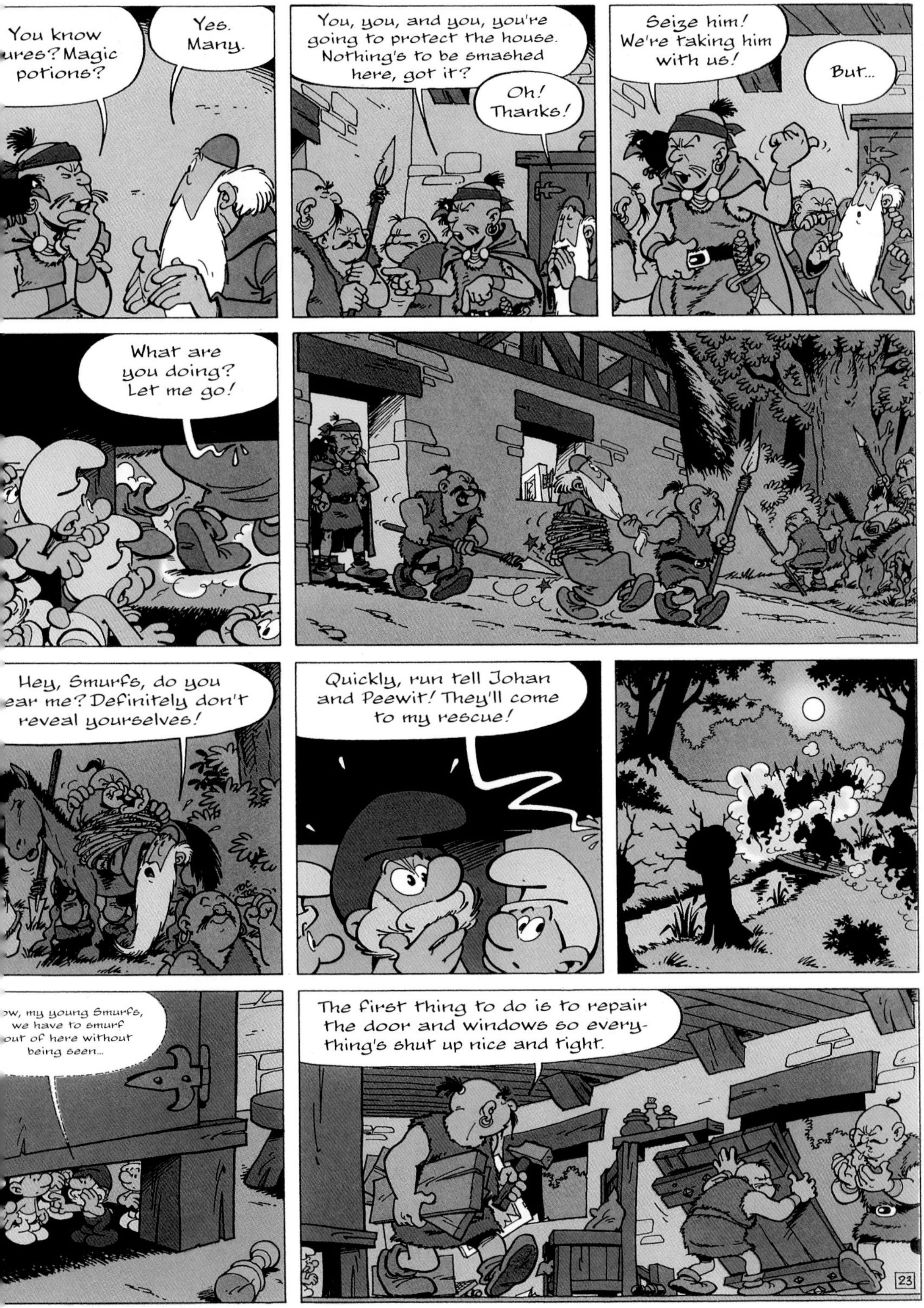
You know
ures? Magic
potions?
Yes.
Many.
You, you, and you, you're going to protect the house. Nothing's to be smashed here, got it?
Oh! Thanks!
Seize him! We're taking him with us!
But...
What are you doing? Let me go!
Hey, Smurfs, do you
ear me? Definitely don't reveal yourselves!
Quickly, run tell Johan and Peewit! They'll come to my rescue!
ow, my young Smurfs, we have to smurf
out of here without being seen...
The first thing to do is to repair the door and windows so every-thing's shut up nice and tight.
23

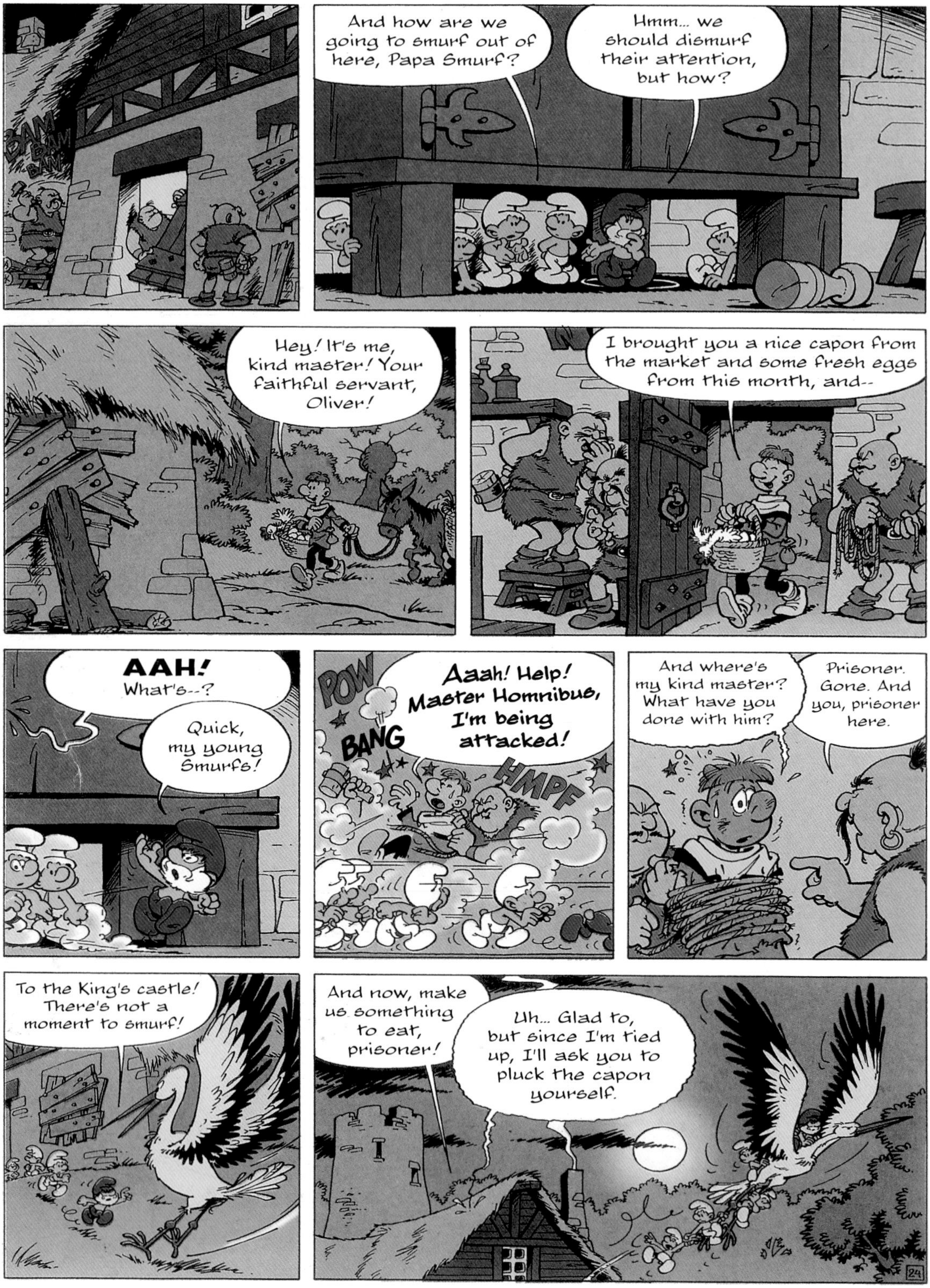
BAM BAM BAM BAM
And how are we going to smurf out of here, Papa Smurf?
Hmm... we should dismurf their attention, but how?
Hey! It's me, kind master! Your faithful servant, Oliver!
I brought you a nice capon from the market and some fresh eggs from this month, and--
AAH! What's--?
Quick, my young Smurfs!
POW
BANG
Aaah! Help! Master Homnibus, I'm being attacked!
HMPF
And where's my kind master? What have you done with him?
Prisoner. Gone. And you, prisoner here.
To the King's castle! There's not a moment to smurf!
And now, make us something to eat, prisoner!
Uh... Glad to, but since I'm tied up, I'll ask you to pluck the capon yourself.
24

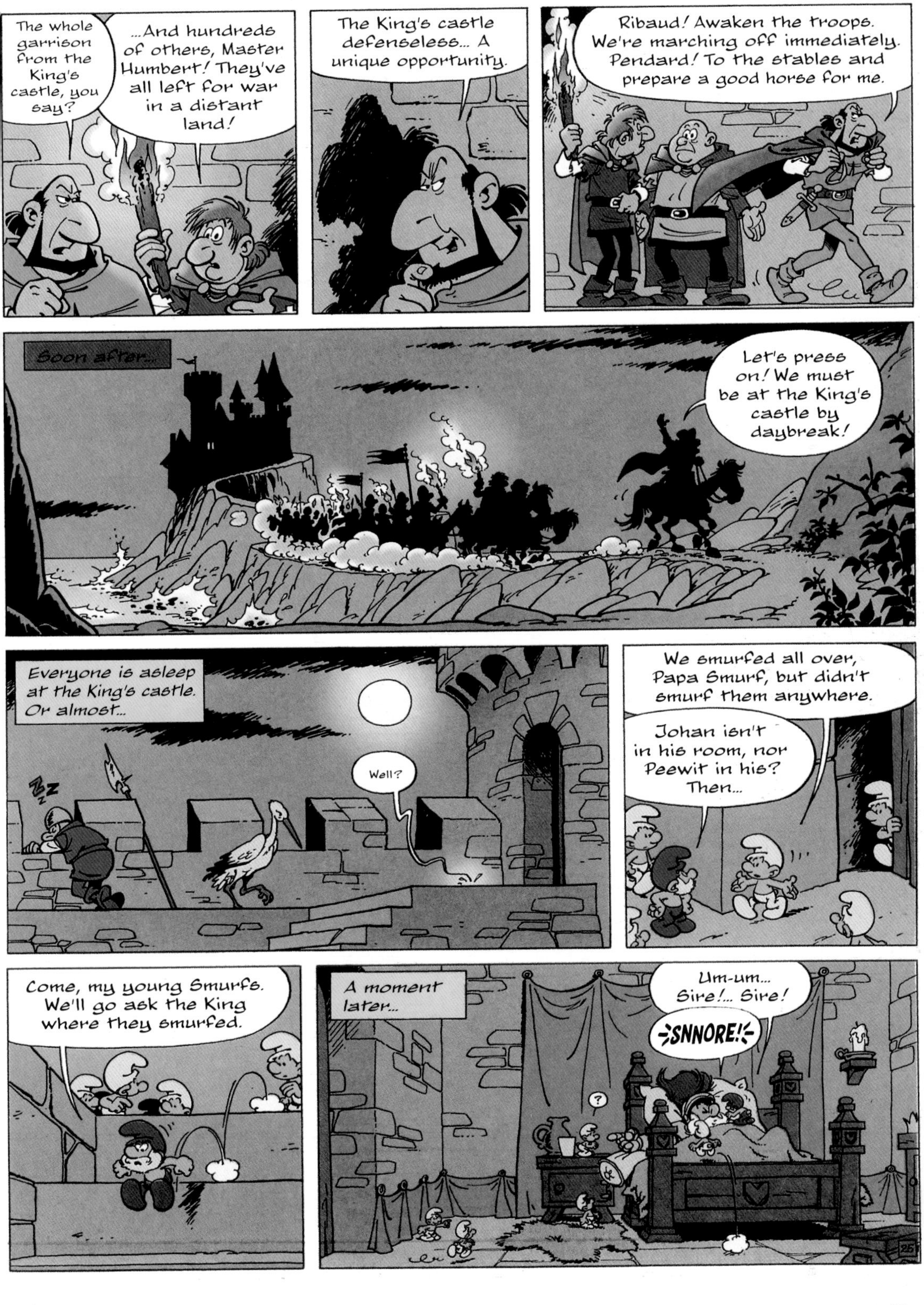
The whole garrison from the King's castle, you say?
...And hundreds of others, Master Humbert! They've all left for war in a distant land!
The King's castle defenseless... A unique opportunity.
Ribaud! Awaken the troops. We're marching off immediately. Pendard! To the stables and prepare a good horse for me.
Soon after...
Let's press on! We must be at the King's castle by daybreak!
Everyone is asleep at the King's castle. Or almost...
ZZ
Well?
We smurfed all over, Papa Smurf, but didn't smurf them anywhere.
Johan isn't in his room, nor Peewit in his? Then...
Come, my young Smurfs. We'll go ask the King where they smurfed.
A moment later...
Um-um... Sire!... Sire!
SNNORE!
?

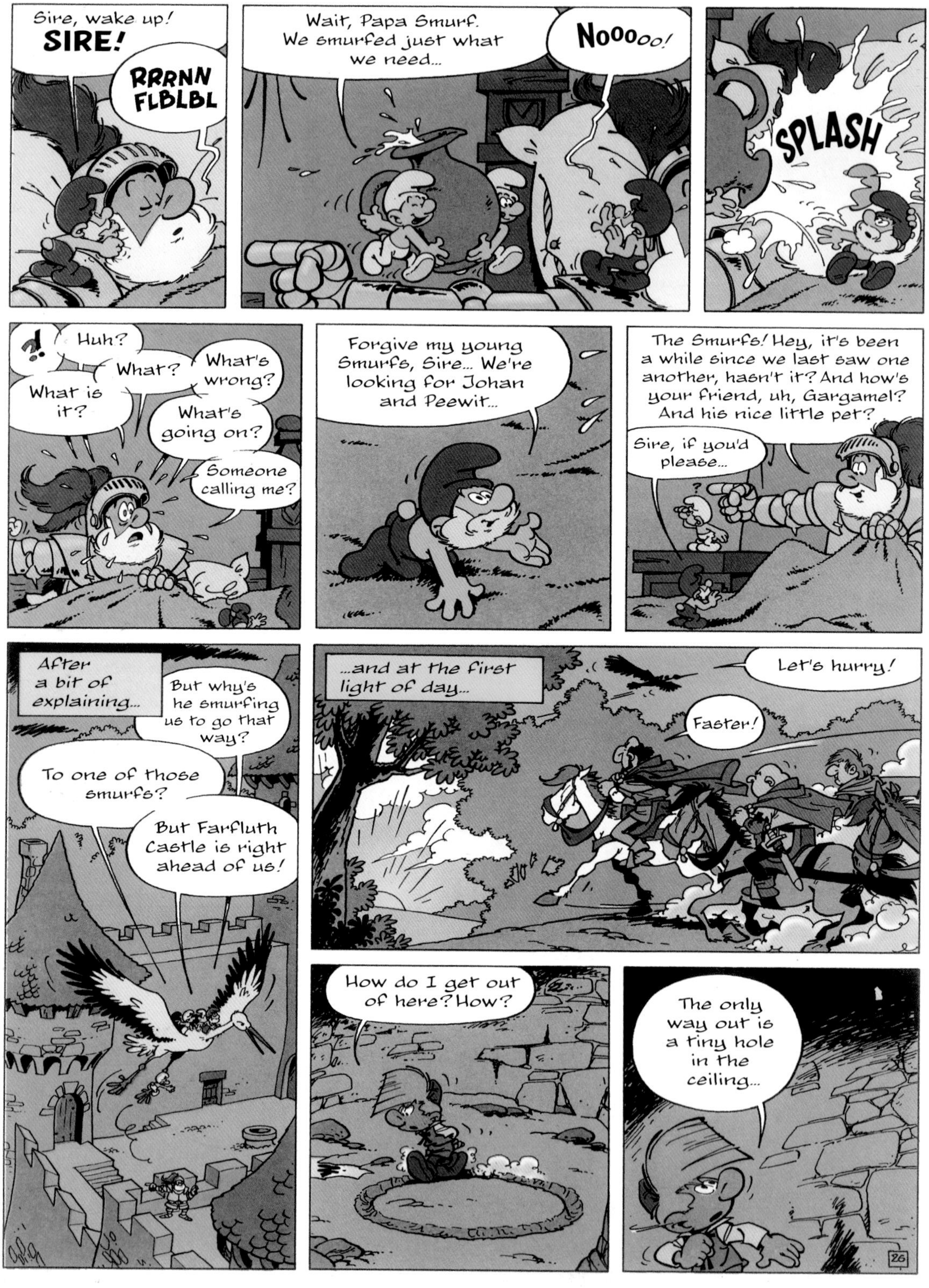

Sire, wake up! SIRE!
RRRNN FLBLBL
Wait, Papa Smurf. We smurfed just what we need...
Nooooo!
SPLASH
Huh?
What?
What's wrong?
What is it?
What's going on?
Someone calling me?
Forgive my young Smurfs, Sire... We're looking for Johan and Peewit...
The Smurfs! Hey, it's been a while since we last saw one another, hasn't it? And how's your friend, uh, Gargamel? And his nice little pet?
Sire, if you'd please...
After a bit of explaining...
But why's he smurfing us to go that way?
To one of those smurfs?
But Farfluth Castle is right ahead of us!
...and at the first light of day...
Let's hurry!
Faster!
How do I get out of here? How?
The only way out is a tiny hole in the ceiling...
26

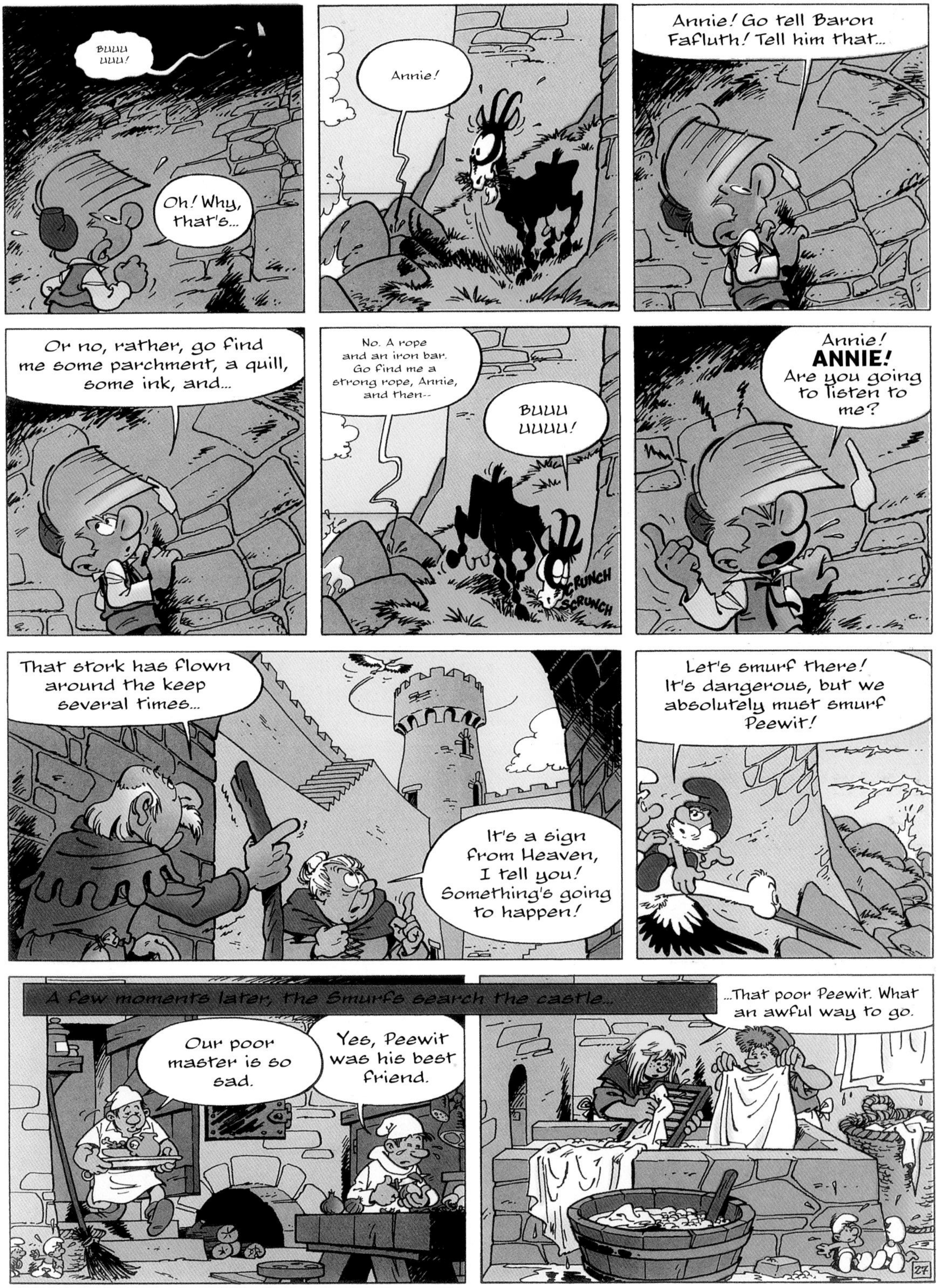
BUUU UUU!
Oh! Why, that's...
Annie!
Annie! Go tell Baron Fafluth! Tell him that...
Or no, rather, go find me some parchment, a quill, some ink, and...
No. A rope and an iron bar. Go find me a strong rope, Annie, and then--
BUUU UUUU!
CRUNCH
SCRUNCH
Annie! ANNIE! Are you going to listen to me?
That stork has flown around the keep several times...
It's a sign from Heaven, I tell you! Something's going to happen!
Let's smurf there! It's dangerous, but we absolutely must smurf Peewit!
A few moments later, the Smurfs search the castle...
Our poor master is so sad.
Yes, Peewit was his best friend.
...That poor Peewit. What an awful way to go.
27

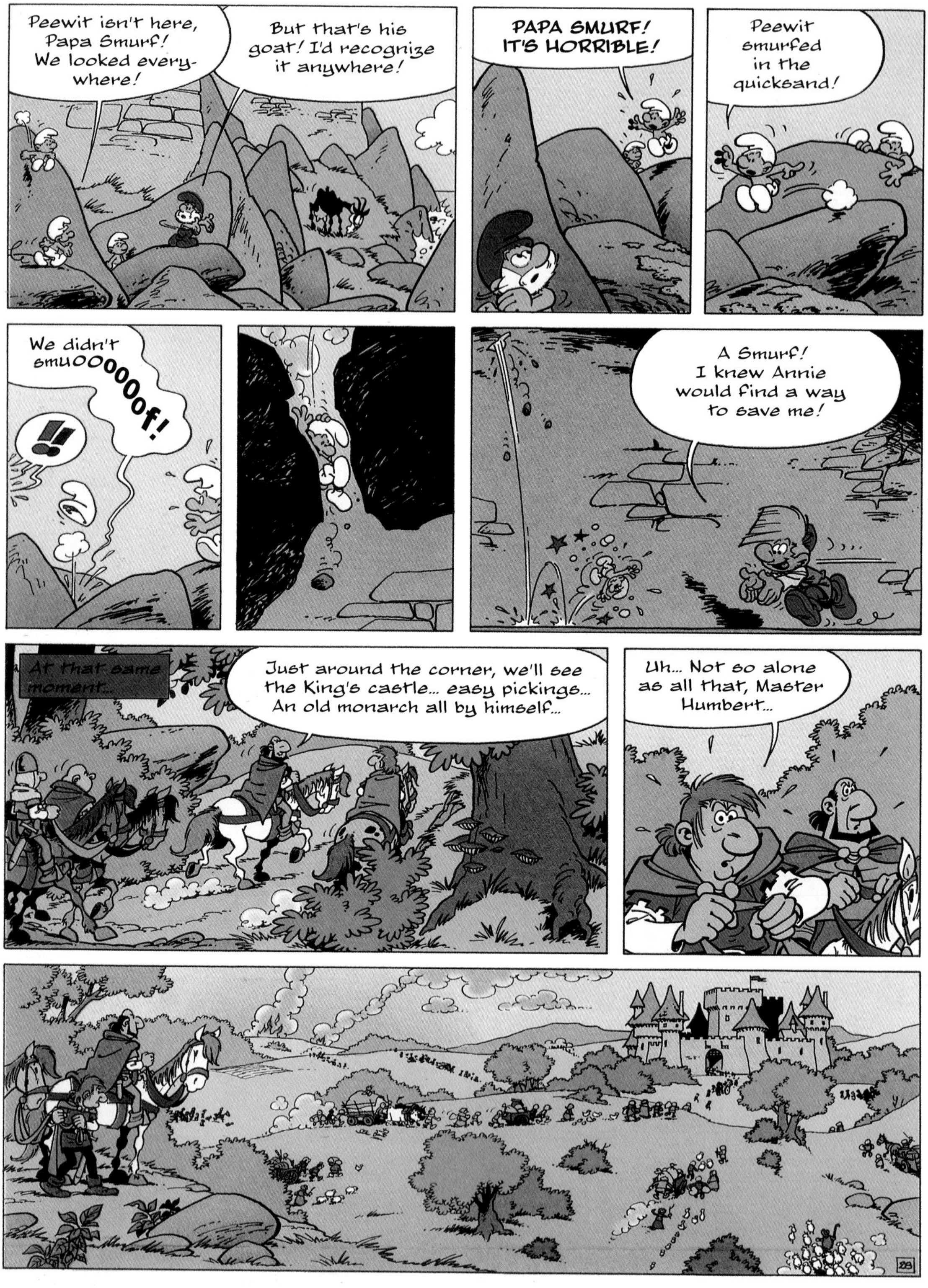
Peewit isn't here, Papa Smurf! We looked every-where!
But that's his goat! I'd recognize it anywhere!
PAPA SMURF! IT'S HORRIBLE!
Peewit smurfed in the quicksand!
We didn't smuOOOOOOf!
A Smurf! I knew Annie would find a way to save me!
At that same moment...
Just around the corner, we'll see the King's castle... easy pickings... An old monarch all by himself...
Uh... Not so alone as all that, Master Humbert...
23

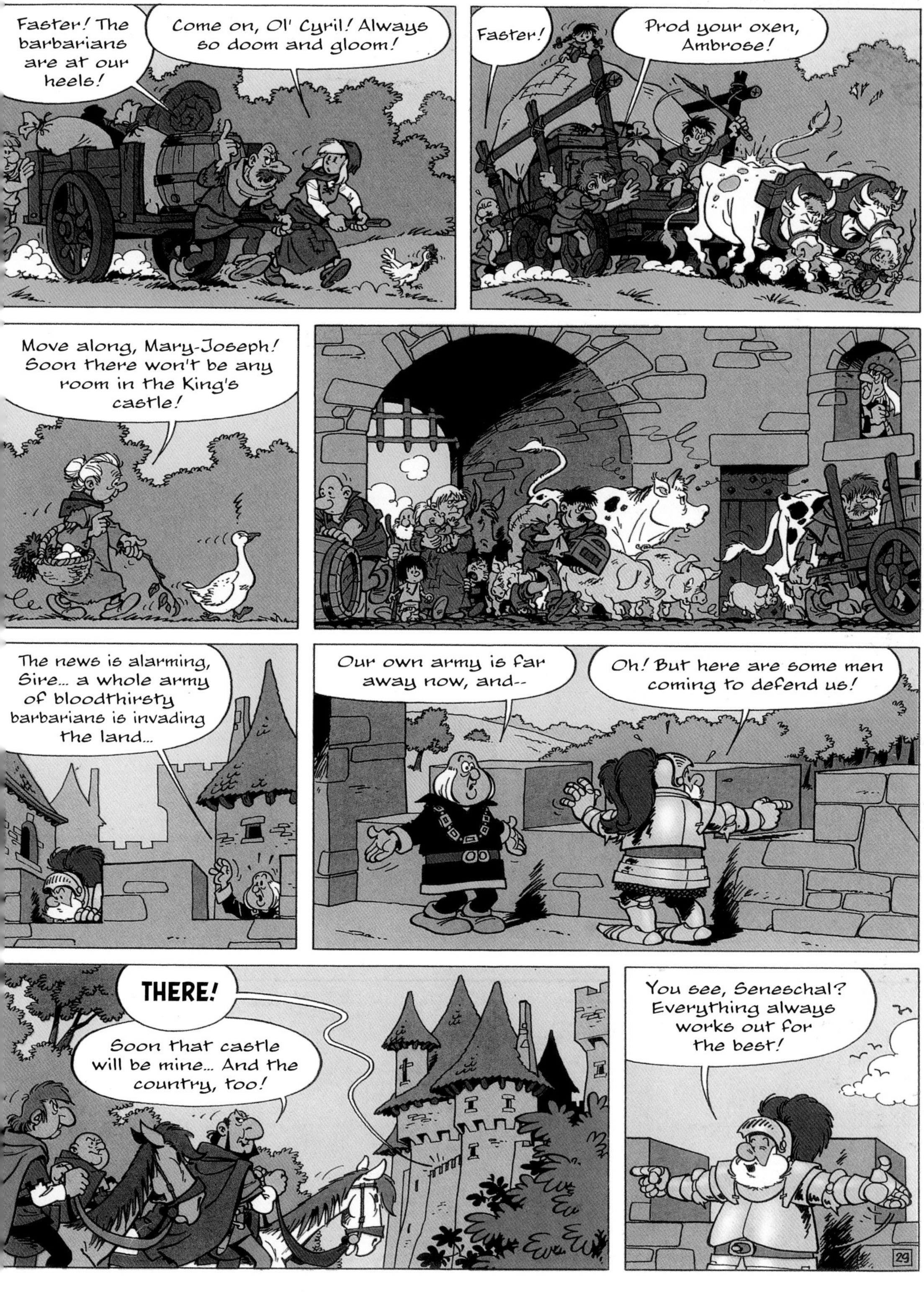
Faster! The barbarians are at our heels!
Come on, Ol' Cyril! Always so doom and gloom!
Faster!
Prod your oxen, Ambrose!
Move along, Mary-Joseph! Soon there won't be any room in the King's castle!
The news is alarming, Sire... a whole army of bloodthirsty barbarians is invading the land...
Our own army is far away now, and--
Oh! But here are some men coming to defend us!
THERE!
Soon that castle will be mine... And the country, too!
You see, Seneschal? Everything always works out for the best!
29

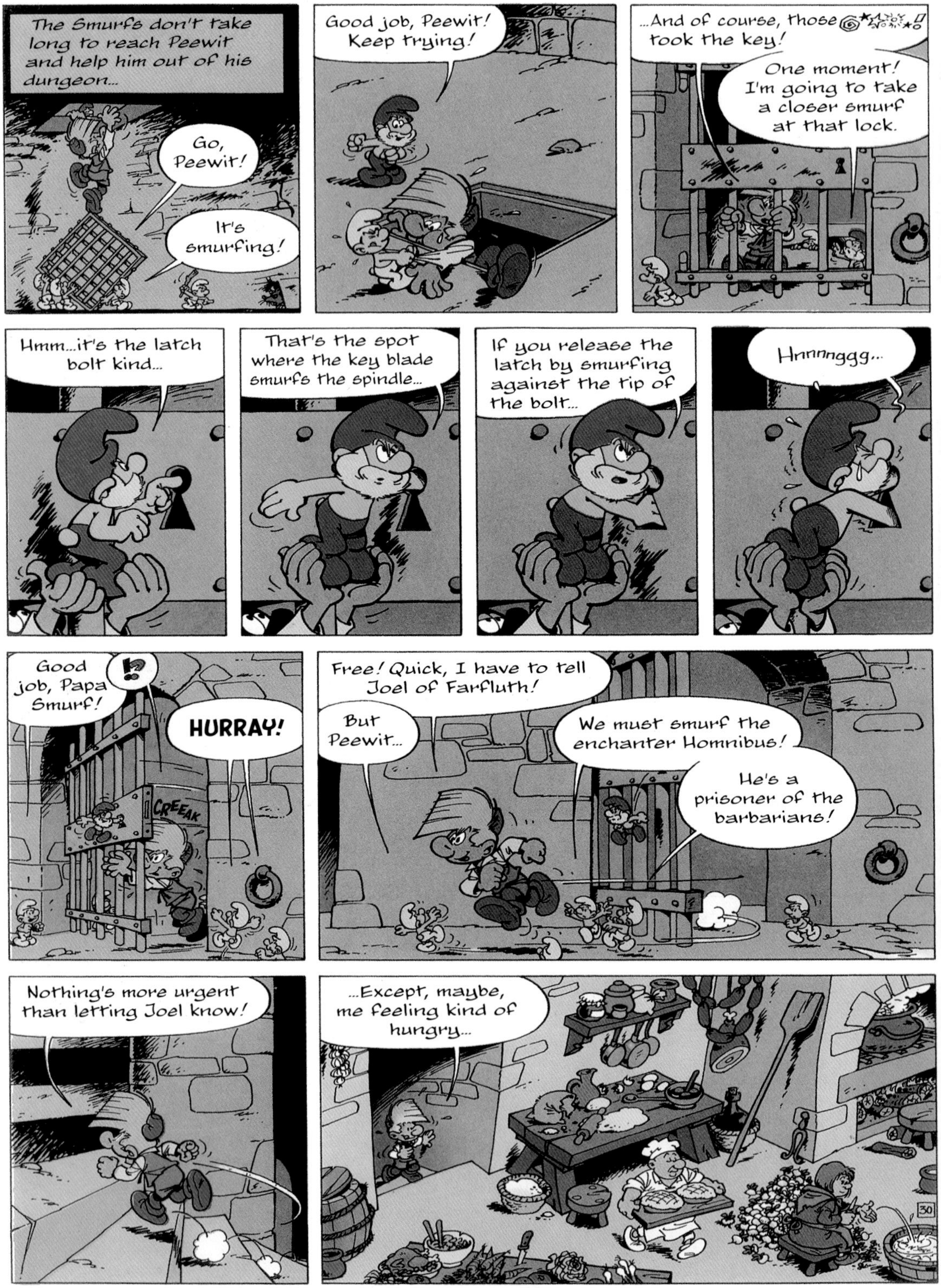
The Smurfs don't take long to reach Peewit and help him out of his dungeon...
Go, Peewit!
It's smurfing!
Good job, Peewit! Keep trying!
...And of course, those
took the key!
One moment! I'm going to take a closer smurf at that lock.
Hmm...it's the latch bolt kind...
That's the spot where the key blade smurfs the spindle...
If you release the latch by smurfing against the tip of the bolt...
Hnnnnggg...
Good job, Papa Smurf!
!?
HURRAY!
CREEAK
Free! Quick, I have to tell Joel of Farfluth!
But Peewit...
We must smurf the enchanter Homnibus!
He's a prisoner of the barbarians!
Nothing's more urgent than letting Joel know!
...Except, maybe, me feeling kind of hungry...
30

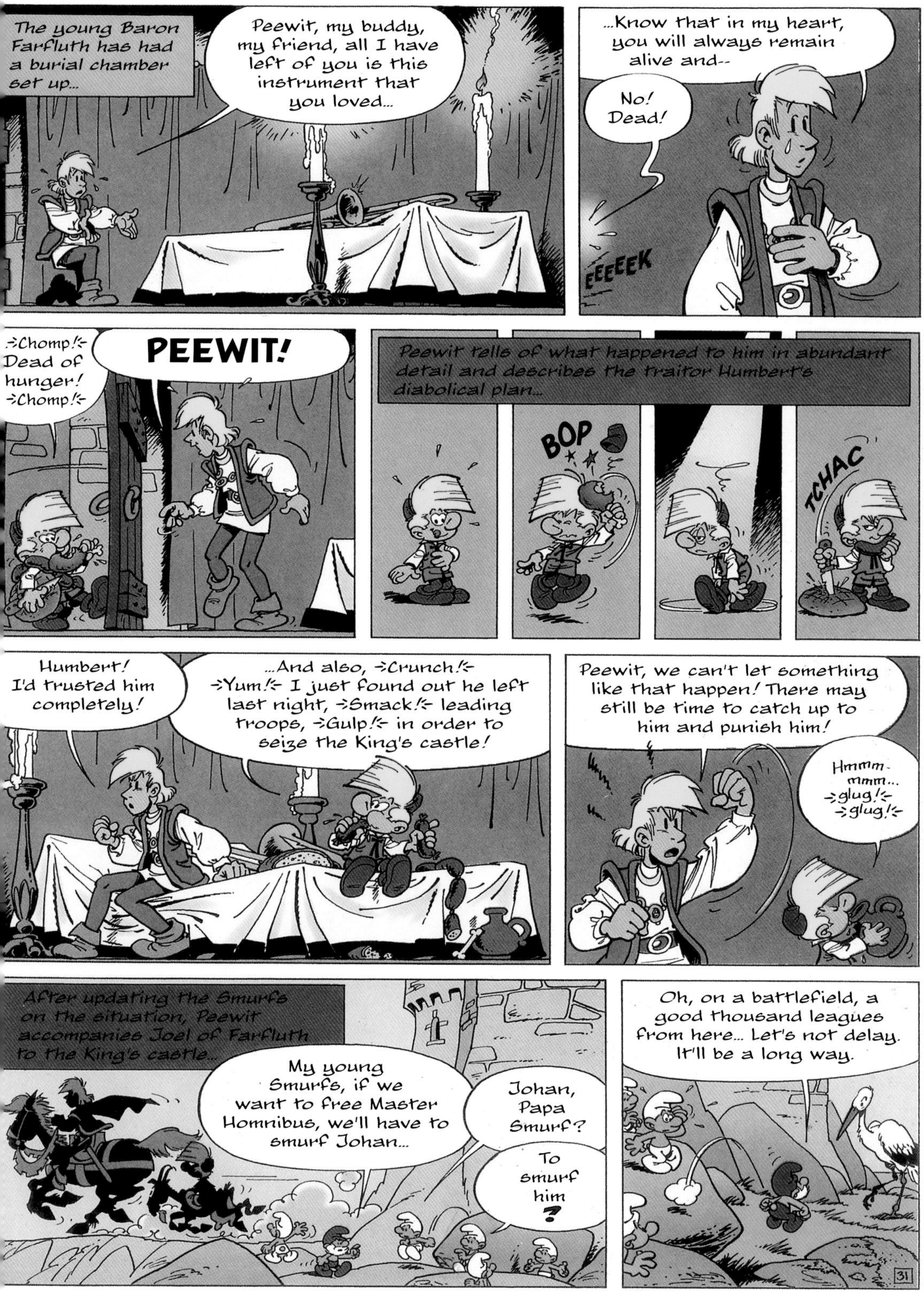

The young Baron Farfluth has had a burial chamber set up...
Peewit, my buddy, my friend, all I have left of you is this instrument that you loved...
...Know that in my heart, you will always remain alive and--
No! Dead!
EEEEEK
>Chomp!< Dead of hunger! >Chomp!<
PEEWIT!
Peewit tells of what happened to him in abundant detail and describes the traitor Humbert's diabolical plan...
BOP
TCHAC
Humbert! I'd trusted him completely!
...And also, >Crunch!< >Yum!< I just found out he left last night, >Smack!< leading troops, >Gulp!< in order to seize the King's castle!
Peewit, we can't let something like that happen! There may still be time to catch up to him and punish him!
Hmmm-mmm... >glug!< >glug!<
After updating the Smurfs on the situation, Peewit accompanies Joel of Farfluth to the King's castle...
My young Smurfs, if we want to free Master Homnibus, we'll have to smurf Johan...
Johan, Papa Smurf?
To smurf him?
Oh, on a battlefield, a good thousand leagues from here... Let's not delay. It'll be a long way.
31

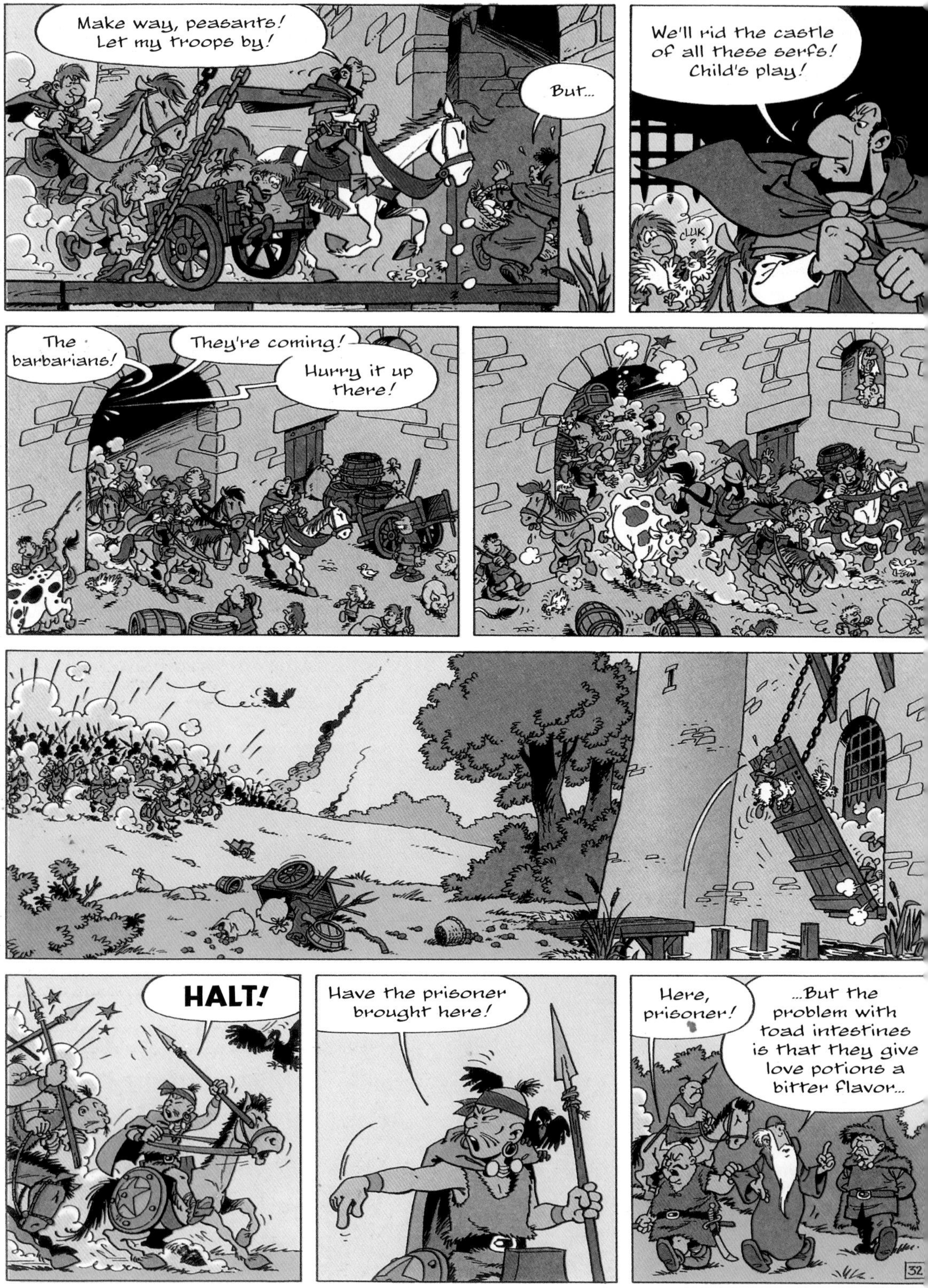

Make way, peasants! Let my troops by!
But...
We'll rid the castle of all these serfs! Child's play!
CLUK
The barbarians!
They're coming!
Hurry it up there!
HALT!
Have the prisoner brought here!
Here, prisoner!
...But the problem with toad intestines is that they give love potions a bitter flavor...
32

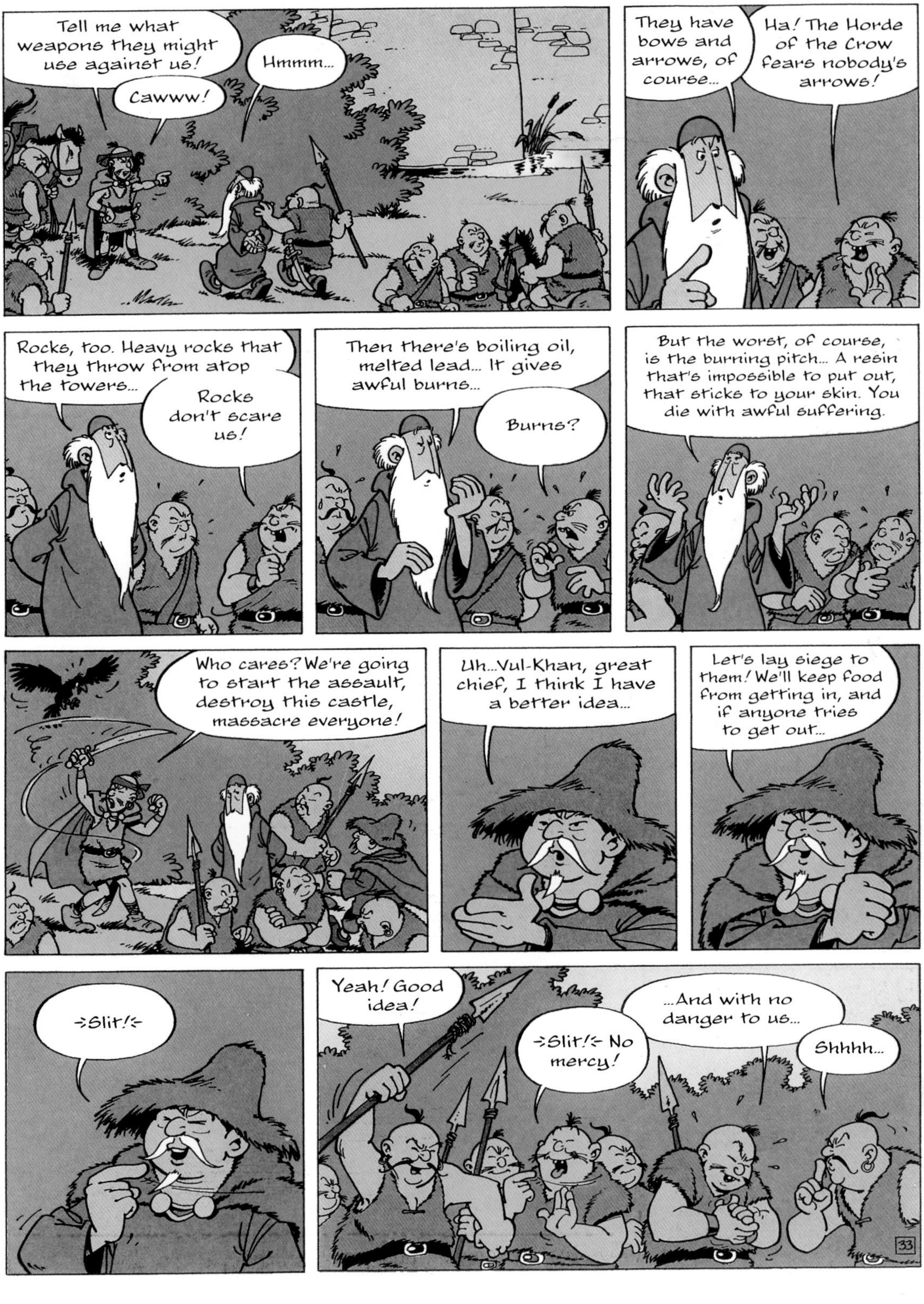
Tell me what weapons they might use against us!
Cawww!
Hmmm...
They have bows and arrows, of course...
Ha! The Horde of the Crow fears nobody's arrows!
Rocks, too. Heavy rocks that they throw from atop the towers...
Rocks don't scare us!
Then there's boiling oil, melted lead... It gives awful burns...
Burns?
But the worst, of course, is the burning pitch... A resin that's impossible to put out, that sticks to your skin. You die with awful suffering.
Who cares? We're going to start the assault, destroy this castle, massacre everyone!
Uh...Vul-Khan, great chief, I think I have a better idea...
Let's lay siege to them! We'll keep food from getting in, and if anyone tries to get out...
>Slit!<
Yeah! Good idea!
>Slit!< No mercy!
...And with no danger to us...
Shhhh...
33

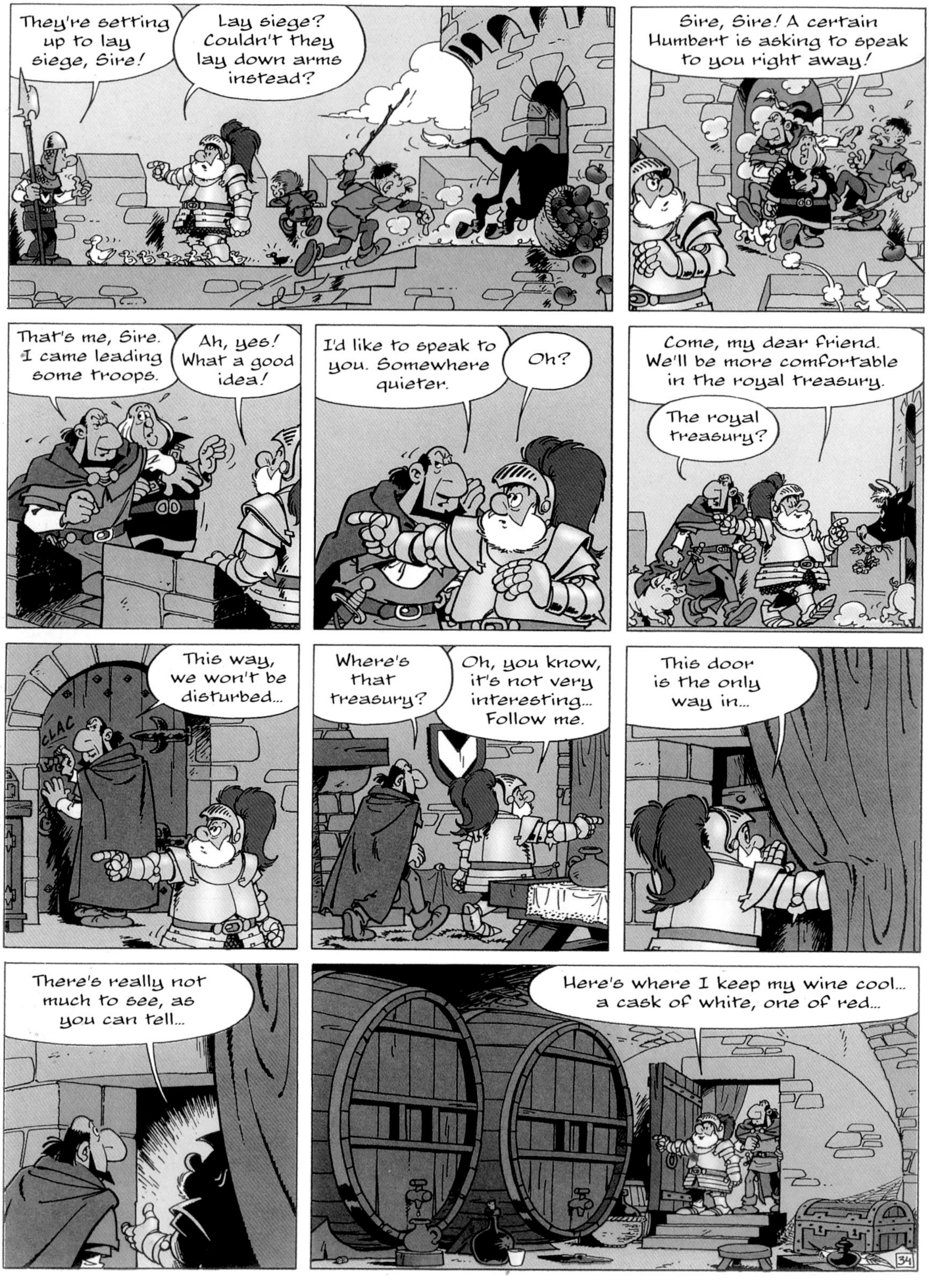
They're setting up to lay siege, Sire!
Lay siege? Couldn't they lay down arms instead?
Sire, Sire! A certain Humbert is asking to speak to you right away!
That's me, Sire. I came leading some troops.
Ah, yes! What a good idea!
I'd like to speak to you. Somewhere quieter.
Oh?
Come, my dear friend. We'll be more comfortable in the royal treasury.
The royal treasury?
This way, we won't be disturbed...
CLAC
Where's that treasury?
Oh, you know, it's not very interesting... Follow me.
This door is the only way in...
There's really not much to see, as you can tell...
Here's where I keep my wine cool... a cask of white, one of red...
34

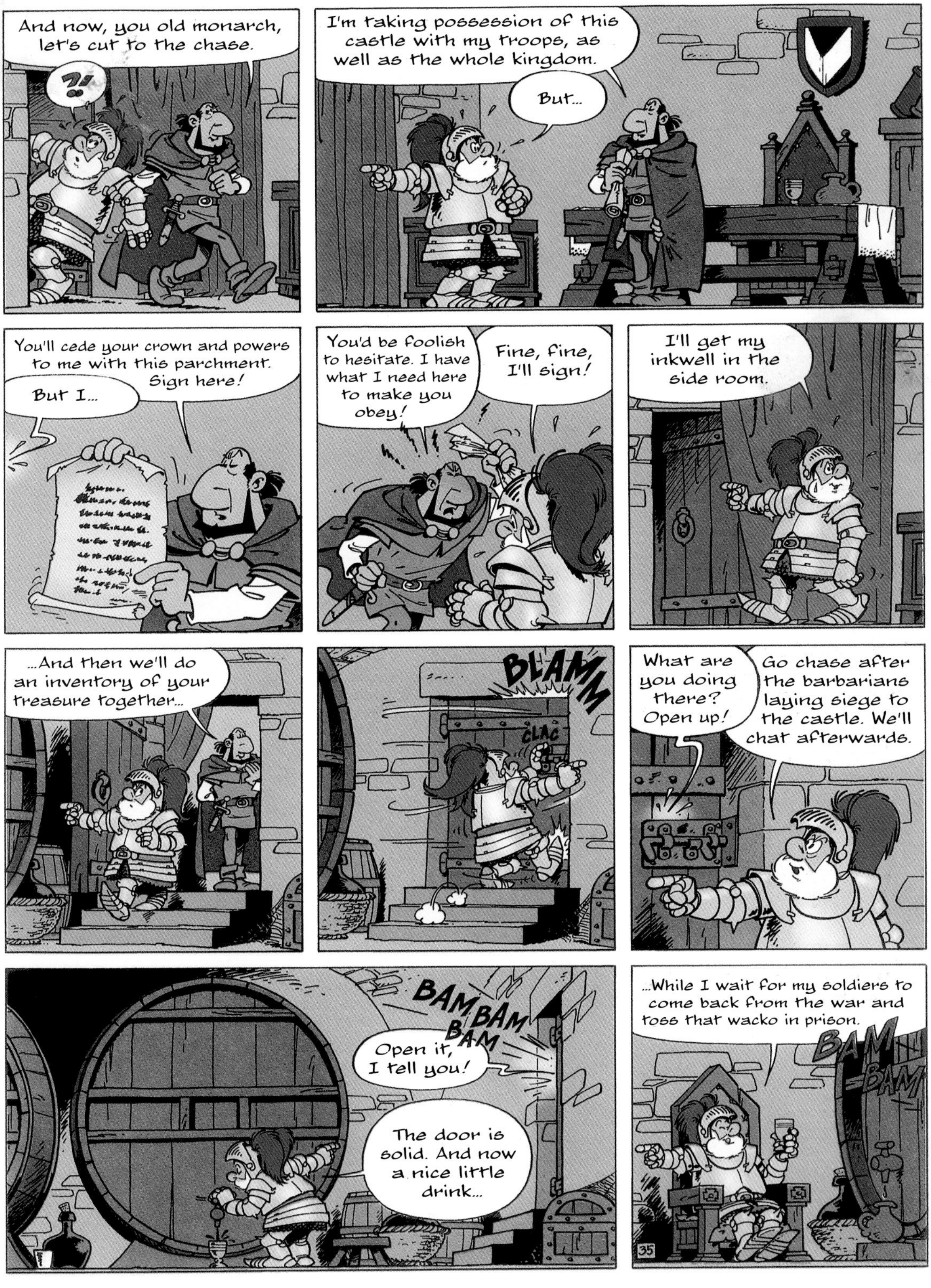
And now, you old monarch, let's cut to the chase.
?!
I'm taking possession of this castle with my troops, as well as the whole kingdom.
But...
You'll cede your crown and powers to me with this parchment. Sign here!
But I...
You'd be foolish to hesitate. I have what I need here to make you obey!
Fine, fine, I'll sign!
I'll get my inkwell in the side room.
...And then we'll do an inventory of your treasure together...
BLAMM
CLAC
What are you doing there? Open up!
Go chase after the barbarians laying siege to the castle. We'll chat afterwards.
BAM BAM BAM
Open it, I tell you!
The door is solid. And now a nice little drink...
...While I wait for my soldiers to come back from the war and toss that wacko in prison.
BAM BAM
35

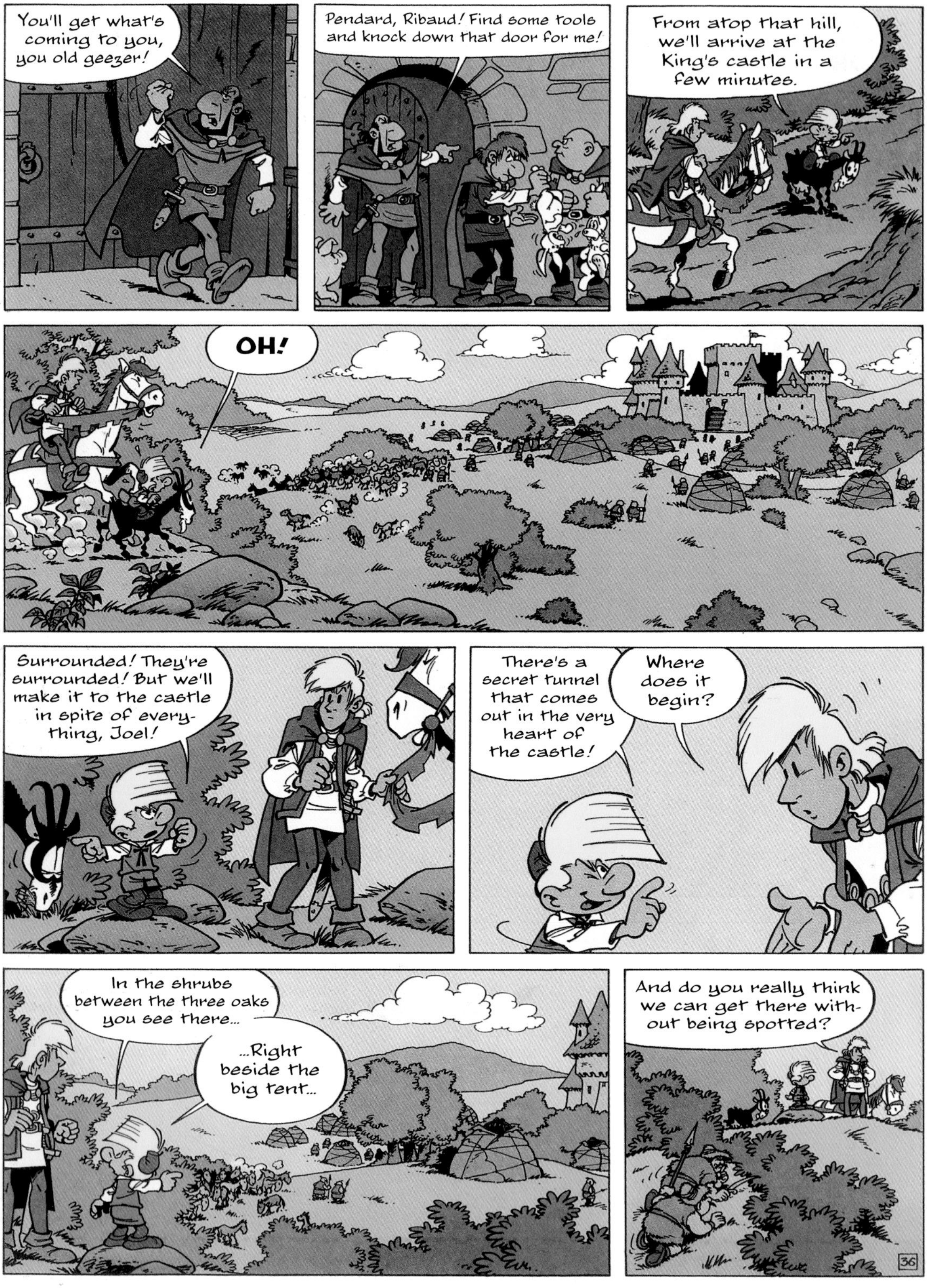
You'll get what's coming to you, you old geezer!
Pendard, Ribaud! Find some tools and knock down that door for me!
From atop that hill, we'll arrive at the King's castle in a few minutes.
OH!
Surrounded! They're surrounded! But we'll make it to the castle in spite of everything, Joel!
There's a secret tunnel that comes out in the very heart of the castle!
Where does it begin?
In the shrubs between the three oaks you see there...
...Right beside the big tent...
And do you really think we can get there without being spotted?
36

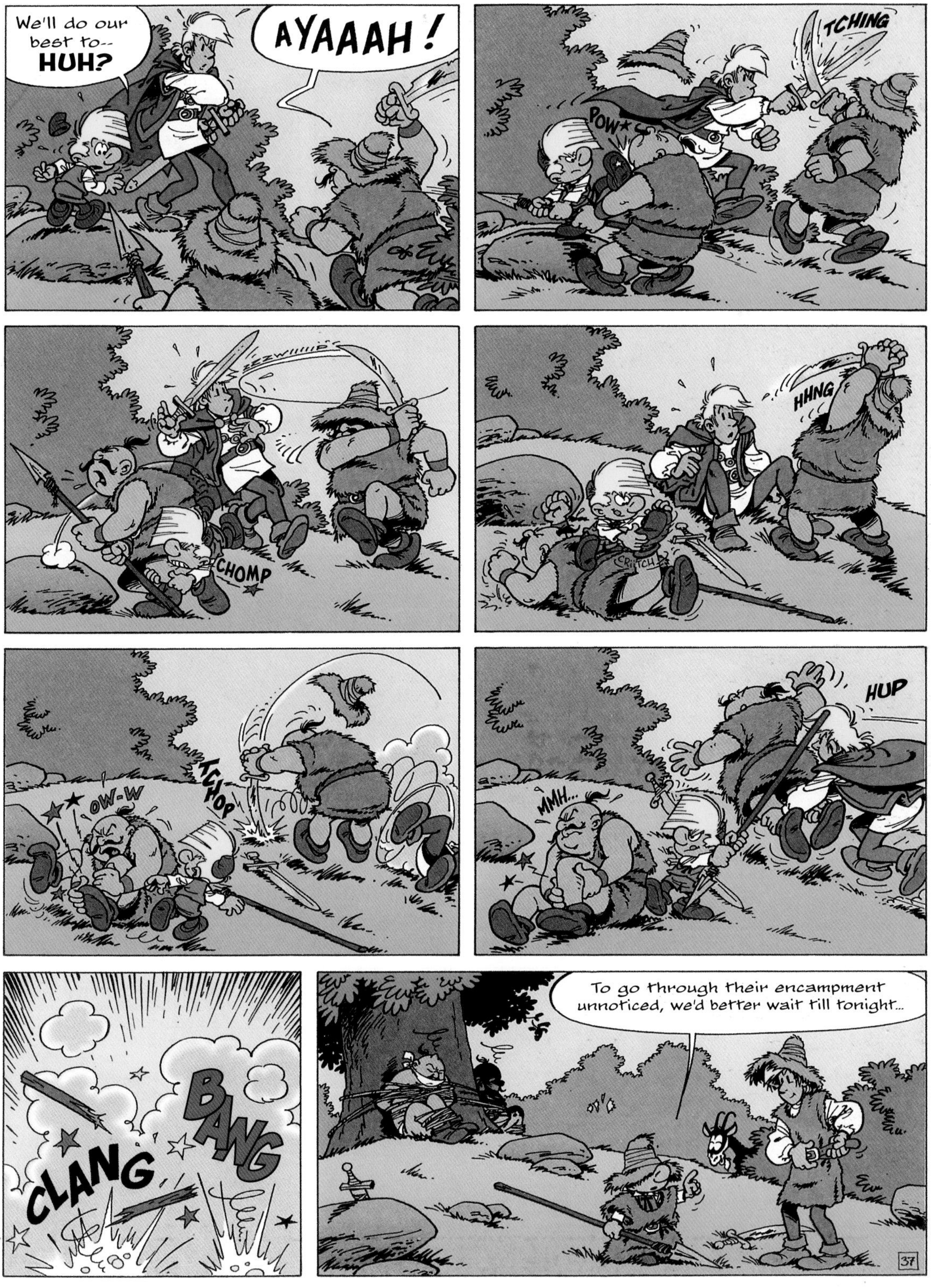

We'll do our best to-- HUH?
AYAAAH!
POW
TCHING
CHOMP
HHNG
CRITCH
OW-W
KCHOP
MMH...
HUP
CLANG
BANG
To go through their encampment unnoticed, we'd better wait till tonight...
37

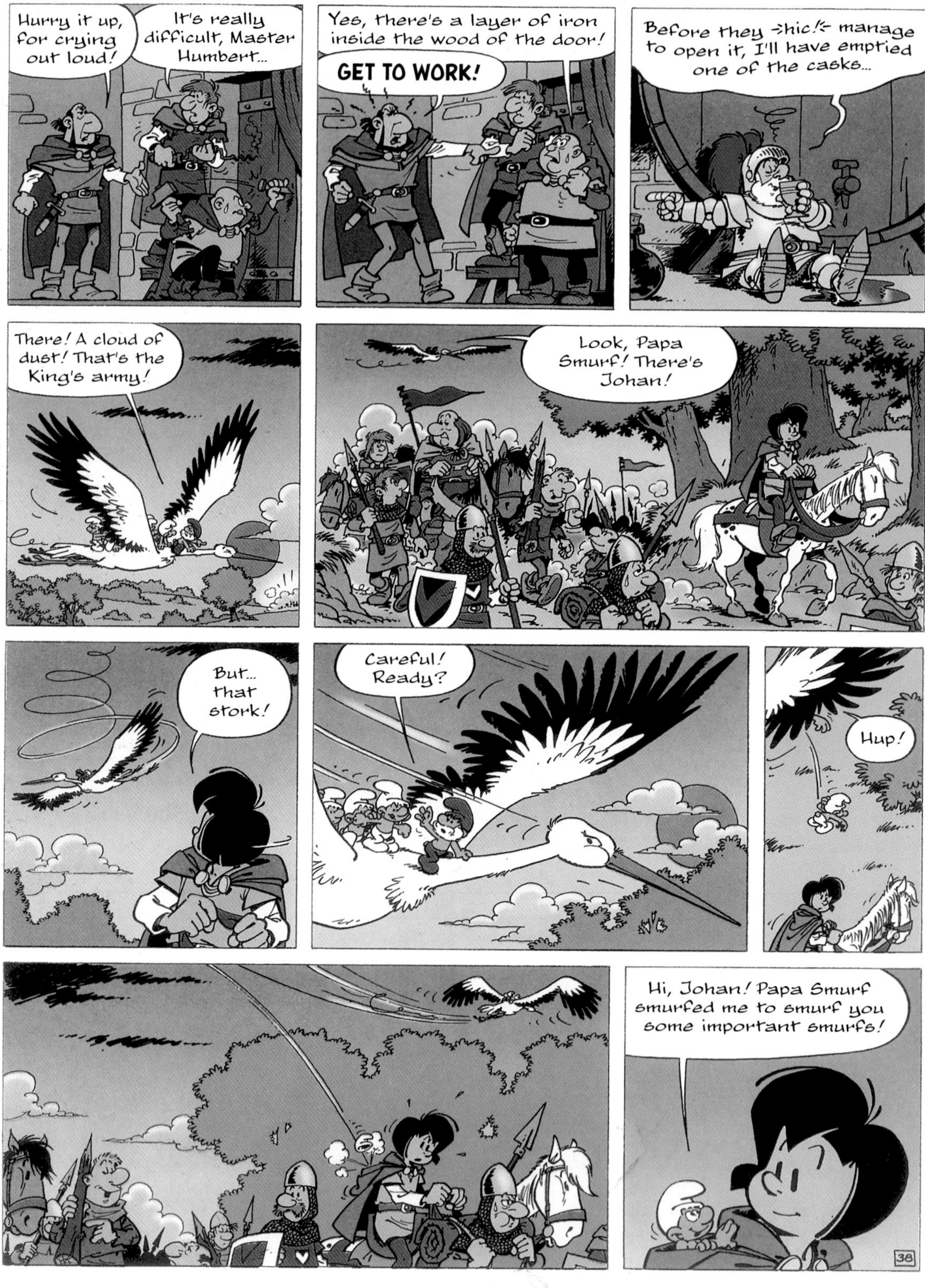
Hurry it up, for crying out loud!
It's really difficult, Master Humbert...
Yes, there's a layer of iron inside the wood of the door!
GET TO WORK!
Before they -hic!- manage to open it, I'll have emptied one of the casks...
There! A cloud of dust! That's the King's army!
Look, Papa Smurf! There's Johan!
But... that stork!
Careful! Ready?
Hup!
Hi, Johan! Papa Smurf smurfed me to smurf you some important smurfs!
38

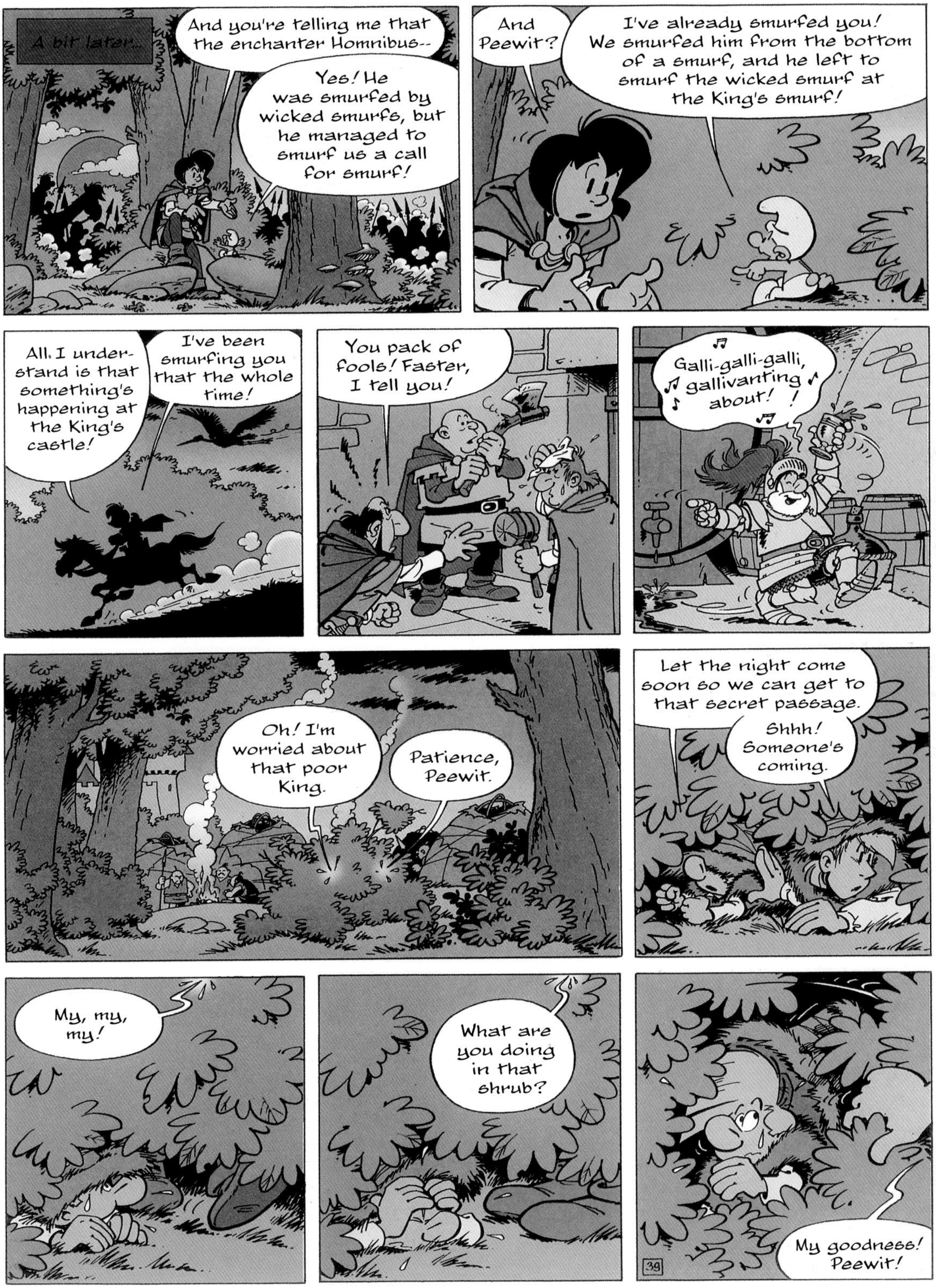
A bit later...
And you're telling me that the enchanter Homnibus--
Yes! He was smurfed by wicked smurfs, but he managed to smurf us a call for smurf!
And Peewit?
I've already smurfed you! We smurfed him from the bottom of a smurf, and he left to smurf the wicked smurf at the King's smurf!
All I understand is that something's happening at the King's castle!
I've been smurfing you that the whole time!
You pack of fools! Faster, I tell you!
Galli-galli-galli, gallivanting about!
Oh! I'm worried about that poor King.
Patience, Peewit.
Let the night come soon so we can get to that secret passage.
Shhh! Someone's coming.
My, my, my!
What are you doing in that shrub?
39
My goodness! Peewit!

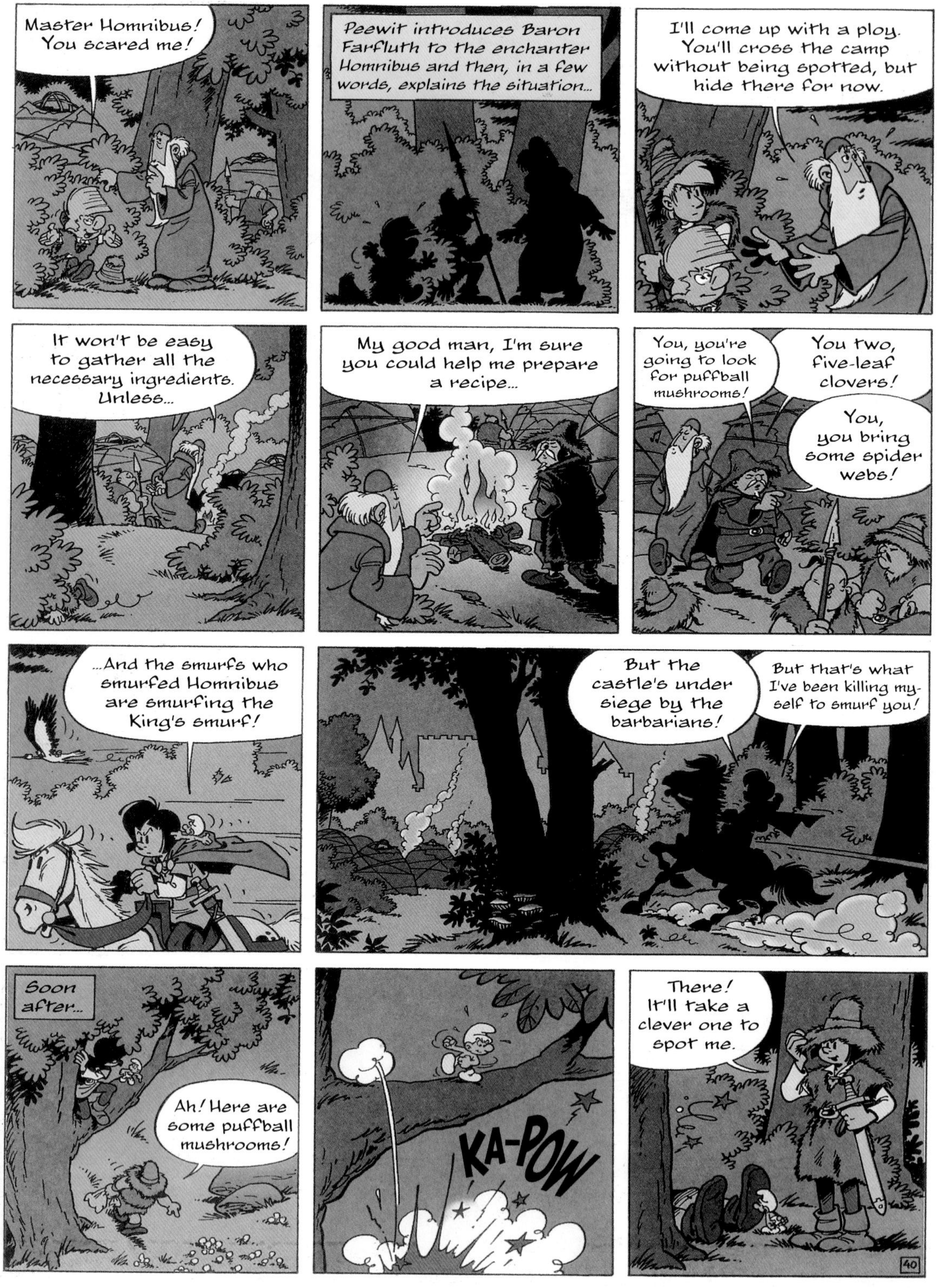
Master Homnibus! You scared me!
Peewit introduces Baron Farfluth to the enchanter Homnibus and then, in a few words, explains the situation...
I'll come up with a ploy. You'll cross the camp without being spotted, but hide there for now.
It won't be easy to gather all the necessary ingredients. Unless...
My good man, I'm sure you could help me prepare a recipe...
You, you're going to look for puffball mushrooms!
You two, five-leaf clovers!
You, you bring some spider webs!
...And the smurfs who smurfed Homnibus are smurfing the King's smurf!
But the castle's under siege by the barbarians!
But that's what I've been killing my-self to smurf you!
Soon after...
Ah! Here are some puffball mushrooms!
KA-POW
There! It'll take a clever one to spot me.
40

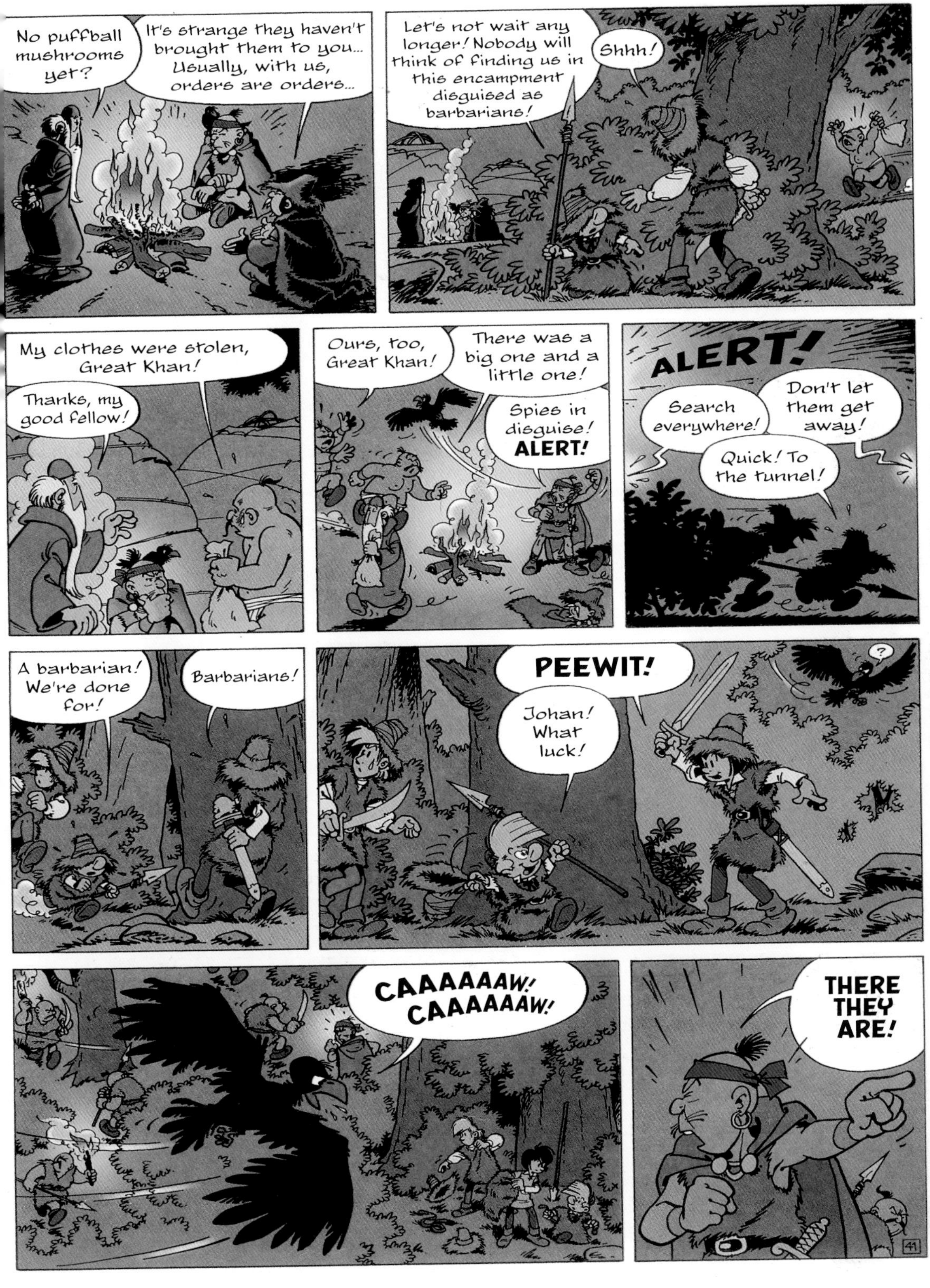
No puffball mushrooms yet?
It's strange they haven't brought them to you... Usually, with us, orders are orders...
Let's not wait any longer! Nobody will think of finding us in this encampment disguised as barbarians!
Shhh!
My clothes were stolen, Great Khan!
Thanks, my good fellow!
Ours, too, Great Khan!
There was a big one and a little one!
Spies in disguise! ALERT!
ALERT!
Search everywhere!
Don't let them get away!
Quick! To the tunnel!
A barbarian! We're done for!
Barbarians!
PEEWIT!
Johan! What luck!
CAAAAAAW! CAAAAAAW!
THERE THEY ARE!
41

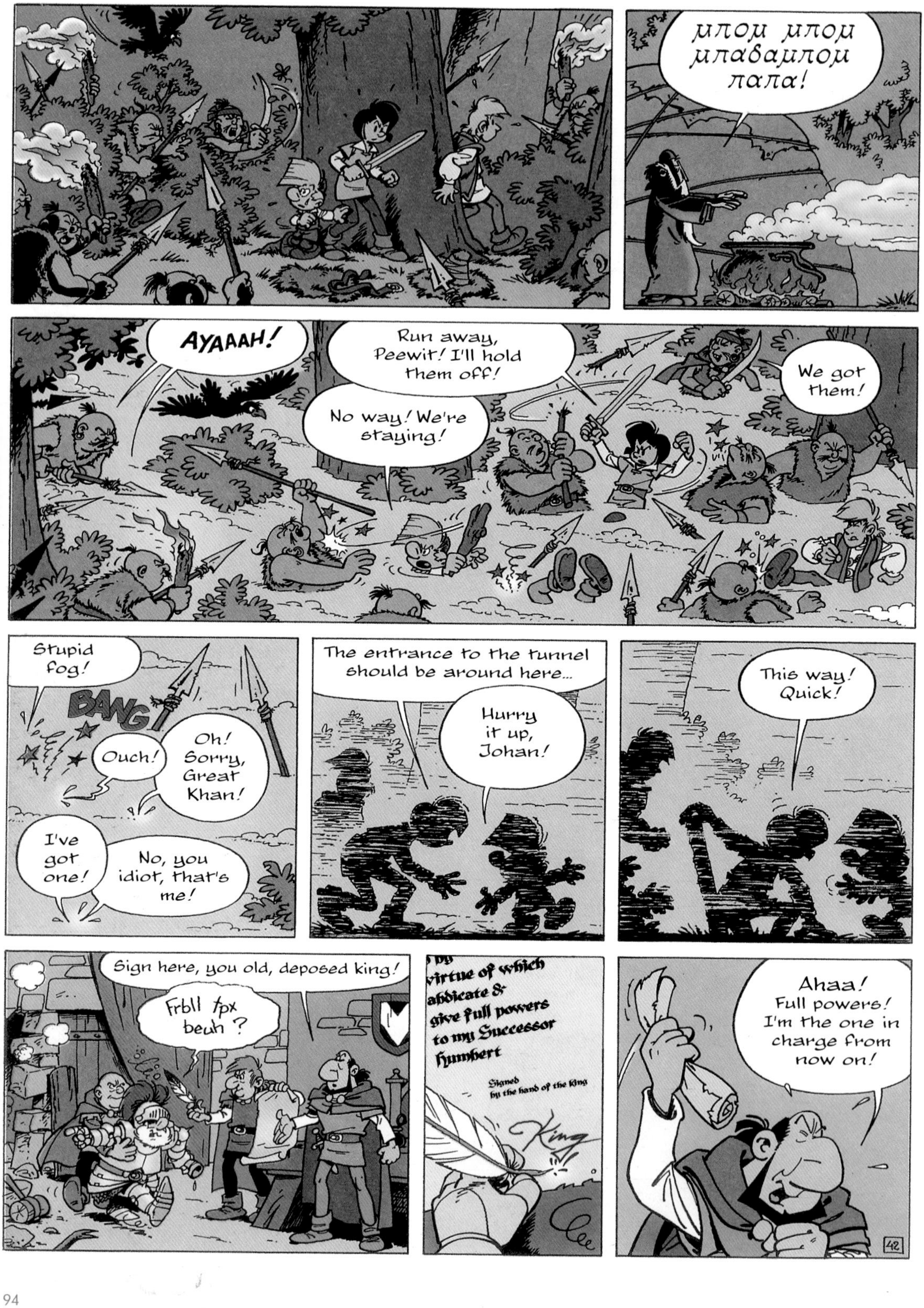
μπομ μπομ μπαβαμπομ παπα!
AYAAAH!
Run away, Peewit! I'll hold them off!
No way! We're staying!
We got them!
Stupid fog!
BANG
Ouch!
Oh! Sorry, Great Khan!
I've got one!
No, you idiot, that's me!
The entrance to the tunnel should be around here...
Hurry it up, Johan!
This way! Quick!
Sign here, you old, deposed king!
Frbll tpx beuh ?
by virtue of which abdicate & give full powers to my Successor Humbert
Signed by the hand of the King
King
Ahaa! Full powers! I'm the one in charge from now on!
42

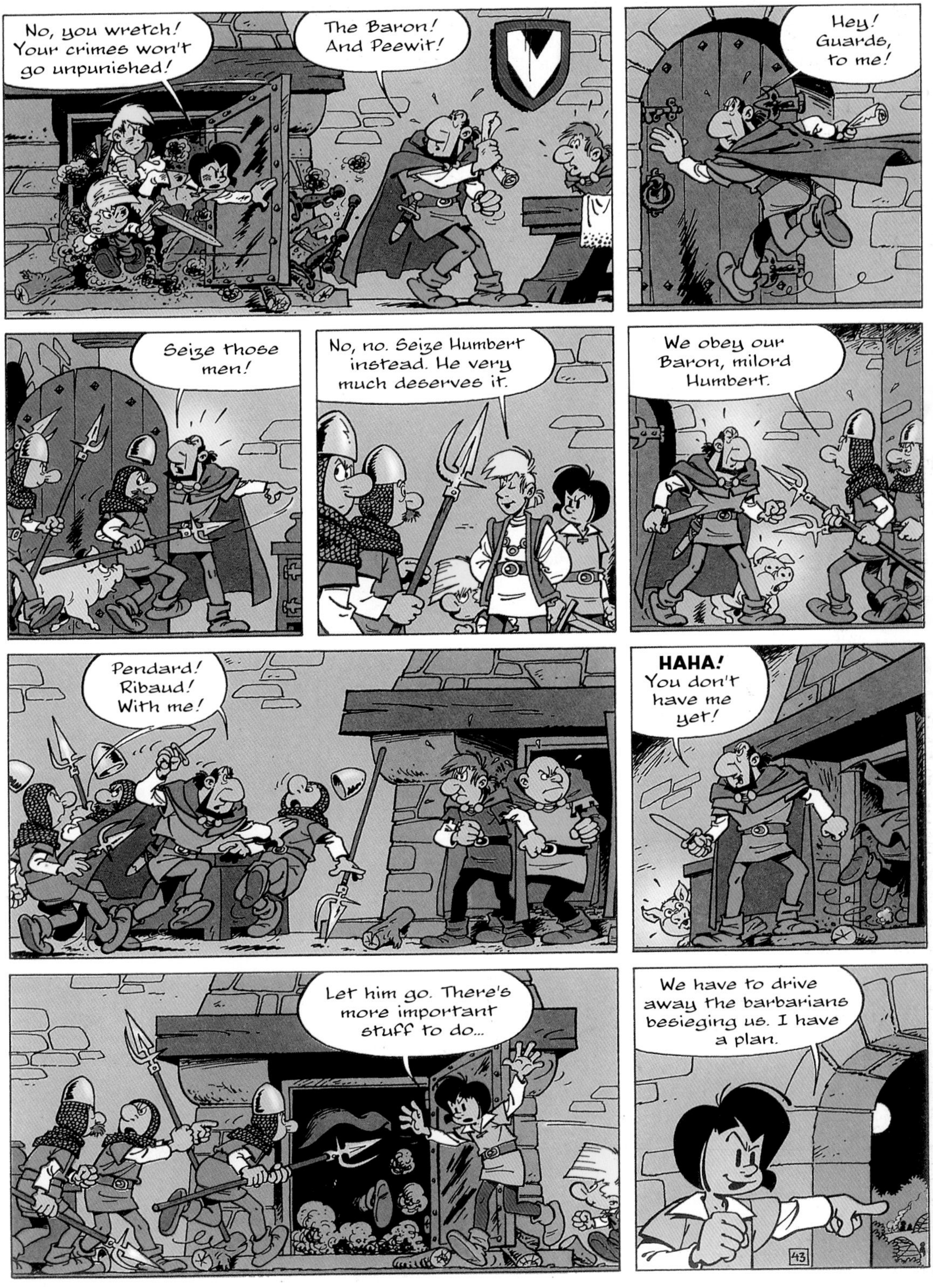
No, you wretch! Your crimes won't go unpunished!
The Baron! And Peewit!
Hey! Guards, to me!
Seize those men!
No, no. Seize Humbert instead. He very much deserves it.
We obey our Baron, milord Humbert.
Pendard! Ribaud! With me!
HAHA! You don't have me yet!
Let him go. There's more important stuff to do...
We have to drive away the barbarians besieging us. I have a plan.
43

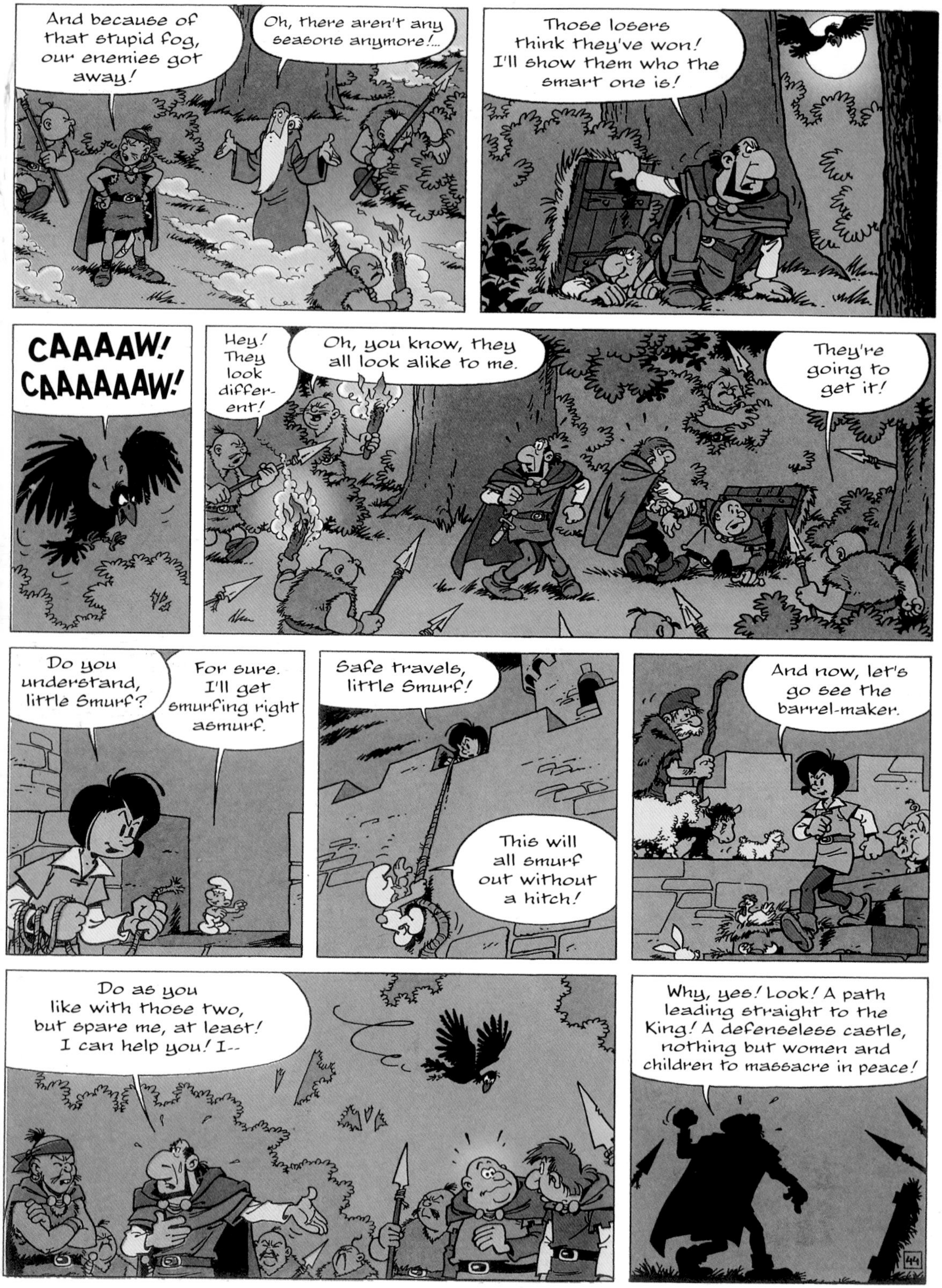

And because of that stupid fog, our enemies got away!
Oh, there aren't any seasons anymore!...
Those losers think they've won! I'll show them who the smart one is!
CAAAAW! CAAAAAAW!
Hey! They look different!
Oh, you know, they all look alike to me.
They're going to get it!
Do you understand, little Smurf?
For sure. I'll get smurfing right asmurf.
Safe travels, little Smurf!
This will all smurf out without a hitch!
And now, let's go see the barrel-maker.
Do as you like with those two, but spare me, at least! I can help you! I--
Why, yes! Look! A path leading straight to the King! A defenseless castle, nothing but women and children to massacre in peace!
44

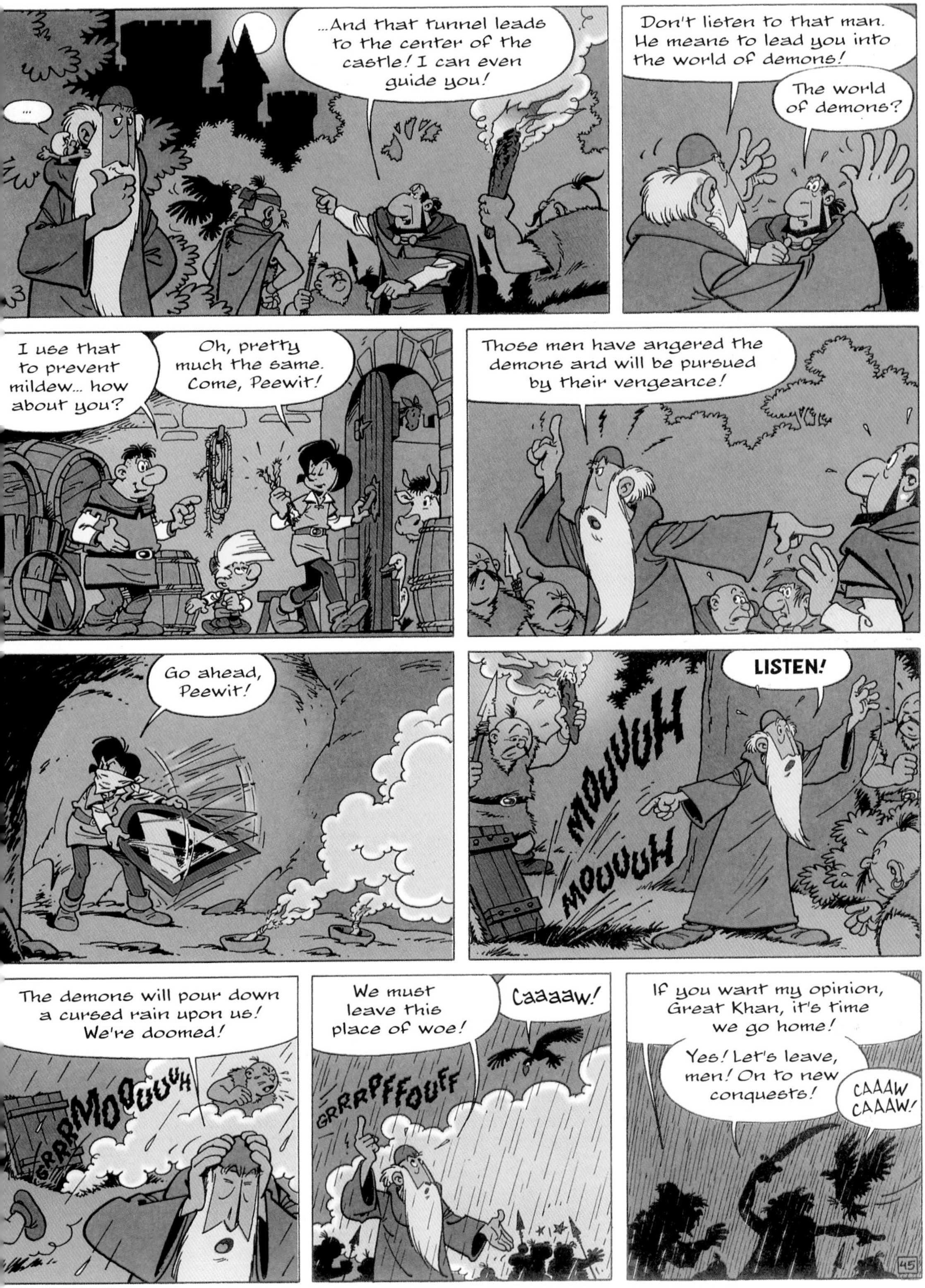
...
...And that tunnel leads to the center of the castle! I can even guide you!
Don't listen to that man. He means to lead you into the world of demons!
The world of demons?
I use that to prevent mildew... how about you?
Oh, pretty much the same. Come, Peewit!
Those men have angered the demons and will be pursued by their vengeance!
Go ahead, Peewit!
LISTEN!
MOUUUH
MOUUUH
The demons will pour down a cursed rain upon us! We're doomed!
GRRRMOOUUUUH
We must leave this place of woe!
Caaaaw!
GRRRPFFOUFF
If you want my opinion, Great Khan, it's time we go home!
Yes! Let's leave, men! On to new conquests!
CAAAW CAAAW!
45

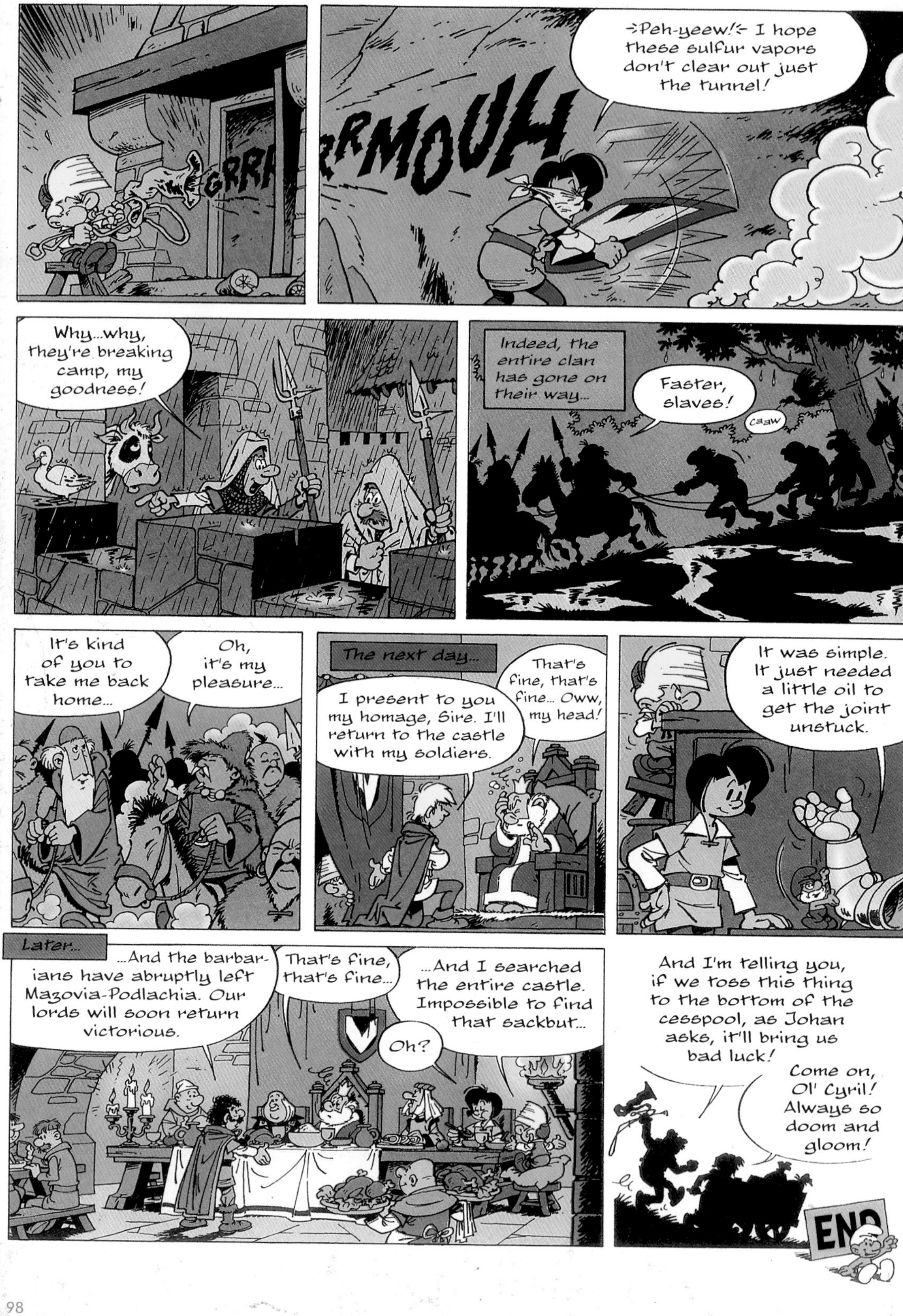
GRRA
RRMOUH
→Peh-yeew!← I hope these sulfur vapors don't clear out just the tunnel!
Why...why, they're breaking camp, my goodness!
Indeed, the entire clan has gone on their way...
Faster, slaves!
Caaw
It's kind of you to take me back home...
Oh, it's my pleasure...
The next day...
I present to you my homage, Sire. I'll return to the castle with my soldiers.
That's fine, that's fine... Oww, my head!
It was simple. It just needed a little oil to get the joint unstuck.
Later...
...And the barbarians have abruptly left Mazovia-Podlachia. Our lords will soon return victorious.
That's fine, that's fine...
...And I searched the entire castle. Impossible to find that sackbut...
Oh?
And I'm telling you, if we toss this thing to the bottom of the cesspool, as Johan asks, it'll bring us bad luck!
Come on, Ol' Cyril! Always so doom and gloom!
END

THE SMURFS GAGS

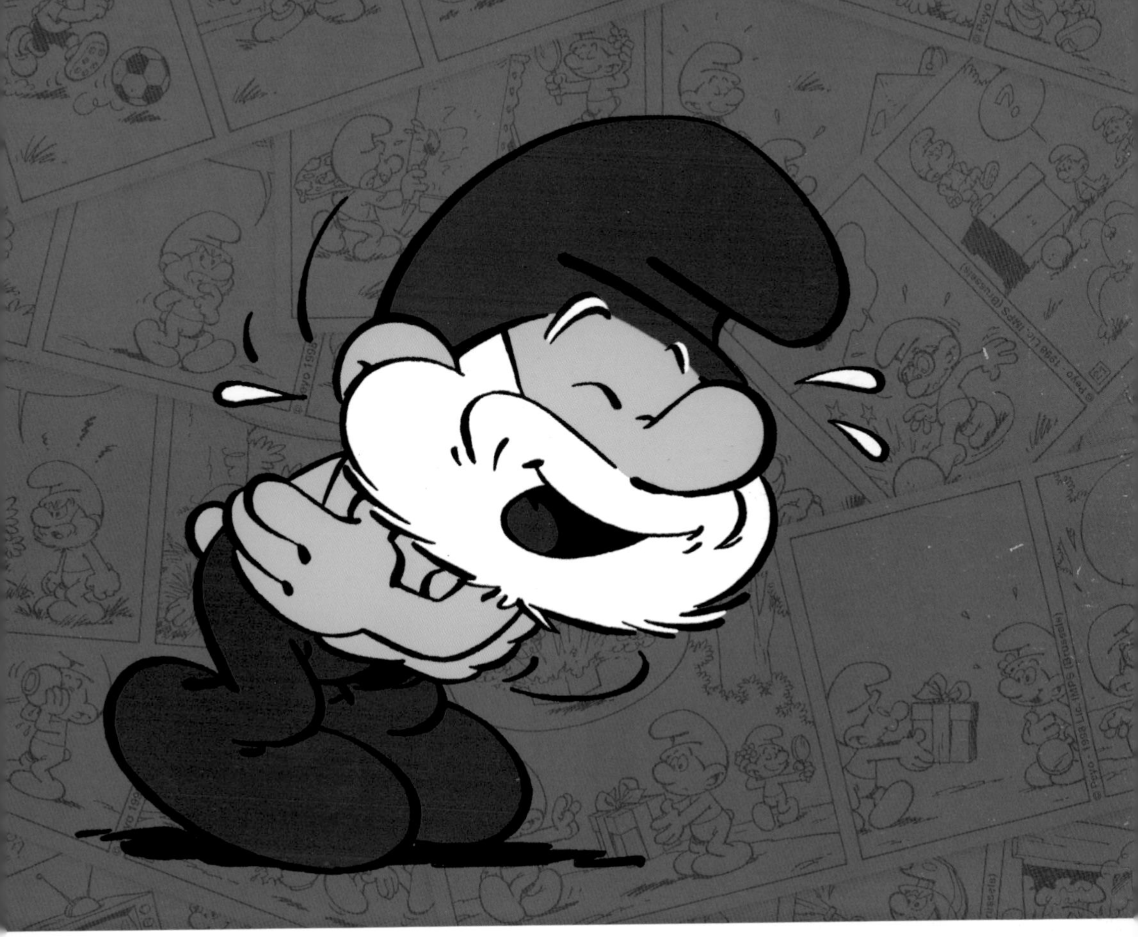

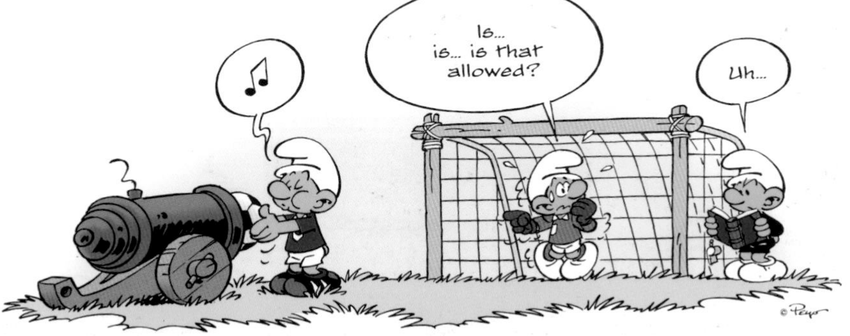
Is...
is... is that
allowed?
Uh...
© Peyo

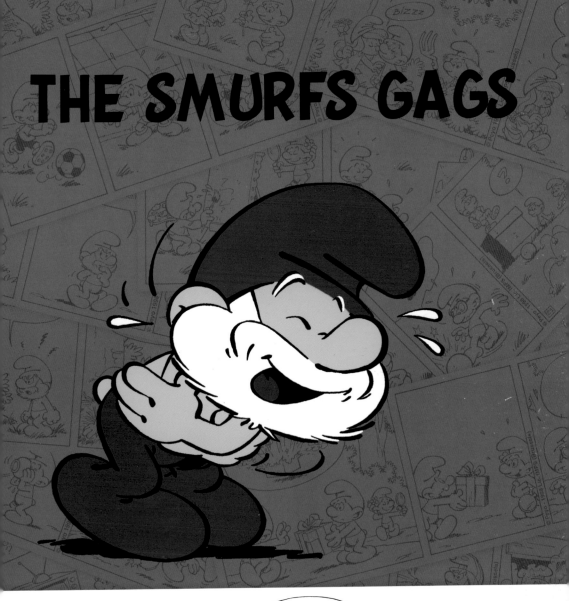

CREATIONS

THE SMURFS 120 JOKES AND OTHER SURPRISES

Okay, to summarize, Azrael...
Let's imagine I'm one of those revolting, filthy, little Smurfs!
153
© Peyo - 1998 Lic. IMPS (Brussels)

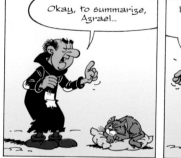

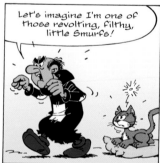

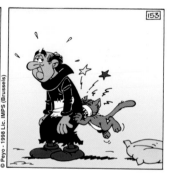

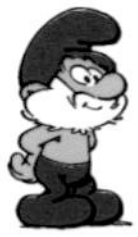

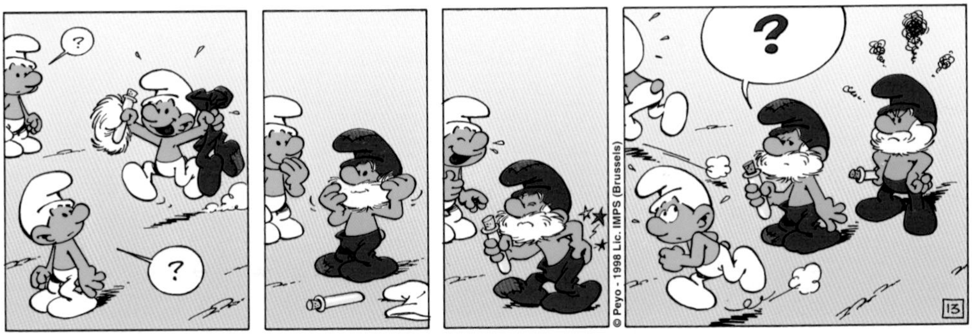
?
?
?
© Peyo - 1998 Lic. IMPS (Brussels)
13

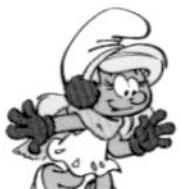

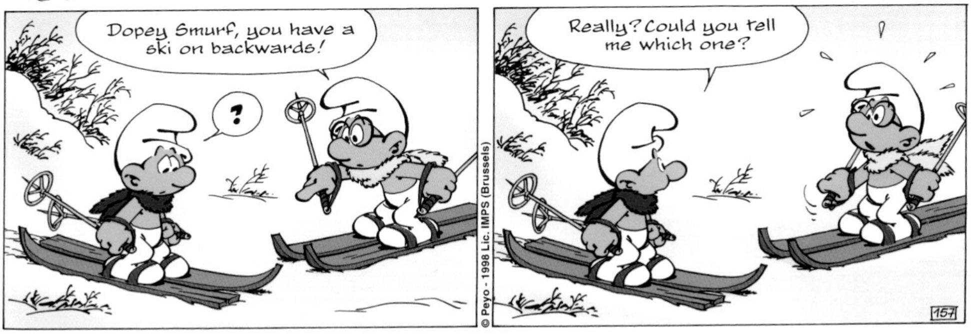
Dopey Smurf, you have a ski on backwards!
?
© Peyo - 1998 Lic. IMPS (Brussels)
Really? Could you tell me which one?
157

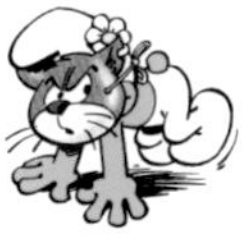

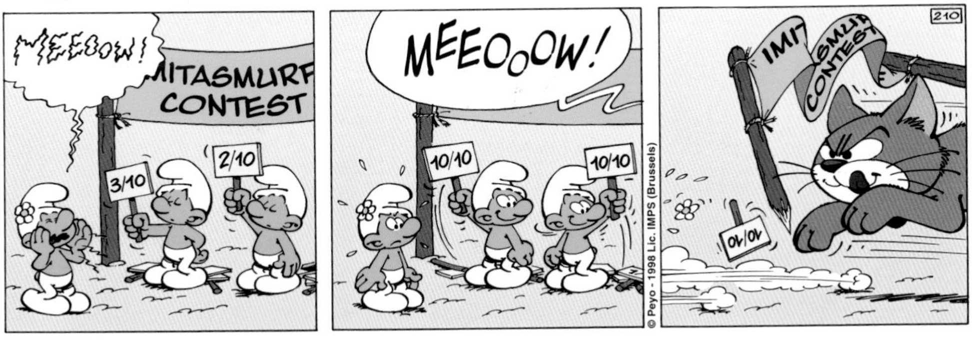
MEEOOW!
MITASMURF CONTEST
3/10
2/10
MEEOooW!
10/10
10/10
© Peyo - 1998 Lic. IMPS (Brussels)
210
IMI
SMUR CONTEST
10/10

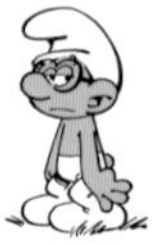

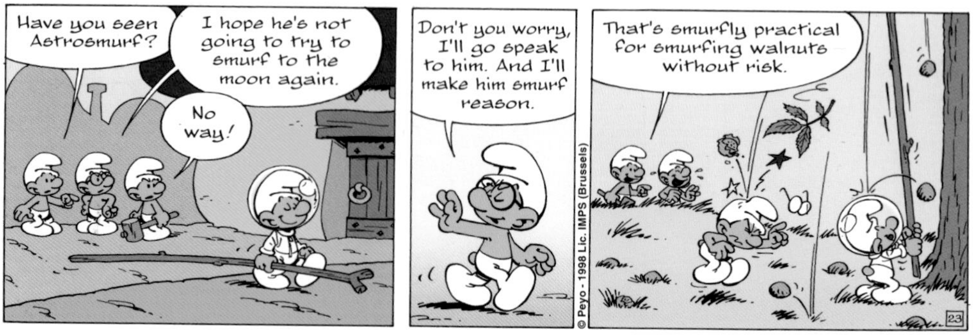

Have you seen Astrosmurf?
I hope he's not going to try to smurf to the moon again.
No way!
Don't you worry, I'll go speak to him. And I'll make him smurf reason.
© Peyo - 1998 Lic. IMPS (Brussels)
That's smurfly practical for smurfing walnuts without risk.
23

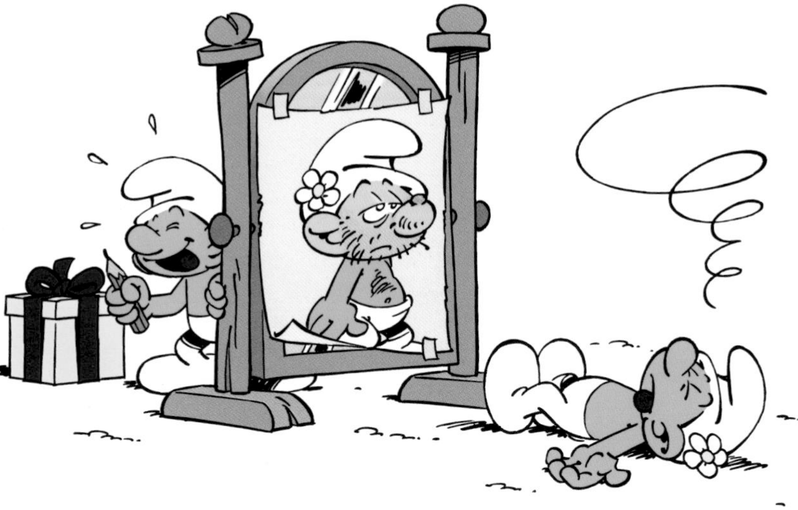

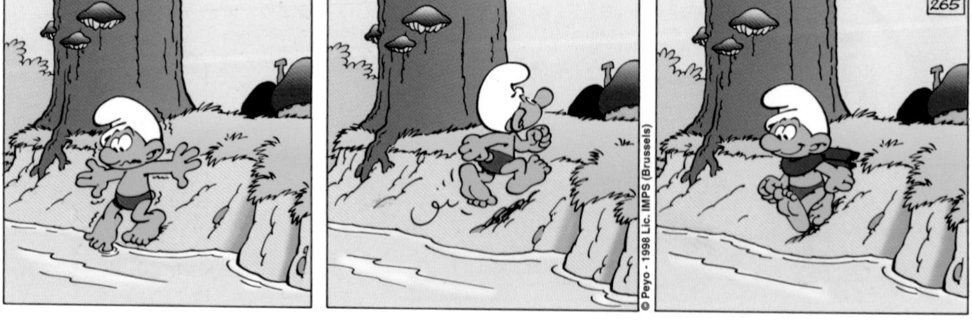

© Peyo - 1998 Lic. IMPS (Brussels)
265

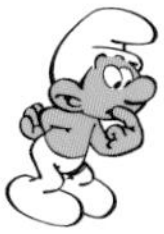

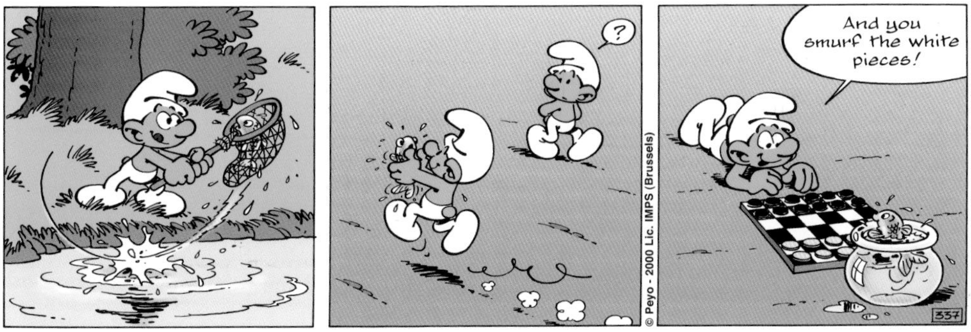
?
And you smurf the white pieces!
© Peyo - 2000 Lic. IMPS (Brussels)
337

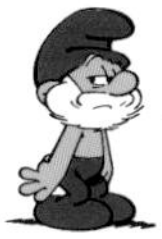

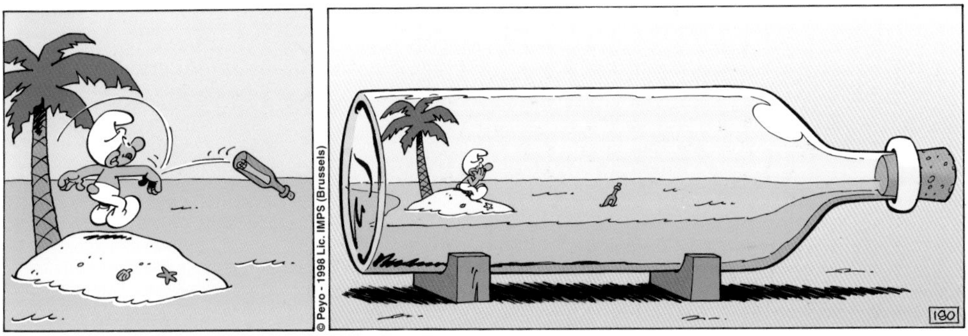
© Peyo - 1998 Lic. IMPS (Brussels)
190

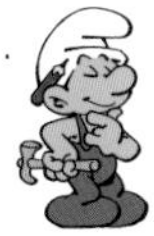

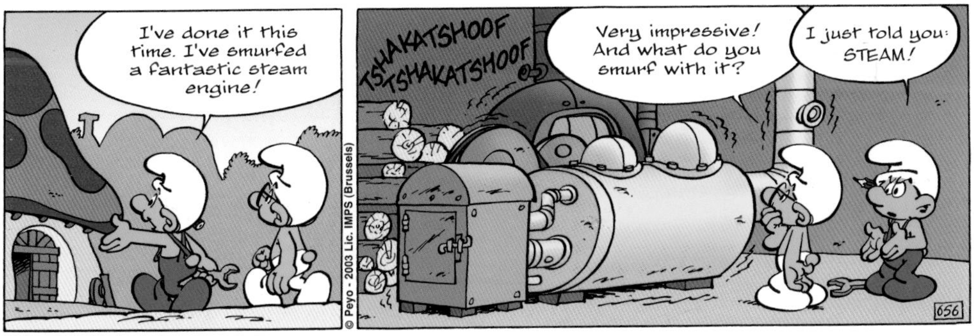
I've done it this time. I've smurfed a fantastic steam engine!
© Peyo - 2003 Lic. IMPS (Brussels)
TSHAKATSHOOF
TSHAKATSHOOF
Very impressive! And what do you smurf with it?
I just told you: STEAM!
656

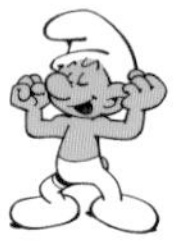

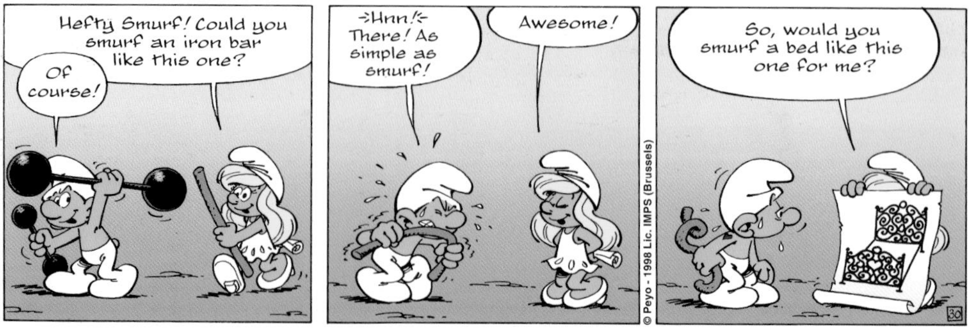

Hefty Smurf! Could you smurf an iron bar like this one?
Of course!
-Hnn!- There! As simple as smurf!
Awesome!
So, would you smurf a bed like this one for me?
© Peyo - 1998 Lic. IMPS (Brussels)
30

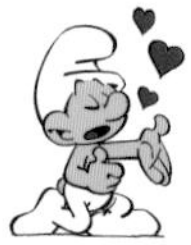

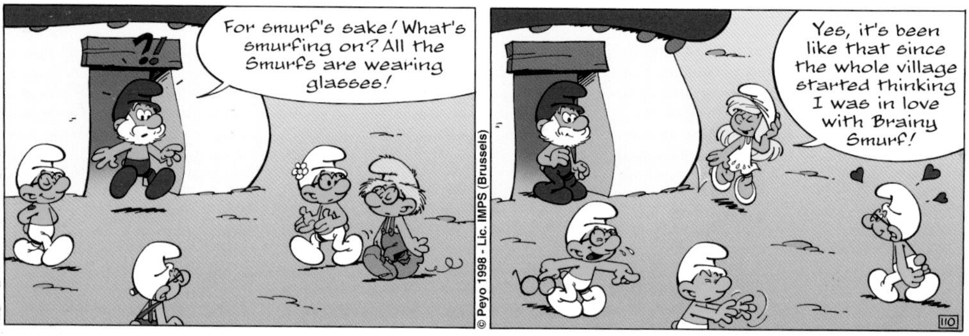

?!
For smurf's sake! What's smurfing on? All the Smurfs are wearing glasses!
Yes, it's been like that since the whole village started thinking I was in love with Brainy Smurf!
© Peyo 1998 - Lic. IMPS (Brussels)
110

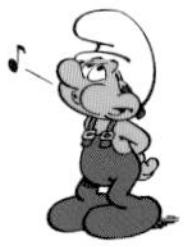

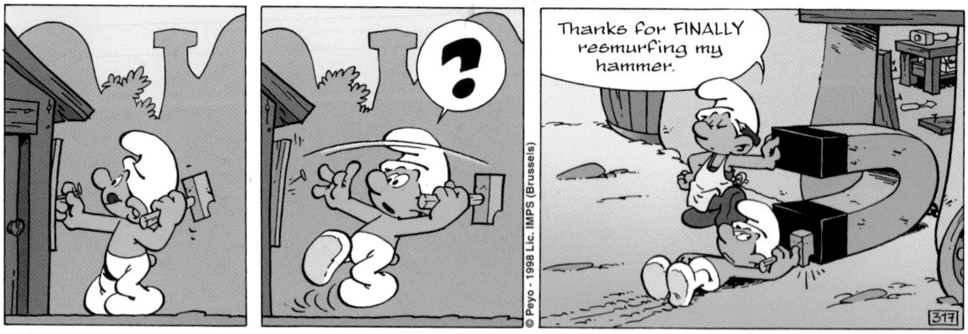

?
Thanks for FINALLY resmurfing my hammer.
© Peyo - 1998 Lic. IMPS (Brussels)
317

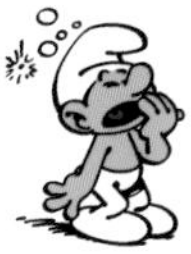

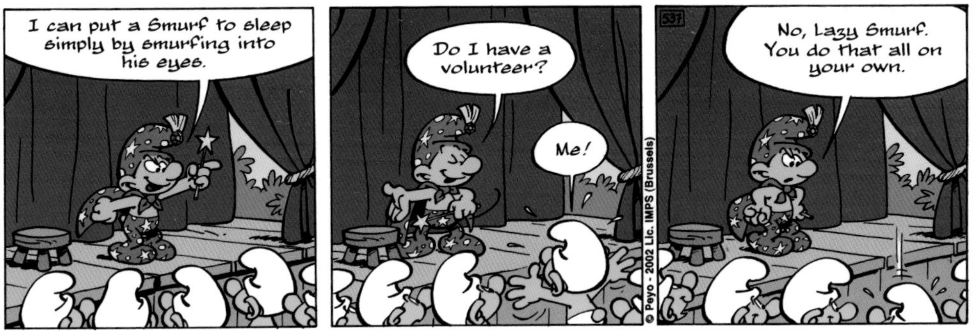
I can put a Smurf to sleep simply by smurfing into his eyes.
Do I have a volunteer?
Me!
© Peyo - 2002 Lic. IMPS (Brussels)
537
No, Lazy Smurf. You do that all on your own.

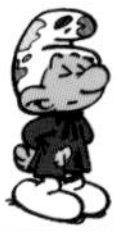

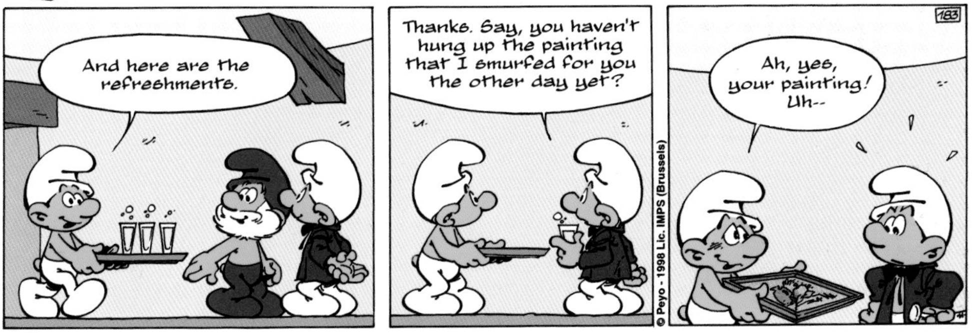
And here are the refreshments.
Thanks. Say, you haven't hung up the painting that I smurfed for you the other day yet?
© Peyo - 1998 Lic. IMPS (Brussels)
183
Ah, yes, your painting! Uh--

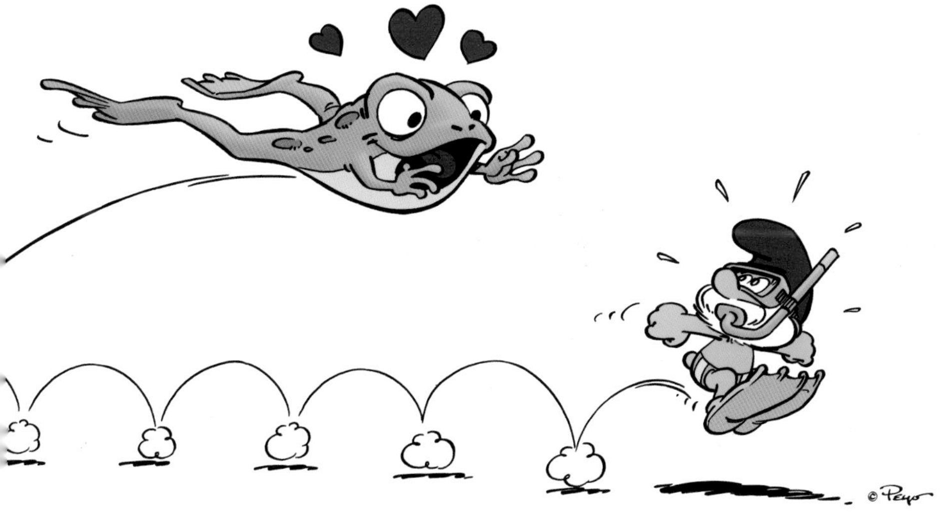
© Peyo

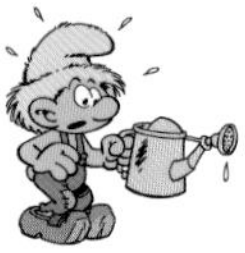

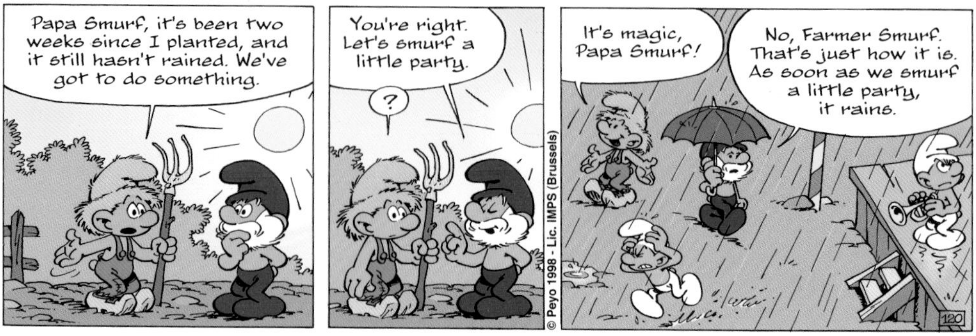
Papa Smurf, it's been two weeks since I planted, and it still hasn't rained. We've got to do something.
You're right. Let's smurf a little party.
?
© Peyo 1998 - Lic. IMPS (Brussels)
It's magic, Papa Smurf!
No, Farmer Smurf. That's just how it is. As soon as we smurf a little party, it rains.
120

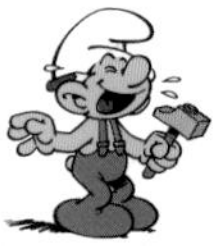

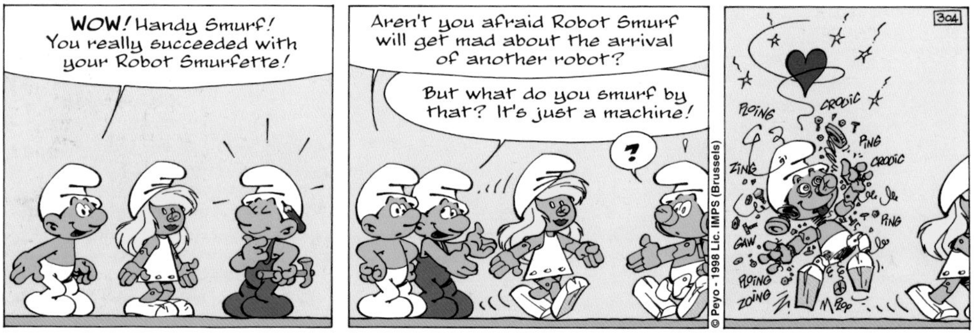
WOW! Handy Smurf! You really succeeded with your Robot Smurfette!
Aren't you afraid Robot Smurf will get mad about the arrival of another robot?
But what do you smurf by that? It's just a machine!
?
© Peyo - 1998 Lic. IMPS (Brussels)
304

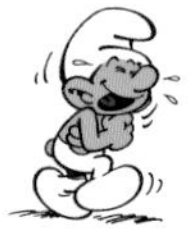

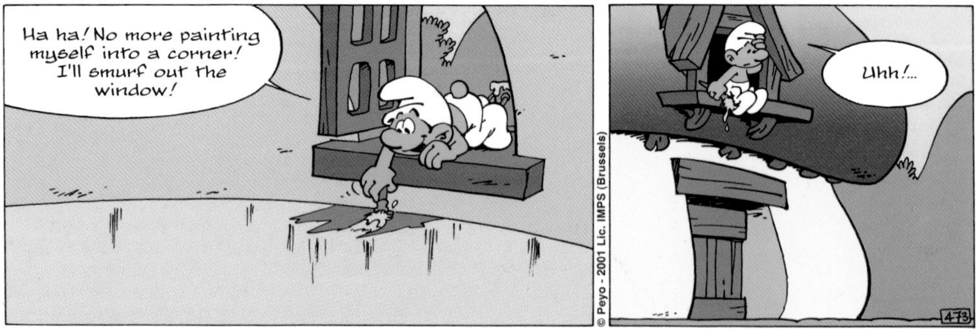
Ha ha! No more painting myself into a corner! I'll smurf out the window!
© Peyo - 2001 Lic. IMPS (Brussels)
Uhh!...
473

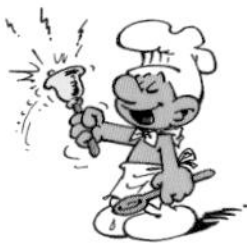

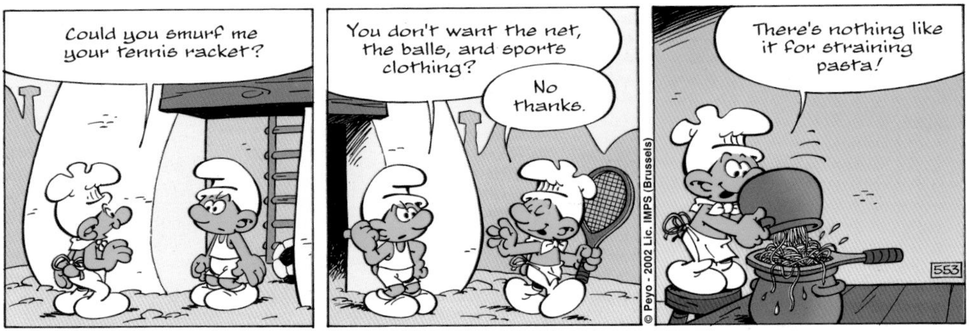

Could you smurf me your tennis racket?
You don't want the net, the balls, and sports clothing?
No thanks.
There's nothing like it for straining pasta!
© Peyo - 2002 Lic. IMPS (Brussels)
553

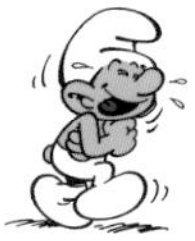

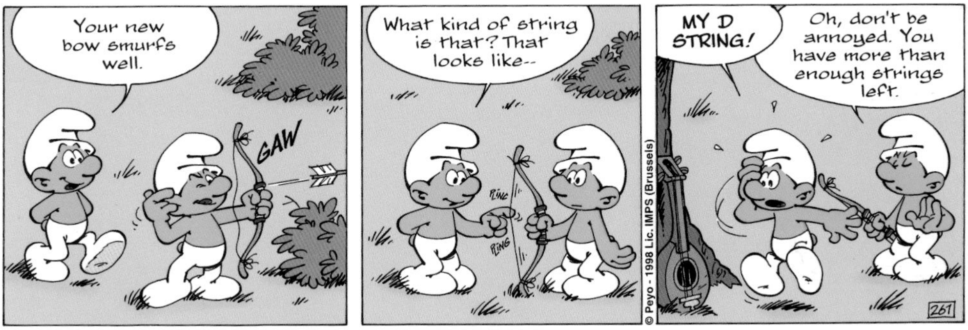

Your new bow smurfs well.
GAW
What kind of string is that? That looks like--
PLING
PLING
MY D STRING!
Oh, don't be annoyed. You have more than enough strings left.
© Peyo - 1998 Lic. IMPS (Brussels)
261

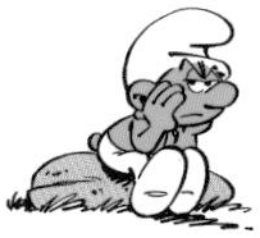

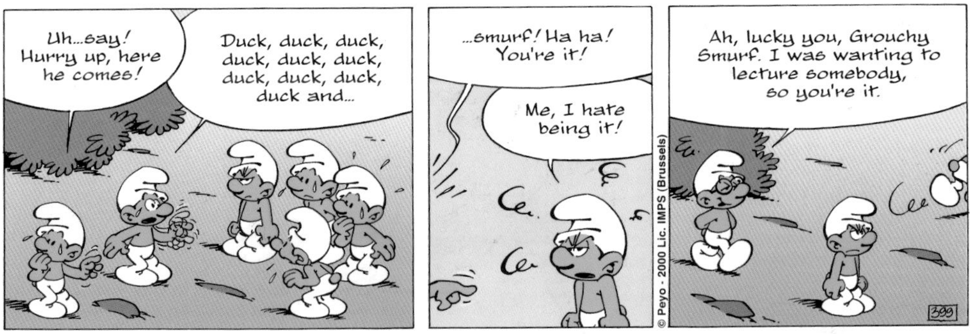

Uh...say! Hurry up, here he comes!
Duck, duck, duck, duck, duck, duck, duck, duck, duck, duck and...
...smurf! Ha ha! You're it!
Me, I hate being it!
Ah, lucky you, Grouchy Smurf. I was wanting to lecture somebody, so you're it.
© Peyo - 2000 Lic. IMPS (Brussels)
399

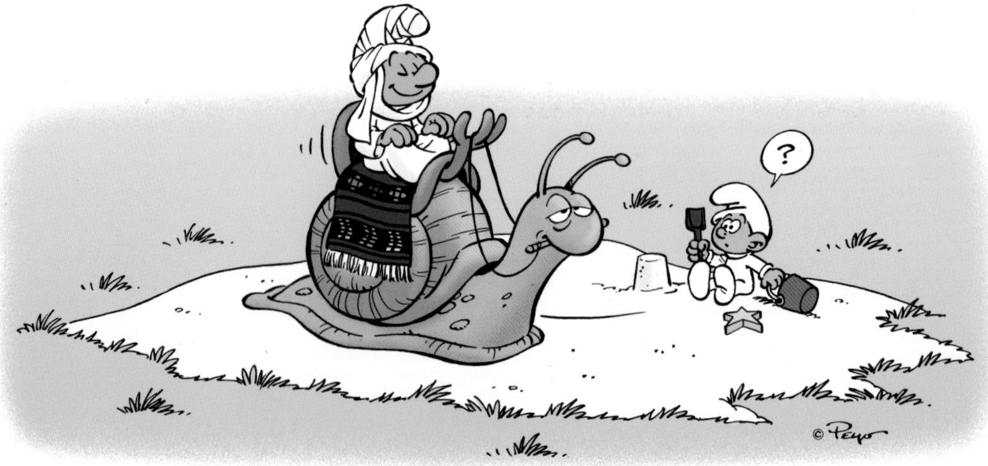
?
© Peyo

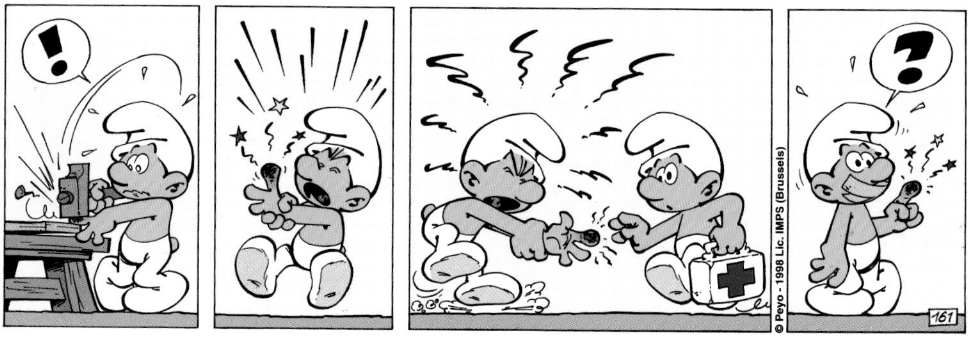
!
© Peyo - 1998 Lic. IMPS (Brussels)
?
161

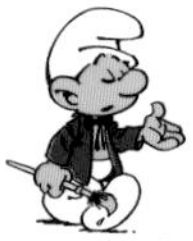

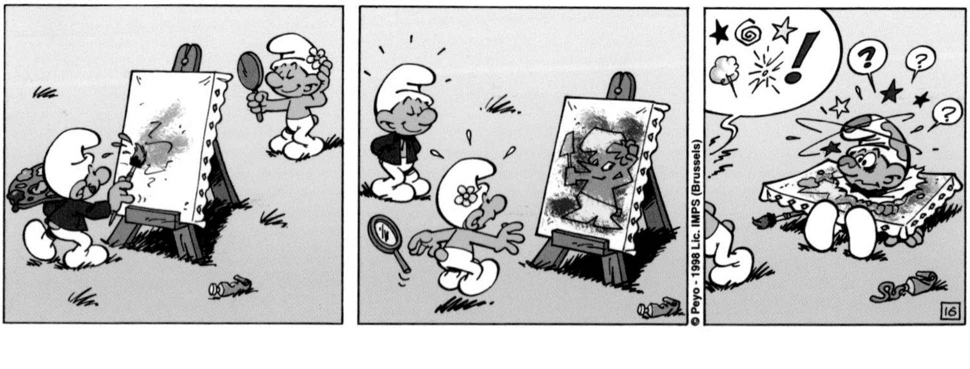
© Peyo - 1998 Lic. IMPS (Brussels)
!
?
?
?
16

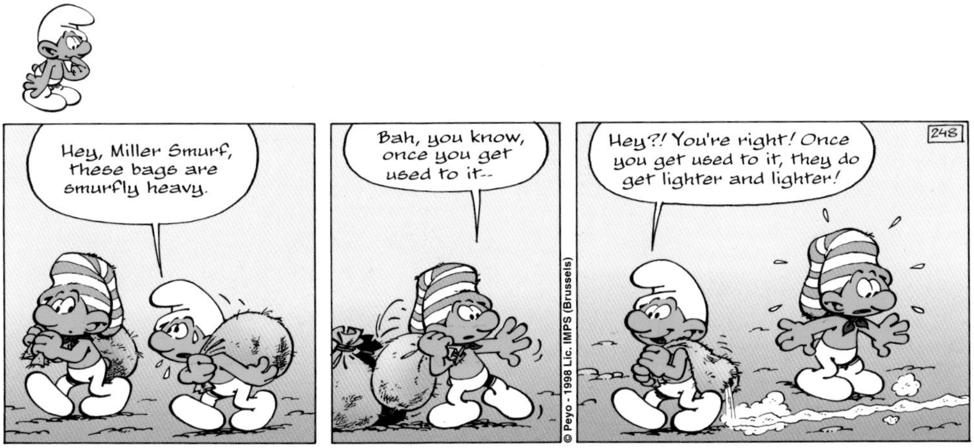
248
Hey, Miller Smurf, these bags are smurfly heavy.
Bah, you know, once you get used to it--
Hey?! You're right! Once you get used to it, they do get lighter and lighter!
© Peyo - 1998 Lic. IMPS (Brussels)

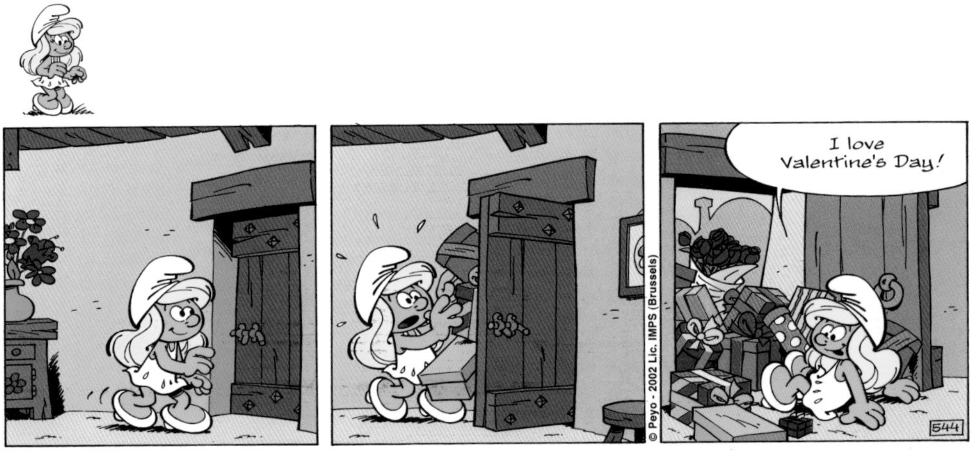
I love Valentine's Day!
544
© Peyo - 2002 Lic. IMPS (Brussels)

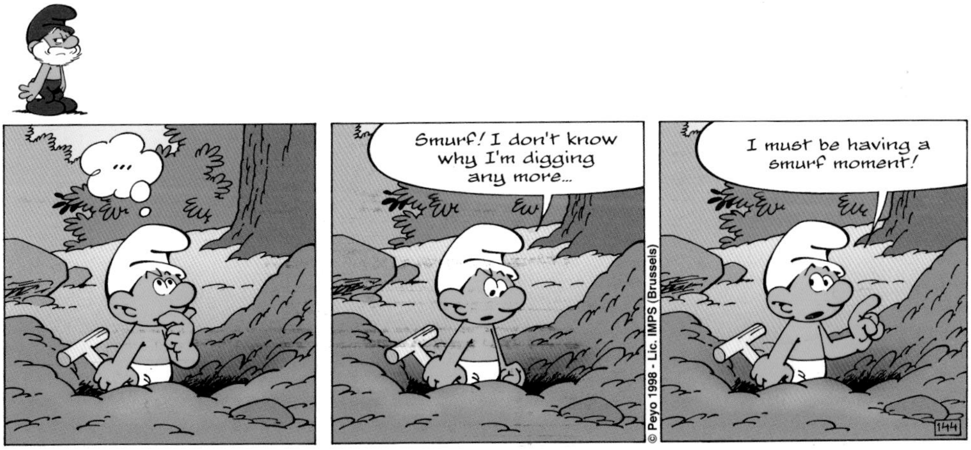
...
Smurf! I don't know why I'm digging any more...
I must be having a smurf moment!
144
© Peyo 1998 - Lic. IMPS (Brussels)

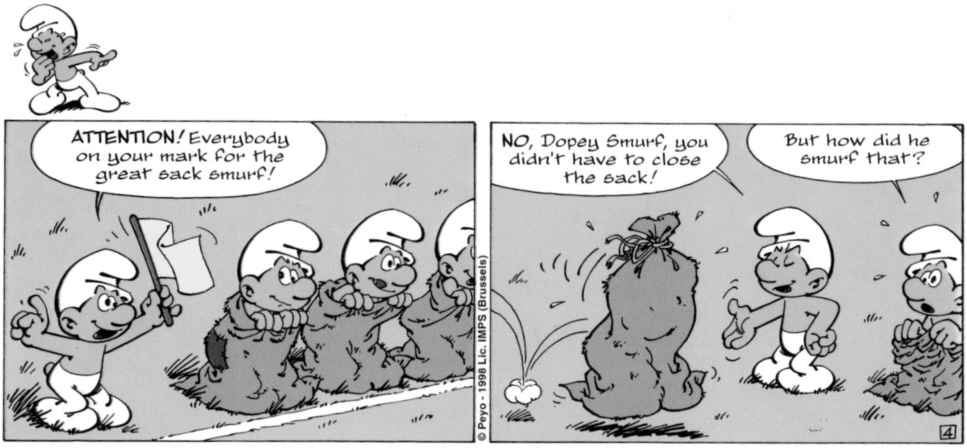
ATTENTION! Everybody on your mark for the great sack smurf!
© Peyo - 1998 Lic. IMPS (Brussels)
NO, Dopey Smurf, you didn't have to close the sack!
But how did he smurf that?
4

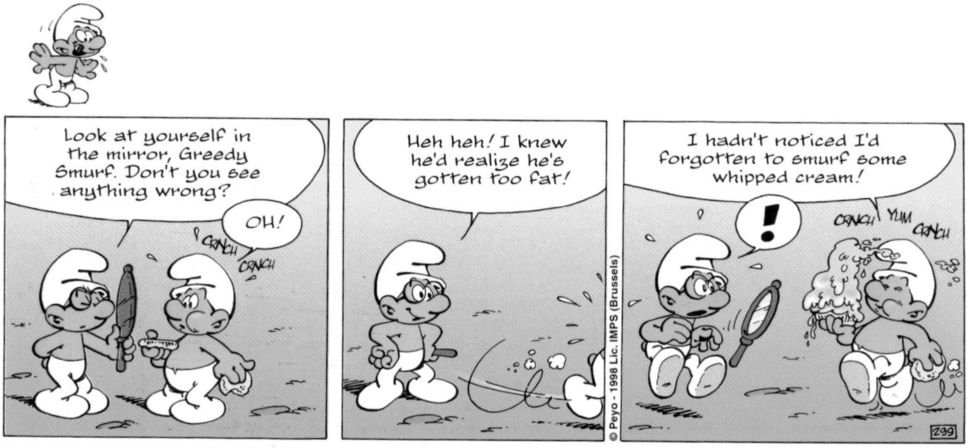
Look at yourself in the mirror, Greedy Smurf. Don't you see anything wrong?
CRNCH
CRNCH
OH!
Heh heh! I knew he'd realize he's gotten too fat!
© Peyo - 1998 Lic. IMPS (Brussels)
I hadn't noticed I'd forgotten to smurf some whipped cream!
!
CRNCH YUM CRNCH
299

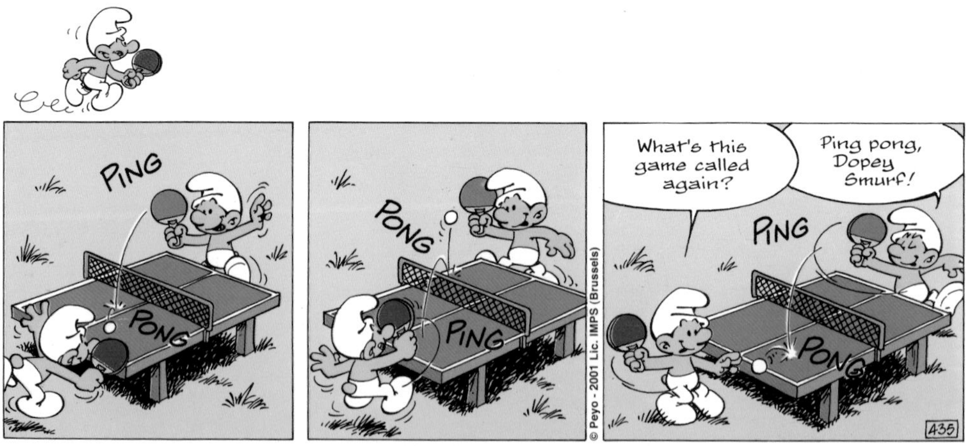
PING
PONG
PONG
PING
© Peyo - 2001 Lic. IMPS (Brussels)
What's this game called again?
Ping pong, Dopey Smurf!
PING
PONG
435

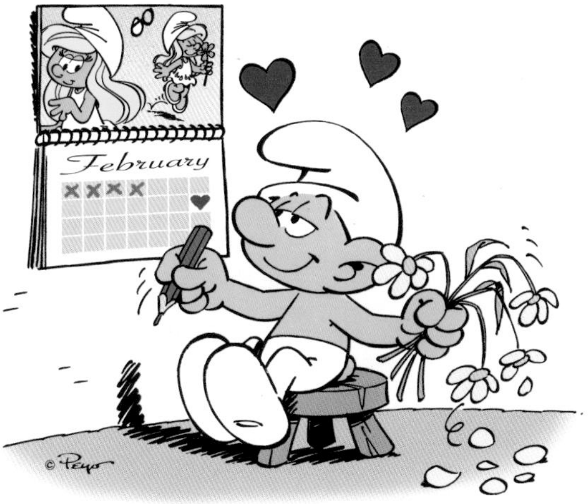
February
© Peyo

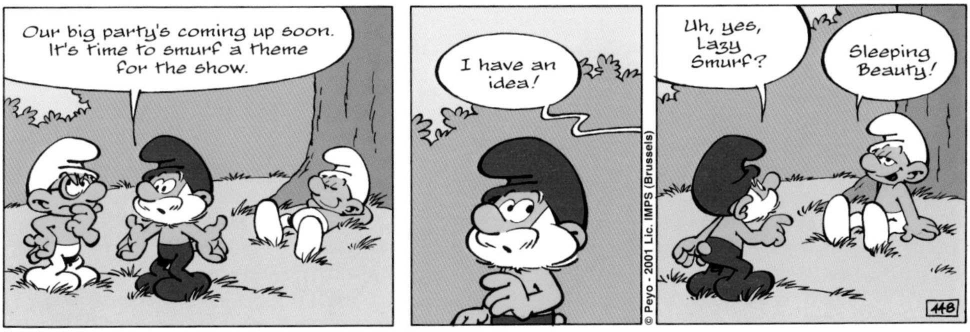
Our big party's coming up soon. It's time to smurf a theme for the show.
I have an idea!
© Peyo - 2001 Lic. IMPS (Brussels)
Uh, yes, Lazy Smurf?
Sleeping Beauty!
118

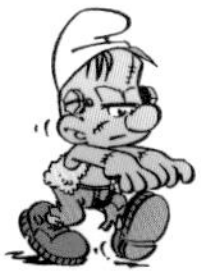

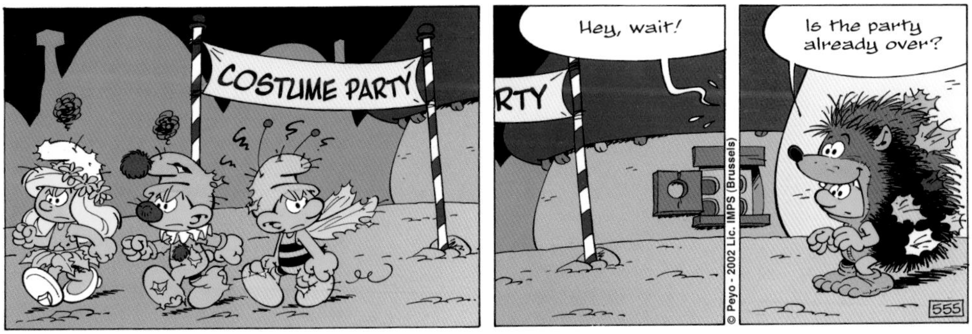
COSTUME PARTY
Hey, wait!
RTY
© Peyo - 2002 Lic. IMPS (Brussels)
Is the party already over?
555

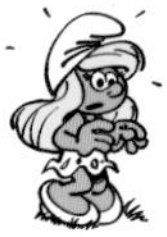

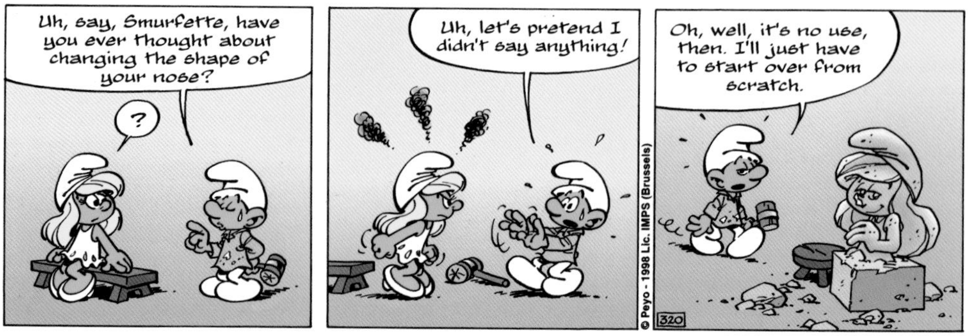
Uh, say, Smurfette, have you ever thought about changing the shape of your nose?
?
Uh, let's pretend I didn't say anything!
Oh, well, it's no use, then. I'll just have to start over from scratch.
© Peyo - 1998 Lic. IMPS (Brussels)
320

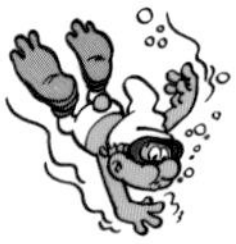

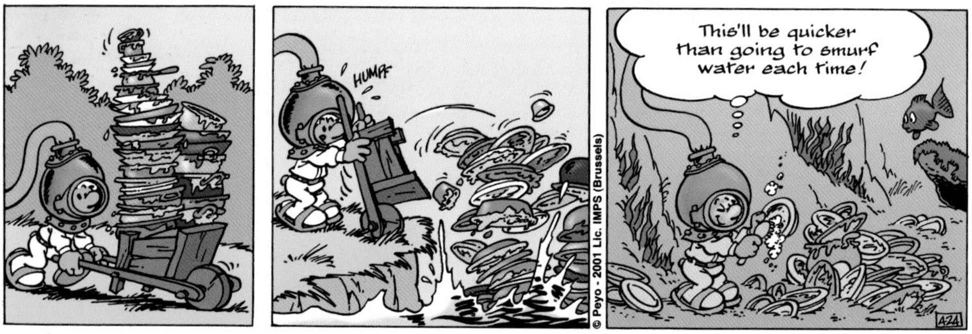
HUMPF
© Peyo - 2001 Lic. IMPS (Brussels)
This'll be quicker than going to smurf water each time!
A24

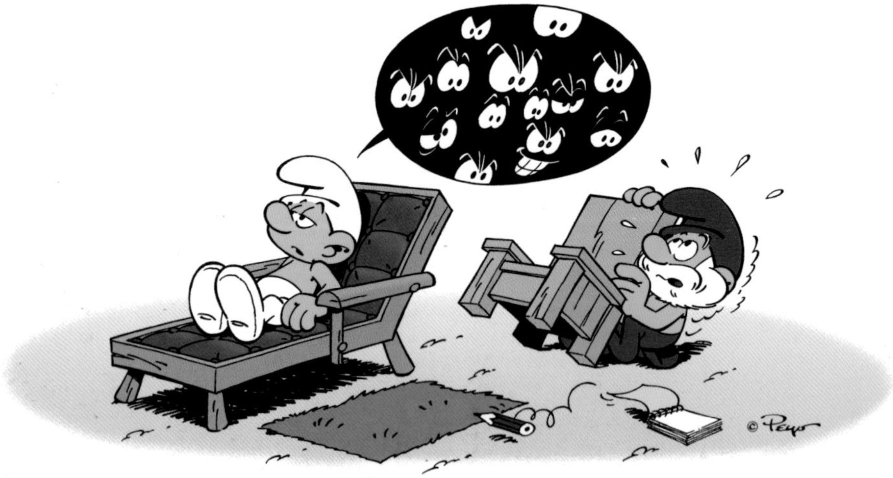
© Peyo

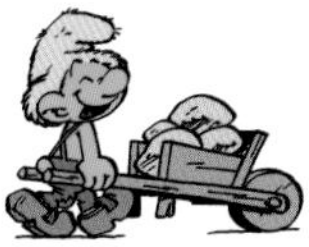

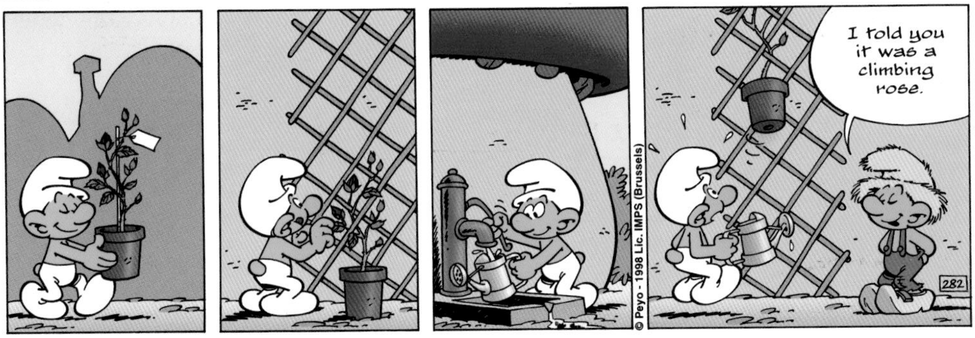

I told you it was a climbing rose.
© Peyo - 1998 Lic. IMPS (Brussels)
282

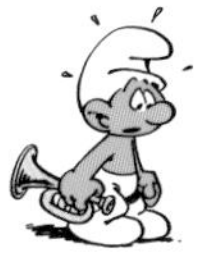

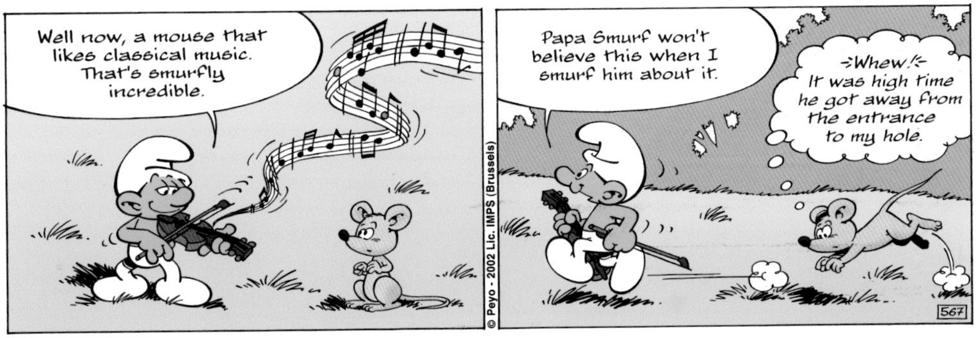

Well now, a mouse that likes classical music. That's smurfly incredible.
© Peyo - 2002 Lic. IMPS (Brussels)
Papa Smurf won't believe this when I smurf him about it.
–Whew!– It was high time he got away from the entrance to my hole.
567

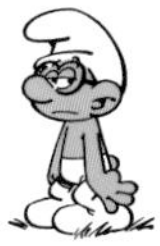

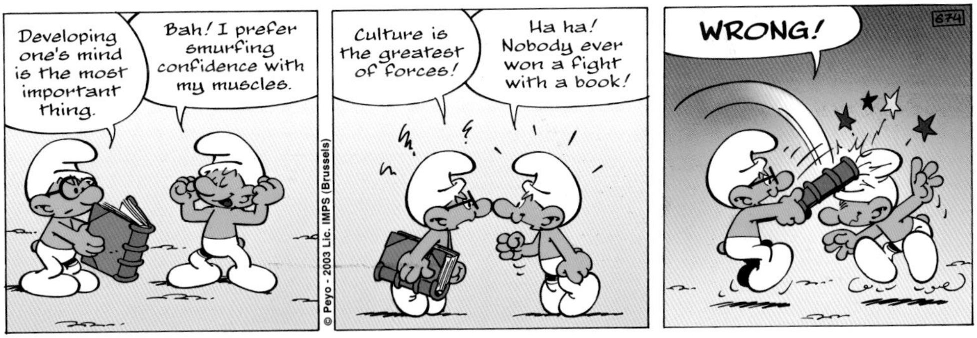

Developing one's mind is the most important thing.
Bah! I prefer smurfing confidence with my muscles.
© Peyo - 2003 Lic. IMPS (Brussels)
Culture is the greatest of forces!
Ha ha! Nobody ever won a fight with a book!
WRONG!
674

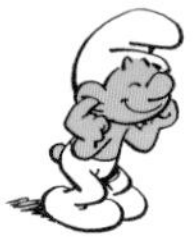

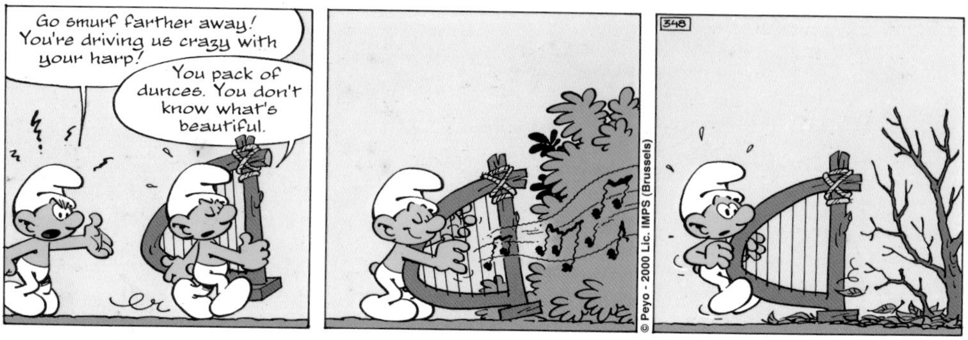
Go smurf farther away! You're driving us crazy with your harp!
You pack of dunces. You don't know what's beautiful.
© Peyo - 2000 Lic. IMPS (Brussels)
348

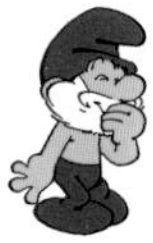

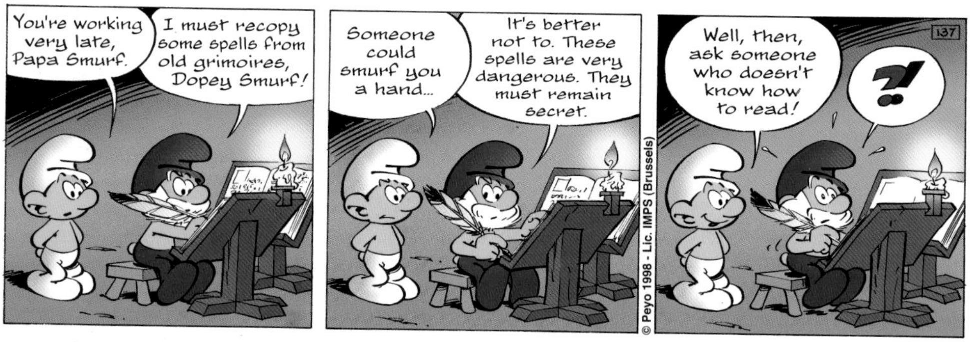
You're working very late, Papa Smurf.
I must recopy some spells from old grimoires, Dopey Smurf!
Someone could smurf you a hand...
It's better not to. These spells are very dangerous. They must remain secret.
© Peyo 1998 - Lic. IMPS (Brussels)
137
Well, then, ask someone who doesn't know how to read!
?!

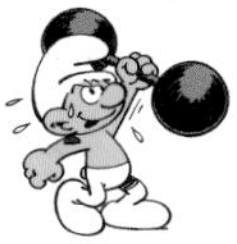

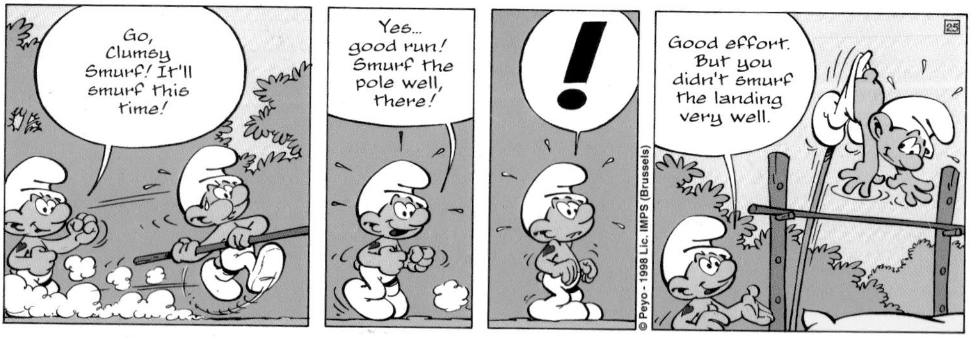
Go, Clumsy Smurf! It'll smurf this time!
Yes... good run! Smurf the pole well, there!
!
© Peyo - 1998 Lic. IMPS (Brussels)
25
Good effort. But you didn't smurf the landing very well.

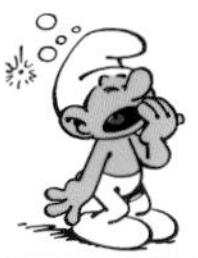

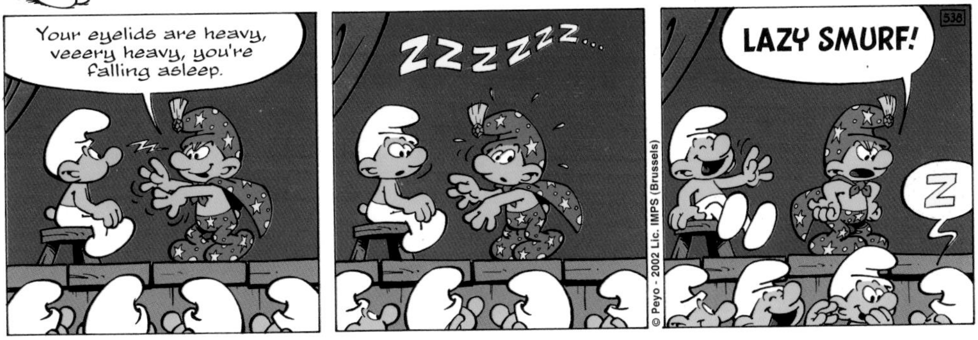
Your eyelids are heavy, veeery heavy, you're falling asleep.
ZZZZZZ...
538
LAZY SMURF!
Z
© Peyo - 2002 Lic. IMPS (Brussels)

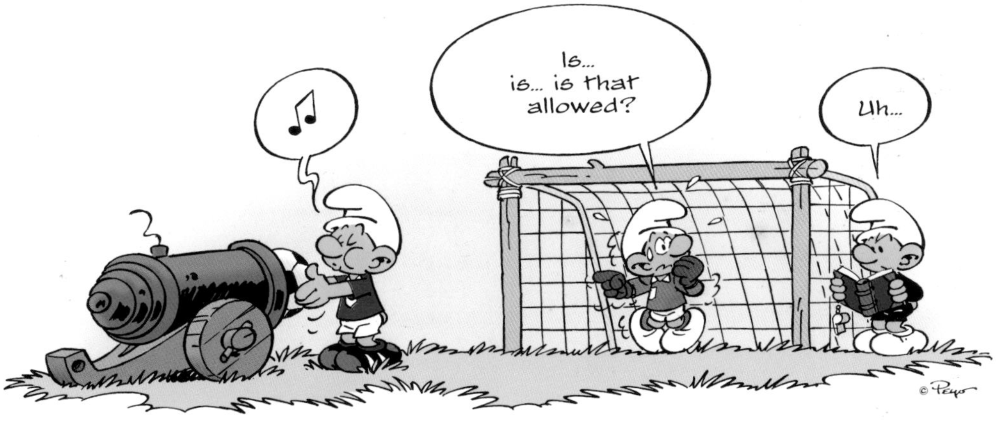
♫
Is... is... is that allowed?
Uh...
© Peyo

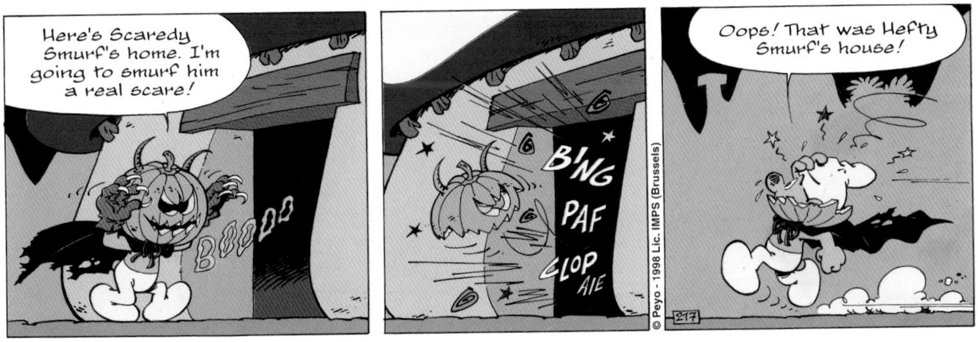
Here's Scaredy Smurf's home. I'm going to smurf him a real scare!
BING
PAF
CLOP
AIE
© Peyo - 1998 Lic. IMPS (Brussels)
217
Oops! That was Hefty Smurf's house!

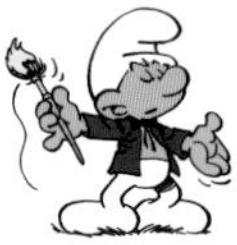

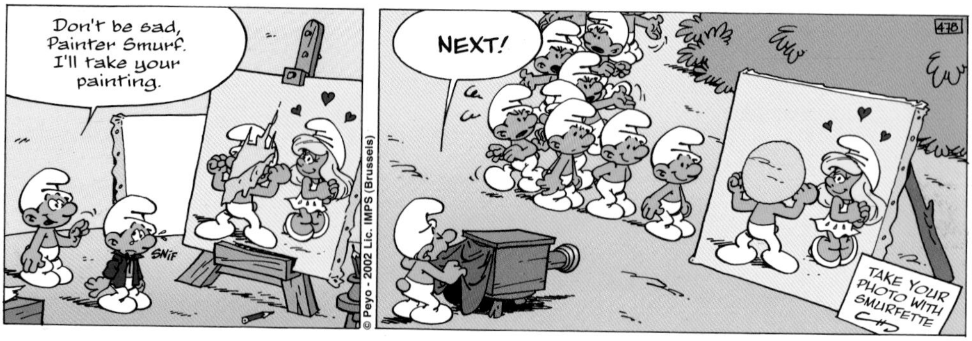

Don't be sad, Painter Smurf. I'll take your painting.
SNIF
© Peyo - 2002 Lic. IMPS (Brussels)
NEXT!
478
TAKE YOUR PHOTO WITH SMURFETTE

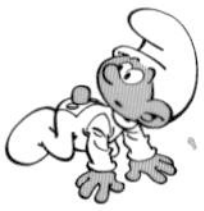

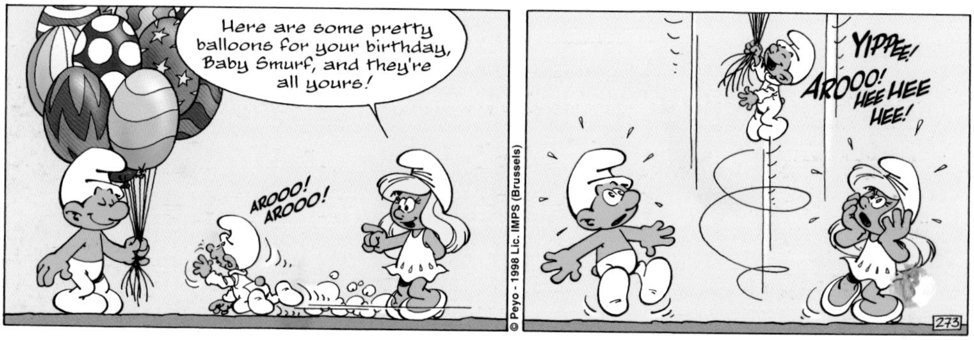

Here are some pretty balloons for your birthday, Baby Smurf, and they're all yours!
AROOO! AROOO!
© Peyo - 1998 Lic. IMPS (Brussels)
YIPPEE!
AROOO! HEE HEE HEE!
273

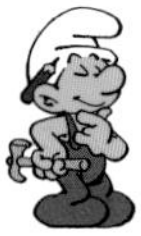

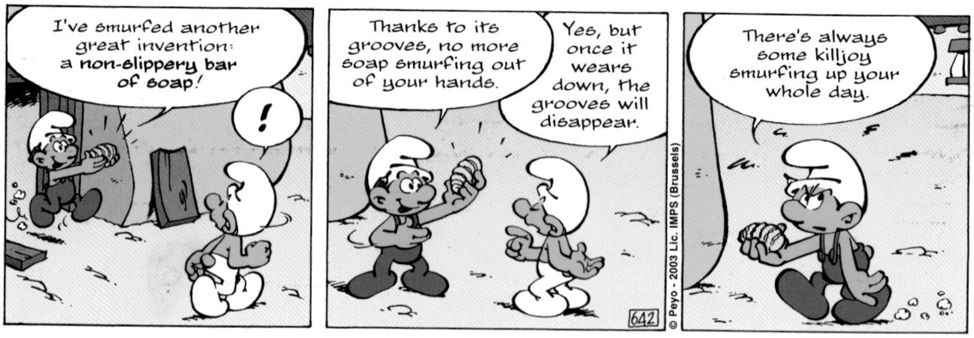

I've smurfed another great invention: a **non-slippery bar of soap**!
!
Thanks to its grooves, no more soap smurfing out of your hands.
Yes, but once it wears down, the grooves will disappear.
642
© Peyo - 2003 Lic. IMPS (Brussels)
There's always some killjoy smurfing up your whole day.

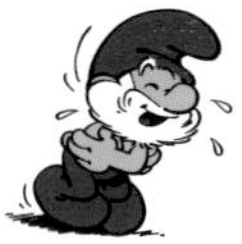

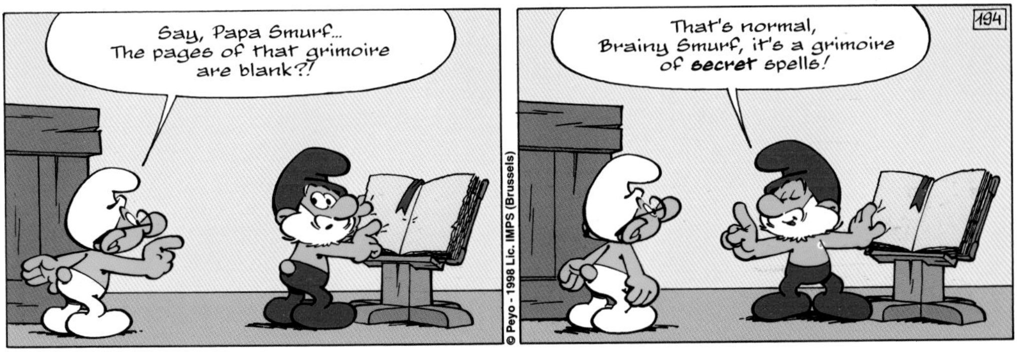
Say, Papa Smurf...
The pages of that grimoire are blank?!
© Peyo - 1998 Lic. IMPS (Brussels)
194
That's normal, Brainy Smurf, it's a grimoire of **secret** spells!

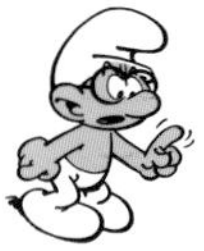

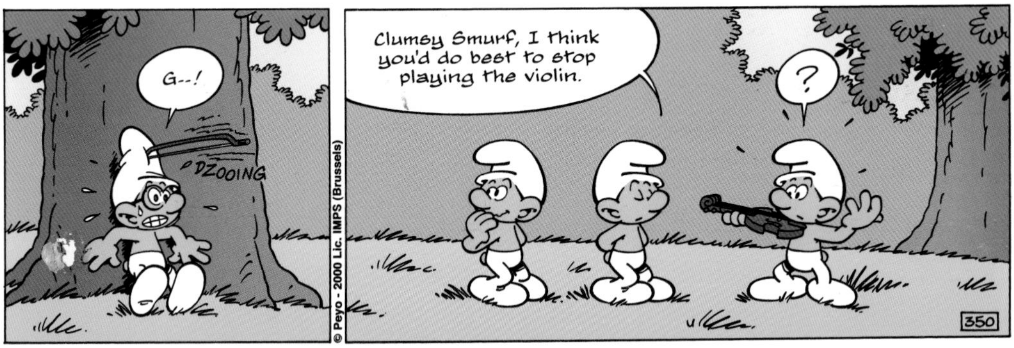
G--!
DZOOING
© Peyo - 2000 Lic. IMPS (Brussels)
Clumsy Smurf, I think you'd do best to stop playing the violin.
?
350

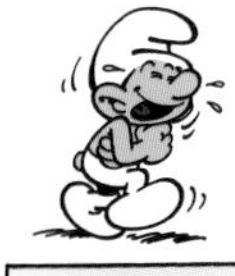

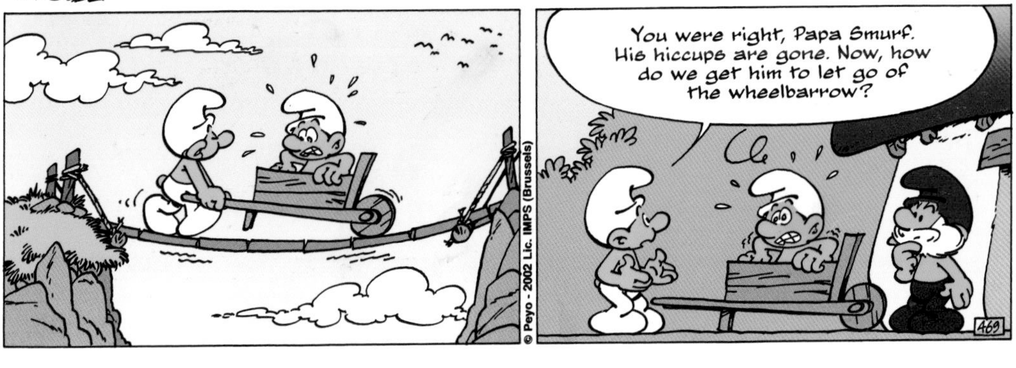
© Peyo - 2002 Lic. IMPS (Brussels)
You were right, Papa Smurf. His hiccups are gone. Now, how do we get him to let go of the wheelbarrow?
469

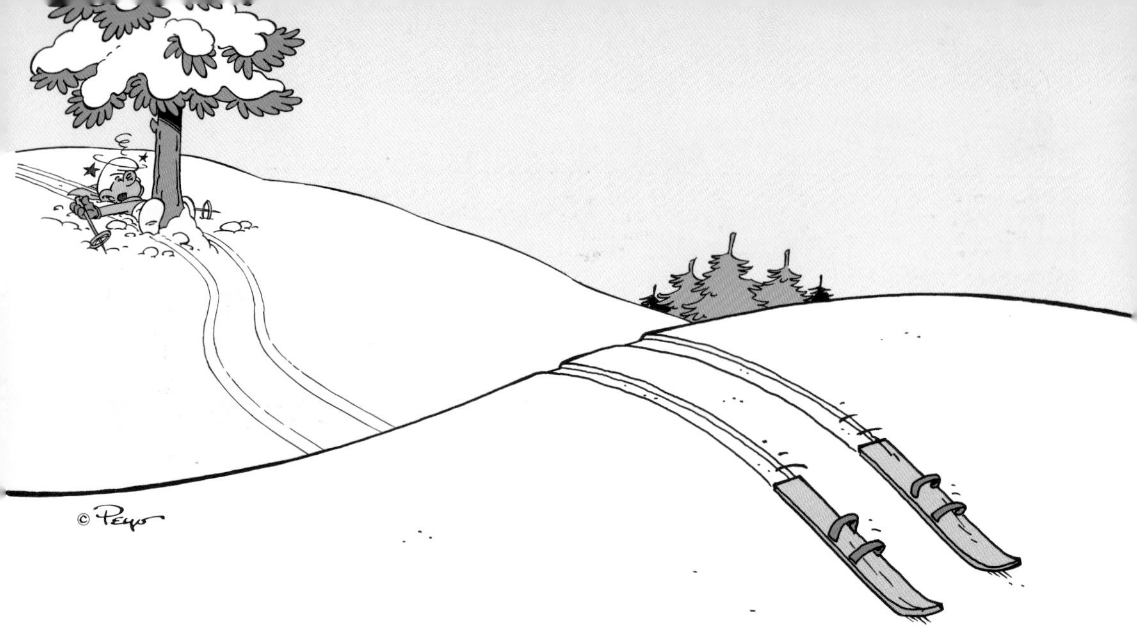
© Peyo

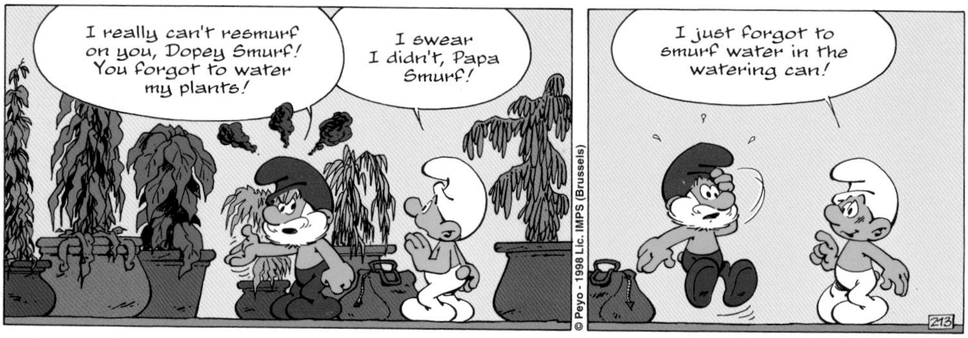
I really can't resmurf on you, Dopey Smurf! You forgot to water my plants!
I swear I didn't, Papa Smurf!
© Peyo - 1998 Lic. IMPS (Brussels)
I just forgot to smurf water in the watering can!
213

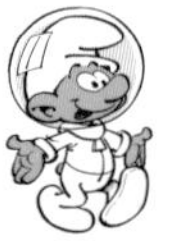

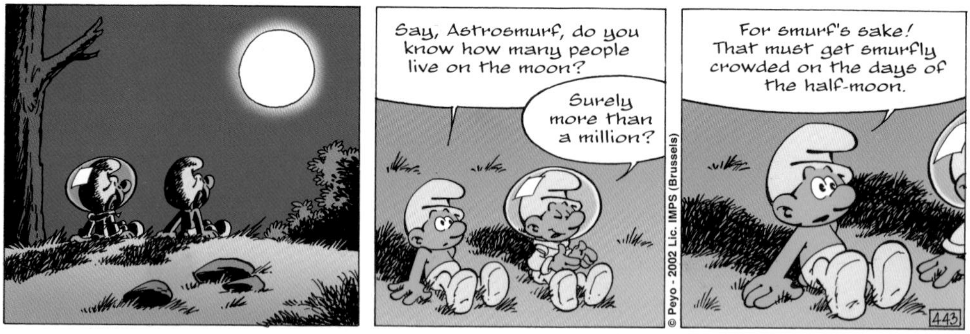
Say, Astrosmurf, do you know how many people live on the moon?
Surely more than a million?
© Peyo - 2002 Lic. IMPS (Brussels)
For smurf's sake! That must get smurfly crowded on the days of the half-moon.
443

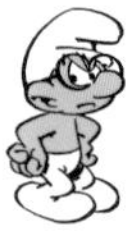

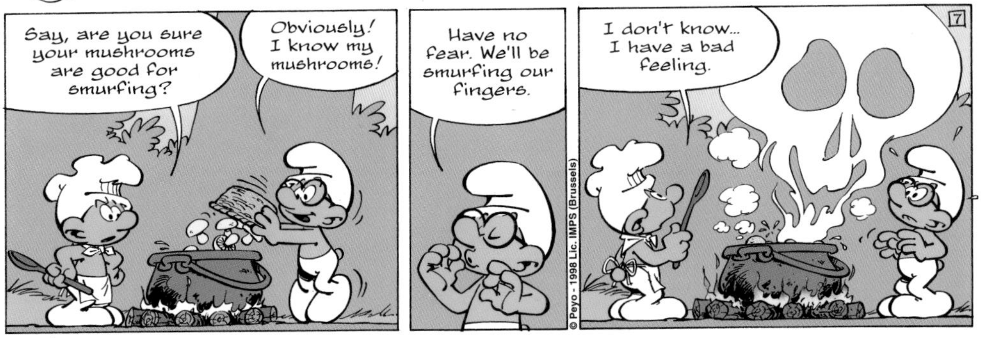
Say, are you sure your mushrooms are good for smurfing?
Obviously! I know my mushrooms!
Have no fear. We'll be smurfing our fingers.
© Peyo - 1998 Lic. IMPS (Brussels)
7
I don't know... I have a bad feeling.

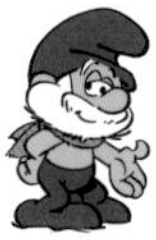

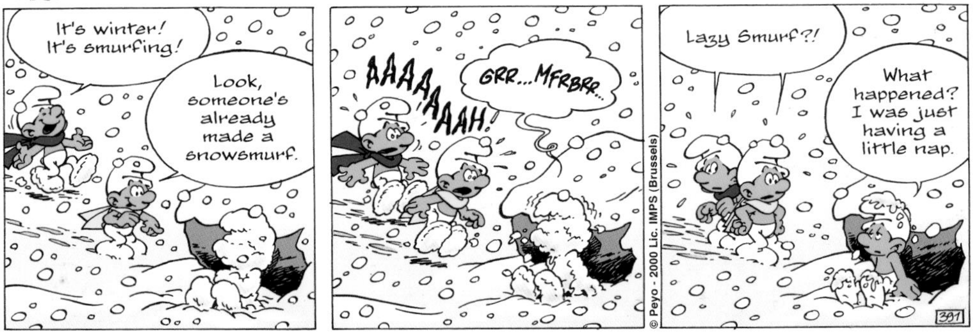
It's winter! It's smurfing!
Look, someone's already made a snowsmurf.
AAAAAAAAH!
GRR...MFRBRR...
© Peyo - 2000 Lic. IMPS (Brussels)
Lazy Smurf?!
What happened? I was just having a little nap.
391

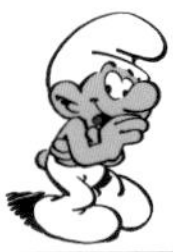

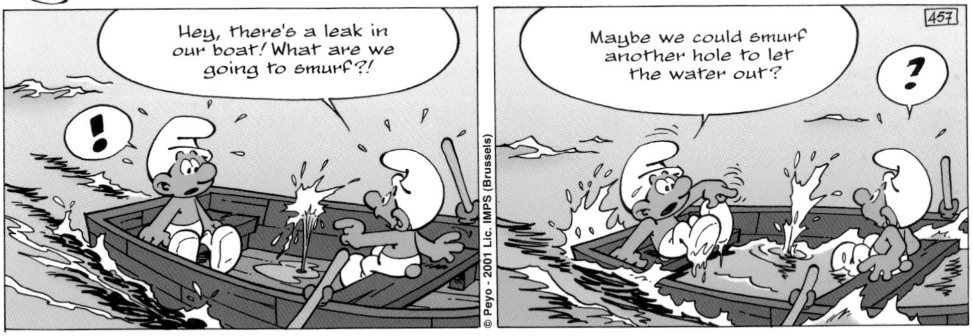
Hey, there's a leak in our boat! What are we going to smurf?!
!
© Peyo - 2001 Lic. IMPS (Brussels)
457
Maybe we could smurf another hole to let the water out?
?

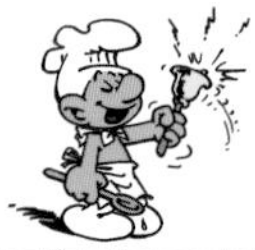

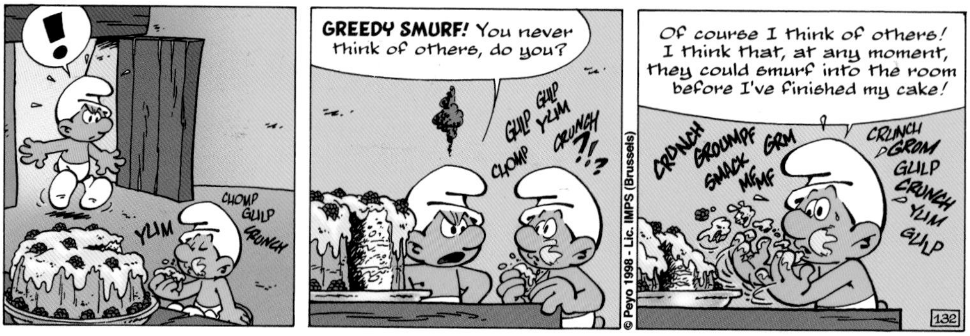
!
GREEDY SMURF! You never think of others, do you?
GULP GULP YUM CHOMP CRUNCH
?!?
YUM CHOMP GULP CRUNCH
© Peyo 1998 - Lic. IMPS (Brussels)
Of course I think of others! I think that, at any moment, they could smurf into the room before I've finished my cake!
CRUNCH GROUMPF SMACK MMF GRM
CRUNCH GROM GULP CRUNCH YUM GULP
132

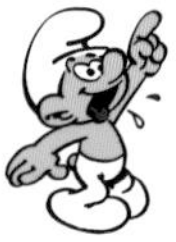

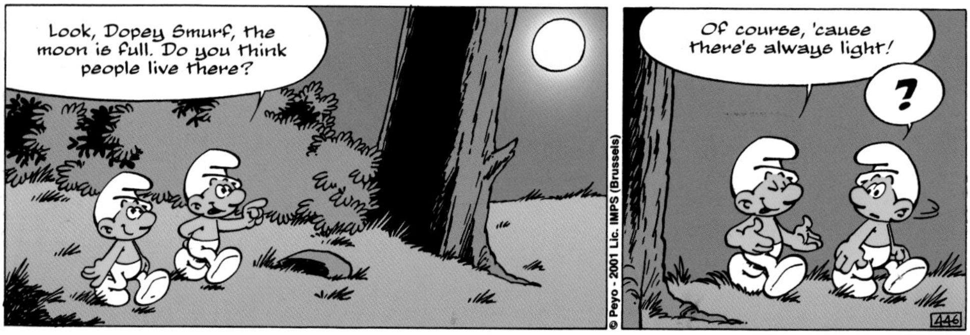
Look, Dopey Smurf, the moon is full. Do you think people live there?
© Peyo - 2001 Lic. IMPS (Brussels)
Of course, 'cause there's always light!
?
446

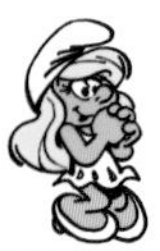

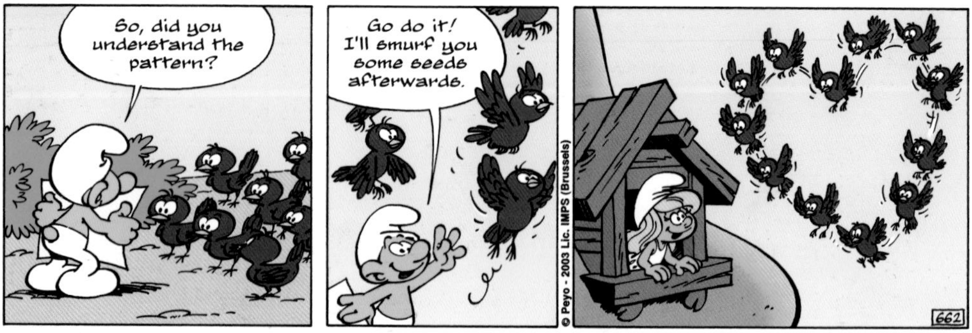
So, did you understand the pattern?
Go do it! I'll smurf you some seeds afterwards.
© Peyo - 2003 Lic. IMPS (Brussels)
662

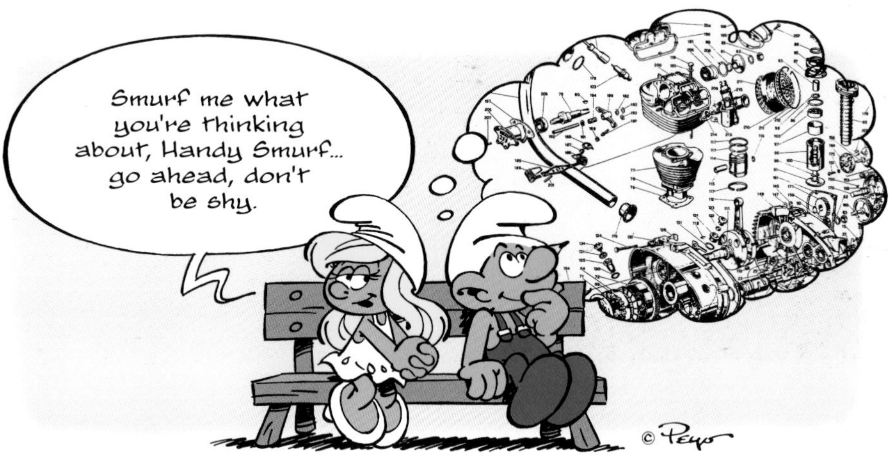
Smurf me what you're thinking about, Handy Smurf... go ahead, don't be shy.
© Peyo

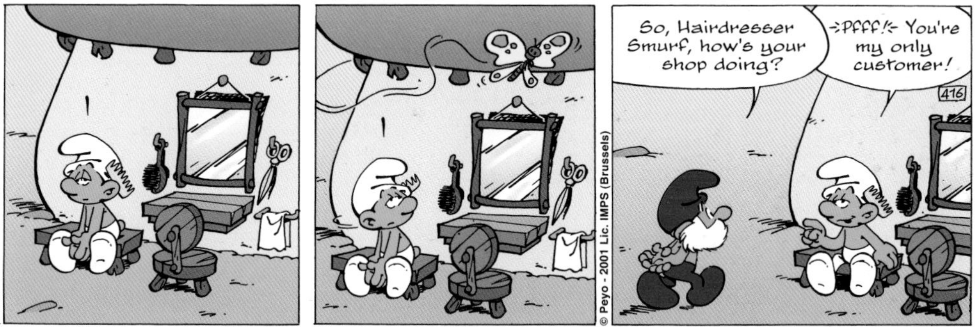
!
!
So, Hairdresser Smurf, how's your shop doing?
Pfff! You're my only customer!
416
© Peyo - 2001 Lic. IMPS (Brussels)

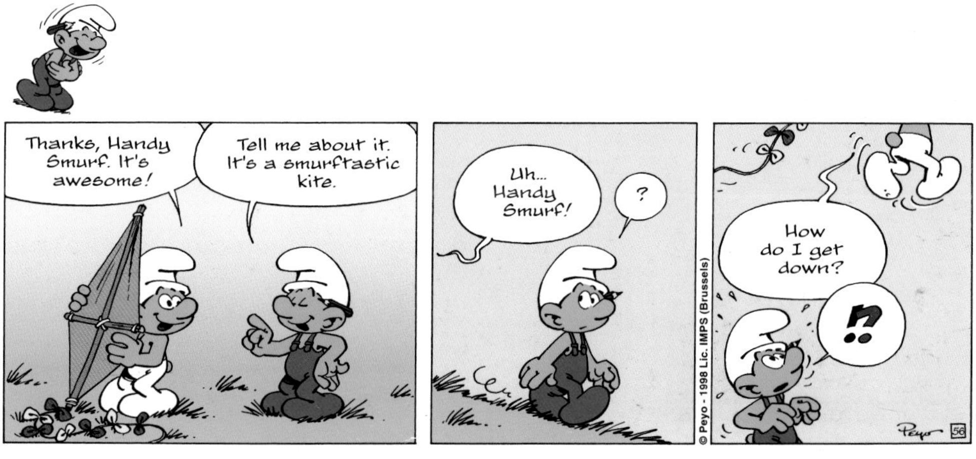
Thanks, Handy Smurf. It's awesome!
Tell me about it. It's a smurftastic kite.
Uh... Handy Smurf!
?
How do I get down?
!?
Peyo
56
© Peyo - 1998 Lic. IMPS (Brussels)

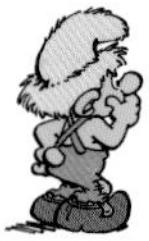

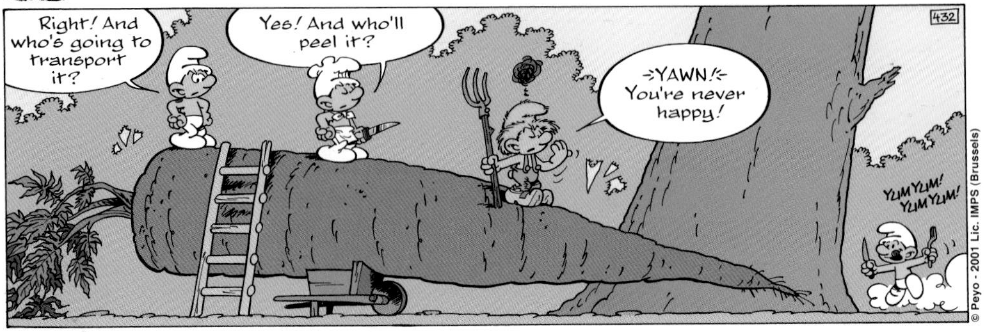
432
Right! And who's going to transport it?
Yes! And who'll peel it?
-YAWN!- You're never happy!
YUM YUM! YUM YUM!
© Peyo - 2001 Lic. IMPS (Brussels)

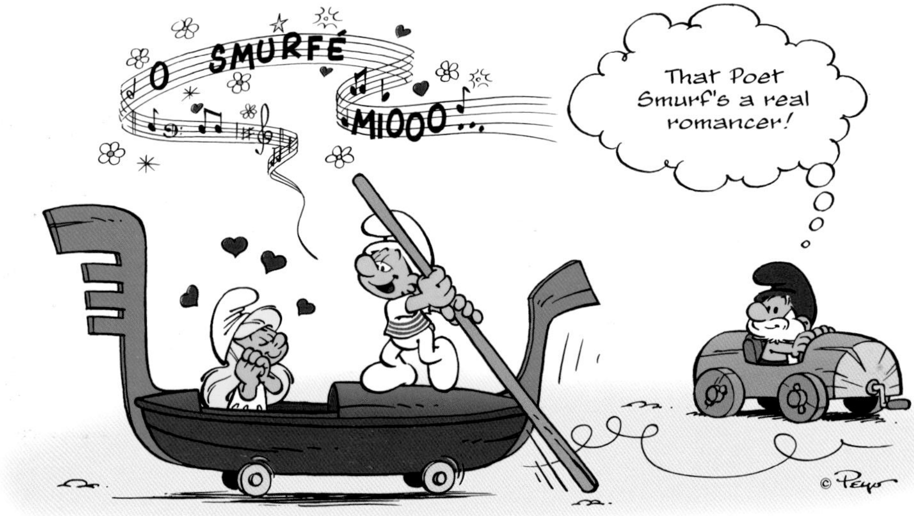
O SMURFÉ MIOOO...
That Poet Smurf's a real romancer!
© Peyo

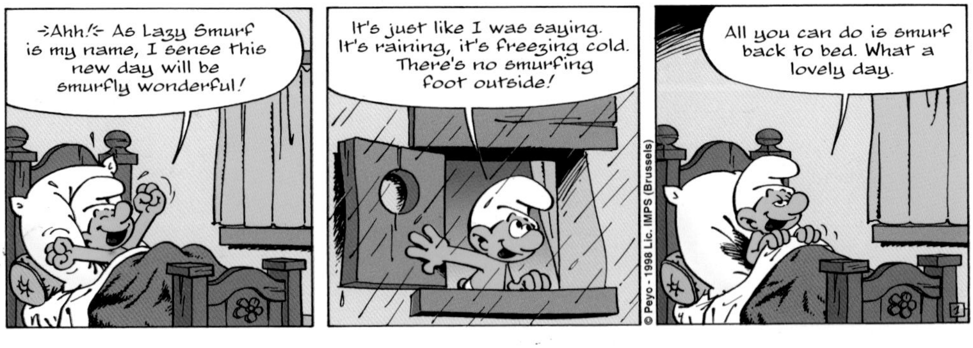
-Ahh!- As Lazy Smurf is my name, I sense this new day will be smurfly wonderful!
It's just like I was saying. It's raining, it's freezing cold. There's no smurfing foot outside!
All you can do is smurf back to bed. What a lovely day.
© Peyo - 1998 Lic. IMPS (Brussels)

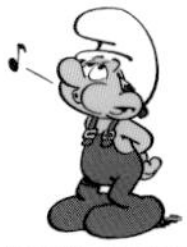

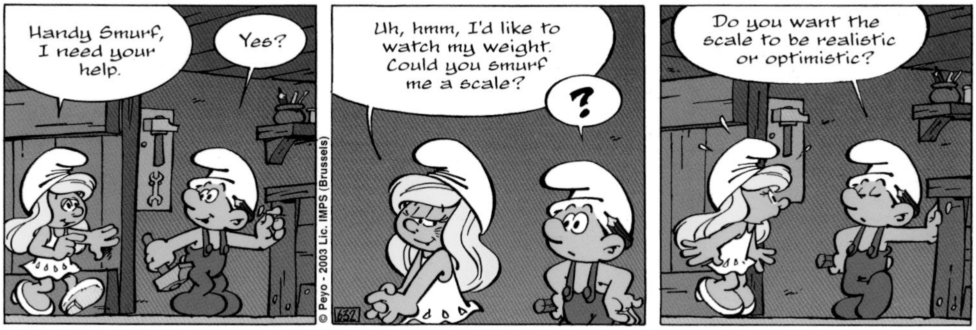

Handy Smurf, I need your help.
Yes?
Uh, hmm, I'd like to watch my weight. Could you smurf me a scale?
?
Do you want the scale to be realistic or optimistic?
632

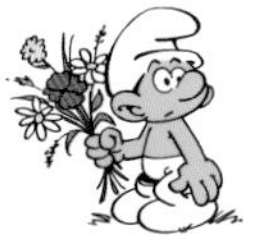

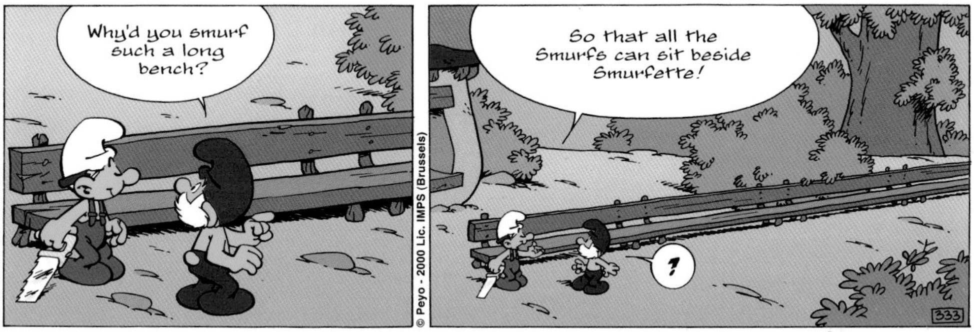

Why'd you smurf such a long bench?
So that all the Smurfs can sit beside Smurfette!
?
333

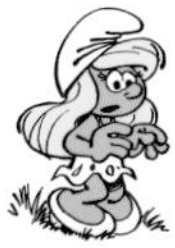

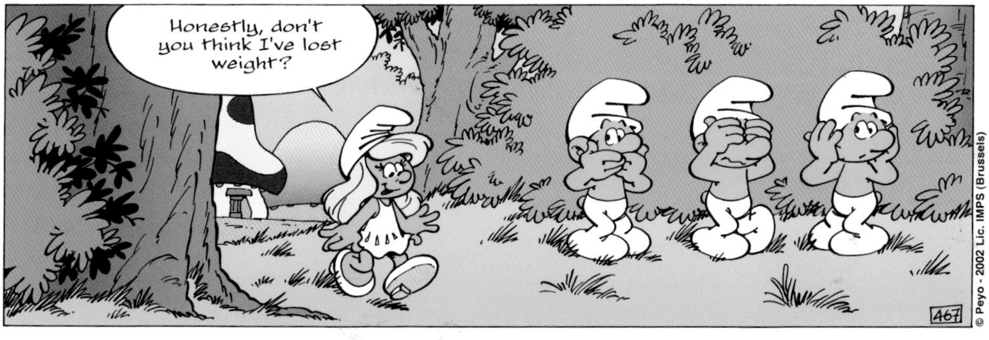

Honestly, don't you think I've lost weight?
467

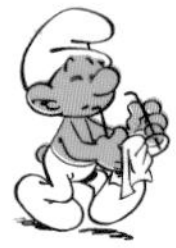

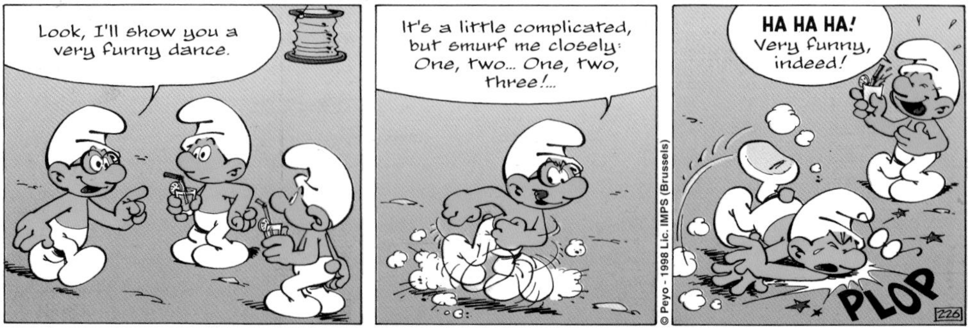
Look, I'll show you a very funny dance.
It's a little complicated, but smurf me closely: One, two... One, two, three!...
HA HA HA! Very funny, indeed!
PLOP
226

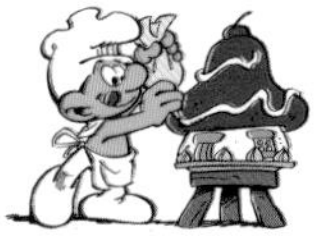

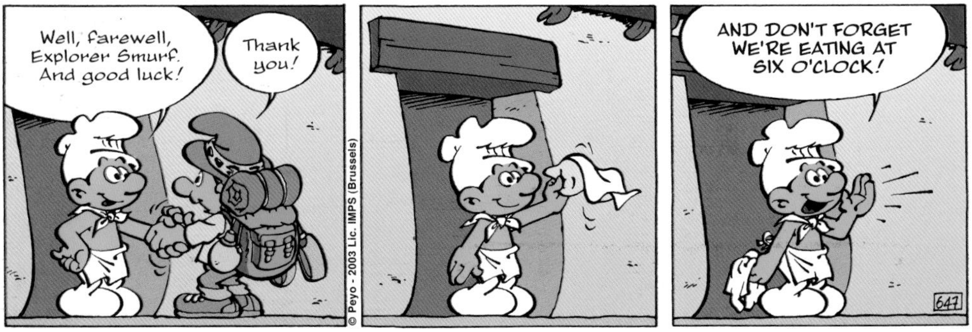
Well, farewell, Explorer Smurf. And good luck!
Thank you!
AND DON'T FORGET WE'RE EATING AT SIX O'CLOCK!
647

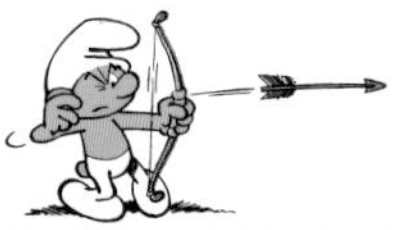

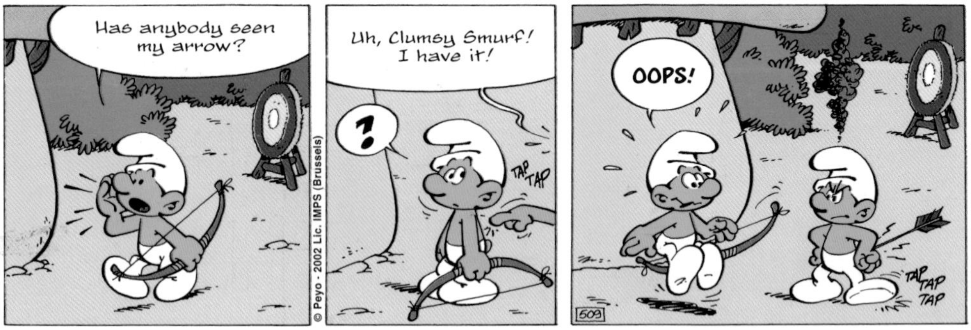
Has anybody seen my arrow?
?
Uh, Clumsy Smurf! I have it!
TAP TAP
OOPS!
TAP TAP TAP
509

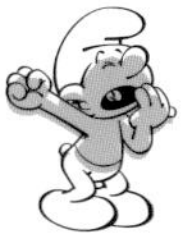

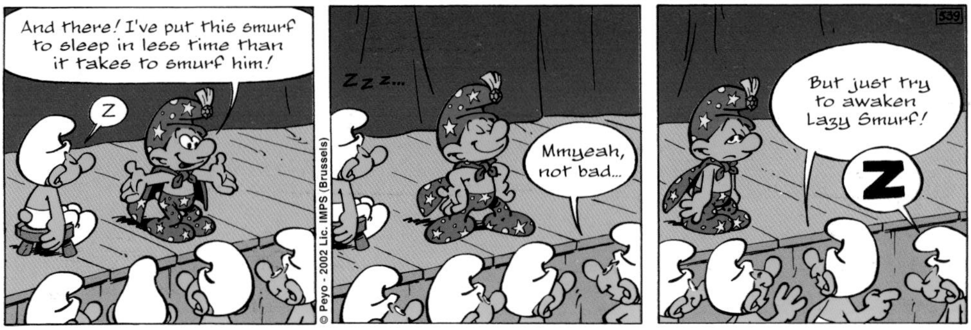
539
And there! I've put this smurf to sleep in less time than it takes to smurf him!
Z
ZZZ...
© Peyo - 2002 Lic. IMPS (Brussels)
Mmyeah, not bad...
But just try to awaken Lazy Smurf!
Z

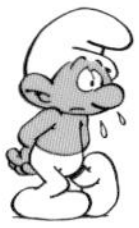

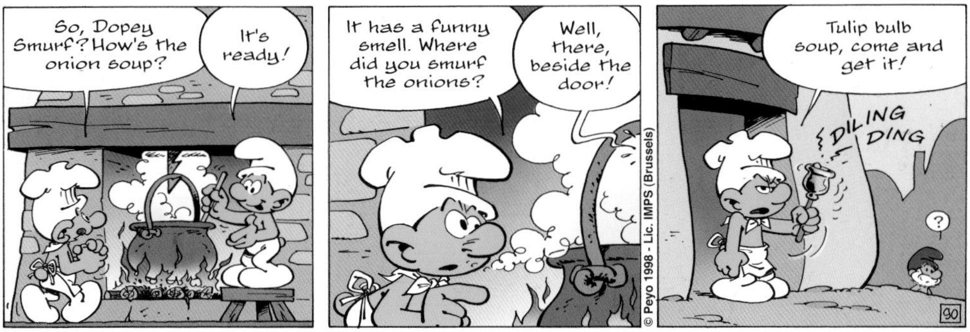
So, Dopey Smurf? How's the onion soup?
It's ready!
It has a funny smell. Where did you smurf the onions?
Well, there, beside the door!
© Peyo 1998 - Lic. IMPS (Brussels)
Tulip bulb soup, come and get it!
DILING DING
?
90

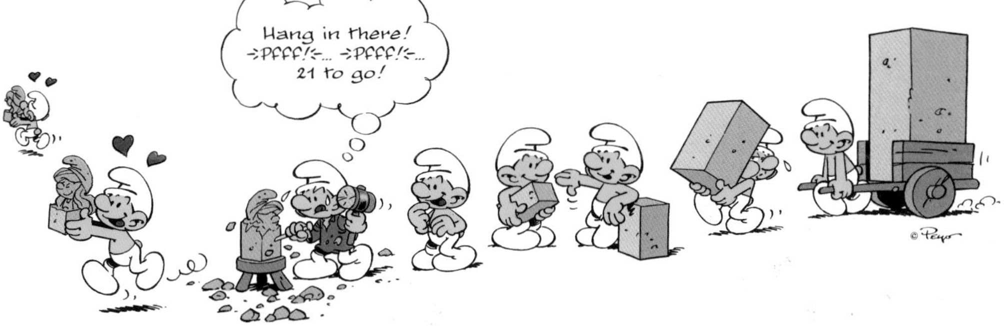
Hang in there!
PFFF!... PFFF!...
21 to go!
© Peyo

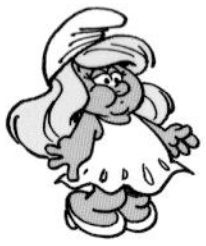

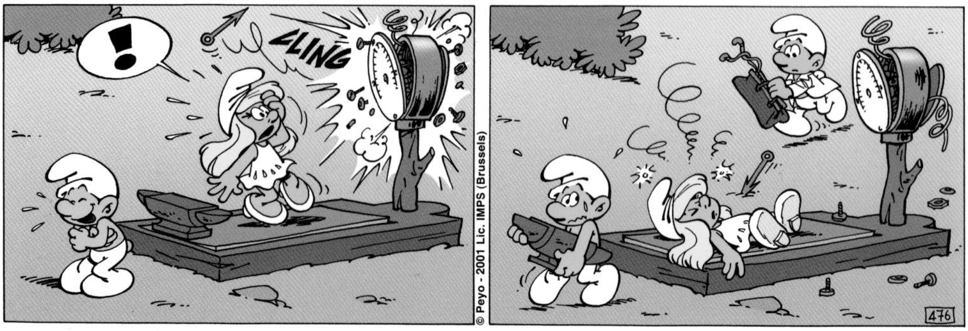
!
CLING
© Peyo - 2001 Lic. IMPS (Brussels)
476

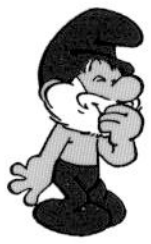

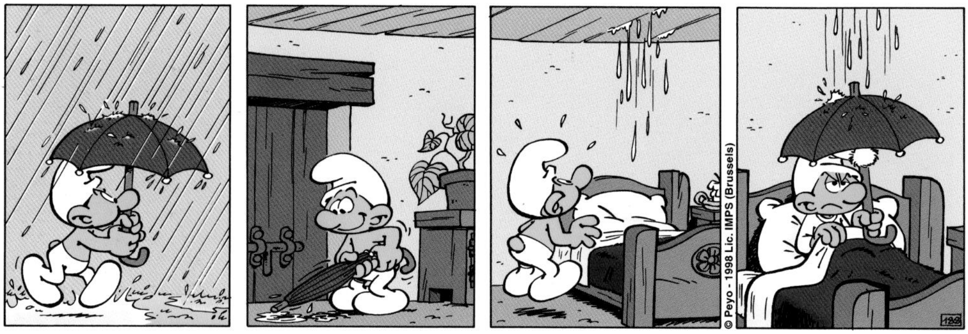
© Peyo - 1998 Lic. IMPS (Brussels)

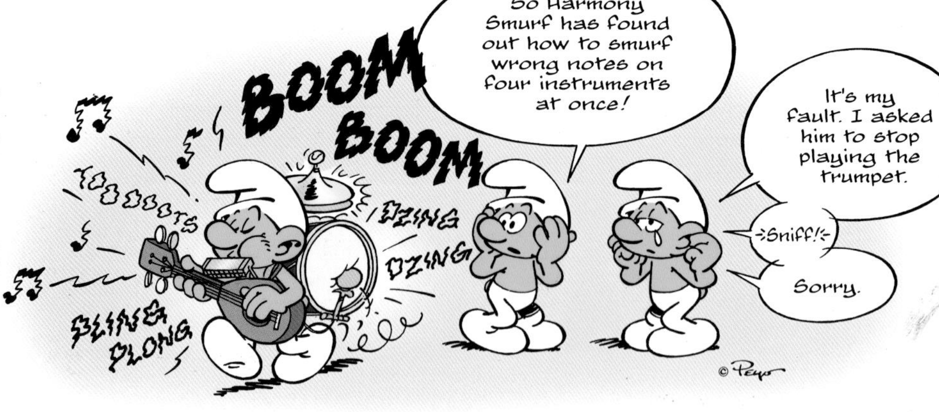
BOOM
BOOM
TOOOOOTS
DZING
DZING
PLING
PLONG
So Harmony Smurf has found out how to smurf wrong notes on four instruments at once!
It's my fault. I asked him to stop playing the trumpet.
Sniff!
Sorry.
© Peyo

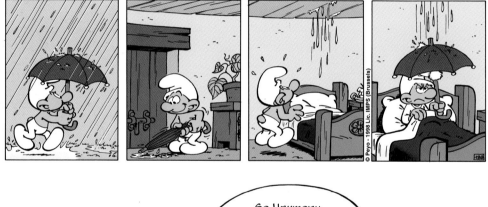

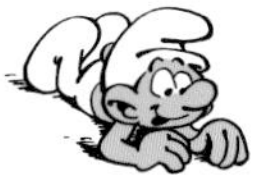

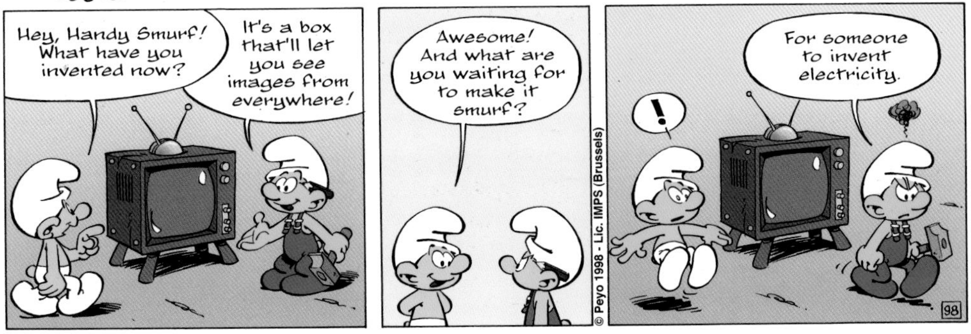

Hey, Handy Smurf! What have you invented now?
It's a box that'll let you see images from everywhere!
Awesome! And what are you waiting for to make it smurf?
© Peyo 1998 - Lic. IMPS (Brussels)
!
For someone to invent electricity.
98

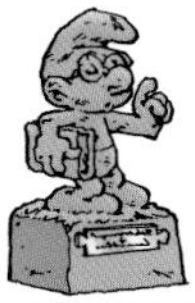

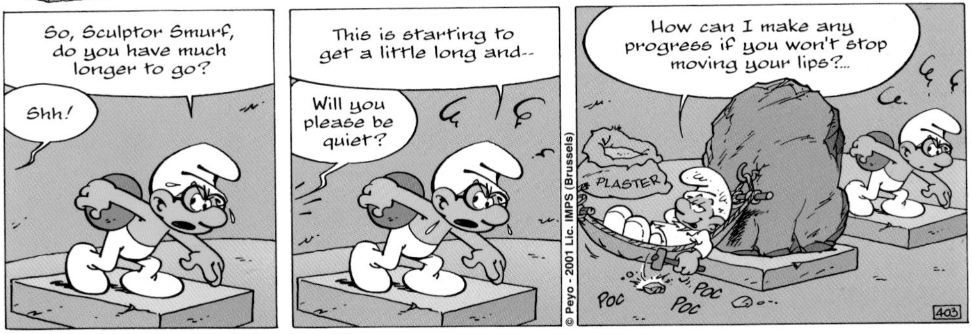

So, Sculptor Smurf, do you have much longer to go?
Shh!
This is starting to get a little long and--
Will you please be quiet?
© Peyo - 2001 Lic. IMPS (Brussels)
How can I make any progress if you won't stop moving your lips?...
PLASTER
POC
POC
POC
403

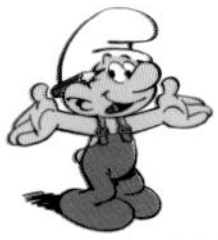

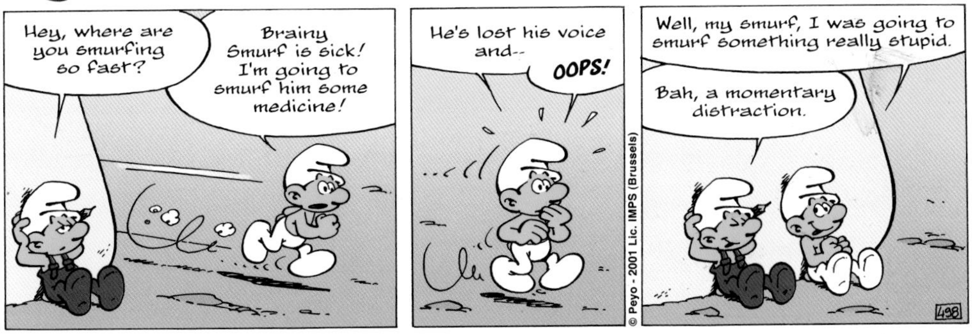

Hey, where are you smurfing so fast?
Brainy Smurf is sick! I'm going to smurf him some medicine!
He's lost his voice and--
OOPS!
© Peyo - 2001 Lic. IMPS (Brussels)
Well, my smurf, I was going to smurf something really stupid.
Bah, a momentary distraction.
498

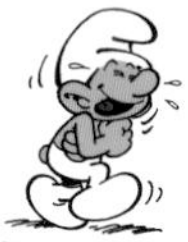

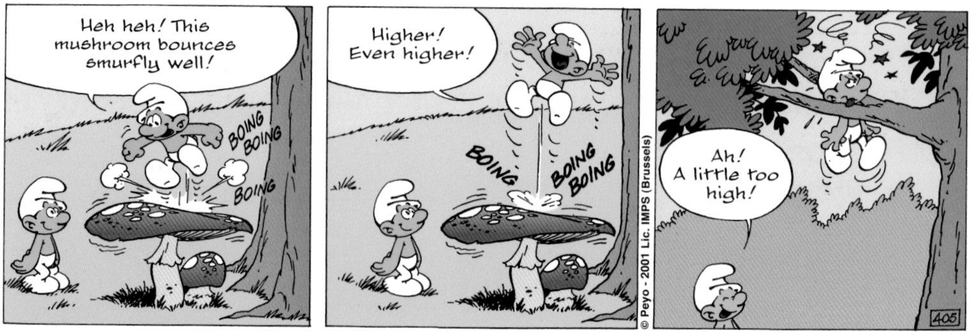
Heh heh! This mushroom bounces smurfly well!
BOING BOING
BOING
Higher! Even higher!
BOING
BOING BOING
© Peyo - 2001 Lic. IMPS (Brussels)
Ah! A little too high!
405

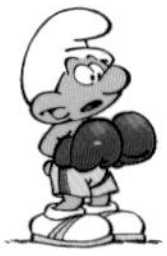

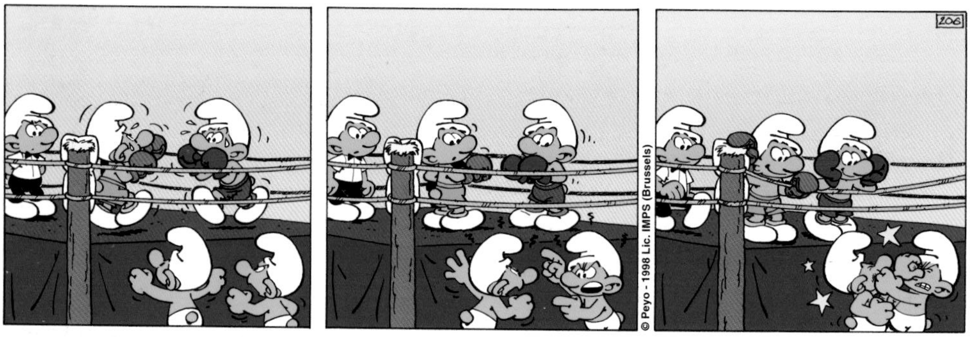
206
© Peyo - 1998 Lic. IMPS (Brussels)

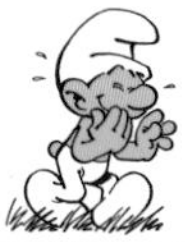

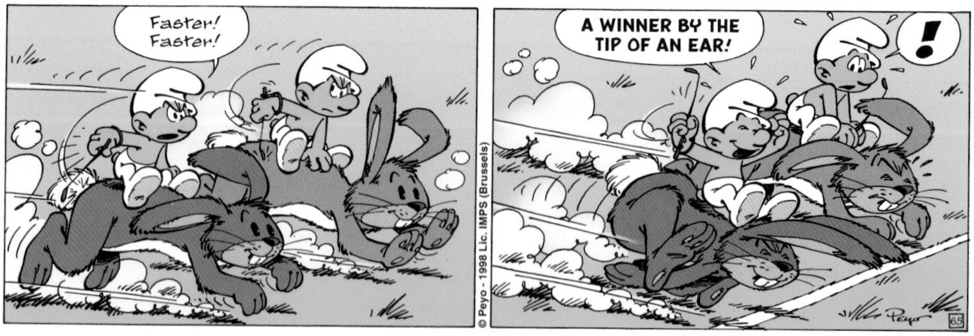
Faster! Faster!
© Peyo - 1998 Lic. IMPS (Brussels)
A WINNER BY THE TIP OF AN EAR!
!
Peyo
65

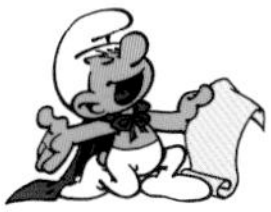

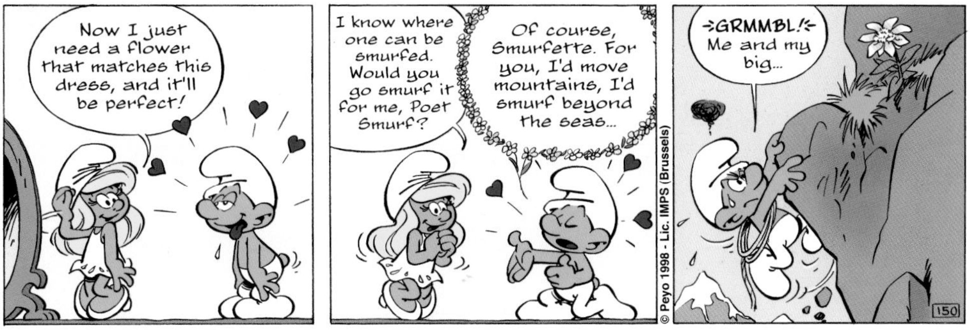
Now I just need a flower that matches this dress, and it'll be perfect!
I know where one can be smurfed. Would you go smurf it for me, Poet Smurf?
Of course, Smurfette. For you, I'd move mountains, I'd smurf beyond the seas...
© Peyo 1998 - Lic. IMPS (Brussels)
-GRMMBL!- Me and my big...
150

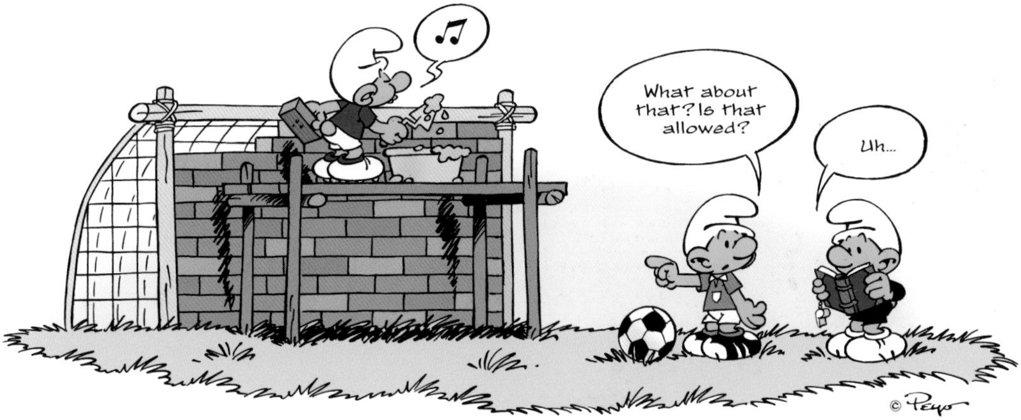
What about that? Is that allowed?
Uh...
© Peyo

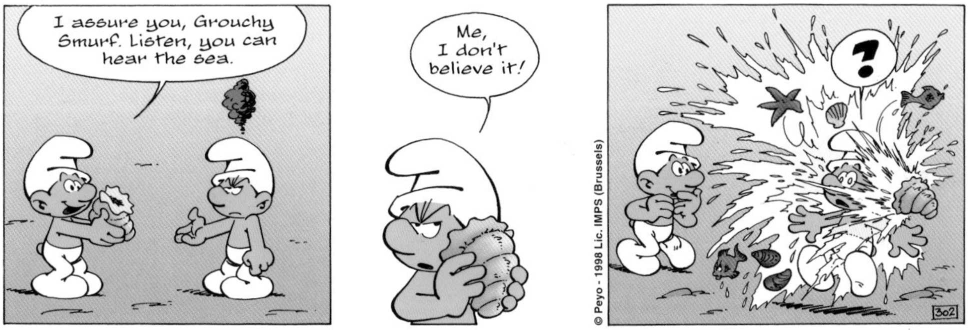
I assure you, Grouchy Smurf. Listen, you can hear the sea.
Me, I don't believe it!
© Peyo - 1998 Lic. IMPS (Brussels)
?
302

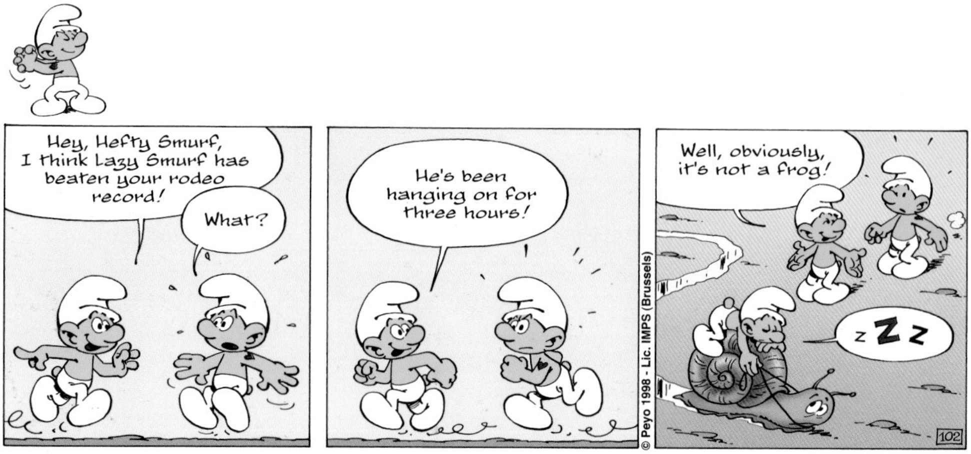
Hey, Hefty Smurf, I think Lazy Smurf has beaten your rodeo record!
What?
He's been hanging on for three hours!
© Peyo 1998 - Lic. IMPS (Brussels)
Well, obviously, it's not a frog!
z Z Z
102

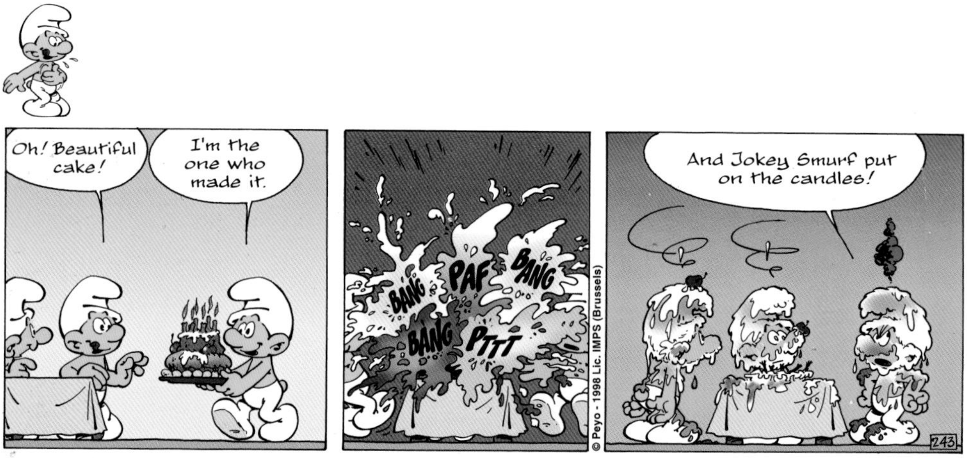
Oh! Beautiful cake!
I'm the one who made it.
BANG
PAF
BANG
BANG
PTTT
© Peyo - 1998 Lic. IMPS (Brussels)
And Jokey Smurf put on the candles!
243

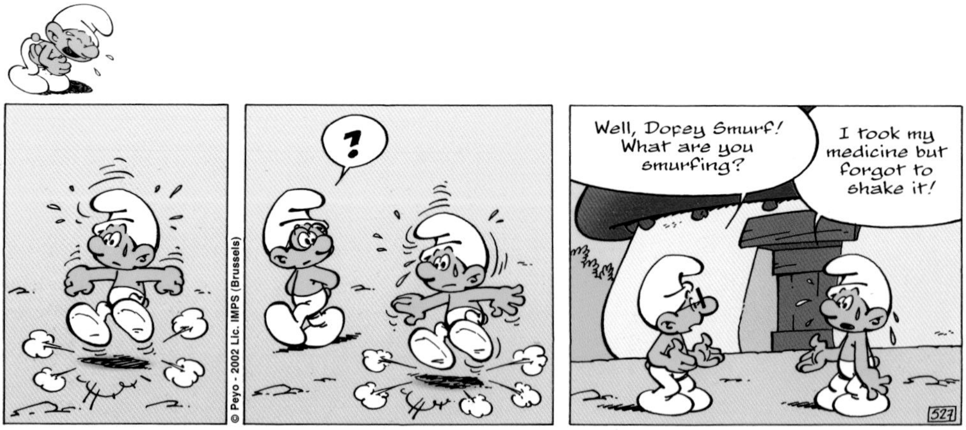
© Peyo - 2002 Lic. IMPS (Brussels)
?
Well, Dopey Smurf! What are you smurfing?
I took my medicine but forgot to shake it!
327

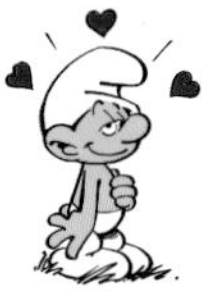

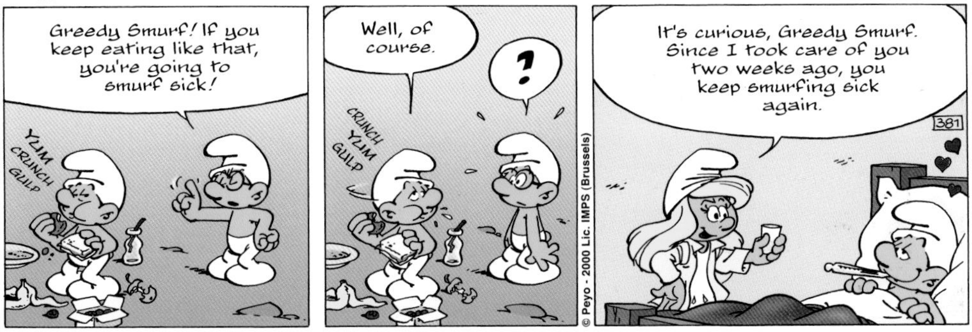

Greedy Smurf! If you keep eating like that, you're going to smurf sick!
YUM CRUNCH GULP
Well, of course.
CRUNCH YUM GULP
?
It's curious, Greedy Smurf. Since I took care of you two weeks ago, you keep smurfing sick again.
381
© Peyo - 2000 Lic. IMPS (Brussels)

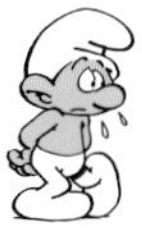

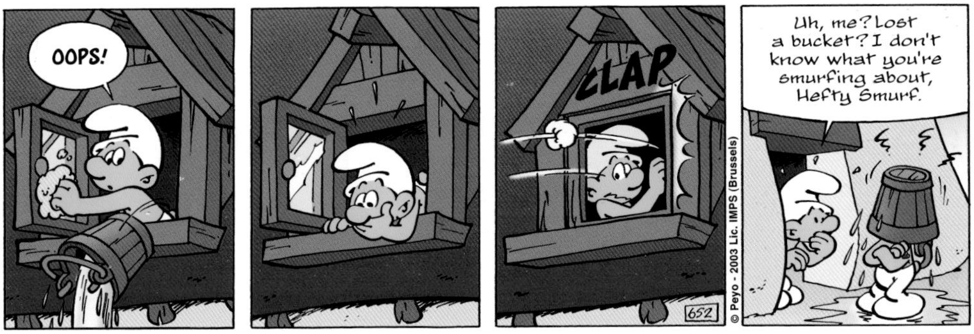

OOPS!
CLAP
652
© Peyo - 2003 Lic. IMPS (Brussels)
Uh, me? Lost a bucket? I don't know what you're smurfing about, Hefty Smurf.

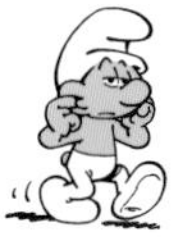

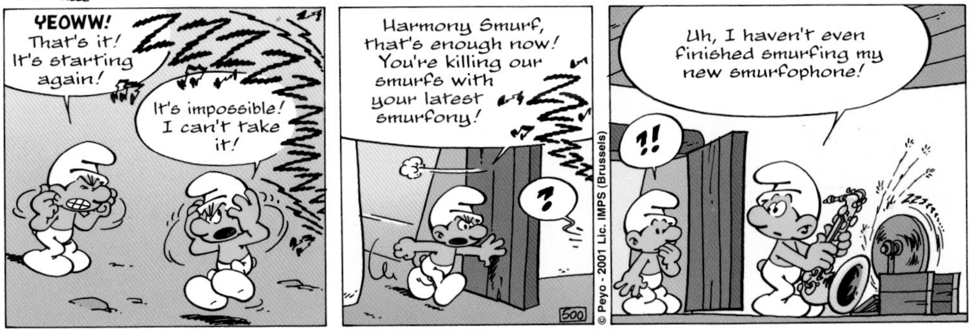

YEOWW! That's it! It's starting again!
It's impossible! I can't take it!
Harmony Smurf, that's enough now! You're killing our smurfs with your latest smurfony!
?
500
© Peyo - 2001 Lic. IMPS (Brussels)
?!
Uh, I haven't even finished smurfing my new smurfophone!

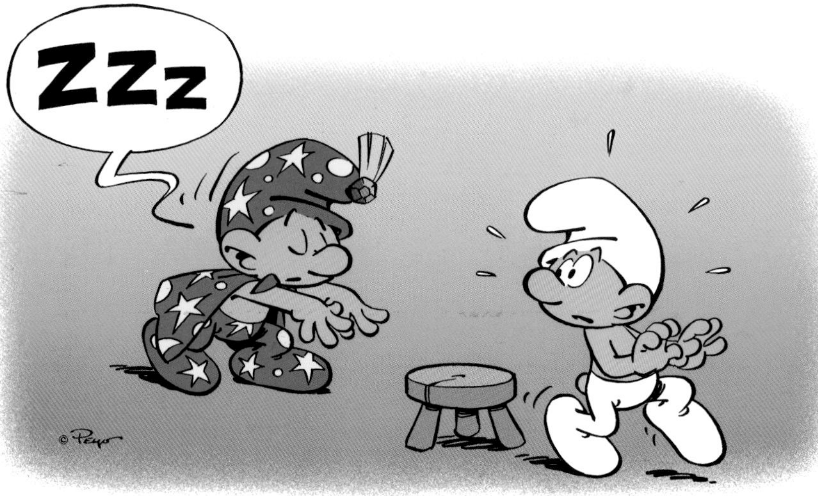
ZZz
© Peyo

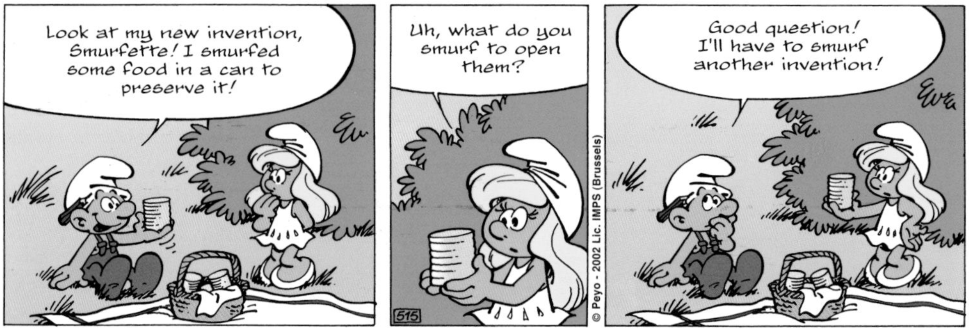
Look at my new invention, Smurfette! I smurfed some food in a can to preserve it!
Uh, what do you smurf to open them?
515
© Peyo - 2002 Lic. IMPS (Brussels)
Good question! I'll have to smurf another invention!

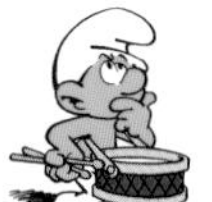

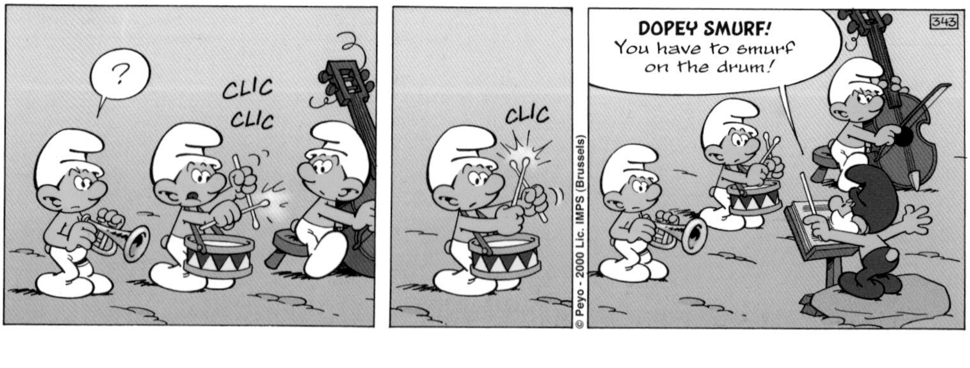
?
CLIC
CLIC
CLIC
© Peyo - 2000 Lic. IMPS (Brussels)
343
DOPEY SMURF! You have to smurf on the drum!

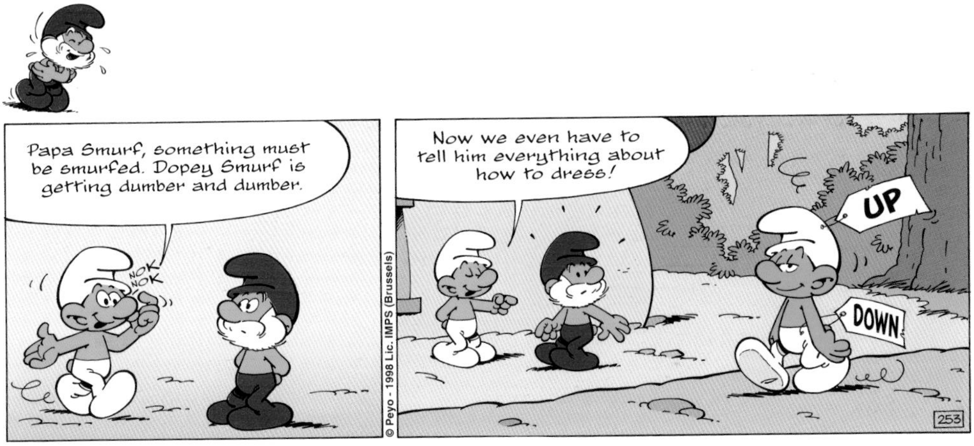
Papa Smurf, something must be smurfed. Dopey Smurf is getting dumber and dumber.
NOK NOK
© Peyo - 1998 Lic. IMPS (Brussels)
Now we even have to tell him everything about how to dress!
UP
DOWN
253

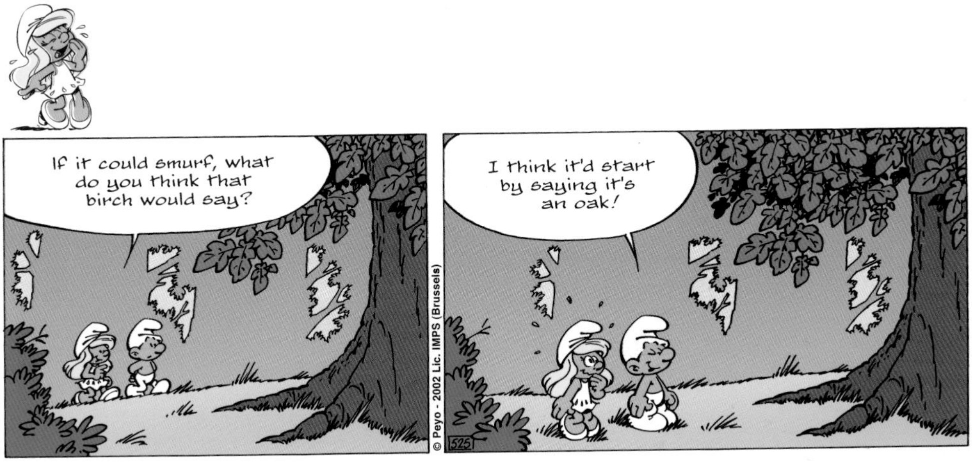
If it could smurf, what do you think that birch would say?
© Peyo - 2002 Lic. IMPS (Brussels)
525
I think it'd start by saying it's an oak!

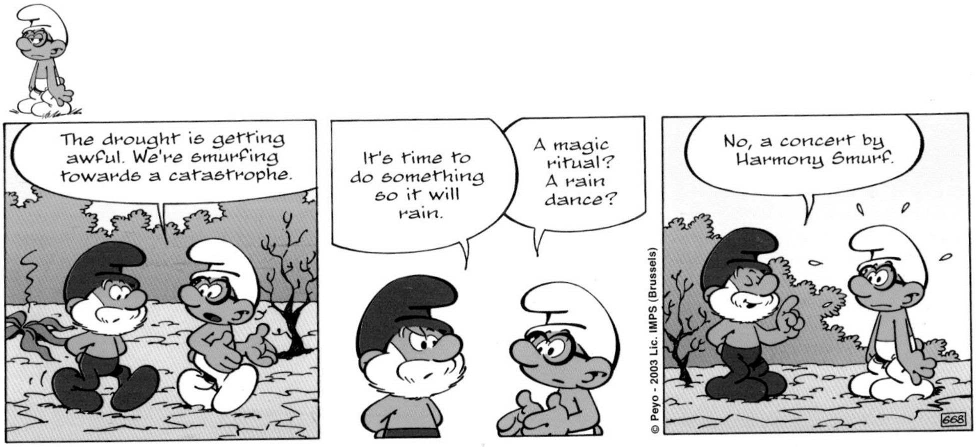
The drought is getting awful. We're smurfing towards a catastrophe.
It's time to do something so it will rain.
A magic ritual? A rain dance?
© Peyo - 2003 Lic. IMPS (Brussels)
No, a concert by Harmony Smurf.
668

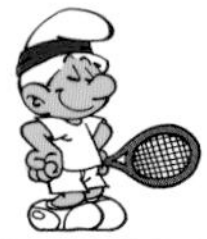

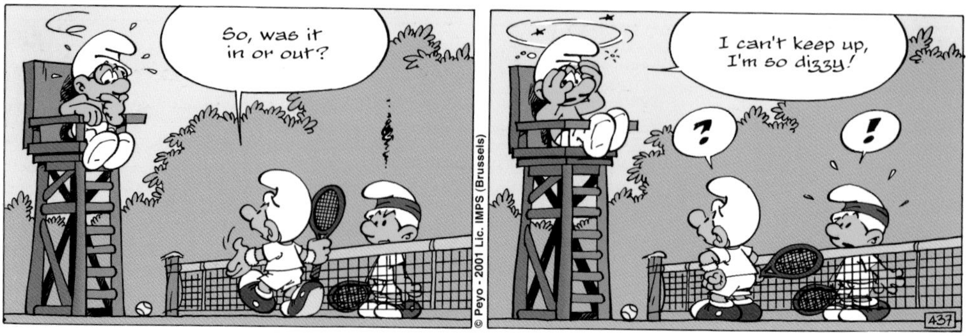

So, was it in or out?
© Peyo - 2001 Lic. IMPS (Brussels)
I can't keep up, I'm so dizzy!
?
!
437

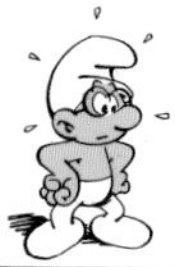

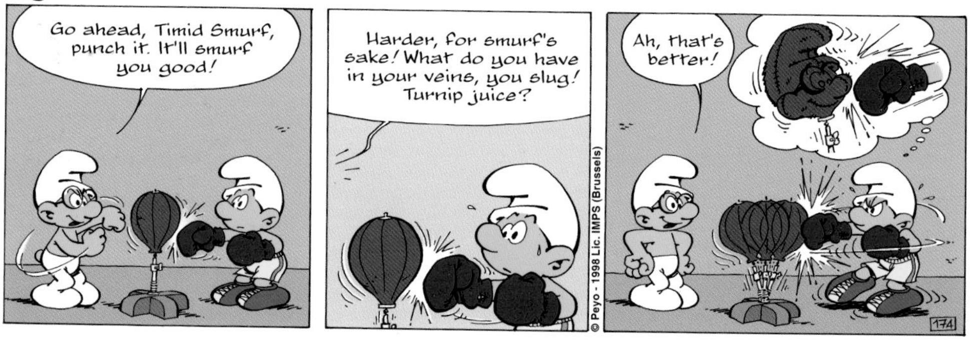

Go ahead, Timid Smurf, punch it. It'll smurf you good!
Harder, for smurf's sake! What do you have in your veins, you slug! Turnip juice?
© Peyo - 1998 Lic. IMPS (Brussels)
Ah, that's better!
174

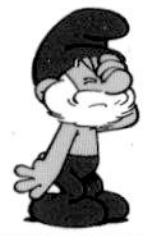

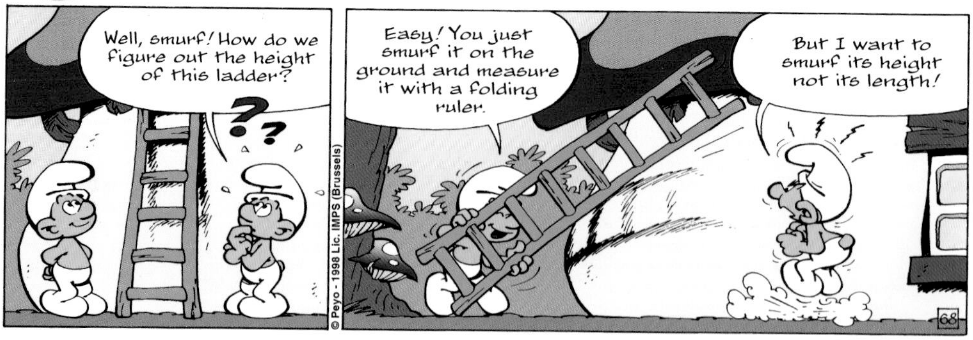

Well, smurf! How do we figure out the height of this ladder?
??
© Peyo - 1998 Lic. IMPS (Brussels)
Easy! You just smurf it on the ground and measure it with a folding ruler.
But I want to smurf its height not its length!
68

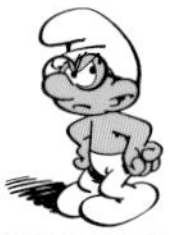

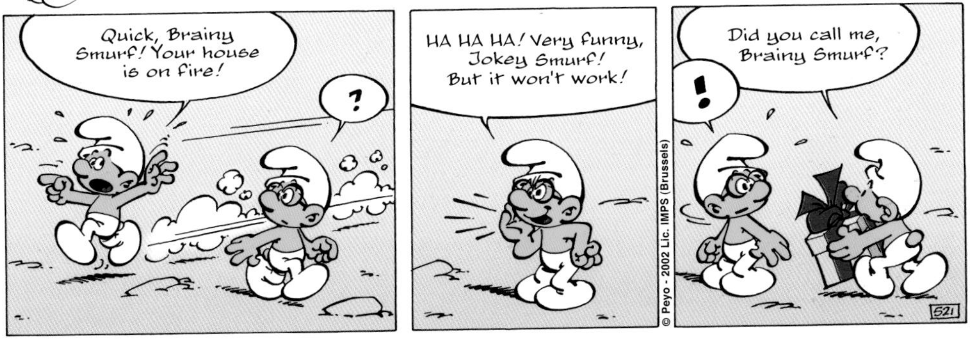
Quick, Brainy Smurf! Your house is on fire!
?
HA HA HA! Very funny, Jokey Smurf! But it won't work!
!
Did you call me, Brainy Smurf?
© Peyo - 2002 Lic. IMPS (Brussels)
521

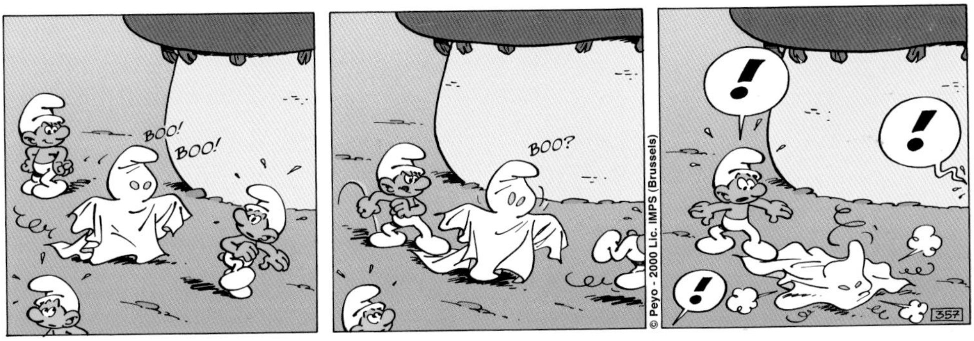
BOO!
BOO!
BOO?
!
!
!
© Peyo - 2000 Lic. IMPS (Brussels)
357

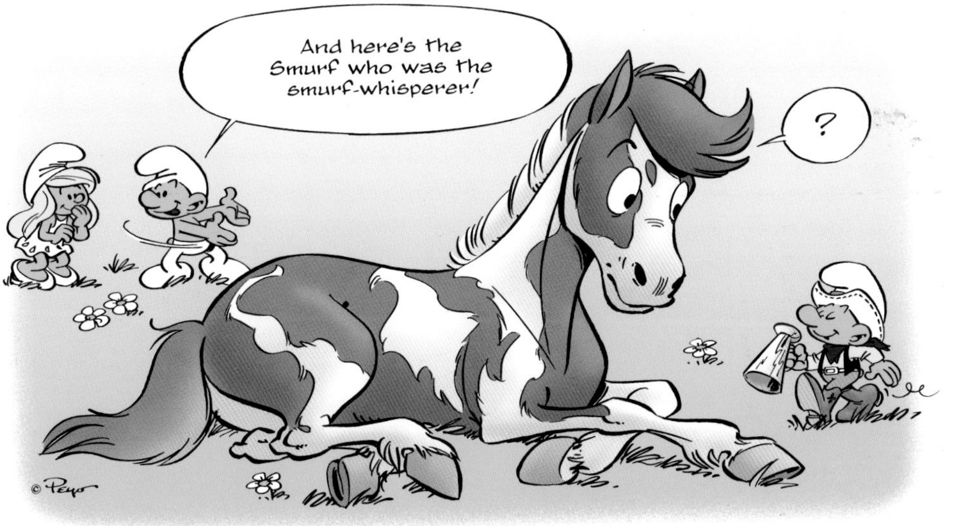
And here's the Smurf who was the smurf-whisperer!
?
© Peyo

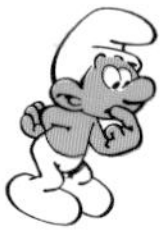

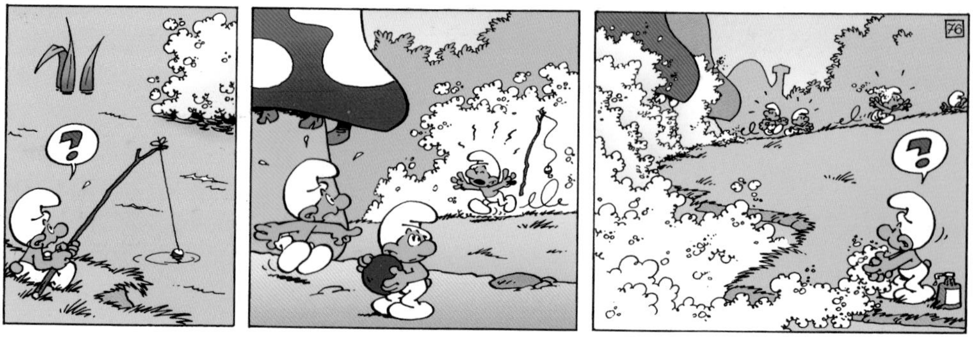
?
76
?

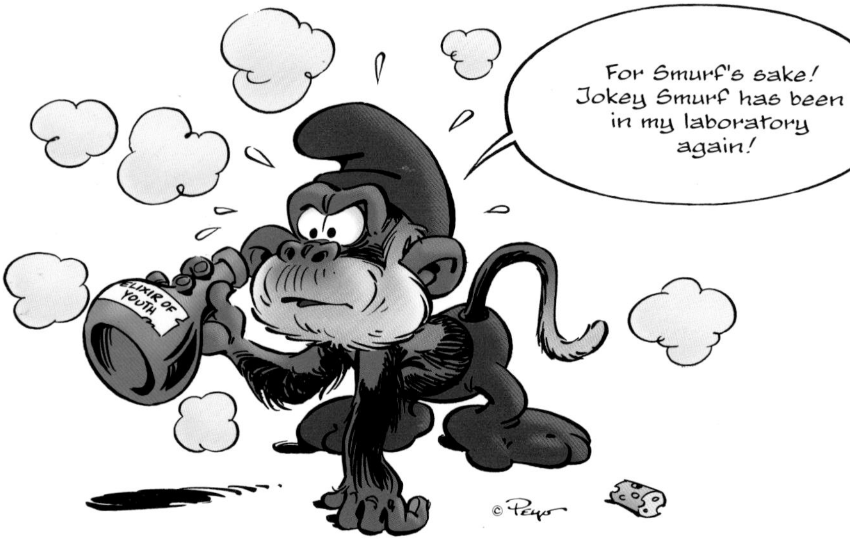
For Smurf's sake! Jokey Smurf has been in my laboratory again!
ELIXIR OF YOUTH
© Peyo

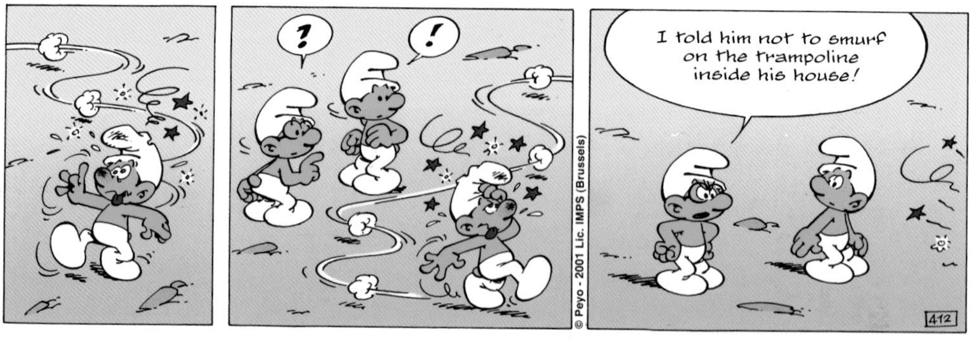
?
!
I told him not to smurf on the trampoline inside his house!
© Peyo - 2001 Lic. IMPS (Brussels)
412

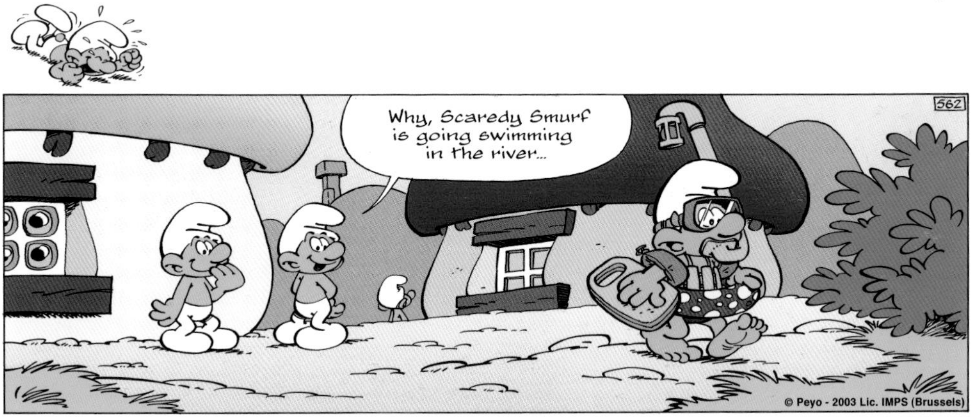
562
Why, Scaredy Smurf is going swimming in the river...
© Peyo - 2003 Lic. IMPS (Brussels)

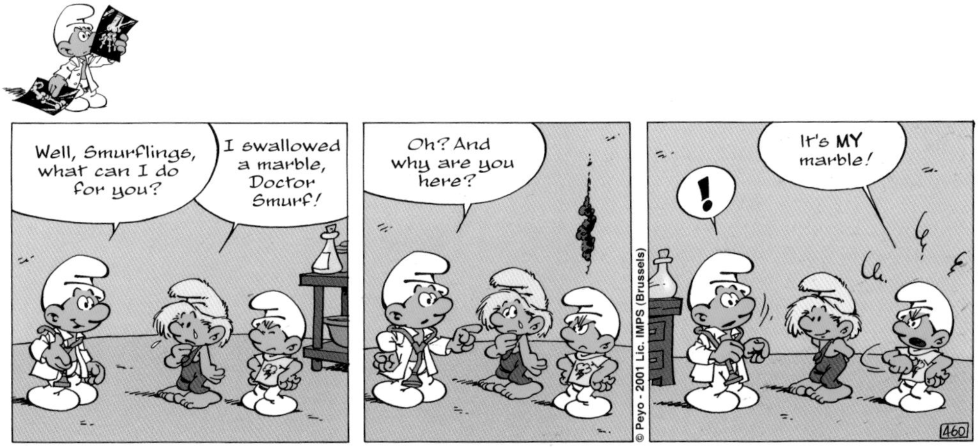
Well, Smurflings, what can I do for you?
I swallowed a marble, Doctor Smurf!
Oh? And why are you here?
© Peyo - 2001 Lic. IMPS (Brussels)
!
It's **MY** marble!
460

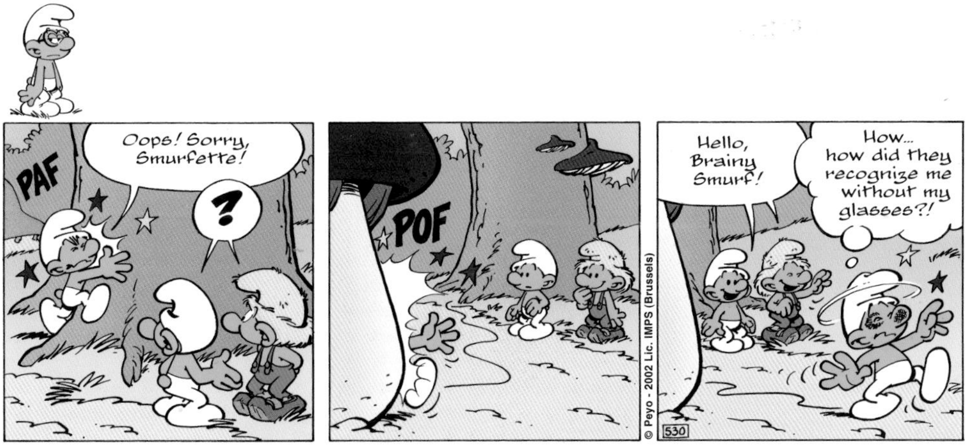
PAF
Oops! Sorry, Smurfette!
?
POF
© Peyo - 2002 Lic. IMPS (Brussels)
Hello, Brainy Smurf!
How... how did they recognize me without my glasses?!
530

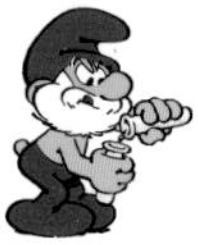

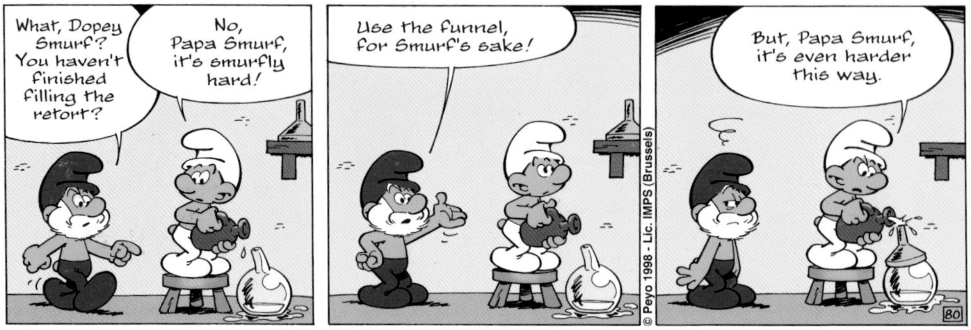
What, Dopey Smurf? You haven't finished filling the retort?
No, Papa Smurf, it's smurfly hard!
Use the funnel, for Smurf's sake!
© Peyo 1998 - Lic. IMPS (Brussels)
But, Papa Smurf, it's even harder this way.
80

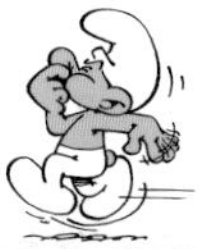

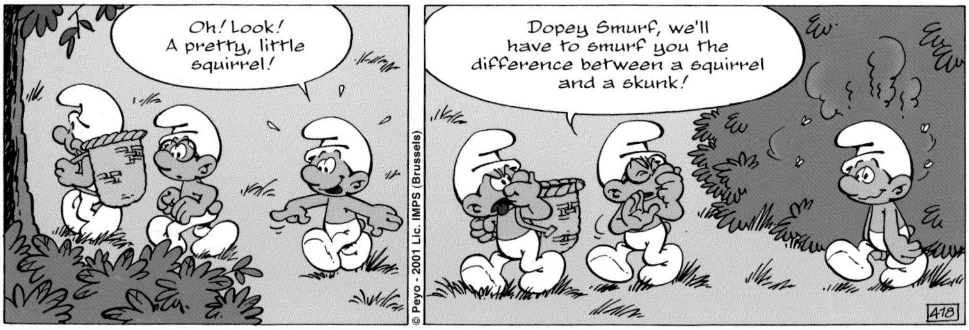
Oh! Look! A pretty, little squirrel!
© Peyo - 2001 Lic. IMPS (Brussels)
Dopey Smurf, we'll have to smurf you the difference between a squirrel and a skunk!
418

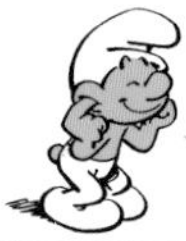

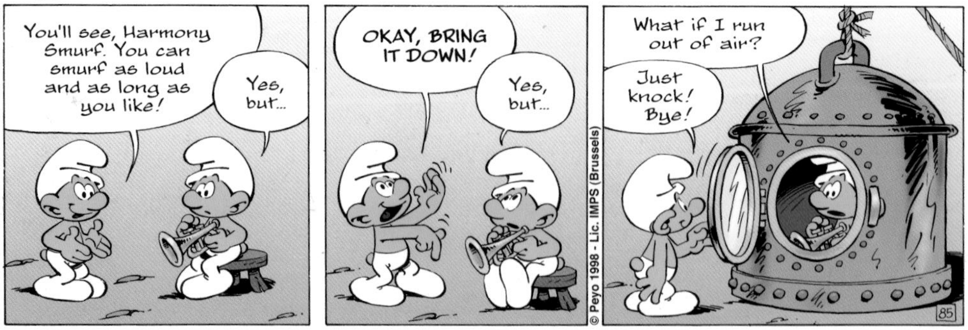
You'll see, Harmony Smurf. You can smurf as loud and as long as you like!
Yes, but...
OKAY, BRING IT DOWN!
Yes, but...
© Peyo 1998 - Lic. IMPS (Brussels)
What if I run out of air?
Just knock! Bye!
85

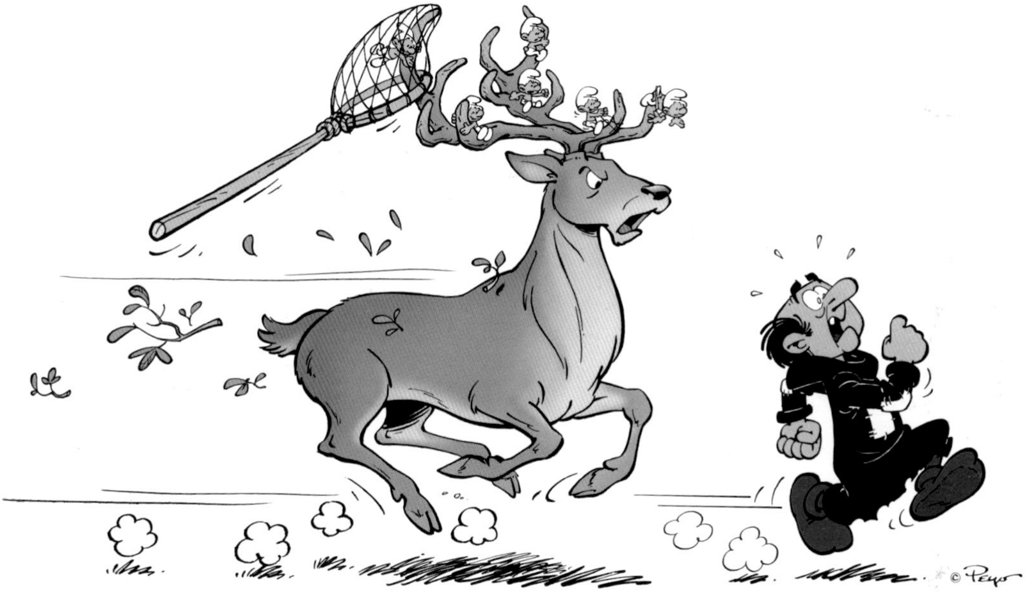
© Peyo

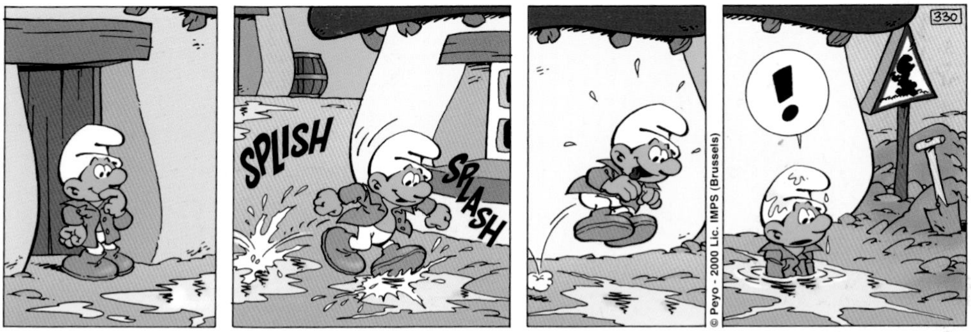
330
SPLISH
SPLASH
!
© Peyo - 2000 Lic. IMPS (Brussels)

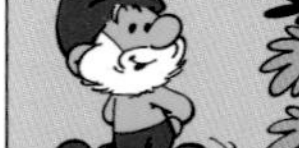

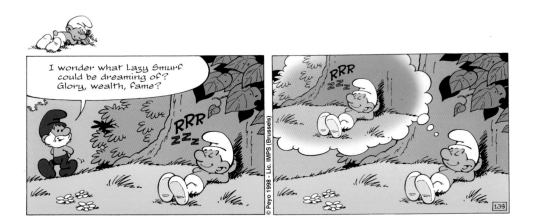

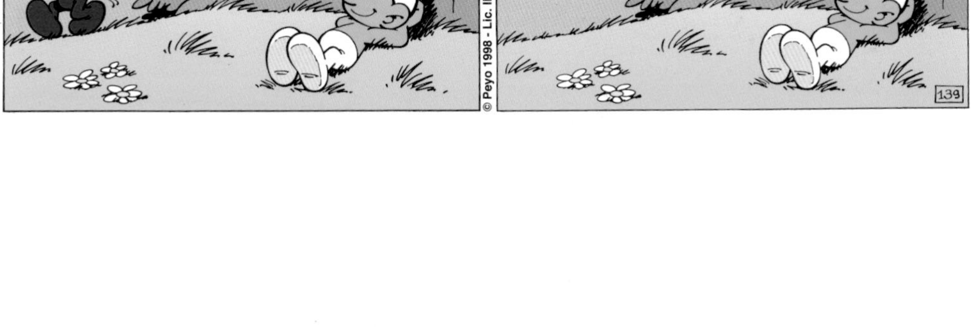
I wonder what Lazy Smurf could be dreaming of? Glory, wealth, fame?
RRR
ZZZ
© Peyo 1998 - Lic. IMPS (Brussels)
RRR
ZZZ
139

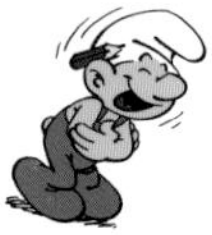

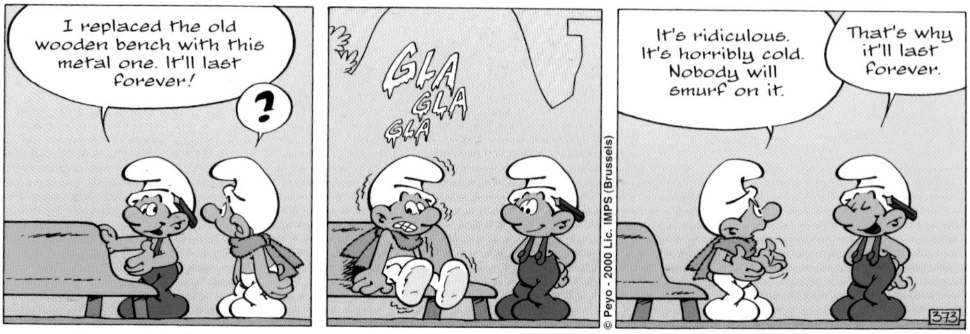
I replaced the old wooden bench with this metal one. It'll last forever!
?
GLA GLA GLA
It's ridiculous. It's horribly cold. Nobody will smurf on it.
That's why it'll last forever.
373

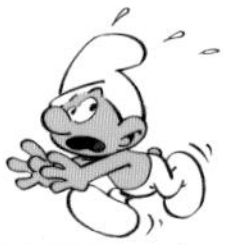

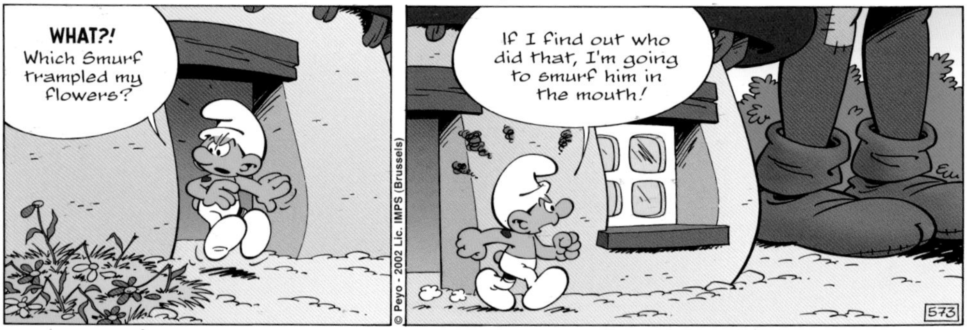
WHAT?! Which Smurf trampled my flowers?
If I find out who did that, I'm going to smurf him in the mouth!
573

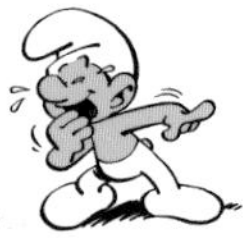

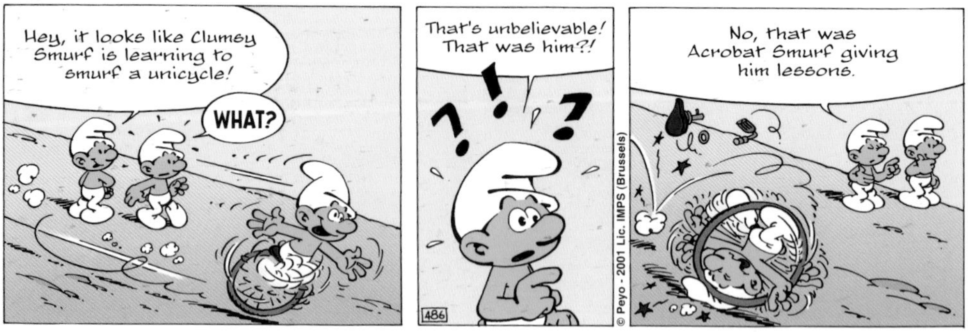
Hey, it looks like Clumsy Smurf is learning to smurf a unicycle!
WHAT?
That's unbelievable! That was him?!
486
No, that was Acrobat Smurf giving him lessons.

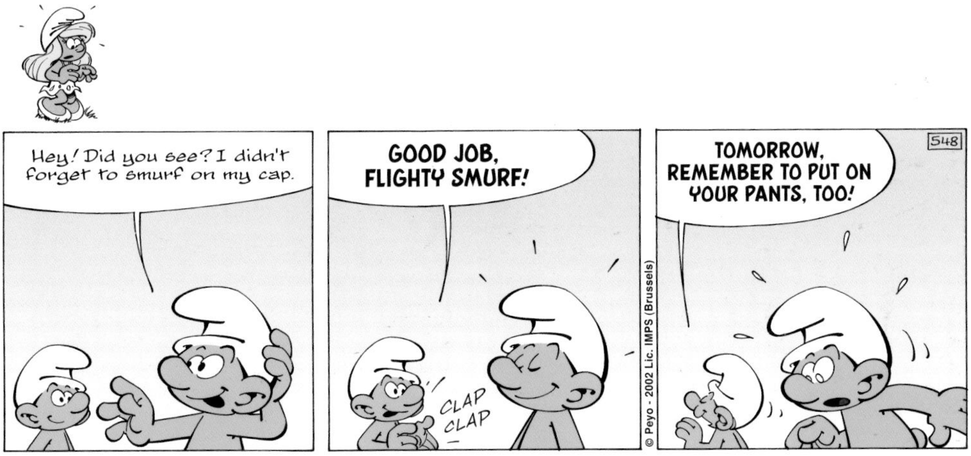
Hey! Did you see? I didn't forget to smurf on my cap.
GOOD JOB, FLIGHTY SMURF!
CLAP CLAP
TOMORROW, REMEMBER TO PUT ON YOUR PANTS, TOO!
548
© Peyo - 2002 Lic. IMPS (Brussels)

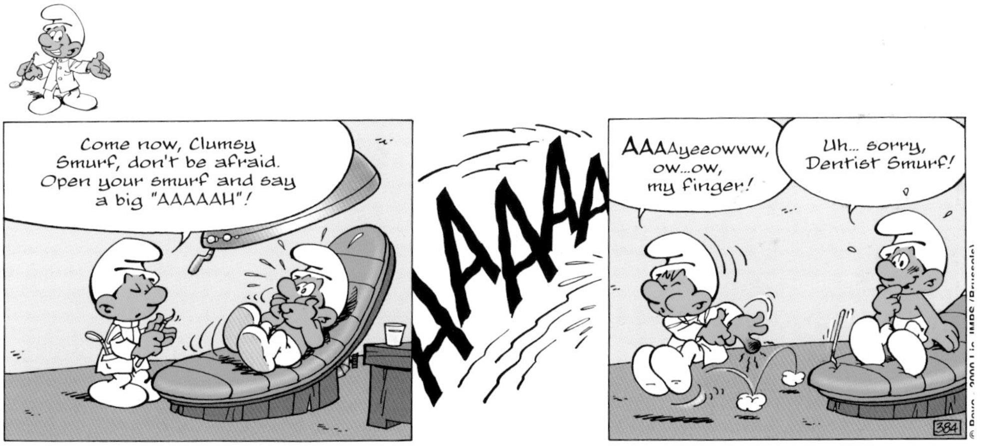
Come now, Clumsy Smurf, don't be afraid. Open your smurf and say a big "AAAAAH"!
AAAAA
AAAAyeeowww, ow...ow, my finger!
Uh... sorry, Dentist Smurf!
384

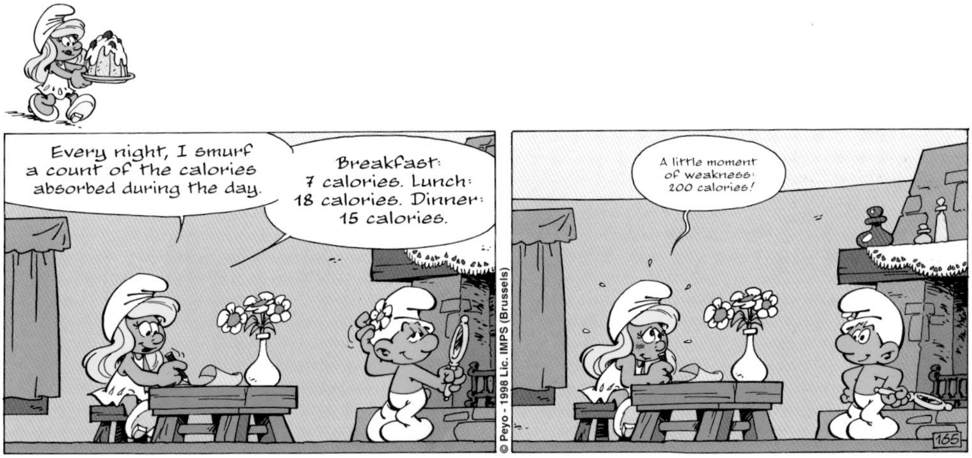
Every night, I smurf a count of the calories absorbed during the day.
Breakfast: 7 calories. Lunch: 18 calories. Dinner: 15 calories.
© Peyo - 1998 Lic. IMPS (Brussels)
A little moment of weakness: 200 calories!
165

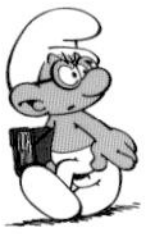

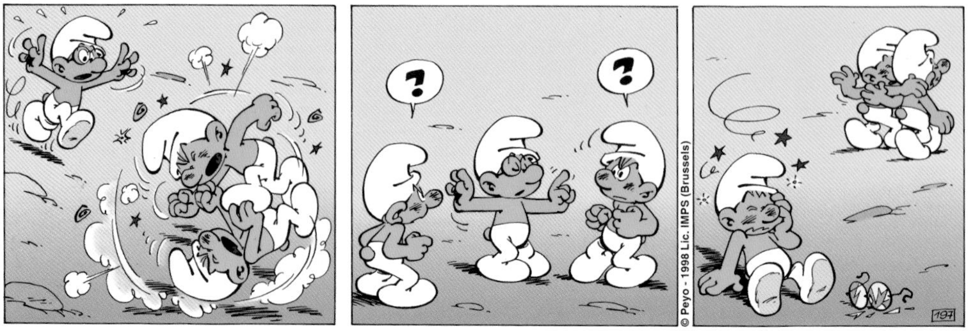
?
?
© Peyo - 1998 Lic. IMPS (Brussels)
197

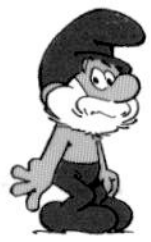

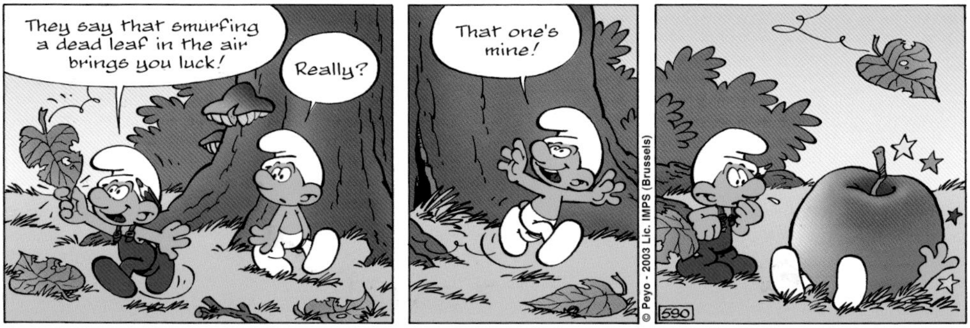
They say that smurfing a dead leaf in the air brings you luck!
Really?
That one's mine!
© Peyo - 2003 Lic. IMPS (Brussels)
590

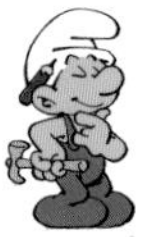

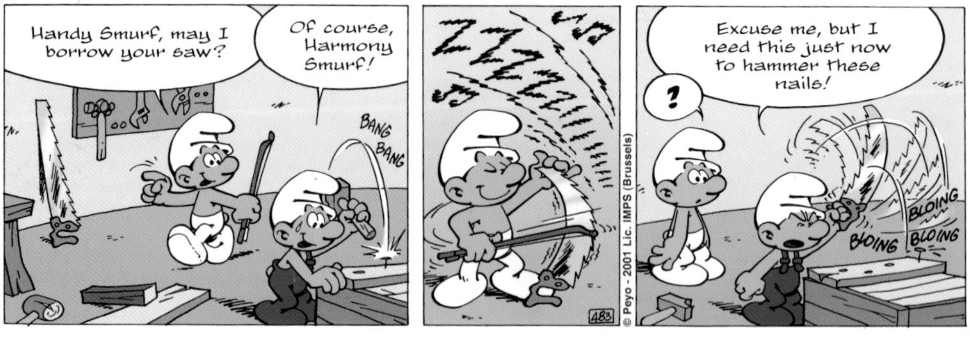
Handy Smurf, may I borrow your saw?
Of course, Harmony Smurf!
BANG
BANG
483
© Peyo - 2001 Lic. IMPS (Brussels)
?
Excuse me, but I need this just now to hammer these nails!
BLOING
BLOING
BLOING

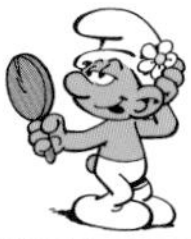

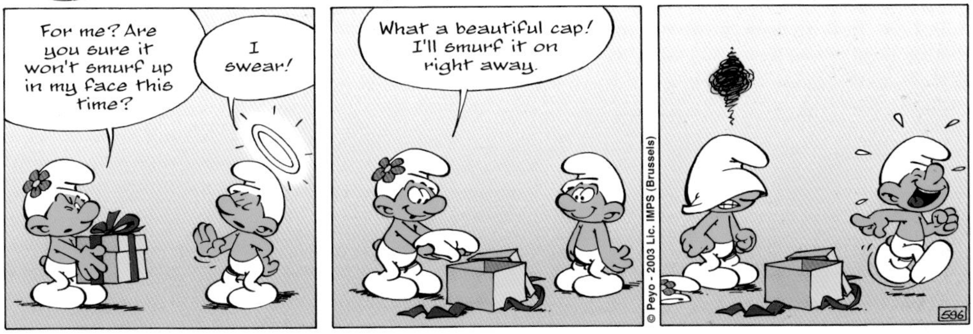
For me? Are you sure it won't smurf up in my face this time?
I swear!
What a beautiful cap! I'll smurf it on right away.
© Peyo - 2003 Lic. IMPS (Brussels)
596

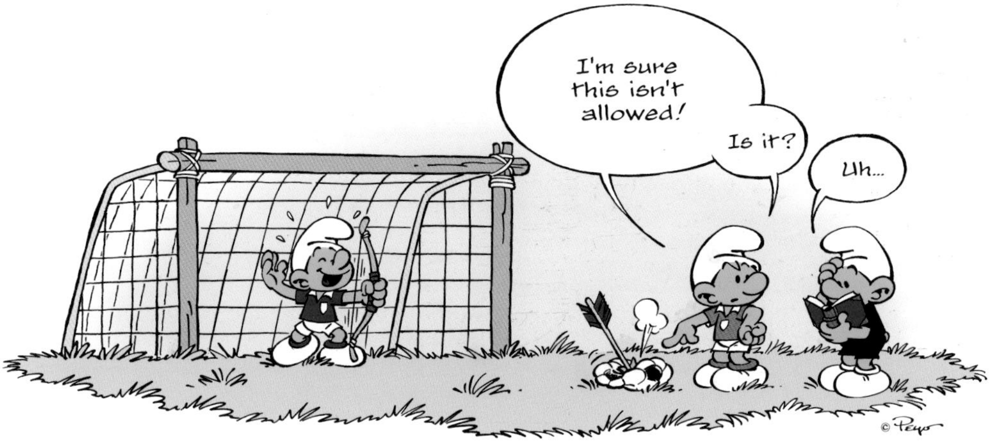
I'm sure this isn't allowed!
Is it?
Uh...
© Peyo

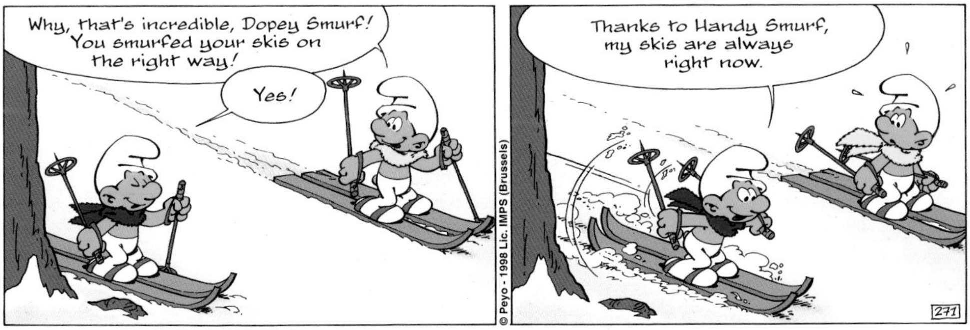
Why, that's incredible, Dopey Smurf! You smurfed your skis on the right way!
Yes!
© Peyo - 1998 Lic. IMPS (Brussels)
Thanks to Handy Smurf, my skis are always right now.
271

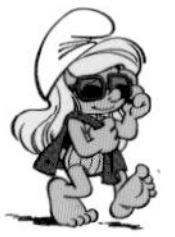

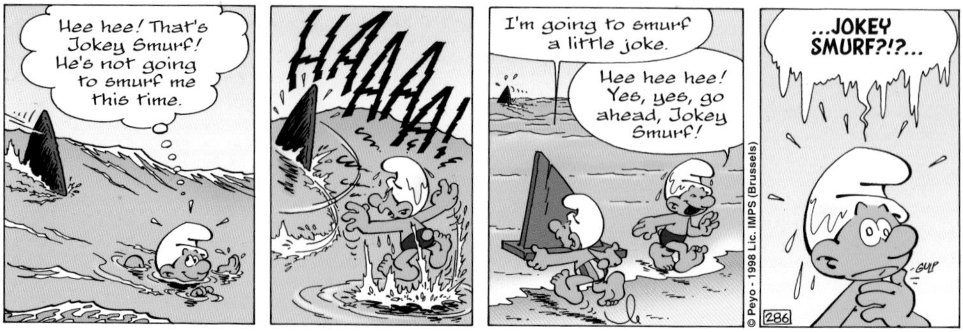
Hee hee! That's Jokey Smurf! He's not going to smurf me this time.
HAAAAI!
I'm going to smurf a little joke.
Hee hee hee! Yes, yes, go ahead, Jokey Smurf!
...JOKEY SMURF?!?...
GULP
© Peyo - 1998 Lic. IMPS (Brussels)
286

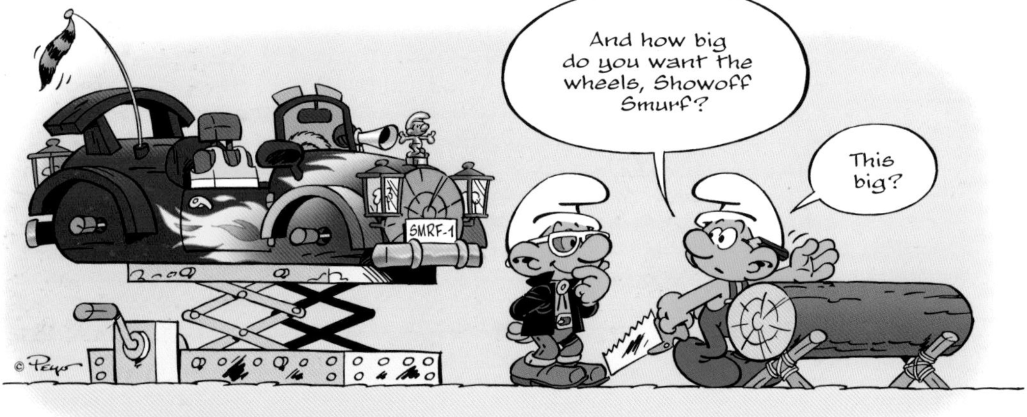
SMRF-1
And how big do you want the wheels, Showoff Smurf?
This big?
© Peyo

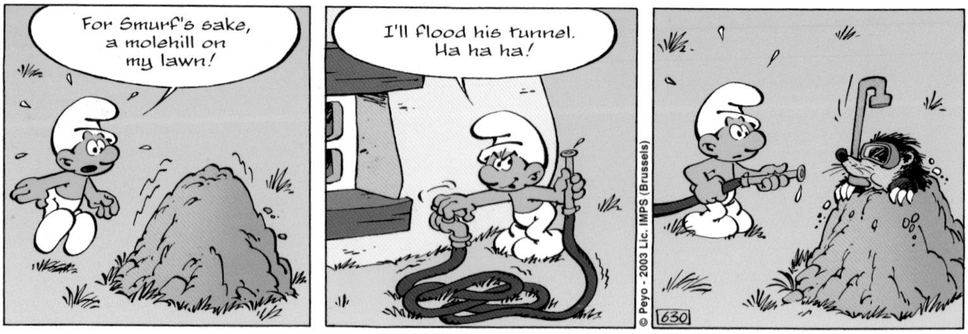
For Smurf's sake, a molehill on my lawn!
I'll flood his tunnel. Ha ha ha!
© Peyo - 2003 Lic. IMPS (Brussels)
630

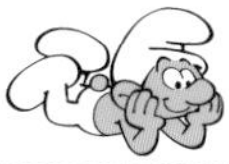

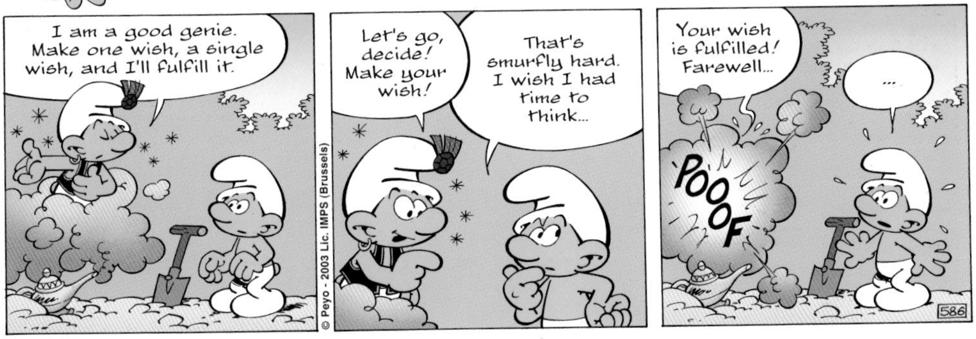
I am a good genie. Make one wish, a single wish, and I'll fulfill it.
Let's go, decide! Make your wish!
That's smurfly hard. I wish I had time to think...
Your wish is fulfilled! Farewell...
POOOF
...
© Peyo - 2003 Lic. IMPS (Brussels)
586

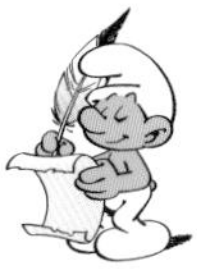

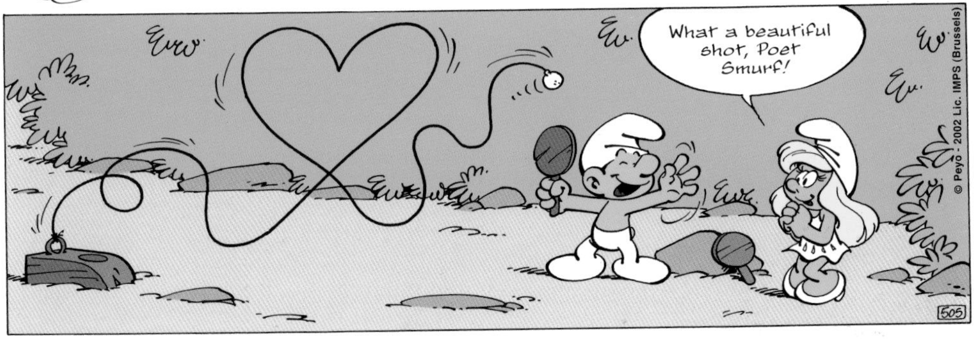
What a beautiful shot, Poet Smurf!
© Peyo - 2002 Lic. IMPS (Brussels)
505

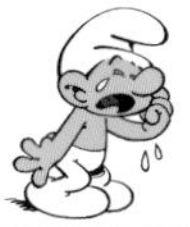

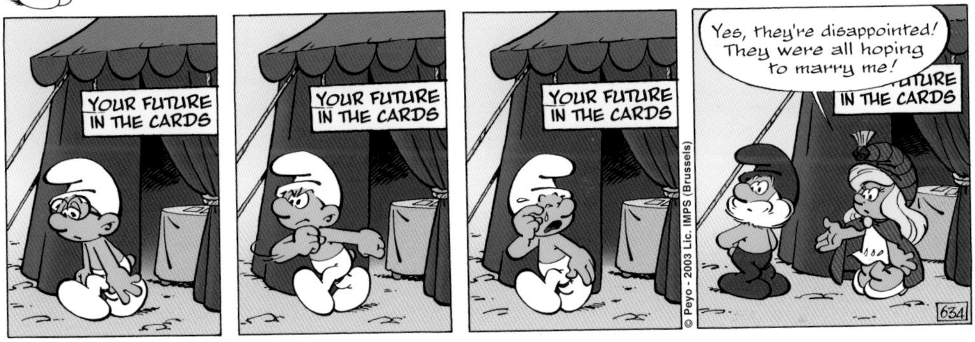
YOUR FUTURE IN THE CARDS
YOUR FUTURE IN THE CARDS
YOUR FUTURE IN THE CARDS
Yes, they're disappointed! They were all hoping to marry me!
© Peyo - 2003 Lic. IMPS (Brussels)
634

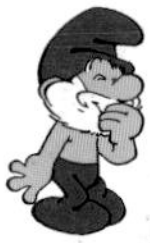

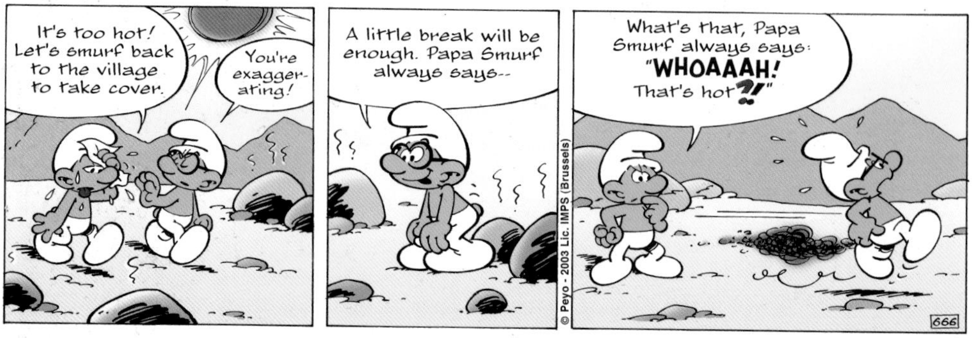
It's too hot! Let's smurf back to the village to take cover.
You're exagger-ating!
A little break will be enough. Papa Smurf always says--
© Peyo - 2003 Lic. IMPS (Brussels)
What's that, Papa Smurf always says: "WHOAAAH! That's hot?!"
666

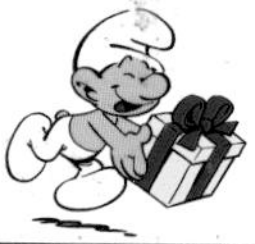

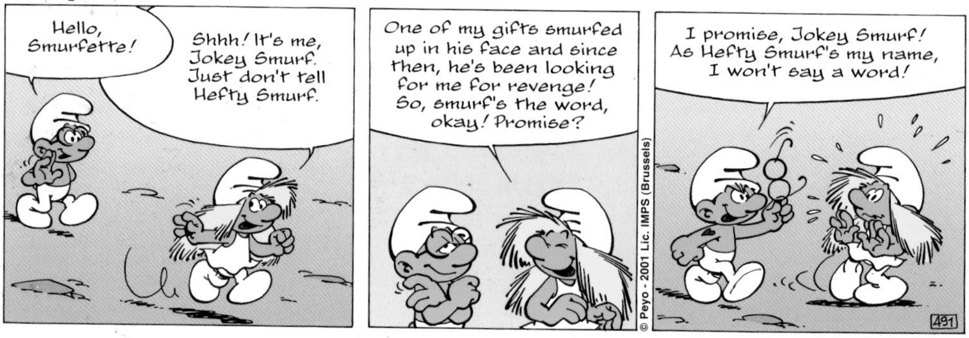
Hello, Smurfette!
Shhh! It's me, Jokey Smurf. Just don't tell Hefty Smurf.
One of my gifts smurfed up in his face and since then, he's been looking for me for revenge! So, smurf's the word, okay! Promise?
© Peyo - 2001 Lic. IMPS (Brussels)
I promise, Jokey Smurf! As Hefty Smurf's my name, I won't say a word!
491

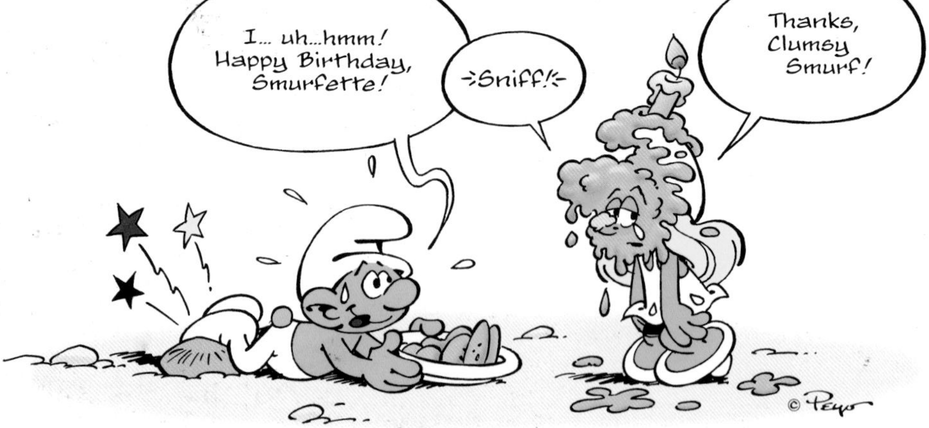
I... uh...hmm! Happy Birthday, Smurfette!
-Sniff!-
Thanks, Clumsy Smurf!
© Peyo

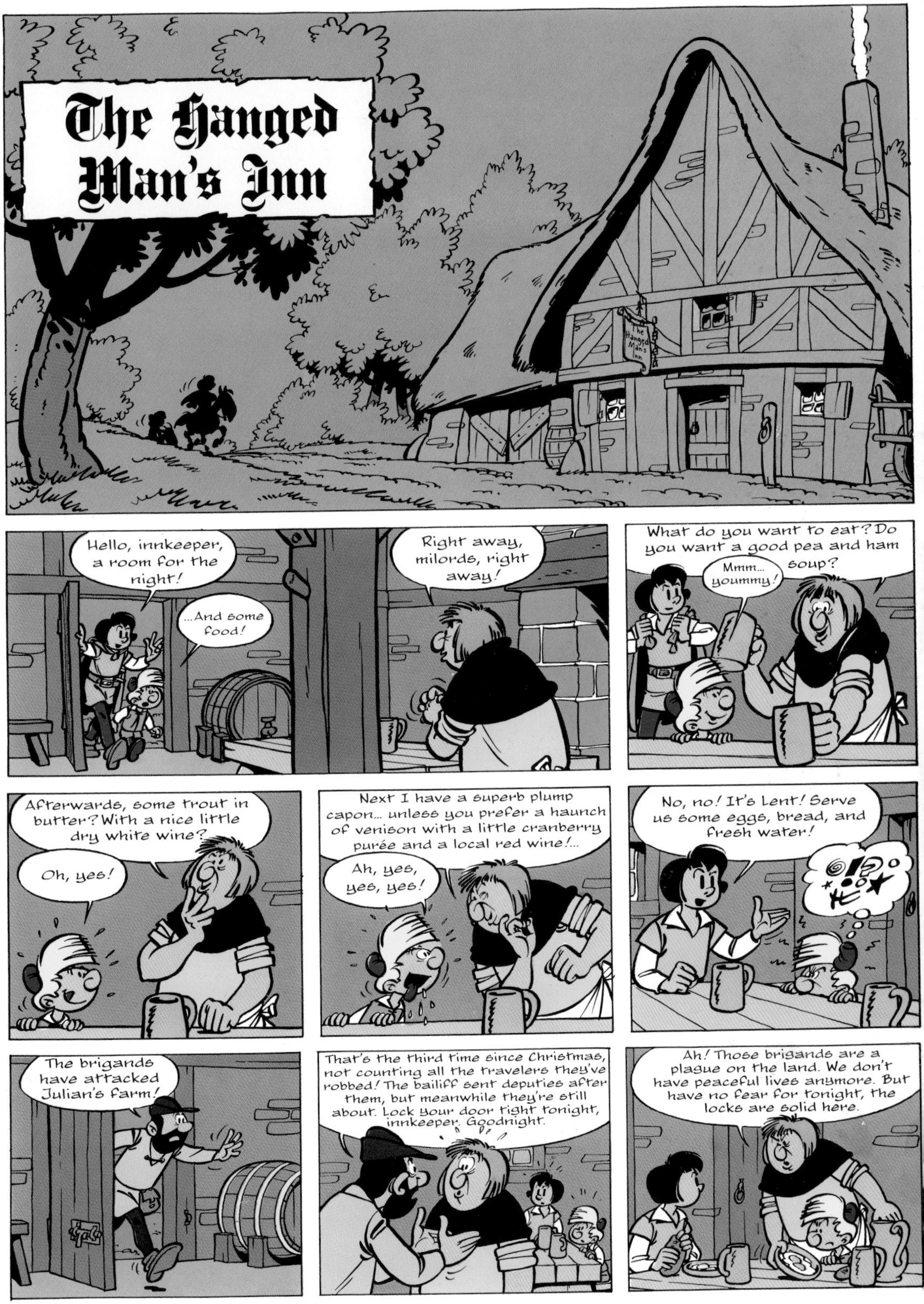
The Hanged Man's Inn
The Hanged Man's Inn
Hello, innkeeper, a room for the night!
...And some food!
Right away, milords, right away!
What do you want to eat? Do you want a good pea and ham soup?
Mmm... yoummy!
Afterwards, some trout in butter? With a nice little dry white wine?
Oh, yes!
Next I have a superb plump capon... unless you prefer a haunch of venison with a little cranberry purée and a local red wine!...
Ah, yes, yes, yes!
No, no! It's Lent! Serve us some eggs, bread, and fresh water!
The brigands have attacked Julian's farm!
That's the third time since Christmas, not counting all the travelers they've robbed! The bailiff sent deputies after them, but meanwhile they're still about. Lock your door tight tonight, innkeeper. Goodnight.
Ah! Those brigands are a plague on the land. We don't have peaceful lives anymore. But have no fear for tonight, the locks are solid here.

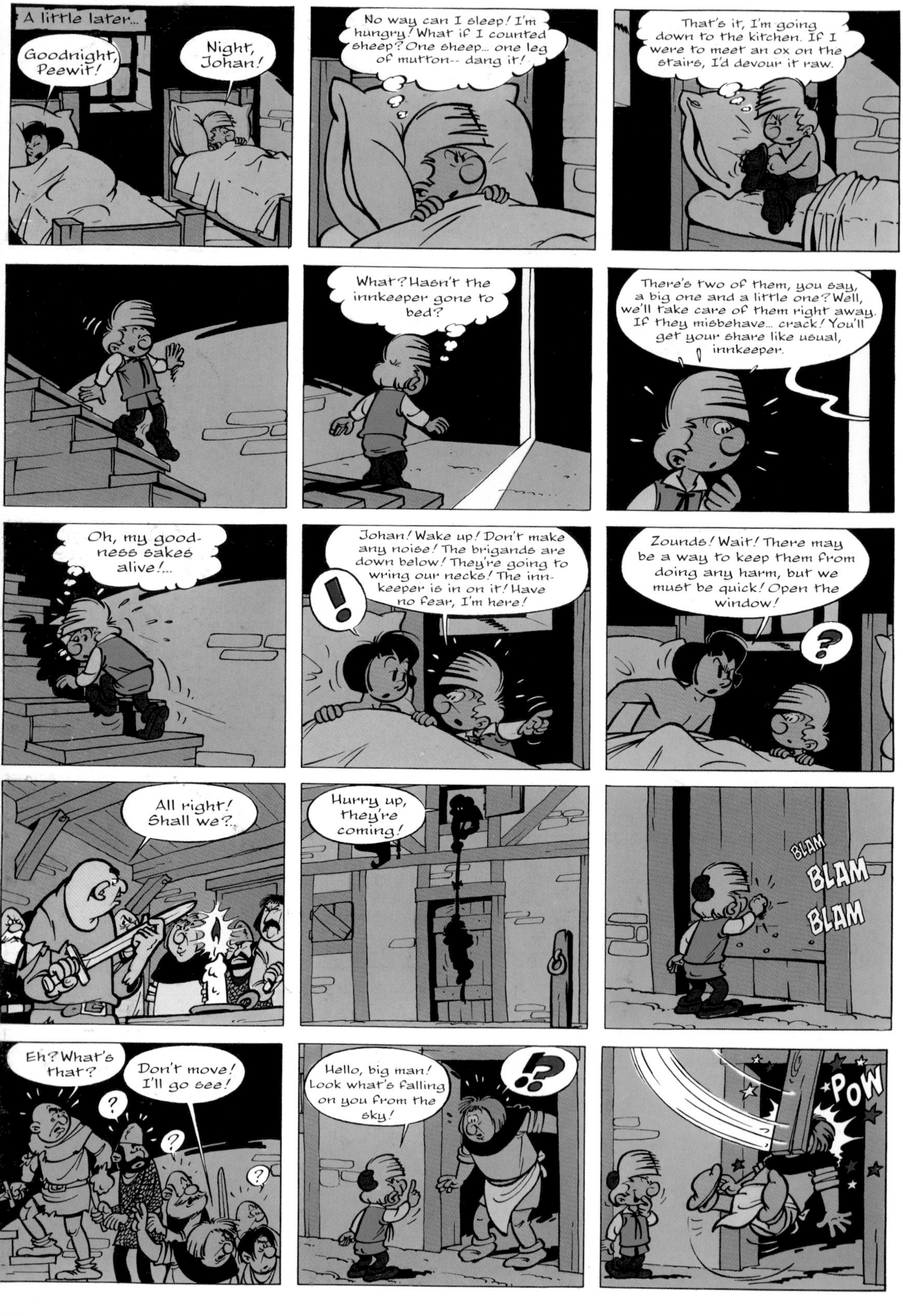
A little later...
Goodnight, Peewit!
Night, Johan!
No way can I sleep! I'm hungry! What if I counted sheep? One sheep... one leg of mutton-- dang it!
That's it, I'm going down to the kitchen. If I were to meet an ox on the stairs, I'd devour it raw.
What? Hasn't the innkeeper gone to bed?
There's two of them, you say, a big one and a little one? Well, we'll take care of them right away. If they misbehave... crack! You'll get your share like usual, innkeeper.
Oh, my goodness sakes alive!...
!
Johan! Wake up! Don't make any noise! The brigands are down below! They're going to wring our necks! The innkeeper is in on it! Have no fear, I'm here!
Zounds! Wait! There may be a way to keep them from doing any harm, but we must be quick! Open the window!
?
All right! Shall we?..
Hurry up, they're coming!
BLAM
BLAM
BLAM
Eh? What's that?
Don't move! I'll go see!
?
?
?
Hello, big man! Look what's falling on you from the sky!
!?
POW

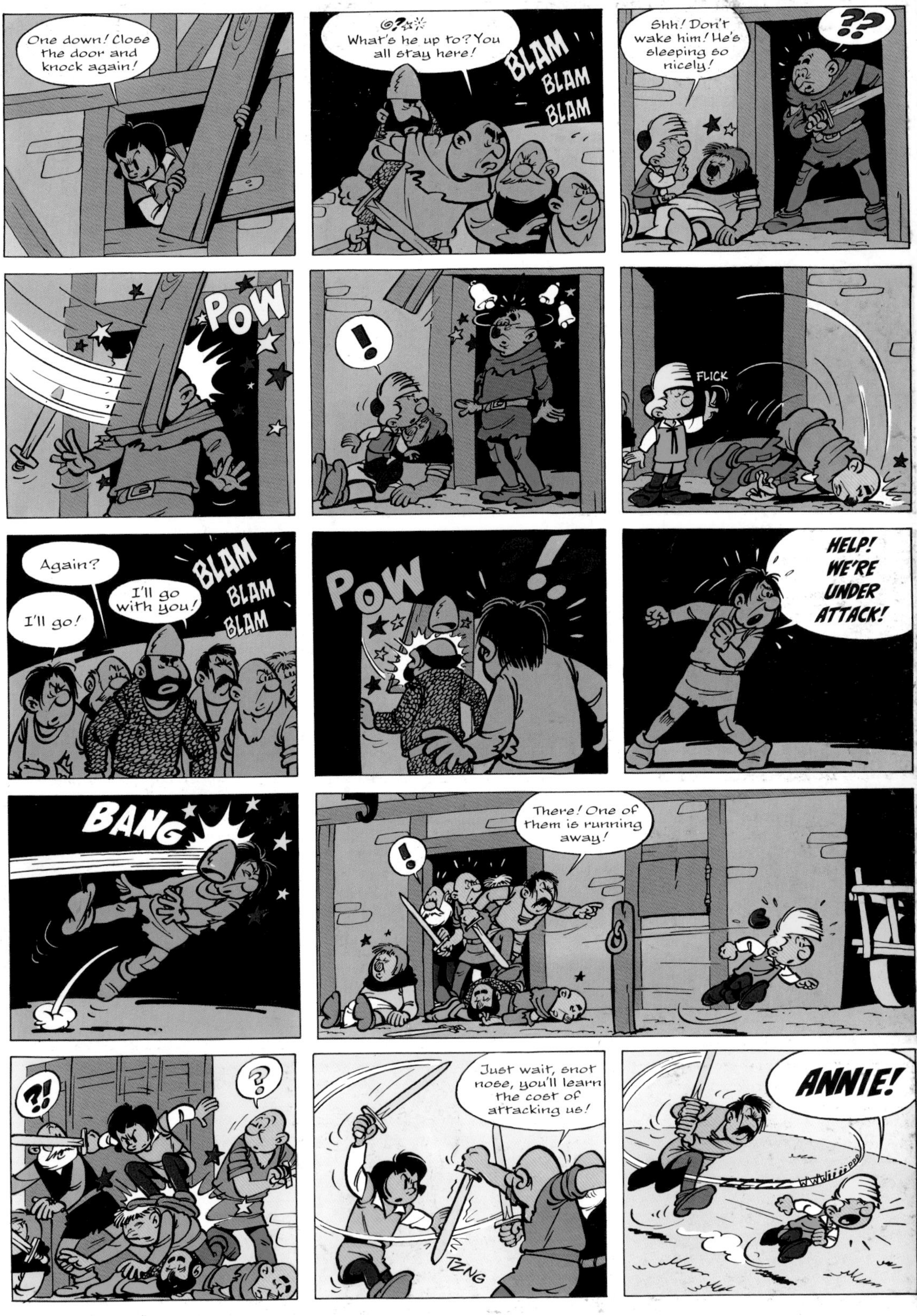
One down! Close the door and knock again!
What's he up to? You all stay here!
BLAM
BLAM
BLAM
Shh! Don't wake him! He's sleeping so nicely!
??
POW
!
FLICK
Again?
I'll go!
I'll go with you!
BLAM
BLAM
BLAM
POW
!
HELP! WE'RE UNDER ATTACK!
BANG
There! One of them is running away!
!
?!
?
Just wait, snot nose, you'll learn the cost of attacking us!
TZNG
ANNIE!

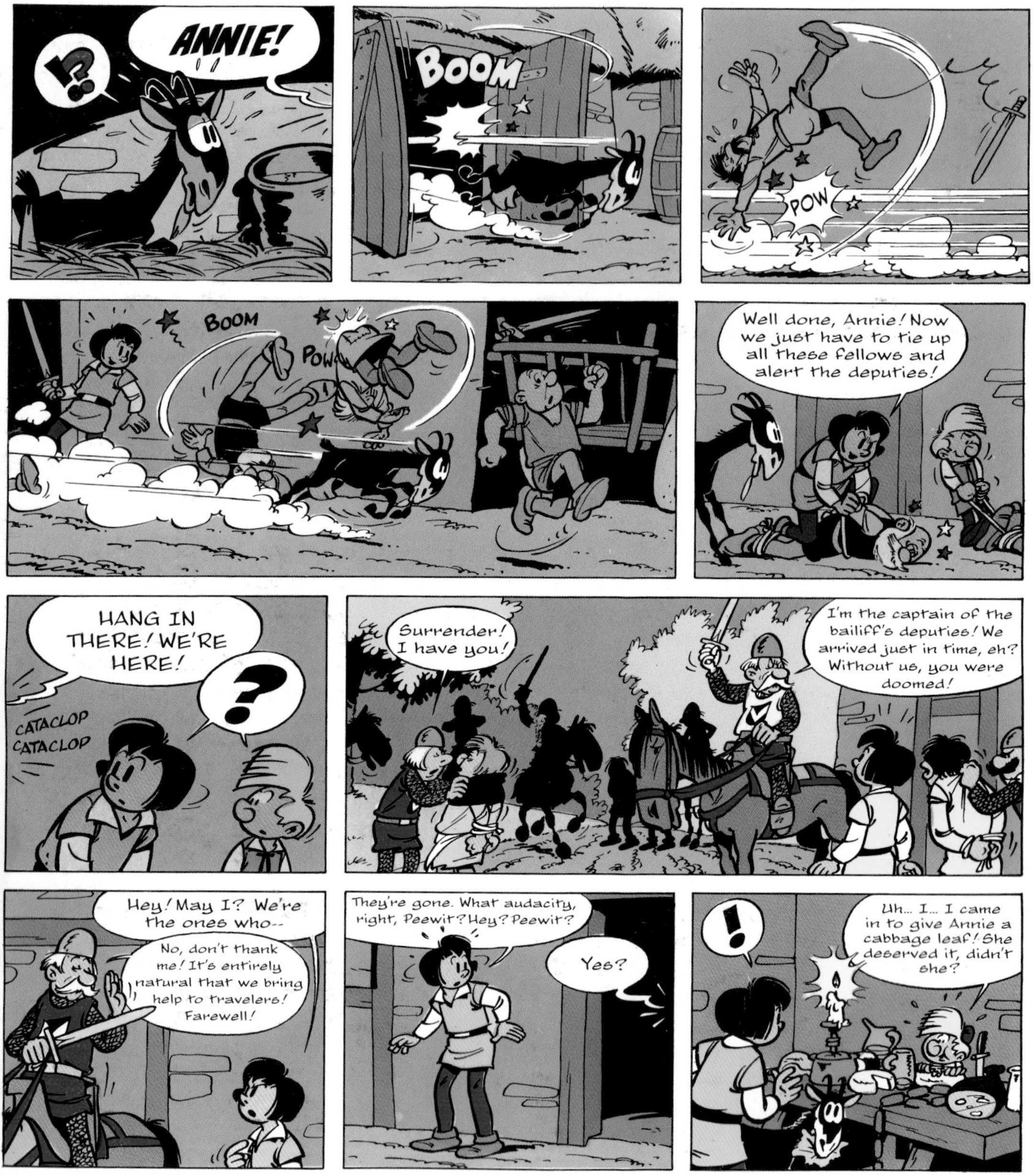

ANNIE!
?!
BOOM
POW
BOOM
POW
Well done, Annie! Now we just have to tie up all these fellows and alert the deputies!
HANG IN THERE! WE'RE HERE!
CATACLOP CATACLOP
?
Surrender! I have you!
I'm the captain of the bailiff's deputies! We arrived just in time, eh? Without us, you were doomed!
Hey! May I? We're the ones who--
No, don't thank me! It's entirely natural that we bring help to travelers! Farewell!
They're gone. What audacity, right, Peewit? Hey? Peewit?
Yes?
!
Uh... I... I came in to give Annie a cabbage leaf! She deserved it, didn't she?

The End

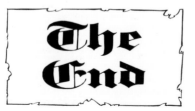